The King

Games We Play: Book #1

LIZ MELDON

The King is a work of fiction. Names, characters, businesses, places, events and incidents are either the products of the author's imagination or used in a fictitious manner. Any resemblance to actual persons, living or dead, or actual events is purely coincidental. The author would love if her characters were real people. She'd hang out with them all the time. Well, not all of them. Some of them are dicks. But alas. They are not real.

ISBN-13: 978-0-9938943-3-6

To my Sun and Stars.

THE KING

CONTENTS

ACKNOWLEDGMENTS

Thank you to my many betas who helped change a somewhat weak rough draft into what it is today. You guys were tough but fair, and I forever appreciate your candor.

I feel that cover art is incredibly important for authors, so a great many thanks goes to James (Humble Nations) at GoOnWrite.com for his beautiful work.

Much thanks go to my editorial team: Monica (@JMWEditor) and Phoenix Bunke. These two basically make sure my rambling is coherent and logical by the final draft. Authors would be nothing without their editors. It goes without saying that my friends and family have been wonderfully supportive.

To Levi, my love, who made sure everybody was logical and rational in a romance—thank you.

Many, many thanks to my twitter tribe of fellow writers. I wouldn't get through all this work without you.

A shout out to my parents who are probably twiddling their thumbs a little while I get this whole writing career sorted out. Thank you for years of support and love. Again, sorry I write smut instead of primatology research papers. This is more fun.

Please enjoy a complimentary copy of *The Fool*, the prologue of the Games We Play duology. Set roughly four months before *The King*, you can download it for free, in any format, from Liz's website:

www.lizmeldonwrites.com/the-fool

The novella is required reading for the duology, though readers who haven't read it can still navigate *The King*—but Liz recommends reading it first.

THE FOOL: A PROLOGUE

A 20K Novella

One night can change everything.

That's what they always say, and for now, vampire hunter Delia hopes it's true. After years of mediocre performances, she's still nothing more than a grunt in her hunter league, stuck on surveillance duty and low-level vamp busts.

So, when her informant drops an amazing lead in her lap, she jumps at the opportunity to take down the region's rumored vampire leader at an invite-only masquerade ball. Clad in a mask and an uncomfortable dress, Delia throws herself into the fray—only to realize she's woefully unprepared for the night that awaits her.

Also… Some ridiculously attractive guy dressed as the Fool keeps distracting her.

One night. One job. One man. One chance to change her life.

All she has to do is not screw it up.

PROLOGUE: THE NIGHT OF THE MASQUERADE

"Oh my god, I'm *so* sorry."

Gerald closed his eyes as lukewarm beer spilled down his back. He deserved this. He deserved the tittering idiot behind him and the soaked shirt. If he'd gone out the back door like every other chump who worked at the bar, he could have avoided this. But no. It was ladies' night and he wanted to scope out the crowd before leaving at the end of his shift.

Instead of gorgeous girls falling all over him, he suddenly had a wet back and a rising temper. Like he didn't stink enough of alcohol after tending bar for the last four hours. Now he got to walk home smelling like he'd drowned in the stuff.

Hands balled into fists, he turned slowly. The culprit was some slim thing with a glazed expression, giggling through her apology as her friends stood by. Summers in Harriswood were both a blessing and a curse, and had been that way for years—centuries, by Gerald's standards. Tourists flocked to the city for the bustling nightlife and the picturesque campsites in the surrounding hills. While the surge of humans every June meant that he landed more shifts at the bar, but he also had to deal with more shit.

Like this. Like the warm beer trickling down his back.

"*Are* you sorry?" he demanded. She blinked, as if stunned he hadn't accepted her half-assed apology because she was a pretty girl. "Are you *really*?"

Her voice was easy to hear over the thumping music, though a human might have needed to lean in to catch her muttering, "Yeah, actually... Sorry."

Shaking his head, he headed for the door, cutting through the tightly packed crowd, then nodding to the vampire who worked security at the front.

"See you around, bud," Gerald said, clapping the vamp's arm. Wyatt waved without looking, too busy dealing with the sidewalk hecklers trying to negotiate the building capacity. It was nice, even briefly, to feel the cool skin of another vamp. Humans could be so stifling sometimes, with their heat and their clumsiness and their... Well, their everything. They were overwhelming. If the general population knew how many vampires lived among them, they'd probably hand out medals for how much restraint most of them showed.

Then again, not all vampires were so successful at restraint—hence the hunter Leagues. Scattered across the country, humans banded together to combat the "vamp problem." Gerald always scoffed at the thought. Vampires weren't going anywhere anytime soon, not after centuries of survival in the Americas. The lineages in Europe had even grander, more longstanding histories.

Since Gerald wasn't so fortunate as to be a part of the larger, powerful local vampire clans, it might not have been the best idea to live in such close proximity to the local league. But he had lived here since the late 1890s and didn't plan to relocate anytime soon. He'd watched Harriswood grow from the safety of his little house by the lake, and he had as much a right to live and work there as anybody, hunters included.

All he had to do was keep his head down, feed outside of town—or with Claude Grimm's clan, who had a deal with a blood donor clinic in Trent—and be a contributing member of society. Hadn't had a single issue with a hunter yet.

Gerald's aversion to the sun made it difficult to get a

weekly nine-to-five job, which was why, as much as he complained about tending bar, he was grateful to find any after-hours employment he could. But the descendants of the head vamps? Fuckers could walk around in the sun all they wanted. Grimms. Donovans. Warwicks. Belmonts. Hewitts. Reyes. All the local bigwigs, who were apparently attending some snooty masquerade at the Banesview Hotel tonight, came from a pure line of vamps who were sun-tolerant. Meanwhile, the lesser clans were stuck in the dark, *wishing* someone like Shane Donovan had turned them instead of some other unimportant asshole.

It was hard not to be bitter sometimes. Those guys were the original outcasts, tainted by bloodlines resistant to sun exposure, a mutation, a genetic defect that had once made them seem more like the physically inferior humans than true vampires—until it became more and more apparent that it was a humans' world and vamps were just living in it. Suddenly that defect had the former outsiders running the show.

After walking for about ten minutes, leaving the club neighbourhood and entering the business district, Gerald realized he was being followed. His tail was pretty good—probably a seasoned hunter—but Gerald liked to think he was better. Switching up his usual route, he cut across one-way streets, behind buildings, and through courtyards. He planned to get through another night with his record intact: no tangling with hunters for him. He hadn't broken any local laws. He wasn't hunting some scantily clad, inebriated barfly. Gerald was being a good boy. The hunter was the one out of line, if anything.

Unfortunately, his shadowy follower was never far behind. Each time he thought he'd given them the slip, there they were, stalking him at about a ten-foot distance. This was fucking harassment.

Teeth gritted, Gerald crossed the street and made for one of the dingy alleys between two corporate buildings. Footsteps followed, and he hurried by stench-ridden garbage bins and metal doors with no handles, then ducked behind the corner of the building on his right. A large paved lot sat behind the two high-rises, perimeter marked by a chain-link fence. Beyond that sat a row of pristine townhouses. Human homes. Most vampires didn't live in the city if they could help it. As part of the Sorrows Clan, a clan of six vampires who allied most closely with the Warwick family, Gerald wasn't required to live in some huge manor with his clan leader in the countryside like the vampires who belonged to the bigger clans.

Silently he waited, pressed against the brick wall, listening for the sounds of his target. He wouldn't kill. Unlike some in the Harriswood area, he didn't delight in senselessly butchering hunters, even when they *were* out of line. Now, if the guy swung first, all bets were off.

But the footsteps had stopped all together. The usual hum of city nightlife tickled his ears, but the sound of his stalker's pursuit had vanished. Gerald frowned, eyebrows slowly knitting together as he pushed off the wall. Was the hunter also paused and waiting, listening for sounds of movement?

Had they reached a standstill?

The longer he listened, the more he realized he couldn't even hear the hunter breathe. They'd been moving at a good pace—the guy ought to at least be panting a little. Vampires had the better deal when it came to that kind of stuff, as it required *a lot* of effort to make him gasp for air. Humans? Sometimes just a smouldering look got them going.

Shaking his head, Gerald ran through his options once more. It was time for this creep to take a long nap—and wake up at sunrise in the alley with a splitting headache. Gerald was missing his late-night shows. His footsteps were silent, soundless after years of careful practice, and he came to a stop at the edge of the building. Careful not to let the hunter see him, he waited, counting to five in his head before he attacked.

The stake impaled him on three.

Straight to the heart—a solid hit. It came out of nowhere. No warning. Just agony. *Now* he gasped, pain radiating through his limbs. Eyes wide, panicked, the golden-haired vampire staggered back, fingertips trailing over the unfeeling brick in an effort to steady himself.

To no avail.

Down he fell, knees buckling and hip slamming into the concrete as he toppled onto his side. He panted like a fish out of water, vision fading in and out of focus. There was no moving the stake. No surviving it. So deeply embedded in him, all his vampiric strength proved useless.

He'd heard all the tales: a stake to the heart meant a slow, painful death. Beheading was more civil, kinder. Thick cold blood gurgled up his throat and spilled over his lips. The viscous liquid inched along his chin and down his neck as he rolled onto his back.

Seconds later, his attacker stood over him—a woman. Statuesque. Beautiful in the moonlight. She had an axe in hand, and Gerald groggily deduced beheading was still an option.

"Do it," he hissed, the pain spreading like wildfire, like he was burning from the inside out. He wanted it to be over. But in the same breath, he was starting to feel cold. Beneath the flames, ice lapped at his altered organs, his hardened bones.

His eyes narrowed when she smiled. In the right light, she would be exquisite, but now, all he could look at were the fangs poking out from beneath her top lip. Beneath the ruby red lipstick. Two points. Sharp—like his.

"Y-You're not..." He swallowed hard, fire exploding behind his eyes now. The worst headache he'd ever experienced in four hundred years of life. Gerald licked his lips, stained with dark blood, before he gasped out, "...not *human*."

His last words.

His attacker cocked her head to the side and raised her

axe, smirking.

"No," she remarked casually, her voice as lovely as her eyes. "I'm not."

And then the axe fell.

CHAPTER 1: PAY DAY FRIGHTS AND DELIGHTS

"So that's three-twenty for the last two weeks."

Delia tried not to make a face as Arthur, friend and League accountant, handed over an envelope full of twenties. She wanted to argue this couldn't be *all* she'd made in two weeks on the job—but then recalled she'd had an awful lot of TV marathons recently, plus that *very* drunken girls' night at Jimmie's with Ali. Not exactly a lot of delinquent vamp hunting going on. Begrudgingly, Delia stuffed the manila envelope into her purse, not wanting to count the cash that would go straight toward rent in front of the man responsible for giving it to her.

Insulting the guy who doled out her pay was at the bottom of her priority list—though she was probably one of the few hunters who thought like that. From what she gathered, most didn't actually *talk* to Arthur when they came by on payday, which she could understand to some degree. The guy didn't exactly radiate sunshine and rainbows, but somehow Delia had ended up in his good books when she first started working five years earlier. They'd been work pals and platonic lunch dates ever since.

"Well, so much for eating this week," she said, shooting him a crooked grin as she straightened up. Arthur raised an eyebrow from behind the glass surrounding his teller booth.

"Oh, come on, it's not that bad."

In all honesty, she kind of felt sorry for the guy. Sure,

as a vampire hunter one's life was constantly in danger, but poor Arthur had to sit in a bulletproof glass box counting money all day every day in the deep, *deep* basement of the Harriswood Library, headquarters of the local vampire hunting league. No sunlight. No windows. Just a computer screen, florescent bulbs, and the occasional jerk coming by to yell at him about budgets or paycheques.

"Well..." She shrugged helplessly as he stared at her. Sure, his job was probably mind-numbing, but at least Arthur had a reason to save for the future. No direct contact with vamps down here. "I don't know. They never really assign me any of the cool cases."

And not for lack of trying to sweet talk scheduling on her part. Delia had been hugging the lower-middle tier of Harriswood vampire hunters for longer than she cared to admit. But then again, the last time she went out on a limb to get the High Council's attention, she had ended up having a vampire snack on her neck at a masquerade.

Fortunately, the Fool, now known to Delia after some research as reclusive and *gorgeous* clan leader Claude Grimm, had only sampled her neck once at the Banesview Hotel's secret vamp-human masquerade. A vampire's bite spread their infection, but the symptoms lay dormant until bite number three. So, while the sun didn't bother her nor did she crave a pint of B-negative, Delia's dreams lately had been absolutely riddled with Claude fucking Grimm. Never in her life had she dreamed so much about a guy— but that's how it went with the first bite. The vamp would haunt your subconscious for life.

Which was, of course, just *fantastic*.

While Delia's first instinct had been to alert her higher-ups that she'd been compromised, Kain had talked her off that ledge. If she told she risked being labeled a traitor and banished—or worse. So Delia covered the marks with concealer and her long brunette waves and kept her mouth shut.

Thus far, Claude had popped in and out of her life at

random, never staying too long—mostly because Delia could lose him in a crowd or hide in a public bathroom until he left. He'd never been invasive, but rather loitered at a distance, sometimes with other people, sometimes alone. Now that she knew him...intimately, Delia figured she simply recognized him more. Despite his tiny League file, most of which was buried in a password-encoded file that no one but the High Council could access, Claude seemed to enjoy social outings in town.

He wasn't physically threatening. Harmless, actually. Possibly infatuated. But in a very real way, Claude Grimm *was* a threat, because she still wasn't sure she could trust herself around him—regardless of the fact that the thought of him infecting her with vampirism usually set off her temper.

If only her dream-self felt the same way. Dream-Delia was all slinky outfits and perfect hair and come hither eyes and *oh yes, Claude, fuck me harder*—it was a nightmare.

"You know," Arthur said, leaning back in his perfectly tuned ergonomic office chair, arms folded behind his head. She tried not to let her eyes flit to his pit stains. "I really think you could be doing so much more. You're a smart person. Totally competent. You need to go for it. Make some noise. Get the assignments you want."

The compliments made her smile awkwardly, so she rolled her eyes in an attempt to look unaffected. "Thanks, Mom."

"I'm serious." He twitched when something vibrated noisily in the breast pocket of his mustard button-up, but ignored it. "You should try to get on that big vamp-on-vamp hate crime."

Her eyebrows shot up. "The *what*?"

Arthur rolled forward, beckoning her closer and lowering his voice. With a soft sigh, Delia crouched a little to put her ear to the window.

"All these other idiots talk like I'm not even here," he told her, "like I'm some inanimate ATM. The other day, a few of the older guys were talking about some decapitated vamp they found in the business district a few months ago. Behind that big bank building, I think."

She resisted the urge to ask him what the big deal was. Why should she—or anyone, really—care that a vamp was found dead?

"Thing is, apparently the guy had the Donovan insignia carved into his forehead," Arthur continued. *That* caught her attention. "Pretty killer stuff, right? The hunters working that case are making some hefty cash."

"Why?" Delia cleared her throat as she straightened up. "I mean, there've been vamp-on-vamp conflicts in the past. Usually we just clean up the mess. No humans were involved, right?"

Arthur shrugged, fishing his phone out of his pocket and quickly scanning it. "Dunno. I don't know how they divvy this stuff up. All I know is who gets paid what, and the guys working that case made more than twice what you did in one week—and that's pretty much all they've been working."

She frowned, a jolt of bitter anger cutting through her. "Are you serious?"

Again, Arthur gave a little half-shrug. "Just telling you what I know. You should try to get on that case though... I hear vamp relations are a bit strained between the clans. Maybe it'll turn into something bigger."

Maybe. If she hadn't been assigned to the case, there was no way scheduling would add her on, and even then, it wasn't like the hunters assigned to it would want to share. Hunters hoarded lucrative gigs whenever they could, especially in a moderately quiet city like—everyone wanted the big payout and the prestige. If Delia was in their shoes, she'd probably do the same. Nobody wanted to do grunt work, even if grunt work solved most of the everyday vamp issues.

Her schedule for next week consisted of two nights of surveillance outside a bar that supposedly employed vamps as bartenders, a cushy patrol night in the swanky suburbs, then a very low-key takedown of a downtown nest full of clanless blood-pushers. No big players. Just the usual slap-on-the-wrist and deportation kind of jobs.

Which was precisely what one could expect at Delia's level of the hunter ladder. She wasn't the only one on it, and she, like everyone else dangling from her rung, lusted after more exciting assignments.

"It's weird," she said, struck by a sudden thought, "that they'd leave the body somewhere so public. I mean, usually the big clans are subtler. It's the little guys we tend to have problems with."

Delia, along with many other hunters, was under the impression that the "little guys" were just doing the bidding of the more powerful clans, but they were the ones hunters usually caught, arrested, banished—the works. Strange that a Donovan would murder a fellow vamp and leave the body for humans to find. Odder still that they'd even waste time carving their convoluted insignia into the dead vamp's skin.

"Maybe they're sending a message?" Arthur tucked his phone away and gave her one last shrug. "I don't know. Just telling you what I heard."

"Thanks." And she meant it. Her League informant Hugh had been annoyingly quiet since his tip about the Banesview masquerade, and he was where she usually got most of her behind-the-scenes intel—intel she had to pay a *lot* for.

"Times are changing," Arthur told her, and Delia stepped back with a smile and a wave, mouthing her thanks again as a group of fresh-faced recruits arrived to pick up their pay. As she made her way to the door, she heard Arthur snap, "What do you mean you don't have photo ID? How'd you expect to get paid, might I ask?"

The soft tread of Delia's old ballet flats accompanied her through the quiet corridors toward the elevators. League HQ extended almost six stories below Harriswood, with its secret entrance in the employee lounge of the public library. Outside of Arthur's bland, depressing workspace, HQ was basically a tiny city with all the essential amenities. Training arenas. A fully-stocked armory. A cafeteria serving world-class grub. Pristine conference rooms. Holding cells. Vamp-disposal rooms. There were even rumors that they were going to build a pool. Totally temperature controlled, most of the halls were lit with bulbs that mimicked natural light. If the rent for the hunters' living suites hadn't been so ridiculous, Delia might have lived there permanently.

Instead, she lived above ground in a one-bedroom apartment near the business district with shoddy AC and noisy neighbours on all sides. Sometimes she preferred it, flaws and all. Delia actually liked what she did for a living most days, but occasionally it was nice to get some distance.

Hunting ill-behaved vampires and keeping people safe gave her an immense sense of purpose—more than she would ever feel if she were still shackled to retail hell. Or if she'd pursued her generalized arts degree. As soon as her aunt, all but famous on the West Coast for her hunting prowess, had invited Delia into the mysterious underground world of vampires, life had never been the same. She'd never figured out what Aunt Julia had seen in Delia's twenty-one-year-old self that made her think she'd do well as a hunter—but five years later Delia was still grateful for the exclusive one-way ticket into her aunt's world.

Most days Delia felt like her eyes were truly open, like she could see the world for what it really was, while everyone else just existed in their vampless, sunshine-and-daisies reality.

Still. There were only so many patrols or surveillance gigs one could go on before the mid-to-low–level assignments lost their sense of awe and wonder. Even if she liked it, some days a job was just a job, especially with no upward mobility in sight. After her royal fuck-up at the masquerade ball, Delia had attempted to embrace the comfortable familiarity of the day-to-day stuff.

A challenge, yes, but damn it, she was trying.

The metallic double doors of the elevator peeled back a few moments after she pressed the up button, revealing walls painted in comforting neutral greens and browns—a stark contrast to the off-white of Arthur's domain. The radio hummed softly through the overhead speakers, and the light panels always reminded her of a sunny day with a hint of overcast.

Delia was digging her phone out of her purse, leaning back against the wall, when a hand jammed itself between the elevator doors, closely followed by a wriggling body. A young hunter whose acne suggested he was *just* out of his late teens shuffled in beside her, face flushed. Even though she got no service this far below ground courtesy of her shitty phone provider, Delia still pretended to be busy texting someone as he hit the button for the second floor—suites, kitchens, common areas—and exhaled noisily.

"Fucking…accountant Nazi," he grumbled, arms crossed as he shifted his weight between both legs. He glanced back at Delia, the movement caught in her peripherals, and gave a breathy laugh. "Am I right?"

His smile faltered at the unimpressed look she shot him, and he quickly faced forward again.

"All right then," she heard him mutter, ever the comedian. Rolling her eyes, she went back to her phone, flipping through the various pages of apps just to look busy. There was an abundance of standoffish, snippy, rude loner-types in the vampire hunter world, and while Delia wasn't one of them, anyone who called a good guy like Arthur a Nazi was automatically out of her good graces.

The elevator continued to rise, blanketed in a tense silence, and as soon as they reached the kid's floor, he was out of there like a shot. Delia pushed the button to close the doors before any other idiots joined her, then it was only another twenty-second ride to the first floor—reception, conference rooms, hunter archives, library, and transport hangar. Once there, Delia slipped out as another group of hunters entered, all of them men. It wasn't until she was off that she thought she noticed the smooth lilt of Kain's Irish accent, but the doors closed before she could look back to confirm.

Shoulders back, she moved through the well-lit corridors with maroon-tiled floors, smiling occasionally at a few of the records staff she recognized, then stopped at a wide-set steel doorway with a keypad off to the side. Hoping she remembered correctly, she punched in this week's code, nibbling her lower lip. A few harrowing seconds later, the pad buzzed, followed by the sound of the door unlocking, and then she was taking the stairs on the other side two at a time. Another door with yet another keypad and a different numerical password—and she was out.

Back to the outside world—also known as the dingy employee lounge of the public library. The few elderly librarians enjoying their lunch didn't even look up as she passed, but Delia didn't stop for pleasantries either. In fact, she didn't pause until halfway down the street, beneath the blaring sun in the sweltering heat of the August afternoon.

Downtown Harriswood bustled at lunch hour, the sidewalks and streets full of office drones breaking for sustenance and errand-running. Flowers bloomed in the baskets hanging from the street lamps, and outdoor cafés overflowed with patrons. Harriswood in the summer was always like this: tourists and college kids. Delia longed for the quiet of fall, but not the bitter bite of winter.

With the rest of her day free, a delicious iced coffee and double-fudge muffin from her favourite café were both singing their siren song.

Grinning, Delia fell back into the sea of pedestrians and let her feet lead the way to sweet indulgence.

*　　*　　*

Unfortunately, on the walk to her favourite coffee shop, adulthood responsibilities got the better of her and Delia made a quick detour to the bank to deposit her measly pay. While she would have rather spent a full twenty on a massive cup of coffee and one of the pricier "fancy" muffins in the display case, she knew she and her bank account would feel better about buying something cheaper. And, just like that, her indulgent midday treat downgraded to whatever spare change she had in her purse by the time she reached the register.

Stepping from the scorching outdoors into the café was like hitting a wall of ice. The frigid blast of the air-conditioning almost warranted a sweater, and, as she brushed her hair away from her sweaty forehead, she noted that a few of the long-term residents—those with a full laptop and work station set up on the small round tables, empty mugs and plates teetering on the edges—had bundled up to combat the climate. Delia, meanwhile, savored the chilly air, loitering beneath one of the air vents by the front door until a pointed throat-clear from behind hurried her along.

While she normally enjoyed wasting away hours in the café, sometimes with Ali or Arthur or Devin—schedule permitting—and sometimes flying solo, today it steadily lost points due to the sheer number of people inside. The majority of them were in line, but, as she scanned the armchairs and booths, she realized that by the time she actually received her order, seating would be limited too. Apparently today was not the day for people-watching in her usual armchair by the corner window.

As soon as she joined the massive line, taking her place next to the display of organic imported coffee beans, Delia felt someone join the queue behind her. The body hovered a little too close for comfort, and she stepped forward a few inches, in no mood to be crowded when she was already at a broil from the summer sunshine.

The line crept forward at a glacial page. As she waited, Delia checked her phone for any messages from Hugh. He hadn't had another worthwhile tip for her since the night of the Banesview masquerade, despite her pestering, and today was no different.

Nothin to report 4 usual price. Raise ur rate and well talk.

As always, Hugh's texts were an assault to one's grammatical senses. Rolling her eyes, Delia tucked her phone away with a huff. There were still eight people in front of her—and the one at the front seemed to be haggling over the quality of the green tea. Delia let out a soft groan.

When it was finally—*finally*—her turn, she was actually pretty ready to get the hell out of there. Her sweaty figure had dried, turning cold under the merciless gusts of AC, and all the constant chatter around her was giving her a headache. But she wasn't going to let the crowd beat her. Not today, tourists.

"An iced coffee," Delia said to the barista behind the cash register, "and..." She leaned to the side, scanning the glass case of dessert treats. No double chocolate muffins left. Of course. "An oatmeal muffin, I guess."

Then Delia realized why the line had been moving so slowly: the barista probably took a full minute to punch in her order, his face screwed in concentration, cheeks stained bright red and a bit of sweat on his upper lip. As she fished her wallet out of her purse, she noted the 'trainee' sticker added to his nametag. Poor guy. When he finally had the amount up on the screen in front of her, she shot him the most reassuring smile she could.

"Fifteen-sixty."

And just like that, the smile was gone. Delia's gaze darted to the price board behind him. "Are you sure?"

The colour on his cheeks darkened as he rechecked his screen, then nodded. "Yup."

Sure enough, they'd upped the prices on her usual "cheap" drink, and she suddenly found herself scrambling to make exact change, not wanting to use her credit card for such a silly purchase.

"Just a second..." The sound of her coins dropping onto the small counter brought heat to her face, and out of the corner of her eye she spotted the barista fidgeting, probably anxious to be kept waiting. Unfortunately, every coin and bill in her wallet only amounted to eleven-seventy. She cursed under her breath, then started scooping it all back into her cupped hands. "Uh, let me... I'll put it on credit, I guess."

Before she had a chance to pull the card out, a large hand reached around her and set a twenty-dollar bill on the counter.

Delia stared, not entirely believing what she was seeing. Sure, people were nicer in Harriswood than in some of the bigger cities she'd lived in, but no one had ever offered to pay the difference on her coffee order before. Taking a quick breath, she turned back to insist that the gesture was appreciated but totally unnecessary, only to find herself looking at a familiar face—a familiar handsome *vampire* face.

"Oh my god," she blurted, louder than she meant to, as she gawked at the man behind her—the man wearing an obnoxious amount of clothing given the weather, and a pair of sunglasses so dark that she couldn't see even a hint of the electric blue eyes she knew lurked behind them.

Claude Grimm. Mask-wearing Fool. Great in bed. The vamp who'd left two permanent puncture marks on her throat. In the months that followed the masquerade, he had always been at a distance—never so close that she could breathe in his scent or feel the heat of his body. Her stomach rolled over and over, mouth suddenly dry as her jumbled brain tried to decide what to do with itself: fight or flight.

She'd been more inclined toward flight in the past, always hurrying away before the vamp had ventured too close. But there was no chance for that now, sandwiched between his hard body and the counter, people on every side, Claude towering over her with a smirk. Her eyes briefly flitted to his lips before she cleared her throat and leaned back.

"I... Uh..."

Smooth.

"Why don't you add a small tea to the order," Claude said, catching her wrist and fishing her money out of her palm. He dropped the coins back into the open change slot in her wallet, displaying more poise in those five seconds than Delia had been able to muster all day. Sliding his money across the counter, he offered a wry smile that seemed only meant for her, one that made her heart beat just a little bit faster. "Is there anything else you'd like to add, Delia?"

"You don't...have to..." Again, words failed her. In her mind's eye, Claude Grimm was the mysterious vamp from the masquerade, all polished and refined and so out of her league. And a *vampire*—absolutely off-limits romantically.

But here he was ordinary. Aside from his clothing, the fitted black trench coat and dark dress pants making him stand out like a sore thumb in the sea of summer dresses and board shorts, Claude seemed so normal. Getting a cup of tea at a local café. It was easy to forget, for a fleeting moment, that he *was* a totally off-limits vampire, what with his warm fingers wrapped around her wrist like a snare. In the daytime.

"Will that be for here or to go?" the barista asked as he handed back the change, which Claude also deposited smoothly into her wallet. The vamp looked from the barista to Delia, lingering on her, and then back again.

"To go, I think?" His black eyebrows rose over the brim of his sunglasses when he turned to her, as if to confirm his decision; against her better judgement Delia nodded. He grinned, then guided her out of the line, toward the far end of the counter where they would grab their order. A cluster of customers hovered around the small countertop, some on their phones, others chatting amongst themselves—not a soul aware of the supernatural creature in their midst.

One she'd fucked.

And couldn't stop thinking about.

Delia gave her arm a tug, trying to free her wrist from his grasp, only to purse her lips when she failed.

"Let go."

"If I do that, you'll run."

"How astute of you." Her eyes honed in on his impossibly dark sunglasses. "Can you at least take those off? You're embarrassing yourself."

"I thought they were quite on trend," he remarked, pushing the almost opaque glasses up so they sat on his head. Vibrant blue eyes met her gaze, and only then, as she consciously tried to frown so that her mouth wouldn't turn up into an appreciative grin, did she realize her mistake. This would be so much easier with his glasses on. Those eyes were like the tide, eager to pull her out to sea.

"We're not in a bar," she fired back weakly, still trying to subtly wriggle free. "Nobody wears sunglasses inside."

"Well, I find the glare today a little overpowering." It was then she noticed he squinted somewhat as he looked around, the skin by his eyes crinkled.

"Is that why you look like a high-priced limo driver?" she asked, eyes sweeping over his outfit. "The sun? How are you even here right now?"

"Comes with being warm-bodied." They both stepped toward the counter as a group of women grabbed their drinks and left, though a few more patrons quickly sidled up behind them, forcing them closer together. Delia's breath caught in her throat. "Though I cannot say I'm entirely comfortable in the daylight, despite what others in my situation boast."

"So why are you here?" If she couldn't overpower him, maybe she could out-talk him. Get him to drop his guard—and the second he did, she'd bolt. There was no way he'd go all vamp-speed here, not with so many members of the general public standing around. Very few humans were privy to the existence of vamps, and Delia was under the impression that the bloodsuckers preferred to keep it that way.

"To see you, of course."

She gave a humorless laugh. "Right."

"I'm quite serious." They moved forward after a frazzled guy in a disheveled business suit grabbed a box loaded with to-go coffees and napkins. "Delia, I've wanted to, well, check up on you for some time now."

"Again, why?"

"You know why."

She bit the inside of her cheek and looked away, inadvertently exposing her neck marks to him. Seconds later, his fingertips brushed along her skin. She slapped his hand away as hard as she could, not caring that it made a few people look their way—and stubbornly ignoring the flutter of longing his fingers elicited with the slightest of touches.

"Delia—"

"Don't say my name like you know me," she hissed, cheeks flushed. "Don't."

They studied one another, the world around them fading to background noise. In that moment, all she saw was him, and her body tingled at the memory of his mouth on her inner thigh.

"I'm sorry," he offered. Her jaw clenched as his eyes wandered down to her lips, remaining there. "I didn't mean to be so familiar. What shall I call you instead?"

"Delia?" a barista called, the sharp sound cutting through the fog and forcing her back to reality. The sounds of conversations and music from nearby speakers hit her full-force, and she found herself temporarily thrown off-balance, moving toward the counter on autopilot. Claude followed, his hand still wrapped tight around her wrist, and she found their order waiting for them. After she shoved her muffin in her purse, they grabbed their drinks and drifted away from the gathering crowd.

"Look," Claude said, raising the hand he clasped up between them, "I'll let you go if you promise not to run." She arched an eyebrow as he added, "I'm here alone. All I want to do is talk."

"Uh huh."

"I won't hurt you." How many times had vamps said the exact same words to their victims? Delia swallowed thickly, condensation from her ice coffee dripping down the plastic cup and coating her fingers. His head ducked down, as if to catch her stare, and he loosened his grip somewhat. "Have I ever actually hurt you?"

Scoffing, Delia pointed to her neck, eyes narrowed. Rather than glare back, Claude grinned again, giving a little laugh.

"That was unintentional, I promise."

"Am I supposed to believe you?" she snapped, hating the way that they were huddled together by one of her favourite chairs. The situation was worlds colliding on overdrive. "It seemed pretty intentional at the time."

"Well, it wasn't. Accidental, if anything, and I think—"

"Oh my god. I can't believe I'm having this conversation with you."

She couldn't believe she was having *a* conversation with him, let alone this one. Whenever she imagined their future confrontation, at a time when she didn't run or swoon or whatever, she'd thought she'd handle herself like a professional hunter. Her aim had improved since then—maybe she actually stood a chance.

"Please." Something in his tone took a bit of the sting out of her glare. Sincerity? She didn't know him well enough to tell whether he was being genuine or not, but his voice brought her back to that night, when they'd kissed at the door of his hotel room. No games, no taunts, no threats. He'd felt real then, like he cared.

"Fine," she whispered, rolling her eyes again for good measure. Beneath the snarky demeanor, she mentally took note of all her exits, assuming there was one in the kitchen if she needed it. "Fine. I won't run."

"I don't want to sound like I'm threatening you," Claude said as he finally released her, "but I *can* catch you if you do."

She gave him one last hard look before grabbing a straw from the condiments stand, noticing the slight tremor in her fingers as she peeled off and tossed its wrapper, then shoved it in her drink.

"Do you want to find a seat, or would you rather walk and talk?" His breath tickled her ear, and she flinched away.

"Walk," she said stiffly.

"Excellent." Claude's lips morphed into a curiously pleasant smile, one that softened her protective armor a little—Delia looked away as fast as she could, hoping the chink wouldn't turn into a full-blown hole. She'd beaten herself up plenty for her behaviour at the masquerade. She'd let a ridiculously charismatic man pull her in and trick her, and it wasn't going to happen again.

Even if he *did* look just as striking as he had that night—more so, if she was being honest.

Ugh. Delia headed for the door, not bothering to wait and see if he'd follow. He did, of course, and pressed his hand to the small of her back when she had to stop and let people pass by the door. Delia stiffened, her breath catching again as heat seeped through her thin shirt. If he felt a damp patch from her sweaty trek through the city, Claude gave no indication, and kept his hand there, as if to guide her, until they were outside.

As soon as her feet hit the sidewalk, Delia took two

long strides away from him, and when he'd caught up, he walked beside her rather than behind. Wrestling her cheap sunglasses out of her purse, Delia shoved them, another barrier between his beautiful eyes and hers, and took a sip of her drink. Out of the corner of her eye, she noted the way his large hand all but engulfed his tea, which he'd yet to try.

"Why did you order anything?" she blurted. When he glanced at her, she straightened out, her gaze fixed dead ahead. "It's not like you eat muffins or drink...tea."

"No, that's true," he said as they skirted a couple of teens taking pictures of themselves on their phones. "But I thought it'd be odd if I didn't get *something*. After all, I waited in line."

Logical. While she was beyond annoyed to be held hostage by a vampire in broad daylight, what irked her more was the casual air Claude adopted when he spoke to her. His tone suggested they were friends—at least—but they hadn't spoken since that night. Delia had seen to that.

"So what's the real reason you were in the café then?"

"I was in the neighbourhood?"

She forced another hollow laugh as they rounded a corner, headed into the fashion district. Blinking hard, she tried to bring herself into the present; griping about Claude in her head had only made her flustered and distracted, totally unaware of her surroundings. Focus. Pay attention. He could be taking her anywhere. Despite the leisurely way he walked, two of her short angry strides matching one of his long ones, Delia couldn't exactly tell who was leading who.

"I've told you why I was here," he continued in the silence that followed. "I've wanted to speak with you for some time, but you've been quite adamant about avoiding me. I didn't *want* to ambush you in broad daylight, but you've forced my hand."

"Sorry I had no interest in speaking to the vamp who tricked me into going up to his room, then *bit* me," she said heatedly, voice low and expression forcibly neutral. He let out a little scoff and her eyes narrowed behind her dark shades, hand tightening around her perspiring drink. "You know, by League standards I'd have a reason to arrest you, no questions asked."

"Not quite, huntress. I *am* a clan leader, after all." Claude smirked, slowing as they neared an intersection. The pair hung back from the group of pedestrians waiting to cross. "Anyway, your lovely League is no more than the brute force for local law enforcement, is it not?" She pressed her lips together tightly, refusing to answer, when he cocked his head to the side. "Yes, that's what I thought. The League might have frightened the general vampire populace once, but I'm afraid they've lost a bit of their edge. So many rules these days."

"We're still killing vamps."

"But not *all* vamps," he mused. "Only those who break the law. It's not against the law to feed, you know, to bite. I don't personally partake in the practice, but many of my brethren have signed treaties allowing them a certain number of humans a month."

"Two," she said tersely, aware of the Grimm clan's deal with an out-of-town blood bank. She'd done her research. And definitely hadn't ogled his on-file pictures. "One for larger clans of thirty or more. Generally, they can't be local to the city the vamp resides in. I know the laws."

"Good—"

"And technically," Delia continued, her mind weaving through the law texts she was forced to peruse about once a month in preparation for the League's online quizzes, "you weren't biting to feed, but to intimidate."

Claude came to a stop so suddenly that she didn't realize he wasn't by her side until she looked to him for a response. He stood about five feet behind her, staring, one arm hanging limply by his side.

"You think I did it to *intimidate* you?" For a few seconds, she thought he actually sounded a little hurt.

Delia placed a hand on her hip in an effort to look unaffected.

"Why else?"

"One might assume it was a part of the sexual act itself," he said bluntly, and her cheeks flamed as a passerby glanced their way. Not wanting him to see her embarrassment, she started walking again, and this time he kept up. Clearing her throat at the feel of his gaze roving across her features, Delia took another sip of her drink, which had all but melted in the mid-afternoon sunshine. Fat beads of condensation built up on the plastic cup, and she found herself wanting to wipe it on her shirt, but caught sight of Claude's cheeky grin and stopped.

"Okay, cut the crap," she said, darting in front of him. He stopped, though not as clumsily as she might have if *he'd* randomly jumped in front of her. Mere inches of space lingered between them, and she swallowed hard, feeling the sweat settling on the nape of her neck as she glowered up at him, her reflection in his sunglasses a little off-putting. "What do you want with me?"

"So suspicious." His grin lingered, but slowly faded when it became apparent he was the only one playing his game, lips setting into a thin line. "Delia, I merely wanted to see you again. Check up on you after... Well, after everything. Can't a man inquire after the woman he took to bed? Especially if she's as fetching as yourself."

She flinched back when he brought a hand up, perhaps to sweep her hair out of her face. Sighing, he let his hand fall back by his side, the other still holding his tea.

"I don't believe you," she told him. Regular guys might call after a one-night stand. It wasn't out of the ordinary by any means—but Claude wasn't a regular guy.

"I don't blame you," he said, the softness of his words willing her knees to buckle. "I haven't exactly gone about it the proper way. But I want to know you, little huntress."

"Why?"

"Why not?"

She swallowed again, unable to come up with an answer aside from, "Because you're a vamp."

"True," he agreed without missing a beat, "but that doesn't mean we can't talk or get to know one another. I have serious doubts that I, or anyone in my clan, is high on your priority list at good ol' *HQ*." The way he said the word made it sound foreign, unfamiliar on his tongue. "It isn't a conflict of interest to have a conversation with me. After all," he paused, and even through his sunglasses she could see him studying her, "there must have been something you liked about me."

A soft breath slipped out, and Delia opened and closed her mouth a few times, words failing her. Of course she'd liked something about him. He was handsome—that much was obvious. At the masquerade, he'd been charming and had kept her from being taken by one of the Donovan daughters. When her whole plan had crumbled to bits, the Fool made her feel like she wasn't a complete failure. At the time, she'd felt desired. Now she only felt confused—and more than a little stupid.

"That's neither here nor there," she finally managed to get out, huffing. "Why are you even remotely interested in pursuing me? I'm a *hunter*. I've killed vamps before and I plan to do it again."

"Yes, I'm familiar with your attempts," Claude said, and an image of her staking him in the back and totally missing his heart flashed across her mind. Delia looked away, annoyed. "Let me be perfectly frank." She jumped when his finger pressed to the side of her chin, turning her face back toward him. He looked down, a flicker of those bright blue eyes appearing over the rims of his sunglasses. "Your chosen profession matters very little to me. Perhaps in the *past*, when League hunters and vampires were mortal enemies, it would have troubled me; but I care very little that you try to kill drug dealers and smugglers and mindless killers."

They stayed like that, still and staring at one another,

until he slowly slid his finger along her jaw, but Delia stepped back when it moved down her neck. It was too much to process—too many feelings and thoughts and emotions to categorize and make sense of. Instead, Delia steeled herself against him, knowing that, for now, deflection was the best defence.

"You want to talk?" she asked, her eyebrow twitching up as her hand tightened around her drink. "You want to have a conversation? Fine. You heard anything about the vamp who was supposedly killed by a member of another clan? As far as I know, there's a peace treaty between all the big name local clans, but rumor has it that—"

"I find it distasteful to get involved with rumors," Claude said sharply, which made her press her lips together, heart pounding. "I try my best not to engage in other clans' business unless I absolutely must. The leaders are all adults. I don't need to hold anyone's hand and walk them through their quarrels."

Delia ducked her head, feeling as though she'd just been disciplined by a superior.

It wasn't a good feeling.

"Well then." She squared her shoulders after a moment of silence. "I guess we don't have anything to talk about."

When she turned away, she did so with some difficulty; it was like her feet wanted to stay planted in front of him. But she managed to put some distance between them before Claude said, "Let me take you out sometime. I promise we'll find more interesting conversation topics."

"No." Keeping a steady pace, Delia looked over her shoulder as she said it. This time, Claude didn't follow. Maybe he'd sensed that he wouldn't get anywhere else with her today—and a part of her was relieved. Her head was starting to hurt.

"I'll try again later, then."

Unable to stop herself, Delia smiled, her steps slowing as she called back, "Good luck with that."

She was halfway down the block, passing a bridal

boutique, when she stopped and stole one last look back at him. Claude hadn't followed her. In fact, he was right where she'd left him, looking down at his tea. Delia paused and watched him toss the white to-go cup in a nearby trashcan before drifting away in the opposite direction, hands shoved in his pockets.

Only then did her smile fall, and Delia headed home with her head down, totally unaware that she was being watched—and not by a gorgeous vampire.

CHAPTER 2: BOYS

Delia wheezed, one leg flailing back in an attempt to knock her attacker's feet out from under him. When that failed, she went for the delicate skin on the underside of his bicep, grabbing hold and pinching as hard as she could. He grunted, but that only made his chokehold tighten around her throat—basically unbreakable.

"Okay, o-okay," she gasped, smacking his arm when her vision started to darken. In an instant the pressure was gone, and the HQ training room came back into sharp focus. Gulping down air, Delia plopped onto the blue exercise mat she and Devin had been training on, and her friend crouched in front of her.

"You okay?" he asked, eyebrows rising in concern. She nodded, rubbing her throat. Even though he'd basically wiped the floor with her, Devin's gorgeous deep baritone had a calming effect—not just on her, but on everyone else in the vicinity. It wasn't a surprise that he was often asked to speak to victims' families or explain the "vamp situation" to unsuspecting humans who were unwittingly dragged into their world. Hell, the Vampire Victims Unit and the regular hunter directors were in a bidding war over where he should specialize.

"You only damaged my pride," Delia told him lightly. Devin grinned at her slight eye roll, then flopped back on the mat himself and grabbed his water bottle. They'd been training for the better part of an hour, though it was pretty clear that he'd surpassed her in hand-to-hand combat skills long ago. Delia suspected that he continued to train with her because he was the kind of guy who refused to leave his friends in the dust, no matter how far he outpaced them.

Devin had joined the League the same year she had, at roughly the same time. He'd been nineteen, she twenty-one, and while Delia came with a hint of prestige because of her relatively well-known hunter aunt, Devin had been referred to as "that skinny black kid from Georgia" for at least a year. Then he went through a growth spurt, suddenly towering over her and the general populous, and his biceps had since outclassed every guy at HQ.

While she knew plenty of hunters who had bulked up physically and steadily ascended the ranks, none of them were quite like Devin. Beneath that muscular exterior, behind the charming smile and deep voice, he was still the sweet southern guy who held doors for people, said please and thank you way too much, and would drop everything to help a friend out—even if it was to go on a 4 AM pizza run after a boring patrol shift because Delia was craving pepperoni. They'd had many early morning meals at twenty-four-hour diners over the years, chatting about anything *not* related to work and watching as the rest of the world came alive again, safe from vamps for another night.

Kain liked to tease Delia about having no friends, and, well, she *was* a bit standoffish when it came to people piercing her personal bubble. But Devin and a select few others had an all-access pass, mostly because she knew they wouldn't abuse it.

"So, do you actually plan your moves at all when you fight, or d'you kind of just wing it?" he asked after taking a large sip of water. She eyed the bottle, her mouth suddenly too dry, and then held out her hand. Devin leaned across the mat once more and retrieved her bottle, and she took a quick swig of the lukewarm liquid inside.

"I plan."

"Really?" He made a face at her outright lie, then

chuckled. "Because I can literally see your brain working out your next move as you go. You need to nail down a few routines, then just use them."

She slouched forward to retie one of her shoes, the laces looking loose. "I like to improvise in the heat of the moment, I guess."

"Yeah? How's that working out for you?"

Delia shrugged. Sure, she was quick on her feet. Track had given her a few shining moments of glory in high school. Tackling HQ obstacle courses usually put her at the top of the heap, but she ranked close to the bottom on any and all combat trials.

"Works fine," she insisted, starting to feel the dull ache in her neck and head from their most recent bout. Her gaze wandered down to his tight work-out tank, which stuck just right to the defined muscles of his midsection— a welcome distraction.

"Hey, eyes are up here, D."

She offered him a sly grin, then looked over his shoulder when one of the guys in the weights area let out an unnecessarily loud grunt as he lifted.

The League training arena was a two-floor monstrosity partially separate from the rest of the underground facility. It contained all the equipment hunters needed to train: barbells and weight machines, squat racks, bikes, ellipticals, treadmills. Delia's favourite part was the enormous track loop that encircled both floors.

"You ready to try again?" Devin asked after a few quiet moments. Nearby, two other hunters were also working on their hand-to-hand combat skills, though the pair seemed more evenly matched than she and Devin.

"Why do you still train with me?" She took another small sip, her neck starting to feel a little stiff on top of the ache. When he didn't answer right away, she added, "You're way out of my league."

They both took a quick chug of water, the rules of a recent drinking game still in effect—take a shot whenever someone used "league" without referencing work. Along with: vamp, stake, council, and any of the major clan names.

"Maybe I feel sorry for you," he said, then laughed when she stuck up her middle finger. "Because I like training with you, D. Do I really need a reason?"

"I'm not going to help you get any better."

"Well, you're not my only sparring partner," Devin argued lightly as he capped his water bottle and set it aside. "And I shouldn't be yours either."

She pursed her lips as he hopped back to his feet, stretching out his quads and calves. He wasn't her only training partner, but everybody else liked to gloat when they beat her. Some seemed to think that put-downs would motivate her to do better, but they only made her bitter.

"Contrary to what you think," she said with an overly dramatic sigh, biting back a smile as she tossed her bottle aside and pushed herself up, legs protesting every slight movement, "you're not the center of my world, friend."

"Delia?" A voice cut off whatever Devin had to say in response, his playful grin dropping in an instant. Behind her, strolling over from the weights area, was a yummy sight if she'd ever seen one: Kain in workout gear. Somehow he managed to make a t-shirt and baggy shorts look good. She crossed her arms, only marginally embarrassed to be seen in a shapeless, grubby t-shirt and bright purple spandex capris that looked straight out of the eighties.

"Kain, hey," she greeted. While Devin was quite large overall, Kain matched him in height but not in width. He was a slim, muscular kind of guy—lean and strong, wiry almost. He'd pulled his shaggy blond-brown hair back into a little bun, and he wore a blood-red tee that Delia had definitely slept in at least once before.

His eyes, sweet and brown like a goofy Labrador's, darted briefly to Devin, who only warranted a nod. Typical snooty upper-rung hunter dismissal. Delia sighed noisily to draw attention to it, but Kain seemed not to notice.

"Can we talk for a second?" he asked, his Irish brogue forcing a little half-smile out of her. She nodded and shot Devin an apologetic look as she followed Kain away from their mat. Her friend waved her off, continuing his stretching routine in silence.

"What's up?" she asked as they loitered around the water fountains. She took the opportunity to refill her bottle, and Kain's stare burned into the side of her face as she did. She glanced up at him. "*What?*"

"Why are you talking to him?"

Her eyebrows furrowed. "What? To Devin? Because he's a nice guy, which you'd know if you stepped off your fucking pedestal for two seconds and—"

"To *Grimm*," he hissed, dropping his voice and stepping closer as he said the name. Her face blanched, palms breaking out in a cold sweat, and she busied herself with the fountain again. It'd been a few days since she'd seen or heard from Claude Grimm, and she'd tried so, *so* hard not to think about him. On the conscious front, she'd been successful—not so much in her dreams. Kain let out a long, annoyed sigh. "Are you stupid, Dels? D'you know what could happen if they find out you—"

"Were you spying on me?" she fired back with a glare. How else would he have known? Kain's expression hardened as he shook his head.

"No." He rocked back and forth between his heels and the balls of his feet, then added, "Not really. Not on purpose."

She tried to slap his arm, but he dodged her hand with ease. Her eyes narrowed. "When?"

"Is there more than one occasion?"

"No, but—"

"The other day," he muttered, shaking his head. "I was on my way to the bank and I saw you two walking together."

"Seriously?"

"You weren't exactly subtle," Kain informed her, his tone more than a little patronizing. "You were practically tripping over your own feet around him."

"Hey, fuck you." She might have been a little thrown in Claude's presence, but she hadn't been *that* bad.

"No, fuck you, Delia," he snapped. "*You* told me who he was. *You* begged for my help, for me to keep your secret. You don't have the right to be angry when I try to look out for you."

Her cheeks tinged with colour at the use of her full name. She was always Dels to Kain, unless he was genuinely exasperated. After a quick glance over his shoulder, he glowered at her, his face taking on a handsome scowl, the kind that had once made her swoon—but that was a long time ago.

"Look," Delia started, pulling him away from the water fountains as a couple of hunters started to drift toward them. They stood close to one another, and only when Delia caught a whiff of his rather masculine cologne did she worry about her training-stink. She pressed her arms down, as if that would keep the smell at bay. "Look. You know I appreciate you keeping my secret. I was a mess that night, and you... I appreciate it."

His face wrinkled with discomfort—never one for getting too personal. "Yeah, I know."

"But you don't need to check up on me," Delia told him in her stop-fucking-with-me-I'm-100%-not-kidding tone. "I don't need you to follow me or warn me about him. He showed up out of nowhere, in the daylight, I might add—"

"Yeah, most clan leaders can do that," he said casually.

She pressed her lips together, irritated. She'd been with the League for almost five years now, but it took a vamp walking around in the sun for her to learn such obviously valuable intel? It was absurd that this wasn't common knowledge, and it made her wonder what other useful nuggets the senior hunters were keeping to themselves—as if the lower and middle tier guys would somehow steal their assignments if they were better informed. It was laughable.

"Well, anyway." She waved it off. "He showed up, I handled it, and that was that."

"What'd he want?" His gaze drifted down to her neck. That fateful night many months ago, Kain had inspected the wound as Delia dry-heaved into a paper bag back at her apartment, fearing the worst. The marks had faded considerably since then. She shifted to the side so he wouldn't be able to see them.

"To talk, apparently," she muttered, hesitating somewhat before adding, "I think he wanted to...to...ask me out."

Kain gawked at her for a long moment, eyes widening and lips quirking up into a grin. "*What?*"

"Yeah, I don't know," she rambled, cheeks flushed as he started to laugh. "It was weird. Like he wanted to check up on how I was doing after we..."

"Fucked," he offered. "After you fucked a vamp."

This time she managed to get him, her punch landing right below his shoulder.

"Can we not joke about that?" She'd yet to come to terms with any of her feelings from that night, but she certainly wasn't at a point where she could make light of it yet with Kain—or anyone, for that matter, if anyone else actually knew.

"Sorry, you're right. I'll be serious." Kain cleared his throat, his laughter slowly dying down. "I just don't know what a clan leader would want romantically with *you* of all people—"

"Hey—"

"Right, right, sorry." He held up his hands innocently and she tried not to glower. "I'm not saying you're, you know... You're a pretty girl, Dels, but some clan leaders are like royalty, you know what I mean? Royalty doesn't go for…"

"Peasantry?" she offered, hating the way her cheeks burned. The topic shouldn't affect her like it did. "Yeah, I get it."

"I'm not trying to have a go at you personally—"

"I *get it*, Kain," Delia snapped. Gripping her water bottle tightly, she looked away, eyes roving the gym landscape. "Move on."

"Stay away from him, okay?"

"Sorry, at what point was I actively seeking him out?" This was getting ridiculous. Sure, she'd read up on the guy in the chronicles section of the HQ library, but she wasn't following him around like a paparazzo creep taking photos. "He just showed up, out of the blue. I couldn't run because you know he'd catch me, and I didn't want to make a fucking scene at a full coffee house in the middle of the fucking *day*—"

"Okay, okay, Dels, fine," he muttered. He reached out to set a hand on her shoulder, but Delia swiveled out of the way, biting her cheeks in displeasure. Kain sighed. "I'm just trying to look out for you. If any of the higher-ups knew you were bitten, you'd be listed as a traitor and disciplined accordingly."

"I know," she said. Some of the anger melted out of her at that. He was right, after all. Nobody knew beyond the rumors what was done to hunters who let a vampire bite them, but it couldn't be good.

"So… walk away if you see him. Don't engage."

"I don't *want* to engage, Kain."

"Okay, well… Good."

Her eyes narrowed at him. "Yeah. I know."

"Right."

"Okay."

Their staring contest went on a fraction of a second too long, and Kain broke away first to scratch at the back of his neck. Nearby, a few curious eyes had darted their way.

"Nice shirt," Kain said suddenly as he nodded down at

her chest. Delia squared her shoulders. She didn't need to look to know what she looked like down there; her baggy t-shirt was old and worn out and soaked with sweat—definitely not flattering. Kain opened his mouth like he had something more to say, going so far as to draw in a breath; but then he turned abruptly on his heel and left, marching for the locker rooms at a pace too brisk for her to match. Delia stood there in a stewed silence, watching him go, before pretending to top up her water bottle again. She zoned out as the water spilled over the top, Kain's words bouncing around in her head until the water started to numb her fingers.

Cursing, Delia pulled back and capped her bottle, then wiped its dripping sides on her shirt before stalking back to Devin in a huff.

Her fellow hunter was in the middle of doing push-ups when she arrived, and when she stopped directly in front of him, he glanced up, his taut-muscled arms unflinching as they held up his body weight.

"You heading out?" he asked, and when she shook her head and all but threw her water bottle on the exercise mat, he pushed up and settled in a seated position, a line of perspiration on his forehead. "Everything okay?"

He didn't need to say things had looked heated between her and Kain—Delia knew they had. He wouldn't either. Devin was too polite to admit to spying.

"Yeah," she said stiffly, planting her hands on her hips, jaw tight. "Everything's fine."

"You sure?"

"Yeah."

Clearing his throat, Devin rose, the movement fluid and smooth. "Look, Kain… Kain's a dick."

Unable to help herself, Delia snorted. "Not news to me, D."

"Don't let him get you all riled up," he went on.

Delia exhaled deeply, like that would carry away the tension. "I'm trying."

"Seriously." Devin smacked her arm lightly, then hopped back on the mat, all nimble elf-like grace—absurd for a man his size. "Kain and all his slutty buddies give the rest of us a bad name." Delia laughed harder this time. "Let's get back to training."

"Fine," she muttered, tossing her head this way and that to stretch out her neck, arms swinging. "I just hope I don't injure you too severely this time, because…"

She launched herself at him—surprise attack!

Seconds later her back hit the mat, forcing all the air out of her body. Delia closed her eyes tightly and groaned.

CHAPTER 3: ROOFTOP RENDEZVOUS

Delia placed a hand on her stomach when it growled so loudly that the folks two towns over in Trent had probably heard it. She checked the laptop she'd set up on an old box five hours ago, the one connected to the camera on the edge of the roof monitoring the building across the street. The two vamps stationed at the front door continued to smoke and chat with one another. If they *had* heard her stomach's desperate plea, they gave no reaction. Tense and still, she watched the screen for a few more seconds, then settled back into her fold-out chair and resumed her multi-hunter Scrabble session with a soft sigh. With her phone's screen set at its lowest brightness setting, she added OVULATE to the board.

Her phone vibrated when Devin wrote *Gross* in the chat window below their game. She smirked.

Their game included three other hunters who were also on surveillance duty that night, stationed on and in buildings across Harriswood like Delia, probably just as bored—though probably better prepared for a long-haul stakeout. All she'd brought was a ham sandwich and a can of soda, both of which she'd finished in the first hour.

According to all the rats, there had been chatter of human trades tonight between a few of the more influential clans. It wasn't illegal, per se, to trade humans, but the humans had to be there voluntarily. At any whiff of kidnapped victims or bound, screaming humans, the hunter present was supposed to record only, then hand the footage over to the League to review and issue a warrant the next day, in conjunction with the police, to rescue said humans.

So, Delia and a few others had been tasked with doing essentially what a security camera could do.

Mel, an eighteen-year-old from Cincinnati, spelled out MISOGYNY on the board, earning her a hell of a score. Seconds later Eric, a thirty-something part-timer, added SENSITIVE. Delia's eyes narrowed at her phone, fingers hovering over her letter tiles. How was everyone getting all these awesome letters? Delia ranked fourth on the Scrabble app's scoreboard, and tonight was determined to at least get up to third.

Ali, a hunter from California who'd connected with Delia their first day of training, spelled PLAYER off the 'e' in Delia's last word, and the round started over again with Delia. She sat there, eyebrows crinkled in concentration and lower lip caught between her teeth, then let out a petulant huff, thumbs tapping at her screen: RED.

Devin's response in the chat box—*LOL*—appeared shortly after. She resisted the urge to throw her phone—again. Another quick glance at the monitor told her there was nothing new going on with her two vamp guards, even when their obnoxious laughter trickled up from the street level. Her gaze went from their faces to their surroundings. All in all, things were looking good.

When she looked back at her phone, Devin had added XENOPHOBE and the screen was covered in fireworks and confetti.

"Fuck," she muttered, eyes narrowed.

"Bad time?"

Delia flew up from her chair, which went toppling over behind her, and assumed a defensive stance: legs bent, arms up, phone gripped tight. Standing there across the roof, right in front of the rusted fire escape she'd used to get up there in the first place, was an annoyingly familiar attractive figure.

"What," she said stiffly, heart pounding as colour flooded her cheeks, "are you doing here?"

"Did you plan to throw your telephone at me?" Claude asked as he strolled across the dusty rooftop. "Maybe zap me with all its radiation?"

He had something in his hand—a bag of some kind. Delia shifted her stance to a less melodramatic pose, knowing that she could probably get to the stake in her purse in a few seconds if she needed it.

But something told her she wouldn't need it.

Probably the fact that the bag he carried had the logo of her usual burger joint on the front of it.

It was sweet.

In a somewhat stalkerish kind of way.

Delia pursed her lips, pushing questions about how he knew her favourite burger—just a good guess?—out of her mind for now. "Why are you here?"

Claude stopped some five feet away, the bag extended to her. He was dressed similarly to the night of the masquerade: black pants, leather shoes so clean that the moonlight glinted off them, and a dark button-up. Green, maybe. It was hard to tell. Delia, meanwhile, was in her usual stakeout attire: faded yoga pants and an old t-shirt.

"Well, I know you've been up here for hours, and I thought you might be hungry, so I—"

"What, are you stalking me?" Delia crossed her arms. Like their meet-up in the coffee shop, she suspected her encounter with Claude Grimm would be harmless.

Physically, anyway.

Emotionally? She might leave in a bit of a loop again.

"Well…" He had the decency to look at least a little sheepish, his handsome features morphing into some semblance of apologetic. "I—"

"Look, Grimm—"

"Claude," he said with a frown. "We're more familiar than that."

"Are we?" Delia adopted her best sneer, though it probably looked as forced as it felt. "Look, we had sex *once*. At a party. And I was drunk."

"Hardly—"

"So you can just..." Her words died on the tip of her tongue, a cold panic gripping her suddenly. Her mouth went dry as she glanced to the laptop screen, then back to Claude. "How did you know I was here? Do... Do *they* know I'm here?"

Claude opened and closed his mouth a few times, his arm finally falling to his side. "From what I gather, you weren't exactly *subtle* in your arrival."

Cursing under her breath, Delia stalked to the edge of the roof and placed a hand on the concrete edge, peeking over to get a better visual on her two vamps. They paused their conversation, and while one grabbed another cigarette, the other looked up, directly at her, and waved. She pulled back sharply, heart hammering.

Could she really be surprised? She made a hell of a racket trying to get that emergency exit ladder down—the damn thing was beyond rusted—but at the time she'd thought she had gotten away with it. After all, the vamps didn't scurry inside their little safe house while she set up her equipment.

Delia turned back and tried to ignore Claude as best she could, her arms hanging limply by her side. In her peripherals, she saw him take a step forward.

"Delia, don't be disheartened," he said softly, then pressed his lips together when she shot him a heated look.

"I'm not." Nor did she need consoling from *him* of all people.

"The trades are going on tonight," Claude continued after a beat. "All the clans know the League has surveillance across the city. One of my people heard a broadcast on the clans' private line about some blonde hunter earlier this evening. Then everyone radioed in once they'd placed a hunter at their location. There are five of you, I believe. I volunteered to check on the location with the physical description that suited you best."

Of course vamps had radio-chatter. Delia bit the insides of her cheeks, then forced out, "And why are they letting us spy on them?"

He'd moved another two feet toward her when she glanced his way again, and he gave her another one-shouldered shrug. "Why not? You ought to know by now the clans like to show when they're being aboveboard. The trade nights are one of the few things they do by the book."

"And your clan?" she asked with a hint of venom. "Do they do it by the book too?"

"My clan does not participate in the trading of humans," Claude remarked somewhat coldly as he all but shoved the bag of fast food at her. Delia raised her chin and looked elsewhere. He sighed. "Humans are of course welcome at my estate. A room can be provided for them in the guest wing if they choose to stay the night."

She half-expected him to add a bit of a leer to that, as to hint at a repeat encounter between them, but when Delia looked back at him, he was still studying her with the same neutral-bordering-on-friendly expression he'd had since he arrived.

"What the hell is this?" she asked, pointing to the bag in his hand in an effort to divert the conversation from the overall League failings that evening. Hopefully none of the higher ups caught wind that all five hunters had been compromised.

Claude pulled the bag back to look at the logo. "Food." When she stared at him blankly, he added, "For *you*."

"Why?"

"Because I thought…" He exhaled noisily again and set the bag down beside her toppled chair. When he straightened, his wavy black hair had fallen across his forehead. Delia's fingers twitched, wanting to sweep it back, but he did it himself once he was upright. "I feel this conversation is going in circles. I brought it because I thought you might be hungry."

Her stomach gave a little gurgle of agreement, but Delia refused to even blink. "I'm not."

"Really?" His head cocked to the side and he seemed to be biting back a grin. "Because I'm pretty sure I could hear your stomach from the other side of Harriswood."

That made her wonder. "Can they hear us talking down there?"

"I was joking, Delia," Claude muttered, then added a little louder, "we don't have supersonic hearing. Though vampires like myself who can walk in the daylight have worse hearing than those who can't."

"Right." This was going nowhere. Shaking her head, Delia suddenly found herself fixing her chair before plopping back down on it, arms crossed and glaring.

No wonder she never got any of the good assignments. Sure, somebody else had been outed first—Ali, probably, given that they said it was a blonde hunter—but Delia should have known better. Tried harder. Not made so much noise as she got into position. Not been so comfortable as to agree to Devin's invite for a *Scrabble* session while working.

Suddenly her eyes were stinging with tears, and she leaned over to reach into the fast food bag and fish out some fries. Once she was upright again, she'd blinked away the impending flood. Claude had busied himself with her laptop anyway, and as she shoved the fries in her mouth, she found him crouched in front of it, hands on his knees, watching the vamps on the screen.

"Are they still hot?" he asked, not looking back at her. Delia frowned, then realized he was referring to the fries that had left smears of grease across her fingers. She wiped them on her pants.

"Sort of."

"I overestimated my ability to get you to eat it as soon as I arrived, I suppose." He shot her a grin, one that made the butterflies flutter in her stomach, then stood and cleared his throat. "I wasn't sure what you liked on a burger, so I didn't get anything outrageous."

Delia shrugged, all her fiery retorts extinguished now that her cover was blown, then reached into the bag to grab the burger and the rest of the fries.

"So what are you going to tell your little vamp buddies about the hunter you checked in on tonight?" she asked once she'd unwrapped the burger. The damn thing smelled so mouth-wateringly delicious that she wanted to devour it in two bites, but she held back from even picking it up. There it sat atop the wrapper, which spilled over the sides of her legs, the little box of fries sitting precariously close to the edge of her knee.

"I don't need to tell them anything."

"Won't they want a report?" she said stiffly, an eyebrow up. "Won't they want *intel*—"

"You know, the League is much less of a threat to the established clans than you think," Claude mused, arms crossed. He towered over her as he stood at his full height, a decidedly generous gap between them. "We each dispatched a few men tonight to make sure you hunters didn't cross the line—"

She snorted in disbelief. "*Hunters* crossing the line? Are you serious?"

"It happens regularly." Claude looked away, his profile rather fetching in the moonlight. Delia blinked hard and looked down at her burger so she wouldn't find herself distracted by his jawline or cheekbones or lips…

Ugh.

"Right."

"Some hunters like the power," he added. "No different than ordinary humans… I've met many young vampires, traveling alone, who have been harassed needlessly by hunters. It goes both ways."

"Well, hunters don't eat vamps, so—"

"Doesn't mean they can't kill them."

A muscle flickered out along his jaw like he was biting down hard on his back teeth. He was right, of course. Anyone, vamp or human, could abuse power in any given situation. Rather than acknowledge it, however, Delia picked up the burger and took a bite. Her eyes drifted closed, but she managed to swallow the moan that crept up her throat.

So. Good.

"Verdict?" Claude asked.

When she opened her eyes, Delia found him watching her again, wearing a ghost of a smile. She forced an indifferent expression.

"S'okay," she told him, mouth full of food.

"You know, in Europe, there are no hunter leagues," he told her after a moment. "Not like the ones here, anyway. Most of the European League equivalents actually *help* vampires."

She swallowed fast, her throat hurting a little at the effort, and shook her head. "That's not true."

The League had offices all over North America. She'd always been told the fight against vamps was a global effort.

"It is true."

"No," she said, setting the burger down on her lap, "it isn't. The Charter says…"

Delia straightened at the sound of vehicles rolling down the street below, and she motioned for Claude to get out of the way so she could get a better look at her laptop. He obliged, taking a dramatic sweeping step to the side, hands clasped behind his back, as what appeared to be two party buses pulled into view on the camera. Seconds later, a whumping bass filled the air, music and laughter and shrieks echoing into the night.

Setting the food aside, careful not to let it fall onto the dirty rooftop, Delia moved to the edge of the building to see for herself, but only after making sure the camera was recording everything. It wouldn't get the audio. There was no way she would have said two words to Claude Grimm if the camera recorded audio. No, its settings were to take high quality video, while the microphones on the street she'd planted during the day recorded the arrival of the trades.

Humans, most of whom had to be around her age, filed off the busses and stumbled toward the buildings across the street. Some were dancing, others were paired up with linked arms.

Everybody was smiling. It was like one giant party down there.

Something in her stomach tightened. She hadn't been assigned to record many human trades, but the last two were definitely more subdued than this.

Maybe this particular clan—Reyes, if she remembered correctly—preferred their humans drunk and high before they sunk their teeth into them.

Her neck tingled at the thought, fingers pressing into the faded marks of Claude's bite before she realized what she was doing. Delia dropped her hand to her side, hand coiled in a fist.

"Are you okay?"

With some effort she glanced at Claude, who had moved in beside her to watch. At least he didn't look thrilled with what was happening down there, though he didn't quite seem to share her disgust.

"Fine," she said tightly. "Does this happen at your place? Do you, I don't know, bus in your meals?"

"No." His jaw muscles flared again before he continued. "Any humans staying with men and women in my clan are there voluntarily. Not for a meal. They are there to be with the vampire because they choose to be. No one is forced… or drugged."

"You think they're drugged?"

"Well, drunk, at the very least."

"Yeah." The whole scene smelled like the inside of a keg.

Not that it was for her to judge. All she had to do was obtain the footage and get out. Still, she couldn't shake the unsettling feeling about the fact that those people were going to be traded between the vamps waiting inside. Bartered and haggled over. Assigned a value. Traded like playing cards. They could only be bitten twice—the third time turned a human to a vamp like clockwork—but she knew there were more *creative* ways to acquire a person's blood. A shiver ran down her spine, despite the summer night's warmth.

As she settled back in her chair and grabbed her food, Claude lingered a few moments longer at the edge of the rooftop until he finally turned away and met her stare.

"Do you want to know why I'm here? The real reason?"

She swallowed her most recent bite with a bit of air, surprised by the question, and coughed until everything went down the right pipes.

"Please t-tell me the thought of human trades didn't just remind you of why you're h-ere," she forced out. It had sounded snarky in her head, but the wavering voice and watery eyes and strained breath kind of ruined it.

"On the contrary," he said lightly. "I wanted to switch to something a little more pleasant…which brought me back to you."

Delia raised her eyebrows as high as they could go. "You think I'm pleasant?"

"Not tonight," Claude fired back, "but I… have thought so in the past."

"Oh." She made a show of rolling her eyes—it was better than the soft smile that threatened to surface. "Right. Thanks, I guess."

"I wanted to, uh…" He scratched at the back of his head. "I wanted to propose a courtship when I wasn't—"

Delia laughed before she could stop herself, one of those biting, incredulous laughs she usually reserved for Kain. "A *what?*"

If he could, Claude might have blushed. Instead, he looked a little embarrassed.

"Apparently *courtship* is the wrong word choice," he muttered, running a hand through his hair.

Still unable to help herself, Delia grinned. "For this century, maybe."

Then, just for a moment, something shifted in the air. It didn't last for long, but as Claude studied her and Delia picked at her fries, pretending not to notice, it almost felt comfortable.

"When I heard you were here, I thought… this was my chance to ask you out on a date where I wasn't sneaking up on you and forcing you to talk to me, which I admit was in poor taste at the café."

And then, just like that, the easy comfort was gone. Delia frowned and dropped the couple of fries she'd been holding back down onto the wrapper.

"*Not* sneak up and force me to talk to you… I'm sorry, but what the hell is happening right now that makes you think you aren't doing that?" She gave another laugh, one with slightly less bite this time. "Let's see, you still snuck up on me, and—"

"I do apologize, Delia, sincerely," Claude said insistently, taking a few steps toward her but stopping when she visibly tensed. "I've been trying to find a way to approach you that didn't seem, well, frightening—"

"I'm not scared of you." Partially true. Claude didn't scare her because he was frightening. Quite the contrary, actually.

"But I seem to keep making a mess of it," he finished, sighing heavily. Those bright blues darted down to her laptop screen briefly before returning to her. "It's been a very long time since I've done…this."

She had another snarky comment that involved stalking women and lurking in the shadows, but the genuinely uncomfortable expression he wore as she drew in a breath made her drop it. Instead, she continued to pick at her fries in silence. Her brain should have been going a mile a minute trying to process everything—that the leader of a pretty established vamp clan wanted to take her out on a date, the same vamp who had bitten her and exposed her to his disease. Instead, she concentrated on ignoring the slight tingle in her neck, but that only seemed to make it worse.

"I think I'm a little out of practice," he offered softly. While she knew she had to reject him, Delia couldn't help but appreciate that a guy so super out of her dating stratosphere was struggling this hard to ask her out. Used to spending time with Kain and his boys, men who *knew* they were attractive and capitalized on it in their interactions with women, this was uncharted territory.

"I'm not asking you to dive into bed with me again," Claude told her as the silence dragged on. When heat rose to her cheeks, he grinned and added, "I mean, you're welcome to, of course, but I'm not here for that. I thought we might get along, even if you're adamant about being the biggest, baddest vampire killer in town."

"I never said—"

"I like you, Delia," he said, his voice akin to a lullaby, "despite all your bark and bite. I don't know why, but I haven't enjoyed someone as I've enjoyed you in some time, and I'd be a fool not to at least ask you for a chance."

She smirked. "Well, you *are* a fool."

The Fool, in fact.

"That I am." Claude's lips spread into a warm smile. "So? What do you think? Can I take you out for dinner sometime? It'll be something more than burgers and fries, I promise."

He knew nothing about her if he thought Delia even *wanted* something more than burgers and fries. She swallowed hard and looked back at her food, then to her laptop at the sound of shrieking. All thoughts of dates and burgers went out the window at the sight of a pair wrestling across the screen, and in an instant Delia sprang to her feet and peered over the edge of the building, her heart racing.

"Ugh…" Delia eased back and crossed her arms at the sight of two people kissing like their only source of oxygen came from the other person's mouth. To make matters worse, one of the face-eaters was a vamp guard from earlier, clearly enamored with his human.

What had she planned to do if it was something worse? Dive off the building, land in a superhero pose, and stake the bastard?

Nope. All she was supposed to do was record. Still, her heart thundered painfully, body gripped with tendrils of adrenaline, as if the life of that woman had been entirely in Delia's hands.

"Boisterous pair, aren't they?"

Claude's voice broke the illusion, and slowly her body started to settle again. Delia brushed a hand over her hair, the nervous sweat in her armpit catching the wind. She glanced down, half-wondering if it was noticeable, half-cursing it for even being there. Professional hunters, the good ones, probably never broke a sweat.

"Delia?"

"I can't go out with you," she said suddenly. Her rejection didn't strictly stem from the fact that Claude was a vamp. It was because, in that moment, she knew that if he had kissed her like that vamp kissed that woman, Delia could have easily ended up in the same position as the night they met at the masquerade—and she couldn't let that happen again, as much as her subconscious mind may have wanted it to.

"Ah."

"I shouldn't even be talking to you," she added as she moved back to her chair, trying her best to inject some much-needed ice in her tone. "It's unprofessional."

"Of course," Claude said as she went for her burger again. It had fallen to the ground earlier, but by some miracle was still on the foil wrapper. As she lifted it to her lap and started reassembling it, she heard Claude clear his throat. "Well, my apologies for all…this."

Despite her salvage attempt, Delia didn't actually bring the burger to her mouth. She sat there like a fussy child, pushing pieces of bun and hamburger meat and pickles with mayo on them around, unable to look up at him.

Why was she feeling guilty? She ought to be angry—indignant, even—that he would do this to her. He was nothing more than a one-night stand, one that had gone straight to hell the second he sunk his teeth into her. A good hunter wouldn't have engaged in conversation at all. A good hunter would have sent the vamp packing the second he arrived, not carried on chatting like they were something they weren't.

But Delia wasn't a good hunter—that much was clear. If she had been a good hunter, she wouldn't have made so much noise when she first arrived. She wouldn't have gotten caught tonight. She wouldn't have suddenly found herself *feeling* something, something that made her stomach tight and her heart flutter, for the man who had been a constant figure in her dreams all these months later—a man who, since the night at the masquerade, had only tried to have a civil conversation with her, despite her accusations.

"Look, thanks for the burger," she said, studying it, each word a chore to get out. "I was getting kind of hungry, and it was nice of you to think of…"

When she finally had the courage to look up again, Delia found herself on an empty rooftop.

"Oh," she muttered as her gaze swept the area, focusing hard on the shadowy corners. "You're gone. Okay."

Easing back down, Delia glanced at her laptop screen briefly before going back to her burger, doing her best to ignore the sinking feeling settling over her.

At some point during their conversation, ketchup had

dribbled onto her loose white t-shirt, probably from the burger, and Claude hadn't once pointed it out.

Perfect.

CHAPTER 4: THAT DREAM WHERE YOU'RE STANDING AT THE FRONT OF THE CLASS WEARING NO PANTS... YEAH, THAT, BUT WORSE

"And as you can see, the outcome as rather grisly…"

Somewhere at the front of the room, the image changed on the screen, causing the one source of light to briefly flicker. Delia, all the way at the back, tried to lean around the head of the hunter in front of her. She would have *loved* to see what was happening, but she'd arrived late to the meeting, Kain hadn't saved her a seat, and the seat Devin had tried to hold for her was currently occupied by Candace Sweetman, secretary for the High Council, who shouldn't even *be* here. She'd had a thing for Devin for a few years now, and he was too nice a guy to tell her to fuck off, so Delia was stuck sitting with Ali at the back.

Ali, who had been pinning wedding gowns and bouquets and decorative plates to her Pinterest board on her phone since the meeting started, totally oblivious to the subject matter of the presentation. Even if the statuesque blonde hunter *could* see over the guy sitting in front of her, it wasn't like Delia could ask her what was going on.

She could hear, of course. Even sitting behind some

seventy hunters, the majority of the in-house hunter staff in Harriswood, she could hear everything crystal clear. Don Wentworth, tip-top of the League hierarchy and head of the High Council, led the presentation today— apparently it was *that* important. In a dark assembly room with hardwood floors and off-white walls and a snack table at the far back, Delia and all the other hunters had learned that the Donovan clan had broken the rules on the night of the human trades. While Delia had spent a boring night on a rooftop trying to stop feeling guilty for rejecting Claude's dinner date offer, Donovan vamps were hijacking and brutally murdering a busload of Warwick-owned humans.

Police had found the bus with all the bodies yesterday, almost a week after the human trades had happened, with Donovan insignia carved into a few chests and foreheads.

"Now, the Warwick clan didn't bring this to us directly because they wanted to handle it internally," Wentworth continued at the front. Ex-military everything, Don Wentworth had a booming voice and a jaw that could cut glass—and always had a way of making Delia feel about two inches tall whenever he berated her for fucking up one thing or another. While she wasn't a fan of the guy, she had a healthy respect for his authority within the League power structure. Seated in chairs facing the hunters was his quartet of underlings: Erik Lechowicz, George Heston, Callum Green, and Davis Warren. Together the five made up the upper echelon of the Harriswood League, the High Council.

Each North American League had such a council, acting as the highest of authority, only subject to the council that presided over *every* League, until its members were no longer physically or mentally able to carry out their duties. When one of the High Council was no longer fit to serve their League, a new hunter was voted into power. Rumor had it that Wentworth was grooming Kain for a position already.

"Unfortunately, this is a matter we cannot let the clans handle themselves," Wentworth said. Delia tried to inch up as much as she could without actually standing. "While we discuss the best strategy going forward, we will be increasing the number of hunters on patrol every night of the week."

The announcement caused some murmuring throughout the crowd. Contrary to what the newbies thought, patrol duty was about as boring as surveillance duty. But with the spike in both vamp *and* human deaths in the last few months, maybe that was about to change.

"Sir?" Delia stood, heart hammering. Where this sudden burst of bravery came from was beyond her, and she felt her mouth go dry when dozens of heads swiveled in her direction. Wentworth peered out into the dark room, his narrowed eyes eventually landing on her.

"Miss Roberts?"

"If you're looking for volunteers to take up extra patrol shifts, I'd be happy to offer my time," she told him, pleased with how even she managed to keep her tone. All the hungry new hunters were probably chomping at the bit to pick up extra shifts, and she wasn't about to let the guys who planned the weekly schedules forget she existed in favor of new blood.

Whispers erupted around her. Nothing obnoxious, but the room wasn't silent for long, not even as Wentworth cocked his head to the side, his salt-and-pepper hair catching in the light of the projector.

"Someone's a keener," Ali teased, and when Delia shot her a look, her friend smirked impishly and went back to her phone.

"Miss Roberts," Wentworth started, and she straightened up as nerves danced through her like little pinpricks. "Thank you for the interruption." Delia felt her cheeks darkening. "Should we need someone to mind the car, I will seek out your expertise."

"Thank you, sir," she said weakly, settling back in her

chair before her legs gave out. A few chuckles broke out around the room. Ali grinned, but Delia assumed it was because of the stunning wedding dress on her phone screen. Kain, on the other hand, was absolutely laughing at Delia, and she glowered at him a few rows up, visible between the heads of the people in front of her. Devin was lost in the crowd, but she knew at least he wouldn't get a kick out of Wentworth embarrassing her.

"You gotta treat scheduling like you treat a cat," Ali told her, eyes still glued to her phone. "If you ignore them, they'll shower you with love. If you pester them, they'll take a swipe at your face."

Delia pressed her lips together, face burning with embarrassment, and said nothing.

The rest of the presentation carried on as if she hadn't just been verbally flogged in front of her coworkers, but Delia didn't hear much of it. She sat there with her head in her hands and her elbows digging into her knees, counting the seconds until it was over. They had moved on from the Donovan attack anyway—something about HR changes and new forms everyone needed to fill out.

As soon as the lights flicked back on, Delia tried to shoot out of the room—only to find herself stuck at the back of the herd. Everyone just ambled toward the door, chatting and laughing and discussing what was happening with the Donovans. Kain pushed through to reach her, smirking as he invited her to the bar tonight since neither of them were working, but Delia waved him off as she cleared a path, no longer caring if she stepped on toes along the way. Behind her, over the din, Kain called her name a few times, but she didn't stop moving until she reached the elevators, and even then, she was a ball of anxious energy.

Anxious, *angry* energy, stuck there in an elevator packed full of hunters. A hunter sardine can.

Wentworth probably got off on humiliating her—the more people watching the better. Today's jab was nothing new.

Once they had reached the top floor, Delia made a beeline for the exit. Even when she was finally outside, the whispers of sunset playing across the sky, she didn't stop walking. No, she pushed on, not really paying much attention to her surroundings, trusting her feet to get her home, wondering if something was subconsciously pushing her closer and closer to career suicide.

The crosswalk light eventually forced her to stop amidst the post-work office crowd, and Delia let out a long, irritable sigh at the feel of her phone vibrating in her bag. At first she ignored it, but halfway across the intersection she pulled it out, temper prickling at the thought of Kain reaching out to poke *more* fun at her.

Instead, it was a text from Devin. She stepped out of the foot traffic by a shop window and checked the message. Sometimes just seeing his name was enough to talk her off the ledge.

Wentworth would have chewed any of us out if we pulled a stunt like that. You know he hates when people interrupt his stupid speeches. Don't let the man get you down, girlfrand.

Unable to keep from smiling, she sent him a quick thank you text loaded with heart-eyed emojis. It was nice of him to say, of course, but Delia knew for a fact that if Kain or any of his buddies had stood up and said something, Wentworth would have applauded their initiative.

Gripping her purse strap tightly, Delia trudged on, no longer angry—just frustrated and disheartened.

It would be easy to stop trying. She'd checked out in high school when a class didn't interest her. College was also a bust, with Delia struggling to pick a program that felt right. She had just stopped showing up to the few brainless part-time gigs she had before the League. Now that she was older and actually had a job that finally gave her a real sense of purpose in the world, she knew she couldn't succumb to old bad habits.

She just needed a chance to prove that she was better than they all thought.

Although she could get home from HQ blindfolded, that didn't always mean her feet chose the fastest route. Once she pulled herself out of her funk, Delia realized she'd taken a turn that wound up in the downtown school district. Harriswood had one elementary school and two high schools, one of which spewed out youths into the downtown area every afternoon. They clogged up cafés and shops and bookstores before going home, and many of the neighbourhood restaurants had a slightly unfair no-student policy enforced after a certain hour.

As Delia approached one of those very restaurants, an Italian place with a price point *way* out of her weekly budget, she came to a stumbling halt at the sight of an annoyingly familiar face. Excitement, fear, embarrassment—a combination of the three coursed through her body when her eyes landed on Claude by the entrance, surrounded by a group of equally attractive men and women. Given it was still daylight, she had to assume they were human, but since *he* could withstand the sun, maybe there was a vamp or two in the mix.

Maybe it was the woman with her hand on Claude's arm, bicep area specifically. Delia's cheeks physically ached from the way she flushed, and she hurried across the street, hoping he hadn't seen her.

It was childish, yes, but tonight wasn't the night for a run-in with Claude Grimm. To his credit, she hadn't heard a peep from him since she'd rejected his advances on the rooftop last week.

Yet it made her feel absolutely ridiculous to be *so* affected by his presence—from a distance, even. As she passed the restaurant across the street, using a group of women in pencil skirts and heels to hide behind, she spared a quick look his way. Claude wasn't looking at her.

In fact, he was holding a car door open for the woman who had been touching him, chatting animatedly with her before laughing.

The suit he was wearing was so perfectly tailored...

Delia shook her head and picked up her pace, quickly disappearing around a corner. Once Claude was out of sight, she let out the breath she'd been holding, then carried on a little slower, her heart pounding in her ears.

She barely made it one block away before something else caught her eye, something that set her heart racing again—but for another reason entirely. Across the street was a high school girl, still in her drab uniform, walking along with her earbuds in and phone in hand. Roughly ten feet behind, a very obvious vamp prowled after her. With the position of the high-rises around her giving him adequate shade, she wasn't sure if he was impervious to the sun like Claude, but he was a pale fucker who was practically drooling as he followed the girl.

This was what a hunter did on patrol. Wander the streets of various sectors around Harriswood, always on the lookout for inappropriate vamp-human interactions. Sure, vamps could feed a certain number of times each month, but that was tracked through the clans. Given the disheveled look of this one, he probably didn't belong to anyone.

But it never hurt to ask. The stake in her purse gave her confidence as she darted across the road, walking toward the man with her shoulders back and her head up high.

"Excuse me, sir?" Delia called, hopping up onto the curb. He looked to her, eyes wild and bloodshot, mouth set in a crooked line. His clothes weren't from this century by any stretch and had definitely seen better days. The teen carried on when Delia came between her and the vamp, stopping him in his tracks. Disgust crept up her throat as his eyes wandered up and down her body. His gaze wasn't sexual—just hungry, probably how she would look if she were eyeing a mountain of chicken wings at the bar.

"Hello," the vamp croaked.

"I'm going to need to ask you a few questions," Delia told him as assertively as she could. "Do you have your clan ID on you?"

The question sent him running. He probably hadn't just taken off as soon as she approached because she was a woman in a plain green tee and slightly too-tight jean shorts. Vampire hunters were all leather and trench coats in the movies. Her flats weren't meant for running, but Delia did her damnedest to keep up, weaving around the bewildered people on the sidewalk as her lungs burned with exertion.

If he'd had the proper ID, by law Delia would have had to let him go. However, lawless, homeless vamps weren't allowed to roll into town and pick off whoever they wanted. Vamps without clans implied vamps without rules—they had no accountability to anyone.

So Delia chased. The vamp dashed across the road, back in the direction of the restaurant where she had seen Claude, but Delia was only *barely* aware of where they were going. Her gaze was fixed to his back, determined not to lose him, and she dug a hand into her purse when he darted into an alley between a theater and a multi-level clothing store.

Much to her surprise, he stopped only some twenty feet from the sidewalk, and Delia slowed, removing her stake and pressing the little button to elongate it. It clicked into place in her hand, and she tried not to let her gasping breaths seem too obvious. She was a fine runner, but this guy was fast.

"If you don't have clan ID, you're going to have to come back to headquarters with me," she told him, flexing her grip on the metallic stake. The vamp studied her for a moment, then broke out into a broad grin.

"No."

"That's the law—"

"You stole my breakfast," he barked with a nod toward

71

the street behind her. "Come here and make it up to me."

She should have fished out her phone and called for someone, anyone, to assist—but there was no time. He might be ten seconds away from bolting again. Besides, this could be her *moment*. After being humiliated in front of her peers, Delia could walk back into HQ with a potentially dangerous killer in her hands, stake pressed to his back in line with his heart, and someone would *have* to acknowledge her efforts.

"If you come with me now, I won't have to force you," Delia said, advancing on the vamp slowly. Stake up, poised at the ready, she did a quick sweep of the area for anything he could grab to use against her. Some trash. A plastic bag. A pile of broken bricks from when the clothing store did renovations—potentially problematic.

But really, she didn't even need to worry about him picking up a weapon: his hands were two of the best weapons out there—and he used them when he swung first. She did her best, diving and bobbing and swiping her stake at him. But the vamp was faster, stronger, and before she knew it, he had her pinned to the wall of the theater, slamming her head against the stonework. Spots flickered across her line of sight briefly.

"One solid minute of fighting," he mused, one hand pinning her wrist to the wall while the other pushed against her throat. One minute? It had felt like a lifetime. His body blocked her free hand from getting at the stake in the other, and hot, foul breath washed across her neck as he added, "You must be your League's *top* recruit."

She struggled, teeth gritted as she utilized every part of her body to resist him—to no avail.

"Now, now," the vamp murmured, forcefully turning her head to the side to expose her neck, "I won't take long. Longer than our fight, but I'll be in and out before you know it."

Warmth bloomed to scalding heat when he opened his mouth, and Delia tried to kick out, only to find his heavy body gave her legs limited movement.

"What's this?" He chuckled, his words cold and baiting. "Seems like someone beat me to it…" The marks on her neck were on fire under his scrutiny. Delia did her best to ignore him, fighting with everything she had even as his hand pressed down on her windpipe. "This won't be bite number three, will it? I'm not sure I'm ready for that kind of commitment. We've only just met."

Blood pounded between her temples, her racing heartbeat like thunder in her ears. This was a mistake. A huge mistake. One of many she'd made recently. Her mouth fell open, gaping like a fish, as she struggled for breath, until suddenly things started to fade. The vamp continued talking to her, even as her vision started to blur, but his voice was like the hum of white noise. Her eyes widened, trying to take in as much light as possible, tears collecting in the corners.

Her stake fell, but she never heard it hit the pavement.

Then, the pressure on her throat disappeared, the weight on her body going with it. The sound that followed was like nothing she'd ever heard before, but later Delia would compare it to two freight trains colliding.

If only she could have seen it.

Instead, her body crumpled to the ground, and the blurred alley was overtaken by a black, black night.

CHAPTER 5: I LIKE YOU BUT YOU SUCK AT YOUR JOB (SUBTEXT)

Delia awoke to the smell of linens that had probably been laundered with a very potent floral dryer sheet—and a pounding headache behind her eyes. She groaned and threaded her fingers through her tangled hair, giving up about halfway through in favour of using a brush instead.

That is… if she could find a brush. Because this clearly wasn't her room—*definitely* not her bed. Her sheets didn't smell like this and her pillow wasn't this thick and high, nor was her mattress so hard that it felt like she'd slept on the floor all night.

A wave of disoriented panic washed over her as she pushed herself up, arms wobbling under her body weight. Was it morning? The soft light suggested as much. Where had all the time gone?

Much to her surprise, Delia found herself in a modest twin-sized bed, with starchy grey sheets and a white blanket. She was still wearing her outfit from yesterday, but someone had removed her shoes and set them at the foot of the bed. Her skin bore the indents from the seams of her jean shorts, and everything felt tight and bunched together down there. She did a sweep of the room before picking out a pretty painful wedgie.

Whoever had picked her up hadn't deposited her into the lap of luxury by any means. The room was small and neat, more like a guest bedroom than anything. There was a waist-high set of drawers between two doors. Leaning to the side let her see into an ensuite bathroom, which also seemed pretty small. The other door, she assumed, led into the rest of the...house?

Groaning again, Delia sat forward, her knees bent, and rubbed her face. Long angry marks wrapped around her wrist where the vamp had pinned her, and her body felt like she'd had the shit kicked out of her—which she had. The headache was manageable and swallowing hurt a little, but nothing was as bruised as her pride.

Wherever she was, it was quiet. There was a very real chance that the vamp had kidnapped her, but given he was clanless, he was probably homeless too. With no fresh puncture marks on her throat, Delia figured it was safe to assume his mealtime had been interrupted again.

Concentrate. Focus on the details.

Her purse sat on top of the set of drawers, along with some fresh towels. If her body hadn't been so sore, she might have panicked more at waking up in a strange place. As it was, all she wanted was a couple of painkillers and a shower—after she relieved her full bladder.

She tried to make as little noise as possible as she went about her business. Once her bladder was empty, she washed her face and gurgled some water, but a shower was out of the question. Hanging around here any longer than necessary wasn't on her list of things to do today.

What *was* on her list was to find her stake. It wasn't in her purse no matter how many times she dug through it, shoving bits of receipts and food wrappers aside. Delia cursed as she pressed a hand to her head, willing away the pain as she wracked her brain for any sliver of memory about the vamp attack.

Nothing. Once he had her pinned to the wall, things went fuzzy.

Her phone battery was dead—classic—and there was nothing in the room she could use to call for help. The small window in the corner overlooked a sunny forested area, with thick pines obscuring her view beyond the immediate foreground.

"Perfect," she muttered, squinting under the sun's glare. From what she *could* tell, her room was on the second floor of a squat building, which seemed longer than it was tall. Birds chattered in the nearby trees, but otherwise everything was silent.

Well. Time to make a run for it. Out the window, if she had to.

Purse slung across her body, Delia kept her phone in hand in case she needed to slam it into someone's face— she and Devin had recently attended a self-defence seminar where they'd learned how to use everyday objects to ward off an attacker. After yesterday's shoddy performance, Delia was eager to prove her mettle.

The door was locked when she tried it, but after a moment of panicked thoughts of picking it or forcing open the window, she realized she could unlock it herself. With the lock. Which turned easily when she tried. Her cheeks flushed as soon as she got the door open.

Idiot.

After taking a deep breath and rolling her shoulders back, Delia poked her head into the hall and found a number of other doors on either side of her—like a floor at a motel. All closed, silent. She spared a quick glance back at her room before slipping out and creeping toward the EXIT sign at the far end of the hall, then took the stairwell down to the first floor. The bland décor followed her from the bedroom to the halls, with light grey carpeting and off-white walls, no pictures or plants or splashes of colour anywhere to be seen.

That is, until she found herself face-to-face with a woman stepping into the corridor at the same time Delia did, she coming out of the stairwell and the woman from a room. Both came to a sudden stop, Delia's hand tightening around the door handle. The new arrival wore a neon-pink silk bathrobe, tied at the front, and a yellow sunhat. Fat black sunglasses dangled from the front of her robe, and orange flip-flops completed the assault of colour.

"Hi," the woman said brightly after a tense pause. She shut the door and locked it, facing Delia with a smile. "Are you going to breakfast?"

"Uh…"

"Tracy," she continued, hand held out expectantly. "Want some help finding the hall?"

Delia swallowed hard and shook her hand, brain suddenly in a fog. "Uhm. Where…? Sure. That'd be great." When Tracy wouldn't let go of her hand, Delia cleared her throat and added, "I'm Delia."

Fucking hell. She could have at least gone with a fake name. She pulled her hand away quickly and smoothed it over her wild hair when Tracy's eyes swept across the mane.

"Is this your first time here?" Tracy asked as they started off together, headed for a set of sunshine-filled double doors at the end of the hall. Delia frowned at the question, which prompted Tracy to keep talking, her voice not exactly the most headache-friendly. "Not to be rude. I haven't seen you around before."

"I… Uh…" Delia braced herself as they stepped outside, the sun taking her head pain from an eight to a twenty in about two seconds flat. She groaned and brought a hand up to shield her eyes.

"Oh my god, are you hungover?" Tracy asked, stopping suddenly and looking at her as she slid her sunglasses on. "I'm so sorry if I'm too chatty. Just a morning person…"

"Apparently," Delia croaked, hoping her succinctness might shut her up.

"Who's your vampire? I can see if they left you a package in the dining hall… Sometimes they do if you're staying the night. You know, Advil and stuff. You can't go in the main house during the day, though. No humans unless accompanied by their vampire." Tracy stared at her, probably because Delia was looking at her like she had three heads, each one wearing a more elaborate sunhat than the last. "I'm sorry. I'm talking too much again. Come on. Let's get some coffee in you and I'll see if anyone has some painkillers to spare."

Delia followed Tracy along the dirt path, fighting with the haze that had settled over her brain, and glanced back at the building she and Tracy had left. It reminded her of military barracks. Even though they were clearly plopped down in the middle of the woods, the grass seemed maintained. Fruit-bearing trees dotted her line of sight. Through the trees, Delia spied two more barracks-esque buildings as she walked, doing her best to take mental snapshots of everything to use later.

Harriswood was bordered by hilly forests on most sides, excluding the lake, so she couldn't be far from home.

"Don't you think?"

"Sorry, what?" Delia had almost successfully tuned Tracy out, but somehow the question broke through.

"That the guest suites should be a little... brighter or something," Tracy said with a sigh, waving her hands about as she talked. "I mean, I told Xavier when I first visited that something should be done. Make it a little more inviting."

"Xavier?"

"He's *my* vampire," Tracy told her, her tone dripping with unnecessary possessiveness. "I don't know how the other clans do it, but then again, I wouldn't want to. I've heard they don't exactly cater to us like the Grimm clan does."

Delia stopped on the spot. "*Grimm?*"

Fucking fuck fucker fuck—

"Delia?"

As her brain started to wrap around the reality of her situation, an all-too-familiar voice called out her name.

"*Oh…*" Tracy studied the vamp hurrying toward them, hands on her hips. "Is *he* your vampire? Well done, girl."

"No, he's not my… He…" Delia exhaled noisily, rife with aggravation, as Claude strolled up to them, a brown paper bag in one hand and a cup of something steaming in the other. Just as he had been when he followed her into the café, he wore impossibly dark sunglasses, though this time he was sans trench coat. Instead, he wore a fresh cream button-up under a navy blazer, paired with dark grey slacks, and, as always, polished leather shoes. Delia crossed her arms as he came to a stop in front of them.

"Morning, Tracy," Claude said, nodding to her companion. "I trust your stay was comfortable. I thought you'd be sleeping."

"I love the mornings too much," Tracy purred with a demure shrug. She spoke with a more girlish intonation in Claude's presence. Delia, meanwhile, wondered if she could lose him in the woods if she got a running start.

"I can't say I blame you."

"I was showing *Delia* to the dining hall," the woman continued, "but I see you've taken care of her needs. Excuse me."

And as quickly as she had forced her way into Delia's personal space, Tracy was gone, padding along the dirt path, her flip-flops smacking against the bottom of her feet with every step.

Once they were alone, suddenly the forest came to life. Birds chirped, bugs hummed, the wind rustled through the trees—and Delia looked just about everywhere except at the man—the vampire—standing in front of her.

"I was going to leave this in front of your door," Claude said at last, "since I wasn't sure how long you would want to sleep."

With some effort, she finally looked at him, body taut with tension. As handsome as he was first thing in the morning, Claude was *not* a welcome sight. She opened her mouth as if to say something, but stalked down the dirt path in the opposite direction instead. This wasn't happening.

She heard him call her name again, shortly followed by footsteps thudding after her.

"Where am I?" she asked stiffly, headed for the trees with absolutely no sense of direction.

"My estate."

Figures. Tracy had said the Grimm clan, and here she was in the middle of the forest. HQ had files on Claude's home being situated in the woods outside of the city. Obviously Claude had come to her rescue last night—*perfect*—and then brought her back here to recuperate. Why hadn't she pieced that together sooner? Her expression hardened, eyes squinted under the sun's unyielding glare, and she quickened her pace.

"Look, I didn't know where you lived," he said, easily keeping up with her. Delia stopped and shot him an incredulous look, to which he shrugged. "Okay, I have a general idea what neighbourhood you live in, but I wasn't going to go door-to-door with your unconscious body hoping I found the right place. I couldn't take you to the League because I would rather stake *and* behead myself, simultaneously, than speak with your High Council, so I put you up in a guest room."

Delia crossed her arms, her whole body screaming to just sit down and curl up in a ball. Pain hummed in every limb, every finger, coaxing her temper out with ease. "A guest room, huh? Not your bedroom, naked? Where I'd wake up with silk sheets in a four-poster bed as you watch me sleep?"

"No need with all the cameras in the guest—"

She let out a huff and pushed forward, moving deeper into the trees. The thought of him seeing her like this, battered and broken and defeated, was enough to put her in a mood. He'd rescued her once already, from the clutches of Bella Donovan at the masquerade, and she didn't need him swooping in to save the day every time she ran into a bit of trouble. Nothing cemented her failings more than feeling like a damsel in distress. So while venting her frustration on him was unfair, Delia couldn't stop herself. Everything hurt, including her ego. It was too bright and sunny and beautiful out for the way she felt inside.

Behind her, Claude gave a weak laugh.

"Delia, I'm joking." Suddenly he was beside her again, but she refused to even glance his way. If she kept walking, she'd have to hit civilization again sometime. Claude darted in front of her, though neither of them stopped moving; he walked backward, countering each of her purposeful steps. He held up his hands in surrender, food and drink in each, and her stomach gave a little rumble of approval.

"Can you just move out of—"

"I thought it would be presumptuous to set you up in my room, or any of the rooms near my room," he told her. "Seeing as the only time you actually *enjoyed* my presumptuousness was the night of the masquerade, I figured the guest suites would be better for you."

"Hooray," she muttered, trying to move around him. The little voice in her head insisted that she should have swallowed her venom instead of spitting it out at him. Delia pressed her lips together, guilt settling like a rock in her gut.

"Delia, stop."

They engaged in a little dance for a few moments, Claude blocking her path and Delia trying to move around him, the urge to run and hide prickling through her body, but she eventually gave up when she nearly tripped over a tree root.

"You're clearly in pain," he argued. "I brought some tea with lemon and honey because I'm sure your throat hurts. Come up to the main house. You can have breakfast, shower if you wish, and then I'll drive you home. Or wherever. Downtown."

She wanted him to stop being so nice to her. Her temper and her pride craved confrontation, yet he deflected every hint of snark with ease, steadily poking holes in her ballooning wrath until it finally deflated enough to let her think clearly. Her body had started to tremble, craving both nourishment and a soft surface to recline on, and when Claude held up the paper bag of what she assumed was some kind of breakfast food and gave it a little shake, she groaned. *"Fine."*

*   *   *

If anyone found out that she had eaten breakfast in Claude Grimm's enormous dining hall, at a table that was three times longer than her entire living room, Delia had every intention of claiming she'd done so to get insider information on a prominent clan leader.

However, if she only had to admit it to herself, Delia was just happy to be indoors in a place with air conditioning—the hike along the hilly paths had left her sweaty and miserable. She shoved a piece of everything bagel slathered with copious amounts of cream cheese into her mouth. Food and comfort. It was all her body needed, and in that moment the plush dining chairs seemed to cradle her battered bones like nothing else could.

Claude had settled on the same side of the table as she did, though a few seats of space sat between them. He had already peeled off his blazer and hung it over the back of his chair, the sleeves of his button-up rolled to his elbows. Drool-worthy, as always. He let her eat in silence, nursing his own mug of what she figured was blood. Delia had been stealing curious little glances at him whenever the urge struck, but this was the first time he'd caught her. She took another bite of her bagel and faced forward, cheeks hot.

"So, are we going to talk about last night?"

Delia choked after swallowing a little too fast, coughing and beating at her chest to get the mouthful down. When she was in the clear, she grabbed the to-go tea and took a quick sip.

"What do you mean?" she asked. When he raised his eyebrows at her, she cleared her throat and sighed. "Oh. Right. The vamp in the alley."

Any time someone used the phrase with her—*are we going to talk about last night?*—Delia usually assumed it had a sexual subtext.

"Yes, him." Claude pushed his mug away and shifted in his high-backed chair so he could face her. "Delia... What were you thinking?"

"I was doing my job," she snapped, dropping the bagel and glaring. "Which isn't really any of your business."

Claude's jaw clenched briefly. "He would have bitten you."

"Not necessarily—"

"He would have taken blood from you regardless," he pressed on, his eyes narrowing. "How could you be so reckless with your own life? I feel fortunate that I was even *there*, otherwise I might not ever enjoy the pleasure of your temperamental company again."

Butterflies did cartwheels in Delia's stomach at his little speech. Sappy idiots. "Hey, I didn't make you to follow me around or ask me out or spend time with me. You decided to do that all on your own."

"No, you didn't," Claude agreed after a few long seconds of tense eye contact. "I made that decision, but I wasn't there yesterday to see you. I had my own plans... It was purely coincidental."

Delia went back to her bagel, considering it a shame to waste something so scrumptious, and once again ignored the indignant voice at the back of her head telling her to *thank* him instead of snarl at him. Claude hadn't needed to lift a finger for her yesterday. He could have let her get attacked and drained, but he hadn't. The thought made her chest tighten and her eyes water. Maybe *she* was the sappy idiot, not the butterflies.

"So?" she forced out, mouth full of bagel and cream cheese.

"So…" He shook his head and sat back in his chair. "So, Delia, what would have happened if I hadn't been there?"

"I would have figured a way out of it," she said stubbornly after she swallowed, but even she could hear the lie. "It's not like I wasn't armed."

"The stake?"

"Which is where, by the way?"

"Probably still on the ground," Claude told her, and he scoffed when she fixed him with another glare. "I'm sorry that I was more concerned with *your* well-being than gathering your discarded vampire-killing tools."

Delia's head drooped a little as she chewed her next bite. When she was done, most of the fire was finally gone, because deep down she knew he was right. She'd been foolish—again—and had put her life in jeopardy—*again*—all because she wanted someone at HQ to pay attention to her—again.

"I was just doing my job," she repeated, her words so quiet she wasn't sure he'd heard. The lengthy exhale he gave told her that he did. "He was following this high school girl. I stopped him, asked to see his clan ID, and then he ran. So I chased. And then he challenged me. I was doing what I thought was right in the moment." Delia looked to Claude, subdued. "Did you get him?"

His hand closed to a fist, then wrapped around his mug. She watched as he took a sip, and when he set the cup back down, dark red liquid stained his lower lip until he licked it away.

"If by *get him* you mean pummeled his face to nothing with a brick, then yes," Claude muttered, "I got him."

She almost thanked him. The words hovered at the tip of her tongue, but she swallowed them down with the last bit of bagel and a final swig of tea.

"Tracy said humans aren't allowed in the main house," Delia blurted, suddenly feeling the need to say something. She had been quiet for long enough earlier, wrapped up in her body's pain and her mind's frustration and her jumbled feelings. Now that Claude had called her out on being a moron, albeit in a nicer way than she deserved, sullen silence didn't seem appropriate anymore.

"They once were," Claude mused. Delia shifted in her chair to face him, but her eyes took to wandering the expansive hall instead. In her peripherals, however, the unearthly blue of Claude's gaze was unflinching. "But I found they got into too much mischief during the day. I'm one of a handful in my clan who can withstand the sun, and with their vampire companions sleeping, usually the humans went wandering."

It didn't surprise Delia that someone would want to explore the Grimm manor. Tracy and Claude had referred to it as the main house, but it was anything *but* a house. A castle, more like, with slate-grey stonework on the outside and tasteful wood flooring on the inside.

The style of the décor changed depending on the room: the entrance hall had been sparse and overwhelming, with old silk tapestries strung from the wall depicting gruesome medieval scenes—not to his taste, Claude had noted when Delia made a face—while the dining hall had a glittering chandelier and gold finishing everywhere, designed to impress rather than unnerve. The whole room dripped with opulence, from the polished silverware to the extravagant gold candelabras spaced out along the table, each with what she guessed were real rubies embedded in the elaborate bases.

And all she had seen were two rooms. From the outside, Claude's "main house" seemed to go on forever.

"So what's the deal with the humans here?" she asked, feeling the need to wear her hunter hat. She squared her shoulders, then winced as pain shot from one side of her to the other. "Are they registered with the League, or…?"

Claude shook his head and sighed like the question exasperated him. "The humans here are friends, boyfriends, girlfriends, family. We found some couples have… extracurricular activities that make it tiresome for the human to go home right after. Instead of dealing with taxis and town cars at all hours, I built the guest suites so they could stay if they wished. Unlike most clans, we do not claim ownership over the humans who stay."

"Huh." Delia pursed her lips and nodded. "And how do the other clans feel about that?"

From what she'd read on local clan politics, the Grimm clan didn't factor in all that much. At the time, she hadn't been able to help wondering why.

"The other clans have no say in how I handle my affairs," Claude told her with a lopsided grin. "I *am* their king, after all."

"*What?*" Delia sat up a little straighter. "I call bullshit on that. There are no *kings*—"

"At one time there were," Claude insisted, his smile growing when she repeated her previous sentiment. *Bullshit.* "I'm quite serious. Kings were once chosen to govern regional clans. However, as the American colonies moved away from their British overlords, so too did the American clans put less and less stock in their kings. Now, I trust them to govern themselves, even if I technically retain the title."

She almost asked he if was sure he could trust the clans to govern themselves, given how reckless and violent the Donovan clan had been lately, but then thought better of it. Asking would be like giving away League secrets. Anything discussed at meetings shouldn't be discussed with Claude Grimm.

Nothing should be discussed with Claude Grimm, but here she was, chatting casually over breakfast. Delia retreated into her seat, wishing she had more willpower to ignore him.

King of the clans. King of the *regional* clans. After all these years as a hunter, Delia had had no idea there were kings now or at any other point in history. She knew of clan leaders who ran their vamp houses with an iron fist, but never of one vamp who had dominion over them all— and it wasn't like Delia hadn't done her reading. Early in her career, she'd spent hours in the archives room at HQ, poring over texts and study aids in a way she had never done at school. She'd wanted to be on top of her game, to prove that she was serious about giving herself over to this life; now, suddenly, it was quite apparent that she still had so much to learn.

But then again, Delia was a mid-level grunt. Nobody shared the juicy, need-to-know details with grunts.

An unwelcome bitterness flooded through her.

"Delia?"

When Claude's fingertips brushed along her arm, she flinched, then twisted out of his reach. "What?"

"I lost you for a second there," he said with a chuckle. He was one seat closer to her now, with only a single chair between them as a buffer.

"I was…" She licked her lips. "I was just revelling in the fact that you're technically a king."

"Well, I've gathered there's much your High Council of simpletons won't share with you." Claude shrugged when she frowned at him. "They treat you all like children… I'm hardly surprised you know so little."

"Great," she muttered. Now even the enemy knew that hunters like Delia were basically just physical entities. Enforcers. Clearly she wasn't the brains behind the operation—not even close. And she didn't *want* to be. She wasn't clawing her way to the top, nor did she want to be groomed like Kain to take over on a High Council position.

She just wanted some fucking respect.

She wanted not to be the butt of a joke in front of seventy of her peers.

Fingertips brushed against her skin again, but this time she didn't flinch back. Slowly she lifted her eyes to Claude, a flicker of her eyebrow asking a wordless question.

"Do you want me to take you home?" he asked, gently, like he was speaking to a lost child. Only she wasn't a lost child. Just a somewhat broken adult, one who needed some time alone with a tub of ice cream, a bottle of wine, and trashy TV to nurse her bruises—on her body and on her ego.

So she nodded, then rose from the gilded table and headed for the door without a word.

*   *   *

"I can't believe you drive a soccer mom mini-van." Delia laughed, unable to help herself. She'd wanted to comment on it the second Claude drove up to the stone porch at the front entrance of the main house, but it wasn't until they hit the familiar downtown streets that she had any will to talk at all. She sat in the front seat, belted in and arms crossed.

"It's discreet," Claude told her almost happily, slowing to a gentle stop at a light. They were only a few blocks from her apartment building now, and with the end nearing, Delia's anxiety dial inched ever upward. There they were, the two of them seated beside one another while the radio played easy rock tunes. It had been nice, actually. Quiet. Relaxed. Just what she needed after the night she'd had—and she didn't want it to be over.

Which was...totally unacceptable.

"If you ever accept my dinner invitation, I promise I'd pick you up in something much nicer," he added when the light changed to green. Delia tried to smile but couldn't, her playfulness falling flat. Apparently the one joke was all she had in her.

"I'll take your word for it."

It probably wasn't smart to give him her address.

Claude had offered to drop her off at the bus station downtown, somewhere very public where all the transit lines converged. But the thought of walking the twenty minutes from the station to her apartment made her want to cry, so she quietly gave up her address and Claude punched it into the GPS.

"Are you alright?" Claude posed the question as they turned onto her street, and she directed him to stop in the designated loitering zone near the front door of her building.

"Fine," she croaked. Today had been exhausting and it wasn't even noon yet, but otherwise fine. "I just need a really hot shower."

"A bath seems more relaxing."

"A bath is for people who enjoy sitting in their own filth," she said, unbuckling her seatbelt and slowly sliding it over her stiff body. Besides, after she freshened up, maybe took a power nap and gobbled some painkillers, Delia had every intention of going back to the alley where she had dropped her stake in order to retrieve it.

Maybe. If she could get off the couch once she sat down.

"Delia, wait…" He locked the doors as she tried to open hers, then unlocked it sheepishly when she scowled. "Sorry."

"What, Claude?"

"I want to help you," he said as he put the van in park and faced her properly. "Your combat skills are subpar, and…" He cleared his throat as a painful blush rose to Delia's cheeks. "I want to help you get better."

She went for the door handle again. "Thanks, but no thanks."

"I'll just keep showing up while you're on patrol then," he announced as soon as she opened the door and slid out.

"No."

"It's the only way I'll stop worrying about you," he continued, leaning across the front seats and popping his sunglasses up on his head. Her breath caught in her throat. It was easier to reject him when he kept those on. "Last night was very telling to me, and I think I can help you improve."

Delia exhaled heatedly, gripping the doorframe. "And why would you want to help a hunter get *better* at fighting and killing vamps?"

"Because what you do is dangerous," he replied, "and many vampires *should* be sanctioned for the crimes they commit."

"I…" She definitely wasn't recharged enough to fight with him about this. So, she shot him a tight smile instead. "Thanks for the ride home. And breakfast. And for… smashing that guy's face in."

Her name tumbled through his lips as a groan, and he sat up as she slammed the door, calling out, "Think about it!"

Shaking her head, she waved stiffly at him through the window, then zipped inside her building without looking back. Once she was in the elevator, Delia punched the button to her floor and all but collapsed back against the wall. With a heavy sigh, she closed her eyes to block out the painfully bright white lighting in the ceiling, wishing it was as easy to block out her increasingly concerning thoughts—about her job, about her abilities, about Claude.

And while she had grand plans of soaking her aching bones in a steamy shower the second she got inside, it seemed once again she was doomed to fail. With the shower running in the background, Delia decided to quickly check her League email, waiting for the water to heat up.

About thirty seconds later, she was passed out on her unmade bed, dead to the world.

CHAPTER 6: TOO MUCH FAMILY TIME

"Well, that's a shiner if I ever saw one." Delia crossed her arms and grinned as Devin sidled up to her, sporting a very noticeable black eye and a sheepish grin of his own. All around them, hunters headed for the meeting room again, having received an emergency mass text to attend a meeting that night, schedules be damned, and to prepare for a lengthy session.

"Vamp got the better of me a couple days ago," Devin admitted as he stopped in front of her. At Delia's prompting, the much taller man crouched down so she could get a proper look. She made a face, resisting the urge to poke at the very bruised skin.

"Looks painful."

"It is."

"Did you get him back?"

"Tenfold," he said, straightening. "One less unregistered son of a bitch running around Harriswood, that's for sure."

She congratulated him, wishing she had her own victorious story of slaying a violent, nomadic vampire. Instead, she asked Devin about his weekend. Hers had consisted of a single patrol shift from 4AM to 9AM on Sunday, a sad attempt at a run, and then eating fast food on the couch and trying to forget the fact that Claude Grimm had rescued her from certain death—well, *maybe*-certain death—only a few days prior.

Otherwise, she had been nursing her battered body and wounded pride. So far, only the former was making much of a recovery. The latter still had a long way to go.

She heard her name as they were about to enter the meeting space, which buzzed with excited conversations beyond the doorway. Both she and Devin stopped just shy of it, moving aside as a few others pushed by to get a good seat. Behind them, Kain jogged toward her—a light, half-walking jog, like he wasn't putting any effort into it. All that changed once he was within an arm's reach, and Delia yelped when he snatched her wrist.

"Where the hell have you been?" he demanded, only to be shoved back by Devin, who positioned himself between her and Kain in seconds. Delia frowned as she shook off the shock. Kain had been calling her all weekend. In fact, he'd called at least once a day since the last meeting, but she hadn't wanted to talk to him.

"Back up, man," Devin warned. Physically, he was an imposing figure to a guy like Kain, who was tall in his own right but not nearly as broad. Still, the Irishman outranked her friend. Kain looked him up and down once, then honed in on his black eye.

"What'd you do, knock your face on a barbell?"

"Okay, okay, okay," Delia said, pushing between the two muscular figures with a groan. "This isn't a schoolyard. Stop it."

Devin looked at her like *she* was being the unreasonable one, and maybe she was, but she didn't need there to be yet another scene involving her for all her coworkers to gossip about before the meeting even started. Shaking her head, she let out a soft sigh and nodded to the door.

"I'll meet you inside, D."

Devin's scowl deepened. "D, I should—"

"Just save me a seat, okay?" She tried to grin, like this was no big deal, but she was stuck in some invisible force field of tension between Kain and Devin that was making her stomach turn. When Devin tried to protest again, she added, "*Actually* save me a seat this time. Here. Put my purse on it."

She had to all but shove it in his hand to get him to actually take it.

"Go on then," Kain called after him once Devin stalked away stiffly, hackles up. "You carry her purse."

"Stop it," Delia snapped, then smacked him hard on the chest as he laughed. He doubled over dramatically, but once he was upright again, still wracked with chuckles, his usually fair face had a tinge of red to it.

"Oh, come on, he can take it," Kain muttered. He rolled his eyes when she glared. "What? He's a big boy."

"A big boy who will literally put you through a wall one day if you push the right buttons." She rubbed her wrist where he'd grabbed her. "What the hell was all that about anyway?"

"You," he said, crossing his arms. "I've been trying to reach you all weekend, and I know you haven't been working. Not really, anyway."

"Okay, stalker." They moved closer to the wall as more hunters filed down the hallway, the noise from the nearby room becoming deafening with the latest arrivals. She shook her head and mirrored his stance: arms folded and shoulders back. "What? Are you mad I didn't answer your calls? I was having *me* time."

"Yeah, well, *me* time didn't happen to include Claude Grimm, did it?"

"Oh my *god*, say it louder!" She pushed at him again, only this time it was obvious just how little impact she had on him. "I don't think the entire League heard you."

"But it didn't, right?"

"Can you fuck off with that?" she grumbled. Heat flooded her cheeks. "*No*, it did not include Claude Grimm. Seriously, Kain…"

Well, Claude Grimm hadn't been the entirety of her 'me time' over the last four days, but he'd definitely been on her mind for much of it, sleeping or awake.

"Look, I only ask because I was worried, alright?" Kain lowered his voice, features slipping into a frown. "I know we took the piss out of you at the last meeting, you know, about the volunteering and stuff—"

"I vividly remember," Delia remarked humorlessly, a familiar heavy weight settling in her gut. Kain's jaw clenched and unclenched briefly, those light brown eyes looking everywhere but her.

"I was worried you went and got drunk afterwards and did something stupid, okay?"

She scoffed. "Glad to know you think so highly of me." Then, when Kain fixed her with a half-smile and a raised eyebrow, she scoffed again. "I wouldn't do that."

"You absolutely *would* do that," he said, sounding annoyingly sure of himself. To be fair, some of her 'me time' had consisted of a bottle of wine or two—at the time she'd rationalized drinking them as a way to dull the pain of her healing.

"Well, I'm fine," she told him after a long pause. "No need to be so dramatic." Delia rubbed again at her wrist, which hummed with a faint ache. "Or rough."

"Main takeaway is that I was worried," he said, then muttered, "though God knows why."

"Who else would be your pity date to the bar when everyone else shoots you down?" Delia smirked, then reached up to pat at his cheek. Kain flinched away slightly, then, perhaps trusting she wouldn't smack him again, leaned in and let her pat him.

"Can you just answer my calls next time? Jesus." He pushed forward and steered Delia toward the door. The next words were said in her ear, his breath making the hairs on the back of her neck rise. "Or at least my messages… Let me know you're still alive."

"Aye, aye, sir," Delia barked, then turned and gave him a mock salute. She flashed a smirk as they parted ways, Kain headed for his boys near the middle of the room and Delia to sit with Devin at the front.

Getting into her seat at these events was like finding one's seat in the middle of the row at a crowded movie theater. Delia had to climb over legs and feet, balance precariously on the chairs in the row in front of her, and mutter a string of apologies as she went. Once she finally fell into her seat beside Devin, she exhaled deeply and plopped her purse on her lap.

"Great seats," she noted, but her smile faded when he didn't offer one in return. "Devin…"

"That guy's a huge ass, Delia," he said gruffly, obviously not caring who heard. "I don't know why you put up with his crap all the time."

"He's not that bad," she insisted, but Delia knew Kain could be an asshole on even the best of days.

"He's a player. He's favoured by the Council. He was promoted faster than he should have been," Devin said, using his fingers to list each item. "He talks down to you. He makes you the butt of every joke in front of his dirtbag friends. He jerks you around and has done so for years. Seriously, D, I don't know why you give that guy the time of day."

She looked away with another exasperated sigh. When he said it like that, the rational side of Delia had to wonder why she stayed friends with Kain over the years too. Something about him had always screamed comfort to her. Before she met and grew close to Devin and Ali in her first hunter year, there was just Kain. Sexy, bad boy Kain who knew what he was doing with a stake *and* in the bedroom. Maybe she just fell back on him these days because he was once an easy habit.

Regardless, they hadn't done anything remotely sexual after he had calmed her down during her post-masquerade meltdown. Apparently he didn't do chicks with vampire bites, which Delia wasn't exactly heartbroken over.

"Okay, okay. Point taken."

"Seriously."

"*Okay.*"

Licking her lips, Delia twisted her body around to get a better look at the room, which was steadily filling up. Ali sat a few rows behind with her fiancé, and the blonde waved when she and Delia made eye contact. Delia waved back, grinning when the woman busied herself with fixing Steve's bushy eyebrows, which he immediately tried to duck out of. Tried and failed. It was like watching a mama lion groom her unwilling cub, but with less tongue.

Soon people were forced to stand at the back, which Delia pointed out to Devin as she thanked him for saving her seat. He bumped her with his muscular upper arm, then offered a small smile. Apparently whatever weird fight they were in had come to an end.

"You know," she said as the last of the hunters filed in, some noticeably out of breath, "one of these days I'm going to harp on you for flirting with some girl you shouldn't. Mark my words. The tables will turn."

"Doubt it," he fired back, his voice dropping to a whisper. "I don't do crazy."

Her eyebrows shot up, even as the lights dimmed. "I'm sorry, but what was Lindsey from accounting, then?"

"Lindsey was drama." Devin faced forward now, and Delia straightened up at the arrival of Wentworth and the rest of the Council. Softly, she heard Devin murmur, "*Kain* is batshit crazy."

She drew a breath to whisper something back, then thought better of it as the room descended into a terse silence. Wentworth wasn't happy. In fact, all the faces of the High Council members looked like they'd taken a whiff of something foul before stalking out of their private entrance. The ceiling pod lights cast shadows across their aged faces, making their frowns all the more dramatic. As always, each of the five members wore their black suits, all tailored to perfection. Delia ran a subtle hand over her beige v-neck tee, hoping it was clean. Beiges and whites were dangerous for messy eaters.

"Good evening, all," Wentworth began, standing

before the crowd with his hands clasped in front of him. "Thank you for coming in on such short notice. Most of you will be here until sunrise tomorrow. Those who have scheduled patrols may leave, but you must return immediately once they are over."

"You working tonight?" Devin whispered, and Delia shook her head, gaze fixed on Wentworth as she absentmindedly nibbled on her thumbnail.

"Tonight we will be casting a vote for an unprecedented development in League and vampire relations," Wentworth continued. "The decision must be unanimous. If by sunrise it is not, we will not go forward. Every argument for and against will be heard. Pizza and drinks are available at the back and will be restocked for the duration of the meeting. Now, if you'll please give your full attention to our guest this evening—Johnathon Warwick."

Whispers erupted across the hall, heated words exchanged as the private door in the front corner opened, and out stepped a familiar face that, for once, wasn't Claude fucking Grimm. No, he was only familiar because he was the head of a local clan and had a small photo pinned on the staff room corkboard—dangerous, but still a small fish.

Johnathon Warwick moved into the room with some caution, followed closely by two vampires Delia assumed were his kids, William and Victoria, rumored to be turned by their father's bite when they were in their early teens. While the men were thin and gaunt, cheekbones so prominent that it was off-putting, Victoria had enough curve to catch more than a few eyes in the crowd, her bright red lips pursed in a petulant frown. All three dressed like they'd strolled out of a gangster movie.

The first invited vamps to League headquarters in— well, Delia wasn't sure a vamp had ever *willingly* set foot in the Harriswood HQ. She swallowed hard and kept her breathing even. Hearts must have been racing around the room, with hunters shifting and murmuring. At the back, those who were forced to stand had surged forward. Wentworth raised his hands like he was soothing a herd of twitchy cattle.

"Easy," he said. Then, in a clearer, much louder voice, he barked, "Order! Johnathon Warwick and his children are *guests* in headquarters tonight. I'll have no foolishness in their presence."

Devin looked like it physically pained him to stay seated. Glancing back, Delia tried to find Kain to gauge his reaction, but there were too many worried and angered faces between them.

"Ladies and gentlemen, thank you for your patience," Warwick began, his accent smoothly English and surprisingly soft. "We approached your High Council yesterday with this matter, and they have agreed to bring it before you. The Donovan situation has grown increasingly worrisome these last few months. Vampires and humans alike are dying. As you know, some of *our* humans, our special friends—" Delia's eyebrows shot up and a few behind her scoffed. "—were brutally murdered on the night of the most recent trades.

"The Donovans are, in numbers, the strongest clan in the region. We would have preferred to handle their recent bids for power internally, but I'm afraid my brother clans fear reprisal from a force as powerful as Shane Donovan and his family. So we turn to you to help us put them back in check. We only survive here because we exist harmoniously, clan and human populace as one. We know the laws, the rules. We know we cannot make ourselves known to the human world, and yet the Donovans have flaunted their status too often as of late."

"We were asked to remedy the situation," Wentworth said from his place beside Warwick, easing into the conversation like the two had practiced it beforehand. "The Warwick clan has requested we pool resources with them and the local PD. The Donovans need to be put in check before more people lose their lives. However, no American League has ever partnered with a clan before. As I said, it's unprecedented."

"And stupid," Devin muttered. Delia shot him a curious look before bringing her gaze back to Wentworth.

"So tonight we will debate the facts." Wentworth gestured to the doorway and off the Warwick trio went, escorted out by two other members of the High Council. "We will go over the histories of the clans and decide whether we need a vampire partnership to address this growing threat. If we cannot come to a consensus, then we will not partner with the Warwick clan. Simple as that. But I will need everyone's opinion. We are a League. We are a family. If we take this leap, we do it together or not at all."

As it stood, Delia had very little interest in joining forces with the Warwicks. In the ten seconds that she had seen Johnathon Warwick in person, he struck her as a bit *too* smooth, like a British used-car salesman made up of too many sharp points and edges and cheekbones. A little voice at the back of her mind whispered for her to use her sole vampire contact and ask Claude to prove or disprove her suspicions.

No. She'd been trying hard not to think about Claude, despite his nightly appearance in her dreams. There was no way she could ask him for help. She couldn't legitimize whatever the hell they had floating between them—even if her subconscious wanted her to.

So Delia put her faith in the League, in her fellow hunters, and hoped that by morning, everything would be sorted.

*   *   *

If Wentworth was right, and the League was supposed to feel like her family, Delia decided that most hunters were the kind of family she could only take in short doses immediately followed by a weeklong holiday. Hours of listening to them all bicker and argue, hunters pounding their chests and whipping out their dicks to see whose was bigger, had given her a migraine.

Just as Wentworth had predicted, the debates lasted until the late hours of the following morning. By the time she'd reach home, the sun would be up and another day would be in full swing—another day that Delia planned to sleep away before her patrol that night. Four hours in the suburbs, nothing major, but she felt like she needed two full days of sleep to muster up the desire to go.

Plus, if she saw one more piece of pizza, she was going to hurl up the twelve slices she'd scarfed down over the course of the last ten hours.

Even though Wentworth had insisted everyone get a say, it became very clear that there were only about ten or so opinions that mattered. Neither she nor Devin were a part of the chosen ones, no matter how hard they fought to be heard, and in the end they were left to fade into the masses and vote when the time came.

The League had unanimously decided to confront the Donovan threat *with* the Warwick clan. That hadn't been the prevailing opinion at the start of the night, but the naysayers were slowly beaten back until everyone agreed that this was in Harriswood's best interest. Be a unified front. Alone, neither the League, the police department, nor the individual clans had enough people to counteract the sheer numbers of Donovan-aligned vampires. An alliance seemed necessary, given the circumstances. Show the other clans that the League wasn't an entity to be trifled with, that they would respond to a threat in kind, if necessary.

There were conditions, of course. The Donovans would need to prove they were a threat to the general population, not just to the *special friends* of the Warwick clan. Patrols would be increased. More surveillance would be installed around Shane Donovan's monstrosity of a mansion on the other side of the lake. All the League informants, Delia's Hugh included, would be tasked with digging up dirt and acquiring sensitive information about the Donovan family and their subordinates.

Which meant the rats wouldn't be trading gigs for cash anymore. Not that Delia cared. Hugh had blown her off over and over again, like he didn't even want her business these days. She knew she didn't pay as well as some of the other hunters, but she'd sort of hoped it would be a money-is-money situation. Apparently not.

All in all, Delia approved of the League's plan to proceed with caution. That was what had swayed her in the end. Delia had voted negative whenever the question of brute force arose. It wasn't a smart approach, not when the Donovan clan numbers beat all the other clans by a little over half. They had to be smart about it, and while no one was asking her opinion, she had enough faith in men like Kain and the High Council to come up with an appropriate solution.

Still, she couldn't shake the somewhat squirmy feeling in the pit of her stomach that the League was now partnered with a vamp clan. Sure, she had been spending an unnecessary amount of time with Claude Grimm recently, but it wasn't the same.

As she and Devin made their way out of the meeting room, both of them heavy-lidded and sluggish in the sea of equally exhausted hunters, she stopped at the sound of both their names being called. Seconds later Ali popped into view, her blonde hair tucked up in a messy bun and her eyes bloodshot. She was taller and skinnier than Delia, even in flats, and, as always, had her cell phone glued to her hand.

"I just wanted to remind you guys about me and Steve's stag and doe at Jimmie's next month," she said. Ali might have been talking normally, but her voice felt a little too shrill for Delia. She tried not to wince. Apparently not everyone was as tired as they looked.

"I already RSVP'd online," Devin told her with a weary

grin. Ali's sharp gaze fixed on Delia, who nodded when cued.

"Of course I'll be there." An opportunity to drink for a cause *and* watch her friend get totally shit-faced before the wedding? Obviously Delia would be in attendance. Ali had been in full militant mode ever since Steve proposed last year, and Delia was desperate to have her friend back, even for one night. There was only so much wedding prep talk she could take before it all started to sound like white noise.

Apparently the bride- and groom-to-be had rented out the bottom floor of Jimmie's Place, a hunter favourite downtown. Of all the drinks purchased, sixty percent would go toward the wedding. Delia had always thought hunters getting married seemed a little pointless, given, well, *everyone's* potentially limited lifespan, but Ali and Steve were determined to make it work.

And Delia had never seen Ali go more hardcore about anything, vamp hunting included, than she had over the wedding.

"Okay, that's awesome," Ali chirped. She brought her phone up and swiped at the screen, then tapped around for a few seconds. "I really need you to RSVP online too so we can get more exact numbers. Okay? Okay. Awesome."

She blew them both kisses before pushing between them and cornering another small group down the hall. Delia's face screwed as she tried to force the higher-than-normal pitch of Ali's voice out of her head.

"Good God was that shrill," Devin said as they rejoined the flow of people headed for the elevators. "Was she shrill? Why do I feel like I'm hungover?"

Delia patted his arm, the ache starting to throb behind her eyes now. "I feel the same."

"So you actually going?"

"Yeah, why not? Should be fun. I like to drink and dance. Ali and Steve are about as broke as the rest of us and yet apparently they decided to drag this huge expense into their lives for no reason at all, so I may as well support them a bit." She felt Devin staring at her when she finished, and it was only then that she realized she was glaring at no one in particular. "Sorry, was that mean? It felt a bit mean."

"Wow."

"I'm just tired," she said, running her hand through her hair. It frizzed, obviously unimpressed with being underground in a mildly humid room for so many hours. At least Devin had had a chance to leave and come back for his quick patrol shift at midnight.

"Yeah, well, try to rein that in at the party," Devin chided as they stopped behind the crowd at the elevators. "You know she's really excited for it. Like, way too excited." Delia noticed him blink heavily, slowly. Poor guy needed a bed as bad as she did. "I'm actually scared to go to the wedding. She seems like she'll shank me if I clap at the wrong time or something."

Delia nodded. "Yeah, I can see that."

Given how tightly-wound Ali was about things, Delia would be surprised if the woman didn't go full bridal meltdown on the day of.

Speaking of full meltdown. As soon as the elevators dinged, she grabbed Devin's arm and shoved her way to the front. No way were they waiting for the next one. Because if she didn't get home and into bed in the next half hour, *she* was going to go full meltdown right there in the depths of League HQ. And for once, she wouldn't care.

CHAPTER 7: DEAD RATS

Hugh was dead. He and six other informants had been found hanging from the Harriswood Library entrance, ropes around their necks and the Donovan insignia carved into their chests. Delia had found out that morning as she was eating breakfast, lazily scooping spoonfuls of soggy cereal into her mouth while perusing her League emails. Pictures were attached as proof, and her heart dropped to her stomach when she recognized Hugh's smarmy face, all purplish red and bloated, amongst the seven.

He hadn't been the nicest of people. Hell, he hadn't been a nice person—period. But Hugh had been her informant for a few years now, and while he'd been annoyingly quiet since his tip about the Banesview masquerade, Delia never wanted anything bad to happen to him. He was a rat. All the dead were League rats, spying on vamps, earning their trust and reporting back to hunters for a fee. Hugh was among the few who actually worked with low-ranking hunters like Delia, though Kain insisted he always overcharged her.

There would be a few hunters feeling as she did today. It was an uncomfortable blend of sadness and anger, plus a pinch of frustration. The League had decided to help the Warwick clan only two days ago, and suddenly seven of their informants were found dead. Did the Donovans have a spy in the organization? Did they have rats of their own?

She didn't want to work with any of the other rats. Hugh had usually steered her in the right direction in the past. His mannerisms, from his horrific smoker's cough to his muttered insults, were traits Delia was at least used to by now. Would she play his weeping widow at the League's small memorial service tomorrow? No, but that didn't mean she felt nothing at the news of his death. In fact, it made her heart hurt quite unexpectedly, and she went through the rest of her morning mindlessly clicking at various social media pages, emails, and shared articles in a fog, trying to distract herself from the pinched feeling in her chest.

Her phone vibrated at noon. After sitting in a crunched up position for an hour or so, her neck, legs, and, well, just about everything was horribly stiff, and Delia set her laptop aside and stretched, then reached for her phone. Devin had texted to ask how she was doing. One of his informants had been found hanging this morning too, so she responded in kind, telling him she was shaken but coping and asked how he was doing. Which seemed to be pretty much the same. From the words Devin used, Delia suspected that he was angrier than he let on.

A dark cloud had settled over the League—a dark cloud flying the Donovan colours. If the rats weren't safe, then nobody was. Informants were promised League protection for their services. Yet here was a very violent, very public display of defiance by the Donovan clan right on the doorstep of League headquarters.

After a long hot shower, Delia settled back down on the couch and loaded up a show to distract herself. While the episode buffered, she grabbed her phone again and clicked on her contacts app to call Kain. Halfway through scrolling, however, she discovered a name she hadn't personally added.

Claude Grimm.

Her lips morphed into a lopsided grin. Bold bastard had slipped his phone number onto her phone—he'd even taken a selfie for the contact photo. Those brilliant blue eyes, electric as ever, stared back at her, his smile touching them so that it actually looked genuine.

It was then she thought back to his offer to help her hone her fighting skills. Delia had pushed it aside last week as she recovered from her injuries, and while Claude himself was more difficult to forget, she'd somehow been able to avoid thinking about it until now.

Maybe there was merit in the offer. As Delia saw it, there were two sides to every coin, just as there were two sides to Claude's offer. On the one side, he probably was at least *partly* interested in helping her because of the unsettling but growing attraction between them. On the other side, there was the possibility that it was a ruse, and Claude planned to use her to gain inside information on League comings and goings. Sure, he might have saved her from a murderous vamp recently, but even Delia's brain had no problem concocting dangerous ulterior motives.

If all that was something a vamp king would do. It seemed more like a task for an underling, frankly.

Maybe, just *maybe*, he actually wanted to help her improve because he was worried for Delia's safety.

If Donovans were attacking League informants, hunters on patrol in characteristically "safe" areas might be next. Maybe Delia *should* beef up her fighting skills. Clearly her sessions with Devin and the League trainers weren't doing much—maybe it was time to look elsewhere.

Her thumb hovered over the call button on his contact page, a surge of adrenaline washing over her, until she tossed the phone aside and watched her show instead. But once again Delia was unfocused, her mind elsewhere as she tried to get into the episode's plot. When the credits rolled, she was right back to Claude's contact page, staring at it while a great internal debate raged over whether or not to call him.

In the end, she succumbed and let her thumb fall, hesitantly bringing the phone up to her ear. The first ring made her heart hammer. She was only agreeing to this because there was the possibility of gaining insider information through Claude. Even if he *was* spying through her, she could play that game too.

Yeah. That was why she'd pressed call. Totally.

The second ring made her mouth dry.

The third made her palms clammy.

She closed her eyes, suddenly hoping he wouldn't answer.

"Hello?" He did after the fifth ring. Delia opened and closed her mouth, but no words came out. She could hear her blood pumping in her ears. "Hello?"

"Claude," she finally managed, then cleared her throat and willed her breathing to even out. "It's Delia." She swallowed hard, hating how the mere thought of him transformed her into a bumbling idiot. "Hi."

There was a brief pause. "Delia." She could actually hear the smile in his voice as he spoke. "This is a surprise."

"Yeah, well—"

"A welcome one," Claude added. Somehow Delia found herself curled up into an even tighter ball in the corner of the couch, constantly fixing her hair like he could actually see her.

"Oh. That's good," she forced out. "I was worried you might be sleeping. I mean. I should have assumed that. Just because you can be up during the day doesn't mean you will be up."

Stop rambling. Delia rolled her eyes, and then tugged at her hair, embarrassed that her discomfort was so obvious. His chuckle made her skin flush.

"I actually had a business lunch today," he told her. "You caught me as I was saying my goodbyes."

"Right. Good." She wasn't sure what to say suddenly, all her people skills disappearing when talking to a guy she was attracted to over the phone like she was a teenager with a crush.

"What can I do for you, Delia?" Claude asked when the silence dragged on. "Have you called to accept my dinner date?"

"No," she said flatly, detecting the teasing edge to his voice. "Actually, I called because…" She closed her eyes. Here goes nothing. "Because I want you to help make me a better fighter."

Now it was his turn to take a pause. She waited, nibbling her lower lip because it was better than gnawing at her nails.

"Look, never mind," Delia muttered, ready to hang up. "Forget I—"

"I'd be happy to help," Claude insisted. The teasing was gone now, and in its place was an emotion Delia couldn't quite wrap her head around. "When would you like to start?"

"I have tomorrow off," she said without thinking— apparently her brain wanted this to happen immediately.

"Done. Would you like me to send a car to fetch you?"

"Fetch me to where?"

"My home, of course," he told her. "I have a gym in the west wing, along with well-maintained trails should you wish to warm up with a run."

Of course this was happening at his place. Why hadn't she considered that before? It wasn't like she could bring him down to the League training hall.

"I can find my own way there," she said after a moment's consideration. "When do you want me?"

The chuckle was back and she braced herself for some sexually charged innuendo…

"Anytime you wish," was his response, which sent a chill down her spine. She sat a little straighter, all business, to will away whatever effect his voice had on her.

"Four o'clock."

"Done." The sounds of midday traffic rumbled behind him, followed by the slamming of what she assumed was a car door. "See you then, Delia."

"Okay."

Seconds later the line was dead, and she tossed her phone aside like it scalded her. Unable to shake her steadily growing grin, Delia hopped up, energized for the first time all day, and went to tidy her disastrous kitchen.

Not because she wanted to do the dishes or scrub the grease stains off the backsplash, but because if she didn't move, the high she felt after a mere two-minute conversation with Claude Grimm would utterly consume her.

And she wasn't ready to be consumed.

Not yet.

CHAPTER 8: ROME WASN'T BUILT IN A DAY

"You sure there's a house out here?" The cabbie raised an eyebrow at her in the rearview mirror when Delia looked up from her phone, on which she had been tracking the car's steady movement toward Claude's forest-enclosed manor.

"Yes," she said tersely. They must have had this conversation six times already, the driver getting more vocal as they made the turn onto the unpaved driveway through the woods.

The car jostled back and forth as it hit yet another dip in the road, and Delia's hand shot out to grip the assist handle over the window until things evened out.

"Feel like I should charge extra for all the trouble my car's gone through," he muttered, irritability rolling off him in waves. "It's not meant to go off-roading."

"We're on a road," Delia countered. A terribly uneven road, sure, but if Claude's soccer mom van could survive it, the taxi could too.

"On the road to nowhere," he carried on as he leaned forward to peer through the windshield uncertainly. He then looked at her in the mirror again, and Delia glared back.

"Would it help if I told you I'm not taking you out here so I can murder you and chop your corpse up into little itty bitty pieces?" she snapped. The dot on her phone screen was almost at the destination, so why hold back anymore? "Will that clear the air? Seriously…"

"You know, I could have made you get out and walk, but I'm a nice guy—"

"Oh my god, *stop*." She grabbed her purse and fished out two tens, then tossed them on the front seat. He didn't deserve the six-dollar tip for all the crap he'd given her ever since they hit country roads, but she wasn't in the mood to wait for change. "I'll just walk."

Thirty seconds later she was stomping along the forest path and the taxi was trying to turn around in an impossibly small space. Delia wondered whether she should stay to help, but then thought better of it. The cabbie had been an ass as soon as she told him her destination. Besides, her pre-training jitters were starting to get the better of her.

Once the high from her conversation with Claude had died down, she'd sat wondering if this was a good idea. Then she'd come to the conclusion that it was a *great* idea. Then she'd second guessed herself and the cycle started all over again.

As she walked, the inner turmoil finally started to ease. Something about being outdoors where it was quiet, where the weather was crisp and cool—it was soothing. Summer evolved into fall in a matter of weeks, though most of the leaves were still green and most of the days still warm. Today she'd gone through all her workout clothes and tried every possible outfit combination a number of times before settling on the one she wore now: black yoga pants, a loose navy blue t-shirt with a slight v-neck, and comfy old sneakers. Dark colours had always been flattering on her—and they hid the sweat.

As she walked, she wondered if track pants might have been more appropriate, then shook her head. While she wasn't there to seduce Claude, she went with the yoga pants that hugged her curves best because a part of her wanted to look at least moderately attractive. They *had* slept together, after all.

She paused at the break in the trees. The dirt road carried on and opened up into a huge circle in front of the main house. To the far left of the manor sat a warehouse, which she suspected housed all of the clan's vehicles. To the right were the trails down to the guest bunkers and dining hall.

Taking a deep breath, she pushed onward, arms crossed over her chest as she marched along the path and up to the front door. Well, *doors*. The entryway was an enormous, somewhat daunting place with mounted lanterns on either side of the two broad doors. The manor—castle, mansion, whatever it was—had a slate-grey rock pattern on the outer walls, but the doors were painted a dark pine green with black iron handles. Drumming her fingers against her thigh, Delia was about to reach for the knocker when she spied what looked like a doorbell hidden off to the side.

Seconds after pressing it, one of the doors swung open. Delia shifted back at Claude's hasty appearance. Inside, the bell was still ringing its melodic tone.

"I wasn't sure whether to... to... uh..." No. This fumbling, bumbling person she became around him wasn't happening today. "I wasn't sure whether to ring the bell or use the knocker thing. So."

"Either is fine," he insisted smoothly, opening the door wider and beckoning her inside. Delia hesitated, her eyes roving the sprawling entryway again. This was it. No going back now. Arms crossed over her chest again, she pushed in, not looking at him as she went—though the whiff of delicious cologne he wore was enough to make her cheeks flush. She bit them in response. *No.*

The entrance hall was much the same as it had been the last time she was there: huge and uninviting, gruesome tapestries of medieval battles hung from floor to ceiling. She turned away from what looked like an impaling scene as Claude sauntered up beside her.

"How did you get here?" he asked, standing close

enough that she could feel his heat, but far enough that she didn't get the urge to bolt.

"Taxi."

"Ah. I'll give you the number of my preferred car service next time. I've found the regular city cabs make a fuss coming all the way out here."

She shrugged, not wanting to admit that he was right. "Sure."

"Shall we?" Claude asked after a brief pause, gesturing to the grand staircase ahead with a slight grin.

"Yeah, right. Let's... Let's do this."

"Oh, *Delia*, don't sound so morose," he teased. He strolled one step ahead of her, casually. "I promise it won't be all that bad."

She bit her lip to keep from responding, instead taking in his outfit with a single up-and-down sweep of her eyes. For once he wasn't in dark jeans or dress pants. Instead, he was wearing a pair of fleece workout pants, grey, a little loose—which made his butt look surprisingly good. He'd paired it with a simple white t-shirt. It was strange seeing him look so casual. In her mind, Claude was forever wearing a suit and tie and leather shoes, dapper and cultured from head to toe.

This version of Claude was less intimidating. Like he wasn't miles ahead of her on the sophistication scale, but somewhere reachable—this vampire king who wore too-white running shoes and drove a minivan to blend in. Delia smirked, then schooled her features when he looked back at her with a slightly arched brow.

True to his word, the west wing of Claude's home housed a gym of sorts. While it lacked the extensive equipment and weights that the gym at HQ had, there were floor-to-ceiling windows that let in so much natural light that it hardly mattered. A few treadmills sat in front of the windows, along with a row of bikes. The lack of equipment wasn't surprising by any means; vamps didn't exactly need to work out. As Delia surveyed the room, she assumed it was mostly used by the clan's human guests. At least everything was clean. Not a speck of dust in sight, nor a mirror to be seen.

"So what is it that you would like to work on?" Claude asked as he hauled a huge, squishy-looking blue exercise mat from its place along the wall and set it in the center of the room. "We have the whole place to ourselves."

Delia joined him moments later, poking at the mat. It seemed much softer than the ones she was used to landing on. "Didn't you come up with some grueling routine for me?"

"No." Claude grinned again, shifting his weight between each leg as they both eyed each other. "I'm trying to stop being presumptuous, remember?"

"Huh." She jumped onto the mat to test it out, then toppled over when she discovered it was much, *much* squishier than she'd expected. Heat crawled from her cheeks to the rest of her face and neck as she got herself situated under Claude's unwavering stare. Trying to seem like she'd done it on purpose, Delia stretched her legs out and tried reaching her toes. "I'm just not great in a fight. I spar with other hunters and they always beat me. I watch training videos and read up on techniques, but I can't get it and I don't know why."

Claude kneeled at the edge of the mat, his hands resting on his thighs. "Well, I can't guarantee I'll make you better, but I'll try."

Why? She wanted to ask it so badly. Why did he care so much? Sure, it was obvious he was attracted to her, but as she started to stretch her stiff leg muscles, she couldn't help but think there had to be something more to it. Men don't just *do* nice things like this without expecting something in return.

"I don't know how you expect me to best a vamp in hand-to-hand combat without a weapon," she said. It was always an issue she had a problem with. "I mean, they're inherently stronger than humans. How am I supposed to win a fight when my opponent is freakishly more powerful than I am?"

"We're in the same situation, you know."

She shook her head. "No we're not."

"Well..." Claude chuckled. "Perhaps not the exact same, but vampires who are sun-resistant like me are actually physically weaker than those who aren't."

"Actually?"

His lips twitched like he was trying to hold back a smile. "Actually."

"Then why are you guys running the show?"

"Because there are more hours in the day for us," he said. After she'd asked the question, Delia could think of a hundred reasons why a sun-resistant vamp was better off than those confined to the shadows, but for some reason, she liked listening to Claude answer. His voice still had that melodic quality to it, even in a setting like this, and she found it easy to be lulled as he went on. "We make more alliances while they are stuck indoors. We blend better with the human populations... Plenty of reasons. Not all strong men can be rulers."

"Or kings," she added softly. Claude nodded, then situated himself closer, the mat dipping under his movement.

"Or kings," he said. A vision crossed her mind of him crawling across the mat and kissing her, slowly pushing her down into the plush blue material and lifting her leg to wrap around his hip, their lips parted and breath heated. Delia blinked hard and looked away, then stood, still a little wobbly. It was like standing on a huge pile of pillows.

"So you seriously think that with your guidance, I can beat a vamp in hand-to-hand combat?"

Claude sat back on his elbows, head cocked to the side. "That's my goal."

"I don't believe you."

"Care to place a wager on it?" He wiggled his brow, his smile both impish and charming; it made her stomach flip in a good way.

Flirtation was just too easy with him.

Not good.

"I'm going to warm-up on the treadmill for a couple minutes," she said, waddling off the exercise mat with some difficulty. How the hell was she supposed to spar on this if she could barely find her footing now?

"I'll be here," she heard Claude say in response. Once she climbed onto a treadmill, Delia started pushing buttons to adjust her speed and incline, all the while the occasional quick glance over her shoulder. Claude was still on the mat, but he wasn't watching her like a creep or pacing back and forth like a caged animal. He lay on his back, hands folded together on his chest, and seemed lost in thought.

Swallowing hard, she faced forward and pressed the treadmill's start button.

*   *   *

"Well, Rome wasn't built in a day, I suppose."

"Shut up," Delia muttered as Claude smirked down at her. She snatched the ice-cold bottle of water from his hand, trying to stop her chest from heaving up and down. So much for looking good in front of a guy she'd had sex with; sweat glistened across every visible inch of her skin. Her cheeks were flushed again, not from embarrassment for once, and loose strands of brown hair stuck to her face, escaping from the rest of the brunette waves tucked into a bun on top of her head. Delia pressed the water bottle to her neck.

While she had cursed the stupidly thick exercise mat when they first started almost two hours ago, she was grateful for it now, its extra padding embracing her aching body as she reclined on it. Everything was sore and she could hear her heartbeat in her ears—a good workout by any measure. Now, if only she had actually gotten the better of Claude, just once, she could feel like she actually accomplished something.

"You will notice improvements with every training session," Claude remarked as he settled down beside her. Instead of a clear plastic water bottle plagued with condensation, he raised a shiny metal thermos to his mouth and took a quick sip. A few small red droplets clung to his lips after, but he licked them away hastily when he caught her staring.

Logically Delia could accept that Claude was drinking blood from a thermos, but it was harder for her brain to wrap around the fact that the two of them were hanging out, casually having a post-workout drink. Biting the inside of her cheek, she looked away and cracked open her plastic cap, then took a gulp of frigid water. When she was through, she'd drained half the bottle.

"Well, I'm supposed to improve *during* the session too," she lamented, allowing herself one little gripe session after not complaining for the whole two hours. Claude took another mouthful of his drink.

"You were improving," he insisted lightly. Delia's eyes swept across his features—not a drop of sweat anywhere. Just gorgeous eyes and a handsome jawline and tousled hair. Bastard.

"No I wasn't."

"Your reaction times *were* a little faster toward the end." He patted her thigh good-naturedly, but Delia stiffened, the heat lingering even after he retracted his hand. "It's all a matter of practice. Soon it will feel like a routine. You'll get faster, less sloppy with your movements. Then it will be second nature. You won't even think about it. Your body will just react."

"Yeah, I've heard that before," she said with a dramatic sigh, letting herself flop back on the mat and study the arched ceiling. Air conditioning blasted out from a vent on the wall as the early evening's setting sun cast golden rays across the gym floor. While they'd been at it for two hours, Delia felt like she'd blinked after her warmup on the treadmill and suddenly she was here, sprawled out on the mat in a sweaty, out-of-shape mess.

"It's true, you know."

She closed her eyes at the sound of him capping his thermos, and suddenly the mat shifted as if he had stretched out beside her. A crack of one eye showed her that he had left a little less than a foot of space between their bodies. While he wasn't sweaty like she was, they were both equally warm. Sighing, Delia tried to fan herself with one hand and pressed her water to her forehead with the other.

"You sound like…" Her eyes wandered the ceiling again. "Well, you sound like every trainer I've ever had. If I just push through the shit part at the beginning, it'll all be a breeze."

His chuckle made her grin. "That's the basic premise of learning something you aren't naturally skilled at."

She cast a sidelong look his way. "Are you saying I'm not a naturally skilled fighter?"

"Implying, more like—and nobody is when they first start out."

"Pretty sure I have some natural rhythm."

"I can personally attest that you have excellent natural rhythm."

A blush bloomed across her already flushed cheeks, and before she could stop herself, she swatted at his arm. "Stop it."

"What?" He laughed, and the mat rustled again as he shifted onto his side. "You set yourself up for that one."

She did her best to not roll into him despite the added dip in the mat beside her. Images of that night, the masks and the champagne and the lazy waltz with his hand pressed to her lower back, danced across her mind, but she beat them back before they took a turn for the scandalous.

"So how are you feeling?"

"Tired," was her first response, thrown out quickly to divert the conversation away from where it had been headed. "I'm sure I'll be pretty sore tomorrow."

Hell, it would be a miracle if she could even get out of bed tomorrow. Strictly speaking, Delia wasn't in *bad* shape—she jogged regularly, did the occasional weight lifting routine with Devin, and could hold her own on HQ's tougher obstacle courses—but apparently a work-out with Claude Grimm was more than she could handle.

"I don't doubt that," Claude said, "but it's a good feeling, I'm sure. Sore, but like you've done something."

She let her head fall to the side to look at him. "Do vamps feel that? Sore, I mean."

"A little." He shrugged. "Not for very long."

It would definitely have made her feel better tomorrow if she knew Claude felt as poorly as she did. They had spent the two hours going over proper fighting stances, with Claude constantly moving her arms and legs and shoulders and hips to the right position, constantly reminding her to correct her posture or tuck in her pelvis. She'd been putting too much pressure on her lower back, apparently.

Once she had her stances relatively down pat, they moved on to actual hand-to-hand combat, wherein Claude gave her pointers about her movements, about her intent. Still, with all his tips, he somehow always got her pinned to the mat, his body heavy and overwhelming and firm—and almost a little too welcome.

At least he didn't seem upset with her. Most instructors were when they finished a session. When hour number two was up, Claude insisted, in a somewhat worn but pleasant tone, that they stop for the evening, telling her they would work on a few routines another time that he found effective against vamp opponents. Weak spots. How she could use her opponent's body weight and strength against them.

Everything he was "teaching" her had already been drilled into her by the League, but somehow Claude's instruction stuck better, as much as she refused to admit it.

"I hate to ask," Claude said, suddenly reaching out and lifting some of the damp hair from her face. She stiffened as he tucked it behind her ear. "But is there any particular reason you decided to take me up on my offer?"

Her gaze swept across his face, wavering between telling the truth and telling a lie. "Because the informants were strung up at the… library."

Truth it was. Claude's eyebrows shot up in surprise. "Oh."

"I figured things are getting dangerous out there," she continued, facing the ceiling again and letting out a heavy sigh. "The Donovans are really ruffling feathers. First on the trades, then with our rats—"

"You call them rats?" He didn't sound particularly impressed with the phrase. Delia shrugged.

"Well, they are." She blinked. "Were. Mine was." Hugh's face appeared in the ceiling brickwork momentarily. "I worried that if they went after rats, what's to stop them from going up the next rung of the League ladder, you know? I'm about two steps up from the bottom. I'm not interested in being found by some kid with the Donovan insignia carved in my skin."

The thought sent a shiver down her spine, even with the heat.

"Shane Donovan…" Claude paused, and in her peripherals she noted that his features had hardened. "The Donovan clan is the largest and the most… present. They've always ruffled feathers."

"But not like this."

"*This* strikes me as very out-of-character for the man that I have known for two centuries," he remarked stiffly. His words prompted Delia to sit up. She crossed her legs and fiddled with her water bottle, wondering if this was the moment to press for information.

"So what do you think is going on?"

"Whatever it is, it will blow over," Claude said. He too sat up, then rose to his feet with more grace than Delia knew she could muster. "It always does. If not... I suppose I will need to act like a king again one of these days."

"But—"

"Delia," he said sharply. She looked up and found his expression unreadable, then inhaled shakily when his fingertips pressed to the underside of her chin. It wasn't a ghost of a caress, a mere whisper of skin against skin. No, he tilted her head back further so that their eyes could meet properly, his touch firm. Her heartbeat quickened with her breathing, but she did her best to keep him from seeing.

"When we are together, I'll never ask you about the comings and goings of your League," he told her, an edge to his tone that made her skin prickle. "I don't care. You are my only interest there. I ask that you give me the same courtesy. Don't pry into clan business."

She held herself there, still and unblinking, his fingers pressed under her chin. "Is that a threat?"

"A request." He pulled away and stepped off the mat, his absence leaving her frustratingly hotter than ever. Delia swiped a hand over her face as if that would erase the memory of him on her skin. "A request from me to you."

She finished the rest of her water in silence. Claude stood a few feet from the mat, his back to her and hands clasped behind him. Something had shifted between them. The playful vibe was dead and buried—and Delia found that she missed it. Stretching her neck from one side to the other, she decided that it was time to go. Two hours in a vamp's house was more than she should spend on any given day.

"Would you like to stay for dinner?" he asked as she tried to get up. Her legs were basically jelly at this point, the muscles in her thighs quivering with every movement. Once she was upright, Delia found him studying her again, the hard lines she'd seen across his face gone. "I can have something delivered."

She shook her head. "Thanks, but I think I'm going to go."

"I'll call you a car."

As much as she wanted to protest, to tell him that she was perfectly capable of calling for a taxi herself, Delia just nodded and stumbled off the mat. A heaviness was slowly settling across her body now that she was up again, the endorphins and adrenaline and whatever-the-hell-else that had kept her going for two straight hours finally abandoning her. All she wanted now was a hot shower and a back massage, both of which she was sure Claude would happily oblige her with if she asked.

But somehow that felt wrong, like she was taking advantage of him. Instead, Delia followed him from the west wing of the sprawling estate to the entrance foyer, only half-listening as he gave the name and location of the pick-up to the driver on his phone.

"Take a seat," he offered, directing her to a wooden bench by the front door. She hadn't noticed it previously—too distracted by the brutal tapestries hanging on the walls to pay attention to much else. "The driver will be here in ten minutes."

"Okay." She drifted to the bench and winced after carelessly plopping down on it—hard as a rock, it sent pain shooting right up her back. Just as she was about to make a somewhat sleepy complaint about the quality of his foyer benches, Delia realized she was alone in the hall. Had she passed out too? He'd been here just a second ago… Frowning, she searched the area for any signs of her handsome vamp instructor, then leaned back against the bench when she found nothing.

"Huh." She frowned and started massaging her temples to ward off the dull ache between them. "Bye then."

A few minutes later Claude was back—and he wasn't alone.

Well, he wasn't with anyone else either, but the giant bundle of flowers in his hand made her sit upright in a flash.

"What are those?" She pointed to the bouquet, her headache becoming more apparent at the sight. Claude peered around the purplish-red petals, an eyebrow up.

"Flowers," he said, and Delia let out a long sigh. "Mums, technically. Really hardy. Should stay blooming as long as you follow the care instructions on the little card inside the bundle."

"Why?" Delia asked, standing and begrudgingly accepting the bouquet.

"Well, I went with mums over something like lilies or roses because you don't strike me as the sort to have the greenest of thumbs—"

"*Why*," Delia reiterated, "are you giving me flowers? This isn't a date."

His hands slid into his pockets, and he rocked back and forth on his heels, head tilted slightly to one side. "Isn't it?"

"*No*," she argued. "It isn't. And you knew that going in."

"Delia—"

"Don't make me regret agreeing to this," she said with a slight groan, cheeks flaming with flustered affection at the feel of his gift in her hands. "I didn't take you up on the whole dating thing because it's a bad idea."

"Not because you don't like me?"

"For many reasons." Her hands tightened around the flowers, which had an agreeable smell and a gorgeous colour. The paper crinkled under her grip. "Claude, if you pull this crap, then I don't want to see you. I think what you taught me today will definitely help, and I'd like to learn more, but only if I'm coming over here to learn. If you keep thinking it's something more than it is, then I have to—"

"Fine, fine." He held up his hands as if to soothe her, smile gone. "Fine. I'm sorry. Give them back."

"No," she said quickly, turning away when he reached

for the flowers. "They're pretty."

He retracted his hands slowly, lips spreading into a small smile again, and then cleared his throat. "Fine. Keep them. Consider them a gift from a mentor to a mentee."

She scoffed. "No thanks."

"Then what will you consider them as?"

"I haven't decided yet." All she knew was that she didn't want to think of Claude as a mentor. Instead, Delia planned to pretend the flowers miraculously just appeared in her apartment tomorrow morning, and she would admire and take care of them because they were beautiful, not because Claude gave them to her.

They stood facing one another in a battle of wills over who would be forced to break the silence first, the air between them filled with everything left unsaid. In the end, it was Claude's phone that broke the standstill, and after checking it quickly, he told her that her car was here.

While Claude went straight for the door, Delia suddenly had a hard time persuading her feet to move. The drive home seemed so long and tiring—she almost wanted to ask for a room in the guest houses and take a six-hour nap.

But she moved eventually, forcing one foot in front of the other. Flowers in hand, she passed Claude at the door and spotted a sleek town car waiting for her in the driveway.

"I'm not paying their fees. These guys are crooks. Way overpriced," she insisted, then turned back only to find herself a few inches from his body. A gasp slipped out before she could stop it, but she refused to stumble back, refused to retreat. He'd done it on purpose, standing so close to her—she could see it in that rare glint of mischievousness in his eye.

"The car service is charged to the clan account, of course," he told her, head dipped down so that she could see his eyes on her lips, the slight movement of his thick eyelashes. All she had to do was close the distance and her stomach would stop its somersaulting. Delia considered his words, then smirked.

"Well, if that's the case, I'll have to save the number."

"Please do." The seductive rumble of his voice was getting the better of her. Abort. *Abort.*

"I'll let you know when I'm free over the next few days," she managed, her voice a little *too* breathy for her liking.

"I'm looking forward to it." Claude straightened up when she took a step back. "Next time I won't go so easy on you."

Delia stopped at the edge of the stone porch, her smile growing. "Even if I ask nicely?"

And with that, she was off, pleased to have the last word. The driver didn't get the door for her, nor was he wearing the ridiculous cap and suit getup that she expected. Once she was in and settled, the car eased away from the manor, effortlessly navigating the uneven road. Just as they were about to head into the trees, Delia looked out the back window, her breath catching when she spied Claude standing at the door and watching her go. As the canopy shadows stretched across the car, he waved to her before stepping inside.

Unable to decide whether she ought to smile or scowl, Delia faced forward and looked down at her flowers, which sat neatly between her knees, and realized she hadn't had the last word after all.

CHAPTER 9: WHITE GIRL WASTED

"To Ali and Stefan—"

"Steven," someone shouted from the back of the hunter herd. Delia blinked drunkenly at them, eyes closing and opening at different speeds, and then waved them off with a guffawing laugh. Devin's hands planted firmly on her hips were currently the only things keeping her from falling off the barstool she somehow found herself on. Apparently she was making a toast too. When the hell had that happened?

"To Ali and *Steven*," Delia crooned, holding up her drink—which slopped over the edge of her glass. Over the music, which the bartender had lowered only a fraction at the start of her impromptu speech, she could hear Devin snort. "May y-your love be as everlasting and immortal-ly as the bloodsuckers you stake along the…the way."

Not her most eloquent speech, but the roar of approval from the crowd was all her alcohol-saturated brain needed to know she'd got the point across. With everyone throwing back their drinks, toasting to Ali and Steve's very successful stag and doe night, Delia threw her head back and downed whatever was in her cup. Her face screwed at the bitter taste of vodka mixed with some sort of sugary fizzy drink.

"I'm surprised you can still taste that," Devin teased as he helped her down.

"I shouldn't get the vodka," she prattled, handing the

glass off to him. Poor guy had been saddled with her for the last hour, but then again, *he* had made the mistake of telling her she'd had too much to drink already. This was his punishment. "Vodka makes m'tummy all weird."

He opened his mouth, but whatever he planned to say was interrupted by a flurry of blonde hair and high heels. Ali shrieked Delia's name before diving on her, sloppily thanking her for such a wonderful speech. Given that Delia's heels were no sturdier than Ali's at that moment, they both tumbled back into the bar, Devin and an equally sober Steve hovering nearby to mitigate the potential damage.

"Ohmygod, you're so, *so* welcome," Delia cried as they broke apart. She slapped a hand on either side of Ali's face, then squished her cheeks. "You so *beau*tiful and gonna make such a beautiful bride."

"I *know*, I *love* my dress," Ali cried back, shrilly elongating every other word. Behind them, both women missed Steve and Devin exchanged somewhat harrowed looks.

"Okay, you gon' mess up m'makeup," Ali whined when Delia started stretching and smooshing her heavily lipsticked lips together. "Le's do some shots, girl!"

Yes. *Yes.* Shots were *just* what she needed!

Squirming around Devin and Steve, Delia made her way over to the portion of the bar that was actually tended. Less than a minute later, the barkeep had a row of shot glasses laid out in a line and Ali had dragged in a few other hunters to partake. Kain jostled Delia's shoulder as he sidled up beside her, his cheeks pink from the booze and his grin toothier than ever.

"To fucking Ali and Steve," Delia toasted again, a glass filled to the brim with a clear acetone-scented liquid and tossing it back. While it burned the whole way down, it made her tummy warm and her mind fuzzy. Suddenly Kain's arms were around her, lifting and carrying her to the dance floor. With the music back at full volume, the party was officially underway once more. Bodies writhed and swayed on the tiny dancefloor set in front of an equally small stage.

Ahh, Jimmie's Place. Delia had puked in the bar's bathroom more times than she cared to admit, and she had definitely danced on the bar top at least once—thrice, probably—in her Harriswood lifetime.

All she wanted tonight was fun—tonight, Delia craved it. After ending September with getting her ass kicked by both Claude and League scheduling, she needed a night to let loose. If anything, she needed a night to forget that she wasn't improving as fast as she wanted with her combat training and that she hadn't been assigned any additional patrol shifts despite repeatedly volunteering for them.

Maybe she should take Ali's advice. Maybe she *should* ignore the scheduling people. Maybe then they'd remember she existed.

It was worth a shot.

Ha. Shot.

Delia wanted to drink, to get wasted, to live in the moment. She wanted to forget the way Claude touched her when they were alone and how it made her feel. He was always so cautious with her, offering only the smallest caresses outside physical training. And all she'd do was flirt, flirt, flirt because she couldn't help it—then she'd go home and berate herself because she should have more self-control.

Six sessions with the vamp king of Harriswood and, surprise surprise, she *was* a better fighter than when she'd started. Last time, Claude had told her he was proud of her as he tucked her hair behind her ear, letting his hand linger—and Delia was out of the Grimm estate like a shot. All those feelings. All those messy, messy feelings. They were starting to bubble up, threatening to spill out of her, when she knew she ought to swallow them down. Feelings-vomit. Yeah. She had a bad case of it.

Alcohol was called for. Very much. In her mouth.

Right now. Booze.

Delia threw her hands up when the song called for it, shrieking and laughing and jumping with the hunters around her. It was easy to forget how pointless she thought hunter marriages were in an environment like this, and the drunker she got, the sappier she became.

By the end of the night she'd probably be sloppily offering to marry Ali and Steve right then and there. It wouldn't count for anything and she would probably cry, but that was the way her night was headed.

Hands snaked around her hips as the song changed to something more sexually charged, and she looked down, half-expecting Devin. He'd been her shadow for a while now, but it was Kain who had wrapped himself around her. His hips pressed to her backside, his lips to her neck, and she found herself a little dizzy in his arms. She wanted to jump around. She wanted to throw her head back and scream-sing with the others. She didn't want this slow grinding bullshit. Not with Kain, anyway.

Delia spun in his arms, throwing them both off balance, then giggled when he caught her. Just as he swooped in for a kiss, she shouted, "I need to pee!" And off she went, making her escape for the bathroom. It was empty—a rarity at a bar, but given the somewhat sad ratio of female hunters to males, it didn't surprise her. Stumbling over to the sinks, she did a quick scan of her appearance. Little black dress that was hiked way up her thighs—she tugged it down quickly—and too much eye makeup. Still, at least her hair was half decent. She ran her fingers through it, drunken brain approving of the way the waves billowed out. Big hair. Little dress. High heels. Appropriate for the night. Difficult to walk in.

She swayed back and forth while standing perfectly still, the room sliding in and out of focus if she stared at one spot for too long.

She didn't have to pee.

Her mouth was dry, and as she ducked down to slurp

water from the tap, she wondered why she had totally bailed on Kain. Without women from the general public to pick from, Delia tended to be his go-to girl. And sometimes she didn't mind. Having a confident guy like Kain all over her meant other creeps didn't try anything funny.

So why had she run?

Claude's bright blues flashed across her mind, and when she closed her eyes, just for a second, she could smell that rich cologne he always wore. The kind that just screamed 100% throw-you-down-and-ravish-you *man*.

Straightening up, she wiped her hand across her lips, collecting the excess water droplets, then fluffed her hair again. What was Claude doing tonight? No. *No.* No Claude.

With a frown she headed for the door.

The bathrooms at Jimmie's were down a hall from the main bar area, the corridor narrow and made more claustrophobic by the dozens and dozens of hunter photos everywhere. She stumbled forward to study them, squinting as her frown morphed into a smile. Her hand bracing herself against the wall, her gaze wandered over the familiar faces—some were dead at this point, the job having finally gotten the better of them. But at least they seemed happy in the photos.

Down the hallway, toward the rear exit, was a stairwell that led upstairs. Delia had never had a reason to use it, but she knew the upper floor was for private groups. Office parties. Meetings. Pub nights for local politicians. If Ali and Steve had been anyone else, the owner would have stuffed everybody into one of those rooms, but because they were hunters and made up the bulk of Jimmie's Place's regulars, they had the run of the main floor for a night.

She was almost at the foot of the stairs, wandering the length of the hall as she admired the photographs, when the sound of feet tromping down the wooden staircase scared her off. Her drunken brain's first response was to scamper back to the party, but she paused near the bathrooms, the distance giving her the courage to turn around and satisfy her curiosity.

Something she shouldn't have done.

Because if she had just kept going, she could have gone back to her friends and colleagues, drinking and laughing and dancing. Instead, she was stuck staring, mouth slightly open, as Claude Grimm and about ten other men—vamps, given their pallor—headed for the door marked with an Exit sign.

"Claude?"

He looked back at the last moment, but was swept outside with the current of those leaving.

Why was he here?

Why was he always *everywhere*?

She saw him twice weekly at his home and most nights in her dreams—wasn't that *enough*?

Eyes narrowed, Delia stalked off after him. In her mind, she stomped down the hall like a queen, when in reality she was more like a pinball, bouncing between the walls on either side of her until she staggered out the door.

He was waiting for her, or so she thought, standing near a sleek dark car with tinted windows. Only two men remained with him, the rest dispersing into the night. His black trench coat was back, and she hated how attractive it made him look. Black coat and black pants and a black shirt, probably button-up—how did all black look so damn good on a man?

The parking lot behind Jimmie's had never been paved, so her thin heels made her extra wobbly as they sunk into the gravel. Her arms shot out to balance herself when she started to tip forward.

"Delia." Claude said her name like she was a mess, and his footsteps crunched across the gravel as he approached. "What are you doing?"

"What'm I doin'?" She tried her best to distribute her

LIZ MELDON

weight evenly between each leg, but somehow her hip still popped out to the left. "What're *you* doin'?"

He ran a hand through his hair. So luscious and thick. So nice. So touchable.

"What? Delia, are you drunk?"

"Don' change the…" Her eyes narrowed as she poked at his chest, only to miss by a mile and hit his arm instead. "The subject. Don't."

He muttered something under his breath as he looked away, then reached out to steady her when she started tipping forward again.

"'M fine," she snapped, brushing him off. Only he didn't let her go, not until she was upright and stable—as much as possible, anyway. When his hands were gone, she wanted them back, craving the warmth against her skin. "Why're you here? It'sa party for hunters, not *you*. You can't be *everywhere*, y'know? Stop…following me."

"Delia, I really don't have the time or the patience for this charade tonight," he told her, his words clipped. His hands slid into his pants pockets as he shook his head. "It must be surprising, but I have a life of my own too, one that actually doesn't involve you."

"So just coincid'nce you're here?" she slurred. Had his skin always looked so smooth? Her hand shot up to caress his cheek, but it only made it to his shoulder, which she gripped. Suddenly standing there wasn't so difficult anymore. "Unprofessionally of you, Claude Grimm. 'S unprofessional. Stalkerishly… Didja wanna see me in a little dress, 's that it?"

"All right, this… This I've had enough with." He snatched her hand as it quested upward for his face, holding her wrist tightly between the two of them. "What is it that you want from me, Delia?"

Out of the corner of her eye, she took some vague note of his associates slinking into the awaiting car. She frowned, not entirely understanding the question. "W-What?"

"Do you want me or don't you?" Claude demanded, shaking her hand and bringing her attention back to his face. Why did he look upset? Was he mad at her? She started to teeter to the left, but his grip kept her upright. "Because you make it seem like you do whenever we're together. *Every* training session. You make it so painfully clear you're interested in me, and not me as a vampire or clan leader as I'm sure you'd like me to think. You touch me. Smile and joke with me. You hint back to the night of the masquerade, but the second I show even the *slightest* reciprocation, I get my knuckles whacked like a naughty child. Suddenly *I'm* the inappropriate asshole who can never seem to do anything right, who needs to learn his place. I can't keep doing this with you, Delia. I can't."

She opened and closed her mouth a few times, but no words came. He'd said all the words in the universe, apparently, and her brain went on overdrive trying to process them. All she knew was that he was still holding her by the wrist, still touching her, slowly drawing her in to him.

And then he was kissing her, hard and fast and firm. She inhaled sharply, her free hand shooting up to push at his chest—only to end up grabbing instead, fisting in the fabric of his shirt. Button-up, just like she'd suspected. Soft. Smooth.

He pulled away abruptly and left her gasping. Her lips stung, pulsing from the force of his kiss. Suddenly he was looking at her, waiting, and she still didn't know what to say. What to feel. What to do.

"I don't..." She licked her lips. No words. Her drunken mind had drawn a blank. But she wanted to keep kissing him. Delia had wanted to keep kissing him for months now, even if finally admitting it to herself felt like a defeat.

Claude released her wrist, but rather than letting her arm fall to her side, Delia threw it around his neck and let herself fall—into him, into another kiss. Her other hand cupped his face and slid up into his hair, her lips parting with his. While the first kiss had been hard, simmering on the edge of frustration, this was fluid and easy, like the dams had finally broken.

Her body arched against his, fitting into a mold that she wished was more familiar. She'd been able to watch him, touch him during their training sessions, but not like this. Not like she wanted.

Claude mumbled her name against her lips, finally pulling back. Delia lurched after him, trying to reclaim the kiss, but he caught her with an easy smile and a gentle hand.

"You're very drunk," he said, to which she shook her head adamantly and tried to get back to his lips. Both his hands held her a foot away from him, however, and suddenly she was cold.

"I'mnot," she managed. Behind him, the parking lot lights seemed hazy. The whole world looked hazy, in fact—the whole world except for Claude. He was clear and pristine, a focal point even as all that booze swirled through her system.

"I feel drunk just kissing you," he confided with a soft chuckle, turning them both slowly and walking her toward the car. His arm slid snugly around her waist, and she curved inward, her hand on his chest. "Why don't I take you home?"

"*You*," she tugged on his shirt, popping a button, "come home with *me*."

He pried her hand off and kissed the top of it, then slipped free to open the car door. Those bright blues met her unfocused greens as he tilted his head to the side, beckoning her to get in. "Ask me again when you're sober."

Her brow furrowed. Ask what again? What were they even talking about? Whose car was this?

Who cares?

"You smell nice," she crooned with a dopey smile,

leaning in and inhaling deeply.

Claude grinned. "Thank you."

Someone inside the car snickered.

"What the fuck's *this*?" came a shout. Delia rounded on the spot and spied Kain blitzing toward them, ten times steadier on his feet than her. Dust flew up from his heels as his boots clomped across the parking lot. She placed a hand back on Claude's chest as if that would keep him from reacting.

"Kain—"

"Are you fuckin' serious, Delia?" he sneered, grabbing at her arm and attempting to yank her toward him. "Go back inside."

Before she so much as stumbled an inch, Claude wrenched Kain's hand off Delia's arm and shoved him back. With ease. Her eyes followed Claude's fingers, mesmerised, while behind them the Irishman staggered and nearly lost his footing.

"None of that," Claude warned. Delia's skin prickled as he placed his hand on her lower back, but in front of Kain it almost felt wrong, like she was breaking some ethical code.

Maybe she was.

"Fuck you," Kain sneered, and Delia had to physically bar him from getting up in Claude's face as he lunged forward. The vamp behind her, meanwhile, stayed perfectly still. "Who the fuck d'you think you are, anyway? Just because you put your teeth in her don't make her *yours*."

She might have been stupidly drunk, but even Delia knew the potential repercussions of what he'd said in that moment. Her eyes widened and she tried harder to push him back—unsuccessfully.

"I don't think you know—"

"Who I'm dealing with?" Kain spat, cutting Claude off. Spittle splattered onto Delia's cheek, but she was too determined to keep Kain from getting split in half by the vamps waiting for Claude in the car to care. "I know *exactly* who y'are, ya right geebag, and I know exactly what kind of game you're playing at."

"Kain, stop," she pleaded. "Jus' go in the inside and—"

"Delia, so help me if you're defending this fucker." This time he actually managed to pull her away from Claude, but the vampire caught her seconds later as she faltered off to the side. When she looked up at him, his expression was no longer carefully neutral, his emotions concealed—he wore his anger like a mask.

"Stay here," he said, leaning her up against the car.

Just as he was about to stalk toward Kain, who stood a few feet away goading him on in a voice bordering on slurred, Delia sprung between them again, a hand on each man to steady herself.

"No," she hissed, her eyes narrowed at Kain before turning to Claude. "No. Stop."

Two thoughts were about all her brain could focus on right now. One: she really wanted Claude to take her home and fuck her into sweet oblivion. Two: she didn't want Claude to put her drunk friend through a wall. Unfortunately, the latter of the two finally won out, as nauseous as that made her.

"Go," she insisted, pointing between Claude and the car. "'S too many hunters."

His hands flexed in and out of fists. As he started to say her name, she placed a finger over his lips and shook her head.

"'M fine." Delia nodded, though the motion made her a little dizzy. "Really. S'okay."

"Get in the car, ya fucking crusty piece of shite." Kain's words of encouragement weren't exactly the helpful push she needed, but one last look from Delia finally sent Claude off. His eyes flickered back to Kain briefly before he unbuttoned his jacket and climbed in, slamming the door behind him. Moments later, the car raced out of the lot, flinging bits of rock and dirt up from its wheels.

She watched him go with a heavy sigh, her head suddenly pounding. This was not what she needed tonight. All Delia had wanted to do was dance. And celebrate her friend's impending wedding. And laugh. And drink heavily. This was not part of the plan.

"You need to tell me *right now* what the fuck went on here," Kain ordered as she stalked back toward him. Before he could get another word out, Delia punched him in the gut as hard as she could. He doubled over, his stomach absorbing most of the hit, and Delia carried on walking back into the bar, steady for the first time all night, as Kain dropped to his knees and groaned.

CHAPTER 10: NOBODY LIKES A TATTLETALE

This was what death felt like. It had to be.

Despite having thrown up twice that morning *and* sleeping a full ten hours, on and off, since the end of Ali and Steve's party, Delia still felt like she was on the verge of kicking the bucket. Her head pounded and her stomach ached, and her fucking phone wouldn't stop going off—but it was all the way across the room in her purse and standing up for any reason other than to run to the bathroom just wasn't happening.

"Ooh my god," she groaned, elongating each word as she buried her face in her pillow. The only good part about the morning was that she had woken up alone. On the second trip to the bathroom to purge all the alcoholic poison from her system, she caught a fleeting look at herself in the mirror. All her eye makeup had smeared across her face and her once perfectly fluffed hair was a total rat's nest. She was still wearing the little black dress from the night before, only without her bra and underwear.

This was, by far, the worst hangover she'd had in a long, long time.

"Kill me," she whimpered at the sound of her phone's message alert going off *again*, shrill and piercing even buried inside her purse.

Who the hell could possibly be...

Her eyes shot open as memories slowly started trickling

back in. Shots with Kain. Speeches on barstools. Picking out dead hunters in photographs near the bathrooms.

Claude Grimm.

Delia groaned and yanked her covers over her head, only to feel hot and claustrophobic within seconds. Huffing noisily, she rolled onto her back and pushed everything off, squinting up at her bedroom ceiling. It was too fucking bright in there, even with her curtains closed.

Claude had been at the bar last night. And she'd called him a stalker.

"Oh my *god*." Both hands covered her face as she emitted something between a groan and a yowl. If her somewhat fuzzy memories served her correctly, she'd been awful to him—and then let him kiss her. And kissed him *back*. Then invited him back up to her apartment.

If the hangover didn't kill her, the embarrassment would. What the hell had she been thinking? She should have let him go. Her now-sober mind could deduce that he was there for business, given the company he kept at the time. Maybe they got a kick out of holding some super secret meeting in a bar full of oblivious hunters— belligerently drunk oblivious hunters, at that. Either way, he clearly hadn't been there for her, but she had accused him of it anyway.

And then he had called her out on it. His face went in and out of focus, but Delia recalled the anger in his eyes, the irritation in his voice. He'd never spoken to her like that before.

They had been seeing each other twice a week for all of September, and each visit had coaxed her into lowering her guard a *little* bit more. It was easy around Claude. He was both sweet and seductive, charming but kind. Sometimes she would forget he was technically the enemy and enjoy her time with him. Then she would remember, usually when he started flirting back, and Delia would slam the brakes so hard it made her head spin.

She did it because she knew she had to. Claude had a

number of traits that made him dating material. He was also infinitely patient with her slow uptake on his lessons. Unlike League trainers, there were no under-the-breath comments or eye rolls behind her back, no jokes made at her expense that weren't good-natured and innocent. It was a whole different learning environment.

But she should have stopped going to him. It shouldn't have continued after the first lesson, yet Delia kept coming back for more. For more flirting, for more muddled feelings. While her fighting skills may have improved slightly, it was still painfully apparent that her decision making skills could use some work.

After lying in bed for another half-hour, mentally berating herself for everything that had happened since the stupid masquerade garden party fiasco, Delia finally dragged herself out of bed to upchuck whatever was left in her stomach. This time, as she washed her face and brushed her teeth vigorously afterward, she felt less like death was upon her. All the physical agonies had been downgraded to a regular hangover, leaving Delia craving something greasy and fried with plans to eat it in bed.

Why not, right? She wasn't working for the next few days, despite signing up to help patrol on a volunteer basis in the staff lounge basically every day in September *and* October. One night she'd tried to just go on an unscheduled patrol by herself in an effort to help—only to run into the hunter who'd actually been assigned that sector. At the time he'd thought she was trying to undermine his authority or something equally absurd, and she'd woken up the following morning with a terse, succinct reminder in her inbox not to infringe on other hunters' patrols. So fuck it. She was going to ride this thing out in style.

Her slow trudge to the kitchen—where Delia planned to eat Nutella out of the jar until she had enough energy to get dressed and go down to the burger place around the corner—was interrupted by the bleating of her phone.

Sighing, she crouched down and grabbed the damn thing with every intention of turning it off.

However, the million missed calls and texts from Kain made her pause, as did the one text from Claude. The texts from Devin asking where she'd gone around the time she was probably drunkenly berating Claude in the parking lot last night could be ignored. Ali's incoherent text made up of random letters that might be words also went unanswered, which left her with Claude and Kain—the two men who had tipped her night from taking a few shots to taking a *lot* of shots. Hesitantly, she checked Claude's first.

> *Hope you're feeling better this morning. I think we should talk about things. I can bring food if you wish.*

Thoughtful bastard definitely knew how to get to her. She had to bite the inside of her cheek to keep from smiling, then flinched when yet another text alert shrieked at her. Kain again. Exhaling deeply, she opened their conversation thread with the expectation of seeing a lot of half-assed apology texts mingled with lectures about her and Claude. Instead, she found something much more urgent.

> *Im sure ur hungover as fuck. Can u just put some pants on? U have 15 min and counting before they make me go pick u up. Wentworth is pissed enough as it is.*

"*What?*" She scrolled up frantically to find the start of his most recent string of texts. Apparently the High Council wanted to see her at three that afternoon—which was, in fact, less than fifteen minutes from now. Tossing her phone aside, Delia raced to her closet and pulled out the most professional outfit she owned: fitted black dress pants and a white button-up blouse. Once dressed, she attempted to run a brush through her hair, then gave up and tried to do one of those trendy ballerina buns on the top of her head. It was sloppier than they made it look on the online tutorials, but there was no time for much else. Lip gloss. Mascara. Some tissues to wipe off last night's eye shadow.

"Fuck, fuck, *fuck*," she hissed, grabbing her purse and her discarded pleather jacket on her way to the front door. Boots and sunglasses completed the somewhat grown-up outfit, and she was out the door and down the stairs in a flurry, not bothering to wait for the elevator. While outside was cool and overcast, sweat had already started to gather on her neck and face—and she missed the bus by a good ten seconds. "*Fuck!*"

So she ran as fast as her hungover body could manage. Somehow she arrived at the library in ten minutes, having cut across traffic and pushed by too many people to count. As she climbed the front steps, the same front steps where Hugh and the others had been found swinging weeks earlier, she was forced to stop by one of the pillars to catch her breath. Each gulp of air burned her throat, and the longer she stood, the more she wanted to vomit again.

No time for sickness. The High Council had requested her. Kain had texted her hours ago to let her know, and she was determined to show them that she wasn't a total screw-up.

No. Delia could be punctual and mediocre, damn it.

It took her another ten minutes to reach the Council chambers, new punch-in door codes and busy elevators not working in her favour. Kain was waiting for her in the reception area, the plush carpeting just the right shade of puke green to bring her nausea back full-force.

"Where the hell have you been?" he demanded, voice low as he pulled her close. "I've been trying to reach you all day."

"I just got out of bed," she snapped as she smoothed a hand over her hair. Kain's eyes swept up and down her body.

"You look like shite."

"And your breath smells like *shite*," she fired back, still upset with his behaviour in front of Claude. But they'd deal with that another time. Delia had to focus on the present. At least her blouse was clean. "Seriously though… Do I look presentable?"

"Considering I know how drunk you were last night?" Kain said, smirking. "Yeah, you're okay."

Behind them, the Council secretary Candace Sweetman glanced up from the computer, her eyes like lasers honing onto all of Delia's faults.

Delia went for her hair again, but Kain batted her hands away.

"Stop. You're making it worse."

"*Kain*—"

"The Council will see you now," Candace drawled, pushing a button on her mahogany desk. The sound of the huge door unlocking made Delia's stomach turn, but she followed Kain toward it with all the dignity she could muster.

Said dignity dissolved into a puddle on the floor at the sight of all five Council members. Wentworth was seated behind an even grander desk than his secretary, while the others stood behind him, stern as ever. This wasn't the first time she had been in the chambers of the High Council, and Delia knew for a fact that the small room with cobblestone flooring was merely for disciplinary matters. The near invisible doorway behind the desk, padlocked and fingerprint reliant, led to a secret room, probably quite ostentatious, where the five members of the High Council held their actual meetings.

When the door behind her shut, bolting noisily, Delia clasped her hands in front of her and tried to concentrate on not crumbling to the floor. Kain, meanwhile, took a seat on the small two-seater couch to her left.

"Miss Roberts," Wentworth began after the twenty most intense seconds of her life. "Do you know why you've been called by the High Council this afternoon?"

"Because…" She swallowed hard, but her mouth was so dry it was like swallowing sandpaper. "Because you're commending me for all the volunteer opportunities I've signed up for?"

It was a long shot, but in her current state she couldn't think of anything she had done wrong recently. Well, anything League-related, anyway.

Wentworth's eyes narrowed.

She cleared her throat.

"Sorry. I didn't mean to be disrespectful." Her voice was getting softer and softer. Delia lowered her eyes to the ground, bracing for the worst.

"Miss Roberts," Wentworth said again, leaning forward in his chair so that it squeaked, "it has been brought to our attention that you have started up a relationship with a vampire." Delia's head snapped up, her world suddenly spinning. "A one… Claude Grimm, head of the Grimm clan. Is that true?"

"I…" She could feel her blood pumping through her body, her heartbeat throbbing in her ears. She was going to pass out. She was going to faint in front of the High Council. Her arm shot out to brace herself, but there was nothing to hold in to. Instead she swayed ever so slightly, then regained her balance, her previously very sickly complexion taking on a dull pink. "I, uh…"

"There's no sense in lying." Wentworth nodded to Kain, whom Delia looked at with wide eyes. "Kain has given us a very thorough report on the situation."

"What the fuck, man?" she blurted, swallowing down the clichéd *I thought we were friends*. He met her eye fleetingly, then looked back to the High Council members. At least he had the decency to look mildly ashamed of what he'd done.

"You should have come to us after the masquerade gathering earlier this year," Wentworth stated. "We could have stopped this dalliance from carrying on as long as it has."

"There is no dalliance," she said quickly, mind reeling. "We're not... There's no crime in being on sort of friendly terms with a vamp. Isn't it a good thing, in this case? I mean, I can ask him whatever I want—"

"You let him bite you," Wentworth remarked. It suddenly felt like someone had kicked her straight in the gut. She couldn't breathe. "You're infected, Delia Roberts, with his *disease*."

"I didn't know... at the time," she protested weakly. Tears were starting to gather in her eyes, and she looked to the ceiling in an effort to push them back down. Her lip quivered anyway, and when she faced the five men who had the power over her very life, two fat trails of liquid streamed down her cheeks. "He was warm. I went to the masquerade to get Claudia because my informant said she'd be there."

"You wanted to take down the purported mistress of all Harriswood vamps... alone?" Wentworth seemed to be trying hard not to smile, what with the way his lips twitched, and the council members behind him all shared a similar expression. "Delia, what a foolish thing to do."

"I realized that there, and I met a guy in a mask who I..." She shook her head, her voice catching. "I thought he was a regular guy, and then he bit me." Her noisy sniffle made George Heston grimace. "I'm sorry. I didn't want it to happen, and I thought I'd be banished, or worse if I said something and—"

"Under the usual circumstances, yes, you would be banished," Wentworth said gruffly. Delia's hands had started to shake. In her peripherals, Kain had settled back on the couch and crossed his arms. He still wasn't looking at her. Delia took the deepest breath she could and squared her shoulders, doing whatever she could to ward off a full-blown weeping meltdown.

"Usual circumstances?"

"The tide is changing amongst the clans," Wentworth

told her. "I'm sure you realized this back when we permitted that vamp scum Johnathon Warwick to attend a meeting. Tensions are escalating, mostly between the smaller clans and the Donovans. We on the Council anticipate there will be more bloodshed, even with our increased security measures. I hope not, for the sake of the people of Harriswood, but there is no telling what is to come. The Donovans have made... unprecedented moves. To our knowledge, the local clans have lived in harmony for years."

As he spoke, Delia continued to take deep breaths. It almost seemed that Wentworth was implying that her punishment for fraternizing with the enemy would be *less* severe than she feared.

But then again, she had been wrong about these sorts of things before.

"I want to help, sir," she insisted, fiddling with the hem of her blouse. "I keep signing up for patrol duty, but—"

"We have another assignment in mind, Miss Roberts." Wentworth stood, then slowly made his way around the desk. While the others of the High Council wore their traditional black robes, Wentworth was in his casuals: a brown v-neck sweater with a white collar poking over the top, worn with a pair of what Delia could only describe as dad jeans. Plus a pair of tan loafers. It was like seeing a teacher outside of school—mildly unsettling. Still, the thought of an assignment given to her directly by Wentworth made her brighten.

"Yes, sir?"

"You're going to tell us everything," Wentworth remarked as he closed in on her, and for the first time, she felt very much like she was being encroached on by a predator. Not even vamps made her feel like this. She shifted, averting her eyes when he stopped no less than a foot from her. "Then you're going to make reports on him and his clan, and anything he tells you about the other clans."

Delia swallowed thickly. This time it was easy to gulp—what with her mouth steadily filling with saliva. She was going to be sick. She was going to be sick all over High Council leader Don Wentworth.

His finger on her chin startled her into momentarily forgetting her queasiness. Stunned, Delia let him tilt her head to one side, then the other, holding it there when he saw the marks Claude had left on her neck. His eyes narrowed before he stepped back and tutted at her.

"Bad form, Miss Roberts. Bad form."

Delia watched him stroll to his desk, then return to his creaky chair. Behind him, the other four men remained unmoved, mere silent observers. Kain was the only one not looking at her, finding his hands more interesting instead. Her eyes watered again, the bile steadily creeping up her throat. She had trusted him implicitly with this secret, this *thing* that burned her from the inside out, that made her feel like she was a walking, talking bundle of misjudgement and idiocy. She had trusted him because he was a better hunter than her. She thought he would know how to save her.

Instead, he had ratted her out to the men who, had the circumstances been different, could have sent her away, destroyed her career—or killed her for treason.

"From the top, Miss Roberts," Wentworth prompted. Delia looked back to him quickly, struggling to find her voice. "Spare no detail, starting from the night of the masquerade—the one we prohibited hunters from attending. Do you remember that? Or does following orders come difficult for you?"

"No, sir," she muttered, holding his gaze, a small part of her challenging him to bring up any other situation in the past—just one—where she hadn't followed orders. He couldn't have, of course; Delia may not have found her shifts stimulating, but she did what she was supposed to do every time.

And while she wanted nothing more than to be given a

special assignment by the High Council—she'd had *dreams* about this moment—the thought of spilling every intimate moment she had shared with Claude made her want to run, to bolt for the door and not look back.

Instead, she talked, her face perpetually flushed, even after she got to the end of her tale—from the moment she met Claude Grimm right up until last night. She felt violated. Like they were cutting her open and examining her insides. Like they were seeing her naked. By the end of it, she was shaking.

"Oh, Miss Roberts..." Wentworth leaned back in his chair and sighed, hands threaded together and resting on his chest. "Technically it is no longer a crime for a hunter to befriend a vamp, but you know you've broken a series of unsaid rules. Vamps are to be monitored and contained, not indulged in."

"Yes, sir." Even her voice shook. She just wanted them to stop staring at her, these men robed in black cloaks, each one dripping with judgement.

"In light of that, the only reason I am suspending your punishment is because you can be of use to the League," the older man continued, head tilted to the side slightly. "Now's the time to prove yourself, Delia. You will continue to see him with the intention of gathering information. We will require reports, of which we will provide the topic. Am I making myself clear?"

With more than a little difficulty, Delia nodded. The grin Wentworth gave made her stomach turn.

"Good. Now, get out your phone and call him. I want to hear you accept his invitation to dinner."

"Right now?" she asked, then pressed her lips together when his gaze hardened. "I mean, yes. Of course, sir."

With trembling hands she dug out her phone, and her fingers moved stiffly as she searched her contacts for his name. When Delia found it, all she did was stare. A pointed clearing of Wentworth's throat made her press her thumb down hard on the screen.

Claude answered on the third ring, and she closed her eyes as he said her name, wishing she could have left a voicemail instead.

"How are you feeling?" he asked. It sounded like he was smiling. "Did you just wake up?"

Delia turned, unable to do this with all these men staring at her, and headed for the corner of the room by the door. Standing there, she wasn't sure she could do this—period—even if she knew she had to.

"Uh, no, I've been up for a while," she said, fidgeting with her jacket's zipper. "Listen, I don't have a lot of time, but, uh, I wanted to take you up on your dinner date."

There was a brief pause. "Really?"

"Yeah." She forced a laugh. "I mean, after last night, yeah, I think it's worth… exploring."

"Well, this is unexpected."

"Is it?"

"A little."

"Look, I wanted to apologize too for, you know, shouting at you. I was pretty drunk." She pressed a hand to her forehead, feeling herself grow hot again as the men behind her shifted about.

Claude chuckled. "Of that I was very aware."

"So, yeah, right," she babbled. "If you want to do the date, uh, thing, I'm off…" Delia looked back to the High Council members with raised eyebrows. Wentworth lifted the huge calendar on his desk and pointed to a square. She sighed shakily. "Tomorrow. Do you want to… uh… meet up or something?"

So cringeworthy.

"I'll pick you up at eight," he told her, "and I promise to drive something better than the soccer mom van."

"Okay, cool," Delia said quickly, knowing she should have laughed at the joke. "I'll see you then."

She hung up before he could say something that would keep her on the phone.

"Good," Wentworth said when Delia faced him again.

"You'll get an email shortly, detailing topics of discussion we're most interested in. I expect the first report as soon as the date is over, be it that night or the following morning."

Both she and Kain were dismissed shortly after, and Delia flew out of the office the second the door unlocked. She blitzed by Candace Sweetman, hurried out of the reception area, and barely made it to the nearest women's washroom—in which she heaved the rest of her limited stomach contents into the sink, unable to make it to the toilet in time.

When it was finally over, she washed her face and mouth, then used a paper towel to clean up the mess as best she could. In the mirror, her eyes were red from crying and her skin was a blotchy mess. She had imagined accepting a date from Claude a few times before, but she'd never imagined looking like this afterward. She had never imagined *feeling* like this afterward, like she was the biggest slimeball in the world—a bigger rat than Hugh. Drawing in a shaky breath, she took a quick sip of water from the tap, then stumbled for the door, ready to make use of the League cafeteria for once.

She stopped, however, when she spied Kain waiting for her outside the bathroom, leaning against the wall across from the door. A white hot bolt of rage shot through her at the sight of him, and without a word she stalked off down the hall.

"Dels," he called, long legs letting him catch up with ease. "Dels, I'm sorry. I had to. You seemed like you were actually getting attached to this guy, and I didn't want something to happen."

She kept going, jaw clenched and hands in fists. When he grabbed her arm, she finally whirled around and shoved at his chest, eyes flashing with anger.

"No." Her voice echoed through the empty hallway. "No, Kain, we are not friends right now. Don't touch me."

"Dels—"

"Fuck you," she seethed, pushing at him again. He let her, arms at his side. "Fuck. You. You weren't worried about me!"

"I was." He caught up again when she marched away. "I really was. I knew they wouldn't banish you... Lots of hunters in lots of Leagues make use of vamp contacts. It's frowned upon these days, but they scare new hunters into thinking it's some huge crime because not everyone knows how to handle—"

"Stop. Following. Me," she growled.

"You always say you want to do more for the League." They both stopped at the elevator doors, Delia stabbing the *up* button repeatedly as he spoke. "You say you can *do* more, and this is your chance, Dels. This is your opportunity to show them you're better than the shite gigs they give you."

"You think I wanted the High Council to know he bit me?" She looked at him, eyes swimming with tears. This time she let them fall, if only to make him feel like an even bigger asshole than he already was. "You think I wanted to stand there and tell them about the sex I had with Claude Grimm? You think I wanted to do that? That I want the High Council to consider me because I can smile and flirt and probably fuck information out of someone?"

"Dels, no one said you had to—"

"Fuck you," she hissed, her voice trembling. The elevator bell dinged to announce its arrival. "I trusted you, Kain, with this huge, life-changing secret, and you went and tattled like we're in fifth grade or something. Like it was no big deal."

He opened and closed his mouth a few times as the elevator doors slid apart. Delia stepped in, arms wrapped around herself, and pressed the button for the cafeteria floor. Just as the doors started to close, Kain stopped them.

"I thought you might be scared," he insisted. "I wanted to help."

"Were you pissed because I sucker-punched you last night?" She pushed at the *close door* button, but Kain threw his back into one side when the doors started to slide shut again, forcing them back. "Is this payback for something I did? Something I said?"

"Delia, *no*. I thought you were in over your head."

She gave a strangled laugh. "Well, thank you for making it ten times worse." She swiped the backs of her hands over her cheeks, collecting the fallen tears. "Now move. I need food or I'm literally going to pass out."

"Fine," he said, moving inward.

"If you get in this elevator, they will have to scrape your carcass off the floor," she snapped. Their eyes met and Delia glared until he stepped back, until the doors finally shut him out entirely.

Until she was finally alone for a good thirty seconds, the elevator traveling smoothly from one floor to another. And when she stepped out, she had dried her tears and forced a half-smile, heading for the cafeteria amidst countless other hunters like nothing had happened.

Like she wasn't being forced to spy on the man she was hopelessly smitten with.

Like she hadn't been assigned to play the whore.

CHAPTER 11: WE'RE BAD AT THIS

For the first time since she'd moved into her building, the elevators decided to work efficiently. Normally a ride from Delia's floor to the lobby felt like it took a good ten years or so, what with the pausing at just about every floor along the way for other tenants, then the occasional heart-stopping moment when it would arrive at the requested floor but the doors wouldn't immediately open.

But tonight Delia was down in record time. The universe had a stupid sense of humor. A part of her thought of staying in the musty box and hitching a ride back up to her floor like she'd forgotten something, but the judgmental looks from the people waiting in the lobby forced her out. Besides, she had no reason to go back—purse, wallet, keys, phone, and first-date anxiety were all accounted for.

Taking a deep breath, she headed for the two sets of double doors that separated her from the vamp waiting outside, all the while knowing that once she stepped out, there was no going back.

As Delia made her way out of her apartment building, Claude spread his arms out, gesturing to the car at the curb. His grin was *almost* smug, and her eyes swept over him appreciatively as she approached. Dashing as ever, of course, in a pair of pressed dress pants and a crisp grey button-up and a dinner jacket. Her wandering gaze paused at his hair, noting that it looked like it had recently been trimmed. Normally there was a pulse-pounding moment when they met up again after a few days apart, a surge of excitement that threatened to take her breath away, which always made her smile. Tonight, she was too wrapped up in her head, and in this new sleazy assignment, to feel any of the usual emotions.

"See?" he said, patting the roof of a sleek little red sports car, head cocked to the side. "I told you I'd bring something better than the soccer mom van for our date."

She stopped in front of him and nodded. "Yup." Her lips pursed momentarily as she took in the car. "You brought the rich douchebag sports car instead."

"Hey." He opened the door for her, a hand out to help her into the ridiculously low vehicle. "Having a Mercedes is more common these days than it once was. I think you'll need to give it a new name."

Once she was in, which took more effort than she cared to admit in her dinner date outfit—heels were a mistake, even if they were chunky wedges—she arched an eyebrow at him and shrugged. "Doubt it."

Smirking, Claude shut the door gently before making his way around to the driver's side. Delia shifted on the hard leather beneath her, hoping she didn't look as nervous as she felt.

She hadn't given him a reason yet to suspect that she hadn't been the one to arrange their first date. Across the street, a hunter whose name escaped her was watching from a bench. One of the rare older guys, he appeared to be reading a paper, his head of thick grey and white hair morphing him into background noise to passing pedestrians.

The first day of October had come and gone. With the leaves finally starting to turn, the sun seemed to be setting earlier and earlier. The season of the vamp was upon them, with more darkness than light on its way. It was almost sunset by the time she buckled herself into Claude's car.

"You look nice this evening," he noted, turning the

keys. The car purred to life as Delia shot him a hesitant grin. She knew next to nothing about cars aside from their stereotypes, and never before had she been a passenger in one so high-end. As much as she wanted to poke fun at the rich douchebag angle she'd introduced, Delia couldn't deny as they pulled away from her building that it was a comfortable way to ride.

"I-I actually went shopping this morning," she said, her cheeks a dull pink when she realized what she'd admitted to—the truth. Delia *had* gone shopping, dragging Ali with her, pretending to shop for a date night with a guy outside the League. Ali had been thrilled at the prospect, but it took a lot of pointed throat clearing to get the vivacious blonde to stop talking about wedding planning. Still, Delia appreciated the company—and Ali's support. Delia wasn't one for pointless shopping, but considering that the bulk of her wardrobe consisted of sweatpants, yoga pants, old jeans, and t-shirts with faded food stains, an outing to the local mall had been a must.

"Did you?"

"I mean, not because of *you*," Delia said, crossing her legs and tugging her skirt down to her knee. "I needed to update things anyway. This was... one of the outfits."

"Well, it's lovely."

She licked her lips and looked away as a blush touched her cheeks. "Thank you."

In her peripherals, Claude was smiling. She wished he wasn't. It only added to the blossoming bubble guilt eating at her insides.

Just as Wentworth had told her, an email had been waiting in her inbox yesterday afternoon when she returned from HQ. At least the topic of conversation that the High Council was interested in was broad. The email had been sent directly from Wentworth himself, instructing Delia to discuss clan dynamics across the years. While he gave no reason as to *why* she needed to dig up said intel, Delia assumed it was to gauge whether any other clans had stepped out of line like the Donovans were doing now. If she could get that out of Claude, something she had serious doubts about, then perhaps they could learn how the clans had dealt with dissenters in the past.

But that was dinner talk. For the moment, Delia focused on appearing engaged and present, despite the fact that her mouth was painfully dry and yesterday's hangover had stayed well into today, leaving her a little nauseous and tired.

"Delia?" The way he said her name suggested it wasn't the first time he'd said it, and she straightened up, realizing she'd been lost in her mounting anxieties.

"Hmm?"

The car idled at a stop light. "Is everything okay?"

"Why?" she asked, hoping to sound nonchalant. Claude shifted gears as the light changed, whipping through downtown Harriswood with the ease of a driver who has traveled the streets many, many times before.

"You seem a little quiet," he remarked. "Nervous?"

"You wish," Delia fired back, though she couldn't quite match his easy smile.

As always, Claude Grimm had hit the nail right on the head. Of course she was nervous. Even if she had conceded to date him on her own, Delia would have been a little apprehensive. Hunters didn't date vamps. They used them—they used each other. Kain's words about older, more experienced hunters having vamp contacts had made her think that perhaps this wasn't so strange a request of the High Council—but then thought better of it. It *was* a strange request, an insulting request, actually. It was the opportunity she'd been waiting for, but this was never the situation she'd imagined.

While the car ride seemed to take forever, in reality they were driving for less than ten minutes before Claude pulled up to the valet parking section in front of the Beltmore Hotel, sister hotel to the Banesview. While the latter was located on the outskirts of Harriswood, the

Beltmore hosted the business elite downtown.

With a hand on her lower back, Claude guided her up the pristine white steps and into the building, nodding and smiling and addressing the staff like he had known them for years.

"I've made reservations at Prewett's," he told her as they strolled through the sprawling lobby. White and gold décor glared back at her, the light fixtures so intricately designed that even they could probably deduce that she didn't belong there.

The austere and gold-plated stylings carried on into Prewett's, the hotel's five-star restaurant, located on the second floor. Claude had reserved them a table next to a window that overlooked a beautiful balcony. While the balcony was empty now, it must have been a treat to sit out there during the warmer months and enjoy the night views of downtown Harriswood. For such a small city, the core boasted several stunning towers with their own unique architectural touches. It was a gorgeous place to live—for those who took the time to actually appreciate it.

Prewett's was almost full by the time she and Claude took their seats, and after her survey of the other patrons, Delia's new outfit felt too simple. She had chosen a maroon skirt, the fabric thin and flowy, down to her knees. Her cream-coloured blouse still had the pressed lines in it from the boutique's gentle care, and she had tucked it into the high waistline of her skirt. Black tights and chunky wedge heels finished off the outfit. In her apartment, it had looked great. Compared to the women at Prewett's, she was a dumpy peasant.

Which was precisely how one wanted to feel on a first date, of course.

"So why did you take me out to eat?" she asked from behind the one-page menu. Each item was grossly overpriced, including the appetizers and desserts. Her plan to split the bill disintegrated in an instant.

"What do you mean?"

"Well, *you* don't eat." She glanced up quickly, then went back to the menu at the first sign of Claude's charming smile.

"I eat."

"Nothing that's on the menu."

"No, I suppose not." The hum of various conversations around them seemed to fade, their table far from the rest to give them some semblance of privacy. "But I can stomach the soup."

"Another trait of warm vamps?" she asked dryly, setting the menu on her stacked pile of plates. "Digesting people food?"

Claude shook his head, still grinning. She ought to be grateful he found her snark amusing; he had more patience than she deserved sometimes. Delia bit her lower lip as she stared blankly at the menu, all the words blurring together, and told herself to stop being snippy.

"No, I can't say it is," he said after a moment of thoughtful consideration. "I've developed a tolerance to it over years of business lunches and dinners with humans. Merely another way of blending in, I suppose."

A part of her was pleased that he wouldn't be slurping a glass of "red wine" for once. Logically, Delia could accept the fact that vamps needed blood to survive, but it still made her stomach turn watching Claude do it.

Their waiter arrived moments later and took their orders. Once he was gone, however, Delia wanted him back, if only to use him as a buffer between her and Claude. Last month, their training sessions had felt natural—*normal*, even. Fun. Now, the air between them was strained again.

Stilted conversation hounded them throughout the meal. Delia had always thought they bantered well, but Claude had to pull her out of her shell tonight, while Delia gave clipped answers to his questions—thank you, anxiety—and occasionally mustered a few awkward ones of her own. At no point did it feel natural to segue into the history of the local clans, and by the end of dessert, she still had nothing to report back to the High Council except that Claude wasn't a fan of the soup of the day.

Something about Claude had also seemed off, however. There were more pauses, more formal questions—more awkwardness to him than usual. They had already slept together, yet the tension lingered. They had spent time alone together for almost a month now, on and off, but Delia felt like they were strangers.

In short, the date was a disaster. The only redeeming quality was the food, which Delia spent a lot of time talking about and praising as she tried not to shovel it into her mouth. Her round filet encircled by scallops had been the swankiest meal she'd ever eaten, and as she did, she could forget for a few blissful moments that she was technically on the clock.

But once they were outside waiting for the valet to return Claude's car, Delia felt a familiar sinking feeling that she had failed—miserably.

Fortunately, it seemed she would have a second chance to get what she wanted—or so she thought. As Claude drove her away from the hotel, he informed her that the night wasn't over.

And then he took her to a movie.

A romantic comedy.

In a theater full of date-night couples, most of the men looked as out of their element as Delia felt. She was on a date with the perfect man, the most attractive guy she had ever slept with, and she couldn't stop *thinking*. Her orders from the High Council hung over her like her own personal storm cloud, edging out momentous first-date events, like when Claude wrapped an arm around her shoulders halfway through the movie and didn't remove it until the credits rolled.

"Delia." Claude stopped her once they left the theater, pulling her aside and away from the crowd. When they faced one another, it was pretty easy to see that she wasn't the only one not having a good time. She bit her lip and looked away, her stomach in knots.

"Claude, I—"

"I wanted to apologize," he said, speaking over her. Her mouth hung open briefly as she gawked up at him. "You seem like you're not having a very good time, and... I'm sorry. I thought the typical modern date was dinner and a movie, but I suppose I'm rusty at courting anyone. So, I apologize if this evening wasn't what you expected."

She continued to stare, mouth closed now, as her brain processed what he had said. *He* was apologizing to *her*? Delia had been the one who was distant and unresponsive all night. If anything, she owed him a huge, skyscraper-sized apology—immediately.

Swallowing hard, she reached out for his jacket and gripped the front, pulling him closer. It was time to bolster her courage, to remember that this was a man who was actually interested in her—and she, deep down, was actually interested in him.

He deserved much better than what she had given.

"If you say you're sorry one more time, I'm going to try out that new move you showed me," she warned, lips curving upward as Claude's turned down. "If anyone should apologize, it's me. Claude, I really am sorry. My head has been totally somewhere else tonight. League... stuff is really heavy right now, and I let it get to me."

"I didn't—"

"I've been a shit date tonight," Delia said frankly. "I was standoffish and disengaged, and I'm sorry. It won't happen again."

It couldn't. For some time now, it had been painfully obvious how different he was from the scumbag vamps she hauled into HQ for discipline. Claude Grimm was just a man, a better man than most, and she planned to take the rest of the night to treat him as such. Fuck the High Council's demands. She was sure she could scour the online archives later for something to send them. For now, she was on a date. With a gentleman. A gentleman who gave her butterflies like she was the star of that stupid rom-com they'd sat through.

"So what do you propose we do?" Claude asked. His arms wrapped around her slowly, pulling her the rest of the way so that their bodies pressed together. All she needed to do was stand up on her tip-toes to bring their lips together too, but Delia let the moment pass. Instead, she leaned back to study his face, unable to wipe the smile from hers.

"I propose…" She paused to think of something they could do that *didn't* involve sex—which, given the feel of his body against hers, was an incredibly difficult task. Still, she pushed through and found the right thought eventually. "I propose we start the night over. Let me take *you* on a date."

*   *   *

Although past experience had proven that Delia wasn't the quickest on her feet, she had to pat herself on the back for this one. For once, her brain had actually come through in the heat of the moment.

"It has been a very long time since I've attended a music festival of any kind," Claude noted as they stood at the gates of Fenton Park, the largest city park, home to the Fenton Festival each October.

"Really?" She felt his grip on her hand tighten somewhat as he surveyed the chaotic entryway. White and orange lights hung from all the trees and carved pumpkins with flickering candles lit the path into the park, while bales of hay with stuffed scarecrows sat stacked for photographs. Delia focused on the complex of scents wafting through the air from various food trunks parked inside, encouraging passersby to make an unexpected pit stop.

"My last festival was Woodstock," Claude told her,

with some hesitation. Delia grinned; if Claude Grimm could blush, he might have in that moment. "Although I was more or less a spectator. I, uh, wasn't part of that particular culture."

"Well, I'm not really part of this culture, honestly," she said as she tugged him toward the entrance station—a table with two volunteers and a mountain of neon pink wristbands. The pair fell in line behind a group of teenagers, all of whom would probably get their hands stamped for being underage.

"This has a culture?"

"Kind of like a weird folky vibe, a little bit—I don't know, hipster but not, I guess," she noted. His thumb had started to caress the top of her hand, which had been clasped with his since they valet parked Claude's car back at the Beltmore Hotel a few blocks over.

"So why did you suggest it?" When she shot him a look, he gave a little half-shrug. "Not that I'm complaining. I prefer this to dropping you off at home, but I'm curious."

"I don't know." A few of the teenagers in front had been let in, while the two remaining were arguing over the validity of their IDs. "I try to make it every year if I can remember and I'm not working. Usually I come for the food, but I get why it's popular."

With summer over and the warmer part of fall fading, the Fenton Festival was like the final hurrah before winter hit. While Harriswood tended to have fairly mild winters, occasionally getting a good dumping of snow in January or February, it would be too chilly to hold any outdoor festivals after October that weren't Christmas-themed.

"Uh, no, put your wallet away," Delia insisted when it was finally their turn to pay. Claude started to protest, but fell silent when she placed a hand on his chest and met his eye. "This is my date, remember? You paid for the other one."

The Other One. The Unspeakable One. In the car

between the movie theater and the Beltmore, they had agreed to pretend the painfully awkward first part of the evening hadn't happened. Delia certainly preferred it that way.

With bright pink bracelets snapped around their wrists, Delia led Claude in through the main gates. Hand-in-hand, they strolled along the row of food trucks stationed by the park's perimeter.

"So what would you usually get?" he asked, tugging her toward him to avoid being swept away in a cluster of very drunk, very loud twenty-somethings.

"Uh… Well…" She bit her lip to keep from spilling that when she came alone, she sampled a little something from each truck—a grand total of fifteen deep fried treats that made her stomach mercilessly angry the following day. "I usually hunt for a really solid funnel cake to end the night with."

Claude slipped out in front of her, their clasped hands hanging between them, and gestured toward the trucks. "Shall we?"

Grinning, she closed the distance between them and nodded, trying her best not to look like a giddy kid about to get their secretly third helping of dessert. Somewhere in the distance, a band had taken to the stage. While it wasn't Delia's music scene—she wasn't even sure she had one, honestly—she could appreciate the fact that it wasn't obtrusive music. It was somehow warm and comforting, adding a much better soundtrack to this part of the date than the classical music lilting through the first.

Delia was perfectly happy hunting for the truck that usually had the best funnel cake until Claude mentioned that there were many, *many* vamps in attendance tonight.

She stiffened. "Really?"

"At ease," Claude chided. He pressed a kiss to her cheek before she could say anything. "No one appears to be hunting. I think they too are here for the music and atmosphere, like many of the humans."

"Right." Like she could believe vamps were in a crowd of humans and none of them were on the hunt. Places like the Fenton Festival were the *perfect* hunting grounds for sluggish, lulled humans, none of whom would have their guard up, relying on unobservant park security to keep them safe. Had hunters been assigned here? Delia scanned the nearest crowd.

"Delia, stop," Claude muttered in her ear. She flinched, then breathed out as he kissed her cheek again. Their hands had broken apart, but his had found its way to her hip, keeping her close. "You aren't working tonight. Let someone else worry about it."

"It's hard to switch off," she admitted hesitantly.

"I believe that." Suddenly his hand was under her chin and he was turning her face toward his. "Is that why you were distracted earlier? You mentioned something with the League, but I won't pry if you're uncomfortable with my asking."

She opened and closed her mouth, knowing that she had enough sense to keep her assignment a secret, even though it made her feel like a terrible human being. He was being so open with her, so earnest, and here she was hiding something from him already.

But that was her job. Even if she wasn't doing this sleazy gig, there was no way she could tell him the ins and outs of her work.

"Never mind," he said gently, easing away from her and taking her hand when she didn't answer. "If you want to tell me, you can. If something is bothering you, I don't mind listening. You can be as vague as you like."

"I know." They started moving forward together, Delia's eyes roving the food trucks. "Thank you. You've been really sweet tonight."

"I did try," he told her as her hand tightened around his. He squeezed back, adding, "I've been on my best date behaviour. It's been quite some time."

"You said that." Taking a deep breath, she shoved the

storm cloud of League and High Council worries away again. Let it hover a few feet behind her for a little while. "Out of curiosity, when *was* the last time you went on an actual date?"

She spied the funnel cake food truck as Claude took a moment to consider the question, his gaze skyward. As always, there was a ridiculous line in front of the register, and she had to stand on her tip-toes to even kind of see the front once she and Claude joined it.

"Well, that would have been with my last wife," he said finally. Delia looked at him sharply, panic fluttering in her chest. "She died almost a decade ago, Alzheimer's, and we were married for a good, oh, twenty years. I courted her before that, so…"

She hadn't realized her mouth was hanging open until their eyes met. Blushing, Delia pressed her lips together tightly and looked away, not entirely sure how to process what she was feeling.

"I'm sorry," Claude told her, his voice catching in his throat as he spoke. "I shouldn't have… That's not very good date etiquette, is it? Bringing up former loves."

"It's fine. Really," she insisted lightly, standing up on her toes as if she was trying to see the front of the line. Really she just didn't want to make eye contact with him.

Delia had skimmed his history at HQ. She knew there had been a Mrs. Grimm at one point or another—only she hadn't realized it was so recent. Well, recent for a vamp. She also hadn't expected to *feel* so much when he said it aloud.

Neither said anything until Delia had her funnel cake in hand, and by then she felt pretty silly about the whole thing. They found a spot to sit on one of the huge rock formations near the young trees the city had planted last year, and Delia dug into her deep-fried mess with fiendish delight.

"I'd offer you some," she said once she'd swallowed a huge mouthful, "but the stuff on top is cherry drizzle, not

O-negative, so…"

Claude wiped something off her cheek, warm fingers brushing close to her lips, and sighed. "You are just *so* thoughtful, Delia."

"And don't you ever forget." She hacked off another piece of cake with her fork, then nudged him with her shoulder. Moments later she was tucked under his arm, eating very carefully to keep the sugar dusting on top of her cake from getting on his clothes.

"I can see why you would want to come here for a first date," Claude said after a long bout of people-watching and cake-eating. Delia set her empty plate aside, stomach ready to burst after all the rich food she'd plied it with that night.

"Yeah? Why's that?"

"It's intimate without being private," he mused. "It's nice."

Delia agreed with a soft hum, resting her head on Claude's shoulder as he started to fiddle with the loose ends of her hair. Hours ago, she had taken a curling iron to it to get some sort of controlled curl. The mirror in the movie theater bathroom had already told her that the effort was wasted. Her hair did what it wanted, but Claude seemed to enjoy twirling it around his fingers—and Delia enjoyed letting him.

Eventually, Claude suggested they check out the latest band, but when they finally reached the concert area, it seemed this band was the most popular of the night. The audience had swelled with people pushing forward and holding up phones to record the performance. To Delia, it all sounded the same: a never-ending stream of banjo and guitar and smooth vocalists. It was nice to listen to, but with no huge monitors to show the stage, anyone standing more than halfway back in the crowd could only do just that—stand and listen.

"Here," Claude said after the first song, Delia up on her toes in an effort to see over the crowd. He crouched down and sidled in front her, gesturing to his back. "Get on."

She almost said no, but she'd thrown caution to the wind ever since they crossed the threshold to Fenton Park. Why not? Grinning, Delia placed her hands on his shoulders, pleased that she had worn an accommodating skirt, then jumped up onto his back. Seconds later he was upright. A giggle escaped her before she could stop it.

"Better?" he called, tipping his head back to try and look at her.

"Much," she said. From there she could actually see the band. It didn't matter that they were far away. In fact, she didn't really care all that much about seeing them in the first place; she just didn't want him to put her down. Her legs wrapped snugly around his midsection, and she shifted down so that she could drape her arms over his shoulders. As his hands slipped under her knees for support, Delia pressed a quick peck to his temple, heat flaring throughout her body. Her whispered thanks in his ear made him smile.

They stayed there until a new band took to the stage, and by then midnight had come and gone. Although staying up all night and sleeping all day was nothing new, Delia hadn't prepped her schedule accordingly. Her second yawn prompted Claude to ask if she wanted him to take her home.

"Not really," she admitted, surprised at her honesty, "but maybe."

She kissed him again, unable to help herself, but this time on his cheek as he carried her away from the crowd. From the festival grounds to the Beltmore Hotel, Claude gave her the only piggyback ride she would ever commit to memory, laughing and chatting as they bypassed other late-night partygoers along the downtown walkways. For once, she wasn't trying to scope out the vamps from the humans—she was in the present, totally fixated on the man carrying her on his back.

It felt kind of nice.

Kind of more than nice.

It felt like relief.

On the drive back to her apartment, Claude thanked her for the date, saying it was quite fun.

"Was it?" she asked as she reclined in the passenger seat beside him. He nodded, gaze fixed on the road.

"I enjoyed myself."

"But only the second half, right?"

"Both," he insisted. "For different reasons, I suppose."

"Hmm." She studied the familiar buildings through the window. Like the last time he drove her home, she almost dreaded seeing her street sign. "Next time you can skip the really expensive restaurant and rom-com. Neither are really my thing."

"Ah, so there will be a next time?" he asked, laughing when she playfully rolled her eyes at him. "Naturally there should be. I have to make up for my dismal choices, don't I?"

"Well, it's not like you'd know what I like on a date." Even if they'd spent time together last month, it wasn't like he actually knew her. Delia had always been careful about not letting too much of her personal life slip.

And to be fair, Delia had no idea what Claude liked, either. Fenton Festival could have been his worst nightmare, but because he was ridiculously patient and considerate with her, he'd never say it to her face. She bit her lower lip, watching him out of the corner of her eye. For some reason, she wanted to make sure he had a good time.

"So…" Claude brought the car to a gentle stop in front of her building, her street quiet in both directions. He shifted in place to face her, his expression suddenly too serious for her liking. "Aren't you going to invite me up again?"

She blinked back her surprise, which peppered her cheeks with colour and made her body warmer than she liked. A tremor of excitement passed through her at the thought, but she swallowed it down, shocked at his presumptuousness.

Seconds later he laughed and snatched her hand, kissing it before she could pull away. "I'm only teasing. Because at the bar the other night…"

"Right, right, let's harp on my drunken stupidity—"

"It was a very enticing offer," he told her, still holding her hand, thumbs stroking the top. The heat from his palms soothed her temper. "I mean, had you been able to stand upright on your own, I might have taken you up on it."

"Okay."

"And if your words were clear, too. As I recall, they were very slurred and your dress was in such a state of—"

"*Okay.*" She yanked her hand back and tried to suppress a smile. "Maybe one day we'll figure out how to get vamps piss drunk, then I can have embarrassing stories about *you* to throw in your face."

"Spend more time with me and you'll see I don't need to be drunk for you to have embarrassing stories," Claude said with a chuckle. Delia pursed her lips, shaking her head.

"Bullshit. I'm sure clan leaders don't do anything embarrassing." At some point, she too had shifted on the seat so that she faced him, one leg bent and drawn under her. "Kings even less so."

"The king title is a formality," he insisted. "Few actually remember I have the power to decree martial law."

"So why don't you?" She paused, sensing a slight shift in the air between them. "I mean, some of the other clans have been misbehaving lately."

"I can assure you, and your League," Claude said somewhat pointedly, "that should a line be crossed, the issue will be dealt with."

She withdrew both hands to her lap. They'd been creeping toward him while they talked, desperate to settle on his arm or his thigh.

"Well, I hope so," she said after another brief pause. "For the sake of the people of Harriswood."

Claude studied her, eyes fixed on her in a way that was almost calculating. But then he blinked and the look was gone.

"Delia, you know I have no desire to discuss clan or League business with you," he said, his tone suggesting he was tired of saying it. All she could do was nod—this wasn't the first time he'd told her, and she had every intention of including that in her report for the High Council tomorrow.

"I know. Sorry. It's habit." She tucked her hair behind her ear. "I don't deal with a lot of people outside the League socially. Vamp and human politics are kind of the main topic of conversation."

Unless there was alcohol involved—then it was open season for whatever her drunken brain could come up with. His jaw clenched momentarily, but, like that look of contention from before, it was gone in a flash.

"I understand," he told her. "At least, I understand now."

"I'll keep my prying to a minimum on the next date," she insisted with a grin. "I promise."

Delia added a wink because she thought it suited her mischievous tone, but instantly regretted it. Who the hell actually winked at anyone in real life? She busied herself with pulling her purse strap over her shoulder and zipping up her jacket to hide her embarrassment.

"And when would you like this next date to be?" he asked. Maybe he'd missed the wink. Delia glanced up with a heavy sigh.

"I'll need to plan it around my schedule," she told him, a half-truth that made her butterflies turn to knots. "Can I let you know?"

Claude nodded. "Of course."

It would have been easy to lean forward and kiss him.

A little awkward with the gear shift between them, given how small the car was, but she could probably swing it. Instead, Delia reached out and pressed her hand to his chest, offering him a very real smile.

"Thanks for everything," she said, swallowing hard when he placed his hand over hers. "Seriously."

Claude lifted her hand to his lips again and pressed them to her palm. Shooting him one last smile, she clambered out of the car as gracefully as she could manage. After she shut the door, Delia heard him roll down the window and call her name. Resting a hand on the car, she leaned down with a raised eyebrow.

"See you soon," Claude said, then, much to her horror, offered her an overly dramatic wink and a wicked smile. So he hadn't missed it. Perfect. With her cheeks hot, Delia flipped him off and kept flipping him off until he closed the window and drove away. Just before he rounded the corner at the end of her building, Claude gave two quick honks, and Delia waved from the curb until the car disappeared.

Across the street, the grey-haired hunter from before was still seated on the same bench. Newspaper folded on his lap, he too waved once she saw him. Jaw clenched, Delia turned on the spot and hurried for the door, her nerves from the start of the night slowly but surely creeping back in and making themselves at home.

CHAPTER 12: KEEPING ENEMIES CLOSER AND ALL THAT

"Well, look at you, high roller." Arthur beamed from the other side of the glass as he slid Delia's pay envelope across the counter. "Why didn't you tell me you'd been promoted?"

She wasn't sure whether to smile or frown, laugh at a joke or take him seriously, so her mouth morphed into some weird half-smile-half-frown thing that felt strained.

"What is that? What is your face doing?" Arthur asked, his exuberance faltering somewhat.

"Oh, I wasn't sure if you were being serious," she said as she shoved the white envelope into her purse. "Are you being serious?"

The accountant frowned. "What? Are you?"

"What?"

They stared at one another, both trying to gauge what the hell was happening, before dissolving into giggles. She was the only one picking up her earnings that afternoon; she'd received a notification yesterday that her cheque was ready. Most hunters visited Arthur the day it was issued, which she knew resulted in a giant headache for her friend behind the counter. ID squabbles. Arguments over the amount—like he was the guy who decided how much everyone was paid. Idiots.

"But seriously, you were in a different category of

hunter when I went to print your stuff," Arthur told her, rolling himself over to a monitor a few feet from the main one. Delia's brow furrowed as he clacked away at a keyboard, then nodded at the screen. "See? New category. Doesn't say why." He glanced over at her through his wide-brimmed glasses. "Got a new super secret assignment?"

"Kind of," she said weakly. She turned away and retrieved the envelope, tearing it open as Arthur continued to type away. While her hunter ID was the same as always, her pay grade seemed to have changed. Suddenly she was getting a quarter more than usual, at least—all because she went on a date with a vamp, then wrote a blasé report about it.

Three days had gone by since she and Claude had had their first date, and she felt just as slimy about it now as she did when the High Council first assigned her to it. If the mark had been anyone else, maybe she could have done it. She could have forgotten that they were using her for some unwarranted sexual prowess. She could forget that she was supposed to flirt and charm information out of a man, that she was supposed to use him for the League's gain, toy with his feelings. If he had been anyone but Claude Grimm.

But Delia actually felt something for Claude. As of that moment, however, she wasn't sure exactly *what*. The lust phase had mostly passed after the masquerade ball. There was no denying the sexual tension, but it was something more than that now. She wasn't just smitten anymore. Not in love. Just floating in some weird middle ground that she couldn't wrap her head around yet.

On the other side of the coin, Delia had made more money than she usually did in a week writing one measly little report—most of which was filled with information she had found in the digital archives, reworded to make it seem like it had come up in conversation.

This was what she had wanted for so long—to finally

move up, to not stay stagnant. For her superiors to see she had worth beyond the mundane tasks they had assigned her week after week, year after year, since she was twenty-one.

It was *finally* happening, in spite of the bite marks on her neck, the ones that should have earned her a one-way ticket to Exiled Traitor Island.

She ought to be *happy*.

"Hey, you okay?"

"Yeah." Delia shoved the pay summary back in the envelope and looked up, finding Arthur studying her curiously.

"You look, uhm, tired."

A polite way of saying she looked like shit. She smirked. "Nice."

He backtracked quickly, as any sane male did when they'd been caught commenting on a woman's appearance. "No, no, no, it's just you kind of seem—"

"I *am* tired," she admitted. "My schedule's a bit all over the place."

She'd been so hyped up on nervous adrenaline after her date that she had barely slept. After sunrise, Delia had decided to stop chasing the ever elusive shut-eye and head to HQ, where she'd holed herself up in the digital archives room with her laptop to write her report for the High Council. Once she'd submitted it and headed for home, she'd crashed hard in a hangry fit, needing food but too tired to make it, and then woke with a splitting headache for her regularly assigned patrol the following evening.

Since then, her sleep schedule hadn't quite balanced out, but since she had the night off she had plans to splurge on takeout for dinner, have a glass of wine in a hot bath while streaming trashy TV, then take the sleeping pill the League nurse had issued and catch up on all her missed hours of quality time in bed—alone.

This week felt never-ending.

"You're not the only one looking tired, I promise,"

Arthur told her as he sidled back to the front of his little accounting bubble. "Kain was in earlier and he looked like he had crawled out of a crypt or something."

Delia hadn't heard from Kain since their run-in on the elevator—and that was totally fine in her books.

Mind you, she also hadn't heard from Claude since their date.

"Can I ask you a weird question?" When Arthur gave a tentative nod, she took a moment to figure out how to phrase it, then just came out with it. "Do you put any stock in that stupid three-day rule after a date? Like it's too desperate to call someone the day after, or the guy isn't interested in you if they don't…" Delia trailed off, the look on Arthur's face coinciding with her realization of how ridiculous the question was. "…call."

"I hate to repeat myself," Arthur said after a brief pause, "but are you serious?"

Her shoulders slumped a little. "No." Delia then shook her head and went for the door. "Thanks for everything."

Delia made it a few feet before she heard him call her name.

"Everybody gets busy," he told her with a shrug. "I mean, you could always call *him*, you know? Nobody thinks it's desperate. We're not in high school."

She shot him a thumbs-up and a half-smile. "Thanks, Arthur."

"See you around," he called back across the vast empty room. Delia nodded before she left, pleased that he hadn't used a somewhat self-conscious moment to poke fun at her.

The rational side of her knew that Claude hadn't called because Delia said she'd let him know when they could see each other again. Still, she actually missed getting the occasional text from him.

Maybe she'd call him when she got home, sometime later tonight—let him know that she'd had fun the other night and was still waiting on her work schedule to come out. Her mouth twisted into a smile at the thought, but the sight of a wall-mounted surveillance camera ogling her made it disappear just as fast. Head down, she made her way to the elevator in silence, all the while fantasizing about the relaxing night ahead.

*   *   *

Delia's hopes of a relaxing night imploded as soon as she rounded the corner and saw who was standing at her building's door, jamming his finger into the wall-mounted intercom talk button.

"Look, I'm worried my friend is ill," Kain sneered. Delia crossed her arms, gripping her phone. Only moments earlier, she had contemplated texting Claude to let him know that she was free to talk for a little while if he wasn't doing anything. That probably wasn't going to be happening anytime soon.

"Oldest trick in the book, buddy," came the prickly response from her super. Delia stopped a few feet behind Kain, her eyes narrowed. "Either a tenant lets you in or you can piss off."

"Fucking bastard," Delia heard the hunter mutter, finger hovering over the communication button. As soon as he punched his finger into it again, Delia cleared her throat, which he ignored.

"You should have said you were a plumber or something," she said stiffly. Kain whirled around, mouth slightly open as if she'd caught him just as he was about to say something. Exhaling deeply, he stepped away from the intercom and ran a hand through his shaggy brown hair. He stank of smoke and was probably responsible for the smoldering cigarette butts scattered around the entryway. Delia looked at them pointedly, but he didn't seem to notice.

"Figured I'd get more sympathy if I said I was worried

about my friend," he told her before raising two fingers at the security camera overhead. "Apparently your super doesn't give a shite if someone's potentially dying up there."

She grabbed his arm and pulled it down so he'd stop flipping off whoever was watching the monitors. "Stop."

"You alright, Dels?" He moved in closer, but Delia skirted around him and shoved her key in the lock. "Haven't heard from you in a few days."

"That's because I'm mad at you," she snapped. Against her better judgement, she let him follow her inside—he probably would have pushed through the door anyway if she hadn't.

"Still?"

"Yeah, *still*. It was a shitty thing you did."

They crossed the lobby to the elevators together, their synced footfalls the only sounds to be heard. Once she'd pressed the *up* button and stepped back, Delia noted Kain's gaze seemed to be everywhere but her.

"I've been under a lot of pressure lately—"

"Oh my god, just go, Kain," Delia said thickly, rolling her eyes as the elevator doors peeled back and stepping inside. He hurried in after her and tapped the button for her floor before she could get to it.

"No, you're right, it's no excuse." He gave her some space as the rickety lift began its ascent, leaning against one wall while she stood firmly at the other. "I was an arse. What I did... I understand why you're angry. I wanted to check in with you and make sure you're okay after the, uh, date thing."

"The date *thing* was fine," she remarked, staring intently at the buttons on the panel in front of her. Some of the numbers had faded, their outlines split and chipped. "Fun, actually."

"Fun?" By the time they'd reached her floor, Kain had another cigarette in hand. "You didn't include that tidbit in your report."

Her eyebrows shot up, but she stepped out and blitzed down the hall before he could catch her look of surprise. Of course he had read her report. The gossip was right. Kain *was* Wentworth's little pet.

"Don't come in if you plan to light that thing up," she told him coolly when he caught up at her door. Kain tucked the cigarette behind his ear, wearing an easy smile when their eyes met.

"I know the rules, Dels."

Sighing, Delia turned the key and pushed the front door open, contemplating slamming it on his foot. However, by the time she decided on doing it, Kain had already shouldered his way inside, and she closed her front door more forcefully than usual, kicked off her shoes, and stalked from the front hall toward the living/dining area. With all the lights off in the late afternoon, her place was shrouded in comfortable shadow. Tossing her purse on the couch, the arms of which had pants and shirts hanging over them, she tidied up—also known as pushing the mess into a single large pile instead of a number of smaller ones—then plopped down in the middle and crossed her arms.

Kain, meanwhile, perched on her window ledge, her usual perch for watching post-work rush hour at the intersection below. It was on that very ledge she had talked to Kain over the phone all those months ago, on the night of the masquerade, when he'd told her to come out to the bar with him and the boys instead of sneaking into the ball.

Had he known? Delia frowned. Time and time again Kain had proved that the High Council put a lot of faith in him. He had known back then that the masquerade would be riddled with more vamps than anticipated. Did he also know that Claudia, every Harriswood hunter's white whale, was a fake?

"Look, I'm really sorry for how things went down the other day," Kain started, and Delia blinked out of her musings, busying herself with her nails. "I didn't think they'd make you describe every detail of the night he bit you—"

"Did you know they had another job lined up for me?" She clenched her jaw briefly. "That they weren't going to, you know, banish me or kill me because I let a vampire bite me?"

"Yes," he said without missing a beat, "because Claude Grimm isn't just some vamp. He's a clan leader. Even if he isn't central to this whole Donovan mess, any information you get from him has value. Lots of value, actually, given—"

"Given that he's the regional king?" When he didn't respond right away, Delia glanced up and found him studying her with a frown. "What? Do I actually know something *you* don't?"

"Did he tell you that?"

"Obviously."

"It's an antiquated title," he insisted, more fervently than necessary. Her eyes dropped to his fingers as he slowly spun his cigarette. With his coat bunched up beside him on the ledge and his shirt sleeves rolled up to his elbows, she could see the mishmash of tattoos up each forearm. She'd thought his whole vibe was so sexy when they first met: a dangerous vampire hunter with tattoos. Now they were a little faded and two of his fingertips were stained yellow from smoking.

After everything that had happened, what she'd thought was sexy before had lost its charm. And without the sex appeal, where exactly did Kain fit in her life anyway? She'd thought he was her support system after Claude bit her, but apparently she had been seeing things that weren't there.

"It's still a title he holds," Delia stated, pleased with the way her words made him scowl. "I think he trusts the clans to govern themselves."

"Well, fine job they're doing," he said with a scoff. "Rats hanging from the library? Humans butchered in the trades? Why doesn't this self-professed *king* do something?"

"He—"

"Because, like the actual monarchy, his title is superficial. It doesn't mean anything in this day and age, Delia. Even if he wanted to assert some authority, who'd listen to him?"

"Vamps are all about tradition," she argued, the heat in her cheeks matching the colour suddenly flaming in his. "If their king puts his foot down, I'm sure they'd toe the line."

"Then why hasn't he?"

"I don't know."

"Isn't that why you're dating him?" he said flippantly. "So you actually know something?"

"Wow…" She pointed in the general direction of the door. "You can leave if you're going to be an ass."

"Alright, alright…" Kain slid off the ledge, hands up in surrender. "I'm sorry. I didn't come here to fight about Claude fucking Grimm. But I don't want you to get too wrapped up in his ridiculous title."

"Thanks, I'll try my best." Sarcasm rolled off her as Delia continued to glare at him, until finally she broke the silence. "Why are you even here?"

"Just checking in," Kain told her. "Seeing how things are with you after the date."

"You read the report," she fired back. "You should know."

Kain slouched back on the ledge, looking a little defeated. "Delia…"

"Are you here asking me because you're genuinely concerned, or because Wentworth doesn't know me well enough to read between the lines yet?"

"Both?"

"Oh my god…" Delia stood and hurried into the kitchen. Once she was there, she wasn't sure why she had marched in there besides needing a break from Kain, so she grabbed a can of Coke and a bag of chips, then meandered back into the living room, only to find her "guest" seated in her previous spot. Jaw clenched, she climbed onto the clothes-less arm of the couch and cracked open her drink.

"You're a shite hostess," he said with a smirk, one she didn't return. Exhaling deeply, he faced her, one ankle crossed over his knee and an arm stretched out along the back of the couch. "Isn't this what you always wanted? The High Council has a special interest in you. A secret operation they cooked up *just* for you. Even more established hunters would be jealous of that kind of attention. You should enjoy it."

"They didn't pick me because of my skills," Delia told him flatly. After taking a noisy slurp of her drink, she set the can on the floor and broke open her bag of chips. "They chose me for circumstantial reasons."

"Who cares?" Kain shoved his hand into the bag when she begrudgingly held it out to him, pulling out a huge handful of chips. "Prove 'em wrong. Show 'em what you're made of. Write good reports. Dig up useful intel. I know you can impress them, Dels."

Shoving a too-big chip in her mouth, Delia chewed thoughtfully for a moment. He had a point. This was an opportunity to prove herself—she just wished it had nothing to do with dating Claude Grimm.

"So, look, this *is* from Wentworth," Kain said, shifting a little closer, "but is there anything you didn't mention? You wrote a lot about clan history, which from what I understand was the assignment, but it didn't feel personal. Kind of like you read up on it and wrote the report." Delia swallowed hard, wincing when the pointed edge of a chip sliced its way down her throat, as Kain went on. "Is there anything else you got out of him? Anything about the Donovans in particular?"

She shrugged. "Not really. He's made it pretty clear on multiple occasions that he doesn't like discussing clan business. He calls it gossiping."

"Are you sure?"

"Yes, Kain," she said sharply, the line of questioning starting to reignite her temper, "I'm fucking sure. It might surprise you, but I can actually read pretty basic social cues." Her eyes narrowed when he rolled his. "You know you guys are asking a lot, right? You're basically twisting my arm into spying on a guy I have this weird history with."

Weird *romantic* history at that.

"He's not a guy, Dels, he's—"

"I know, I know, clan leader and king of the—"

"He's a vamp," Kain said tersely. "Think of him as one the next time you go out with him."

Difficult as it was, she tried to keep her face neutral, ignoring his patronizing tone to focus on what actually mattered to her. "So the High Council wants me to go on more dates?"

"Well, you didn't exactly give them much that they don't already know in this report," Kain told her. "I think you'll be getting an email sometime tonight about the next topic."

She pressed her lips together to hide her sudden smile, but given the expression on Kain's face, she wasn't successful. Clearing her throat, Delia dug into the chip bag again. It didn't matter that Kain was here and he was being an ass. She got to go out with Claude. *That's* what mattered. "Oh darn. Go out on more dates with a gorgeous guy. Get taken to the finest restaurants. Drive around in his sexy car. Sucks to be me."

Kain took a playful swipe at her leg, catching her with the tips of his fingers as she tried to dart out of the way. Both of them were smiling this time when their gazes met, though perhaps for different reasons. Delia slid off the armrest onto the couch, legs folded up against her chest and head leaning on the backrest.

"Dels, this is serious." Kain took another handful of

chips. "I mean, I know you don't feel like the High Council values you, but they're testing you here. Try to do a good job."

"Oh, thanks, Kain," she drawled, pushing aside thoughts about her outfit for the next date. "No, I mean, I thought I'd fucking wing it and see what happens."

"You know what I mean." He broke a chip in half. Crumbs scattered onto her cushion. "Don't get wrapped up in a guy like Claude Grimm."

"You mean don't fall for him?"

He shrugged, brushing the crumbs onto the floor. "Yeah, I guess."

Somewhere outside, two cars had erupted in a honking battle, probably at the intersection down the street. As Kain looked back to the window, Delia bit her lower lip and set the chip bag aside. Even though she'd put on a front for Kain, the idea of more dates where she had to play the spy wasn't exactly appealing.

More dates, on the other hand, more time with Claude, *was*. Maybe she could fake her way through those reports too. If the worst she got was a talking to from Kain, maybe she could actually do it: go on a date with a man who made her giddy *and* pride herself on being given a personal assignment from the High Council.

She wished she could talk to Kain about it, but it seemed that ship had long since sailed. Devin would be the ideal one to discuss her mess of personal and professional feelings with, but the fewer people within the League who knew she'd been bitten, the better.

"So, are we friends again or what?" Kain asked when the symphony of car horns finally died down. He poked at her leg, grinning. "I don't like when you're mad at me."

"We were always friends, Kain," she said with a slight shake of her head, though the words felt empty now. "But I haven't forgiven you for what you've done. And I probably won't."

He'd lost his chance at a real friendship the second he

ratted her out to the High Council. But if keeping Kain in her life meant she had an in with the men who controlled her career, then she'd keep him around. Gone were the bar nights. Gone was the flirty banter. Gone were the thoughts about how attractive he looked in workout gear. As far as Kain was concerned, Delia's feelings had shifted to strictly professional.

"Guessing an afternoon quickie probably wouldn't help with that, eh?"

She frowned at him, trying to gauge whether or not he was serious, but Delia got her answer when he flashed what she was knew to be his seductive grin. It usually worked best on her when she was drunk. In the daylight, it was sleazy.

"Go," she ordered.

"Come on, Dels, I was only trying to lighten the mood…"

Taking him by his sleeve, Delia eventually managed to shove Kain out of her apartment. As soon as he was gone, a peaceful quiet descended, the emptiness curling around her like a welcome embrace. With a long sigh, exhaling all of the day's stresses with it, Delia flopped back down on her couch and demolished the rest of her chips.

So they wanted her to date Claude Grimm again. Dig deeper. Get more information from him. There was no other way around it—Delia *had* to look at it as an opportunity. She suddenly had permission to spend time with a forbidden man and explore her feelings for him, *and* she had the High Council's attention. She'd just have to get better at masking archive information in her reports.

Later that evening, as she drew herself a bath and powered down all her electronics, Delia vowed that by tomorrow morning, she would have figured out a way to both date Claude Grimm *and* work her way up through the League without dissolving into a frazzled, sleepless disaster like she'd done over the last couple of days.

When she eventually did, it was like finding nirvana.

Because once she gave herself permission to move forward, to brush aside the anxieties and fears and insecurities, Delia could actually enjoy herself.

*   *   *

Which was precisely what she did. In the weeks that followed, Delia dated the hell out of Claude Grimm and wrote lengthy, fluffy reports around the questions the High Council sent her. She drew information from the archives and padded it with watered-down drama from her reality TV favourites, knowing Don Wentworth wouldn't share her taste in guilty pleasures. There were no more inquiries from Kain. No more meetings in the High Council's disciplinary chambers. For the first time in her life, Delia got her cake and ate the absolute shit out of it too.

And for once, Delia was happy.

CHAPTER 13: KISS IN THE RAIN (BUCKET LIST ITEM #3)

"Maybe you should stop being a hunter," Claude mused as he glanced over his shoulder at her. A few feet behind, Delia paused on the crest of an unearthed tree root, arms out for balance, and frowned. The crunch of his feet on the forest floor, littered with the decay of fallen leaves, stopped, and the dark-haired vamp turned back, hands in the pockets of his charcoal-grey sweater.

"Why do you say that?" she asked, fingertips brushing the trunk of the nearby tree. He offered her what she could only describe as a kind smile, a patient one, the sort he used whenever she wasn't *quite* getting it.

"Well, think about it," he started as he took a few steps toward her. She looked up at the sound of a woodland creature skittering along the branches overhead—a squirrel, fatter than ever as winter approached. When she faced Claude again, that stupid smile was still there, and she reached out to push at his chest. The contact changed his expression for the better. "You've spent the last half an hour listing all your employee grievances about the League. You've worked there for years with no real upward mobility, nor have your superiors given so much as a hint that you might be going somewhere career-wise beyond this little secret project…"

She swallowed hard. It had sort of slipped out during her ranting that the High Council had finally offered her a better paying gig, but she clammed up before telling him it was all thanks to the bite mark he'd left on her throat. True to form, Claude hadn't questioned it or pressed for more information. He always seemed happy to take whatever she would give, somehow.

Delia hadn't been able to help herself. When Claude had asked her if she wanted to tell him about her experiences as a hunter, it was like he'd opened the floodgate to Rant Central. There were so few people in her life she could complain to, and most of them were hunters. They already knew the whole story, a few of them experiencing something similar. Claude was a fresh sounding board, a blank canvas on which she could paint her annoyances and spill her grievances.

"You're young, Delia," Claude told her with a soft sigh. "If you aren't happy with your job, then you have all the time in the world to change it. Pursue another passion. Find something that you're good at."

"I've always thought *this* was what I would be good at," she said weakly. A gentle gust of cold November wind rustled through the forest, rattling the empty branches and dragging her hair across her face. She combed it aside, scolding herself for not bringing a band to tie it back with.

Claude had only told her to dress comfortably—he hadn't even slightly hinted they'd be going for a late afternoon hike through the more rugged and unkempt parts of his property. They'd been hiking for so long that she wasn't even sure if they were within Harriswood limits anymore, but, for once, she didn't mind. Forest walks weren't usually her thing, but talking to Claude definitely was.

"Come now," Claude said, reaching out and brushing a few of her rogue brown curls back where they belonged. Her skin warmed at even the slightest touch. "There must be something else you're skilled at? Other career paths you might have considered?"

She shrugged and looked away, eyes wandering the wild terrain. There was no path to be seen. Claude simply led and Delia followed, not once concerned that he would get them lost.

"I didn't really care much about school when I was in it," she told him, "and everything else, all the stupid part-time, dirt-paying jobs, never held my interest. I don't know. My aunt was a great hunter. She brought me into this life, pulled all the right strings to get me an interview with the recruiters, and I would feel like I failed her if I just up and left it."

"You can't do something for a living to please others," he said. "Do it to please yourself. If you aren't happy with what you're doing, do something else. Surely you must have passions outside of hunting vampires?"

Her gaze drifted upward to the grey, overcast sky, the forest canopy all but gone. "I don't know. I've never felt drawn toward anything. I don't have a favourite band or movie or book. I can't see myself doing anything else. I don't think I have other passions."

Besides eating and watching reality TV in bed, that is. Not exactly the passions of a mature adult. Oh, and jogging—but any thoughts of becoming some track superstar were dead and buried. Besides, she wanted to do something in life that actually gave her purpose.

"Perhaps," Claude remarked, taking her hand and helping her off the thick exposed root, "you've just never tried. We all have passions. Some are hobbies, some turn into careers. Perhaps you're so apathetic because you feel stuck in a place where you're going nowhere."

"I'm not apathetic," she countered. Claude's hand tightened around hers when she tried to tug it away, and they both grinned at one another as she fell back into her usual place by his side. "I'm... I don't know. I fought really hard to prove myself when I first joined. Then more recruits started filtering in, better hunters than me, and now it feels I've just kind of faded into the background no matter what I do."

"If it doesn't make you happy, perhaps you shouldn't

do it."

"But it *does* make me happy," she argued, faltering, then muttered, "sometimes."

The people she worked with made her happy. Her assignments, while usually mind-numbingly boring, gave her that sense of purpose she craved. But ever since she'd been assigned to spy on Claude, something had changed. League emails in her inbox gave her a rush of panic. Knowing that Wentworth wanted to see her made her physically queasy.

Working a better gig was supposed to make her happy, and it did, for a time, but after over a month of dating Claude *and* drafting fake reports on him, Delia found she preferred the former to the latter. She went willingly to each and every date, happily, because it meant she got to see Claude, one of the handful people in her life who didn't make her feel small.

The High Council insisted she see him twice a week, but as of the last three weeks, Delia had gone rogue and seen him more often. Four dates a week wasn't unheard of, and she had already planned a speech to tell Wentworth should she be caught: it would be odd for a couple building a relationship not to see one another if they had time, so why limit it to twice a week?

There were dates at the coffee house. Walks in the park. Horror movie marathons in her living room— though he had yet to stay the night. He had, at the time, commented on the fact that she'd let the mums he gave her wilt into oblivion. No more bouquets for her. Two weeks ago they had gone ice-skating, a pastime that they were equally bad at—a pleasant surprise.

Halloween had come and gone, and while Delia had been assigned a random patrol in the suburbs, she'd received an email the day before instructing her to bring Claude along. She had replied back with objections to save face when really she had planned to ask him to come anyway. They'd strolled the neighbourhoods with huge houses and spectacular lawns, pointing out ridiculous costumes and watching for misbehaving vamps.

With Claude by her side, not a single thing went wrong her entire shift—a rarity, given that vamps, like teenagers, were notoriously ill-behaved on Halloween. There was a slight moment of tension when Claude had showed up at their designated meeting spot wearing that ridiculous, bell-laden fool's mask from the masquerade, but Delia had made sure it went back in the car where it belonged before they took a single step together.

It didn't feel like work anymore, this special assignment. Most of her reports consisted of information she dug up from the archives, the wording changed to the point that it was unrecognizable from the source material, along with the occasional real-life twist from her TV favourites. She couldn't actually remember the last time she'd asked Claude one of the High Council's suggested questions, or used a direct quote from him that wasn't concocted out of thin air as she wrote.

Their hike through the woods that afternoon wasn't a High Council–mandated date. In fact, Claude had only called two hours ago and told her his evening meeting had been cancelled, which meant he was free if she was.

She knew that the cancellation of his meeting—which League sources had deemed a region-wide clan meeting— meant her report topic for her date tomorrow would probably change. In fact, she could already guess that the High Council would want to know *why* the meeting was postponed; there was probably already a revised email sitting in her inbox.

Delia could guess why it was put off. Clan tensions had mounted in recent weeks, with more violence erupting between the Donovans and the others. What she gathered from the little Claude shared with her was that the Grimm clan steered clear of the drama, with many of its members preferring to set off on winter vacations now if it meant avoiding the conflict.

"Have I lost you?"

Delia looked to him quickly, cheeks flushed at being caught daydreaming. "Hmm?"

"You've gone quiet." Overhead, the winds had started to pick up, rattling the trees and blowing Claude's dark locks this way and that. They curled the longer they grew, and he'd left his hair natural today, making it seem fuller than usual. Worthy of a good finger-combing.

Her gaze swept over his thick tresses before flitting up to the sky briefly. The clouds had darkened, bringing with them a chilly breeze. Delia fought back a shiver as she moved in closer to Claude—the only vamp she knew personally who radiated heat.

"You gave me a lot to think about," she told him. "Sorry."

"Don't be." They both paused to navigate a dangerous prickle bush between a cluster of trees, skirting around the outstretched thorns on the curved branches before tackling a thick, half-rotted log. Once around the obstacles, Claude wrapped an arm around her shoulders. "Is there anything in particular that made you think?"

She shrugged, knowing she couldn't share what she'd actually been thinking, even if she wanted to—always a great start to a relationship. "One thing, I guess."

"Only one? I thought I was more interesting than that."

Delia returned his smirk. "There's that presumptuousness again." He drew her in briefly to kiss her temple. It was the only place he kissed her these days—her temple, her cheek, her hand. Delia licked her lips and shot him a sidelong glance. "You said I was young."

Claude nodded. "You are."

"And is that... I don't know..." Delia paused, trying to find the right wording. "Is that weird for you?"

"No," he remarked without missing a beat. "Does it bother you that I'm substantially older than you?"

"How substantially?"

191

"I'd hazard a guess at, say…three hundred years, possibly," Claude said, smiling when her eyebrows shot up. "What? Surely you knew that was a possibility. Young vampires don't run clans."

"Or rule regions, I guess," she muttered, to which he nodded. "Fine. So you're old and I'm young. You're fine with that?"

A bird fluttered by overheard, the whap of its wings causing her to look up. All black. Large. Maybe a crow or a raven. It carried on, not paying attention to the cuddling explorers below.

"In my lifetime, I've had four wives," Claude admitted, this time with some hesitancy. She knew he'd been married before. Hell, he brought it up on their first date. Still, even with prior knowledge, a rush of something hot surged through her, something that settled as a heavy lump in her throat as Claude spoke. "One was a vampire, the others human. I never saw their ages as a reason not to pursue them. I've always thought humans, no matter the age, have as much to teach me as I have to teach them."

"What happened to them?" she asked without thinking the question through. A pained look flashed across his face, but only for a moment.

"They died," Claude said flatly. "Every last one of them. Old age. War. Alzheimer's." He coughed and looked away, but seconds later he faced her again and the pain in his eyes was gone. "I've grieved. I've celebrated each one as I said goodbye. Don't the League archives have a section on my marital status?" When Delia opened and closed her mouth wordlessly, he gave a warm laugh and squeezed her shoulder. "Come now, I don't believe for a second that you didn't read up on me after the masquerade."

She pursed her lips at him, sensing a welcome shift in the direction of the conversation. "So the age thing, it's a non-issue, huh?"

"As long as you don't look like a child," he told her,

"or act like one, I'm fine. Is it an issue for you?"

"I hadn't even considered it before now," she said honestly. Freeing herself from his grasp, Delia whirled around in front of him, walking backward, trusting Claude not to let her fall over some thorn bush as she matched each of his steps. "I think…" She pressed a finger to her chin, squinting at him. "I think it's a deal breaker."

He cocked his head to the side, mischievousness washing over his features. "Oh, little huntress, age is but a number. Have I not proven my stamina yet?"

Warmth spread from the nape of her neck to the crux of her thighs. When she shook her head, Claude tutted at her and rolled up his sleeves, slowly, one at a time.

"Well, I do sincerely apologize," he said, his voice edged with a purr that left her wanting. "I'll need to rectify that *immediately*."

His arm shot out, a hand reaching for her, but Delia ducked out of the way just in time and took off with a giggle. Weaving her way around the trees and over grasping roots, she ran with the silliest of smiles on her lips, not caring if he saw, not caring that he could have caught her in seconds if he actually tried.

Delia pushed on, forcing her legs to go as fast as they could on the unfriendly terrain, until her foot slipped into something that wouldn't let go. She toppled forward with an embarrassing half-shriek, stopping herself with her hands against the hard earth.

"Mind the animal dens, little huntress," Claude teased, sliding an arm under her waist and hauling her upright. "You wouldn't be much good to your High Council with a broken leg, would you?"

"I think you underestimate the strength of my shin bones," Delia said breathlessly. Arms outstretched to each side, she watched with growing affection as Claude dusted the dirt and underbrush from her clothes, taking more time than needed to ensure her thighs and breasts were spick-and-span. It was the first time he'd been so physically forward on their dates—and she liked it.

In fact, she liked it so much that she had every intention of kissing him, planning to catch his face as he stood and press her lips to his.

Just then, however, the skies opened. With no canopy to speak of, they were soaked within the minute. Scowling, Delia shuffled forward and tucked her head under Claude's chin.

"Poor thing," Claude rumbled. Delia's hand flattened against his chest, enjoying the vibration of his voice as he continued. "Come on then. Let's get somewhere dry."

"And where, exactly, would that be?" She started walking somewhat begrudgingly. "I have no idea where we are."

"Well, *some* of us were paying attention," he said. Suddenly the rain stopped, and when Delia looked up, she saw he'd taken off his jacket and was holding it over her head in the form of a makeshift umbrella. "We actually aren't too far from the guest quarters."

Her eyes dropped to his lips, wet with little rain droplets while he shielded her from the worst of it. Those kissable lips, the memory of them still seared to her skin...

"Well, come on then," she said somewhat unsteadily, forcing herself to carry onward. "*Some* of us can actually catch a cold in this weather."

They trudged ahead, a curtain of thick rain following the pair through the forest. Steadily the ground went from hard and unforgiving to mushy and clawing. More than once Delia got her hiking boots stuck in the mud, and more than once Claude had to help yank her leg out. When they finally reached the manicured sanctuary of the Grimm grounds, she all but ran for the lawn, temporarily forsaking the shelter of Claude's jacket if it meant getting out of a forest that wanted to swallow her whole.

On the trek back to the main house, bypassing the dull guest quarters and the mess hall with the bright red door, Claude invited her to stay for dinner, but she declined. She was scheduled for a mini patrol from four until seven the following morning and Delia needed a semi-decent night's sleep if she was going to drag her body out of bed at that hour. And given the effort she'd expended today, she suspected she'd crash the second her body settled onto something even half comfortable.

"Trust me, I'd stay here if I could," she insisted as they plodded along. "Little baby shifts like this one sometimes don't feel worth the time and effort it takes me to get ready."

The only reason she had been scheduled, she figured, was to fatten up the numbers out on patrol—the League's scheme to maintain the tentative order in Harriswood, despite escalating clan tensions.

They had almost reached the circular driveway in front of the main house, rain-soaked lawn squishing underfoot, when an enormous bolt of lightning cracked across the sky. It must have connected somewhere nearby—the sound was unlike anything Delia had ever experienced before. She could practically feel the heat of it. Seconds later, thunder rumbled overhead and Delia was surprised it didn't shake the ground.

When another streak of light stabbed the sky, she grabbed Claude's hand and hurried for the huge parking garage on the other side of the house. An embarrassing yelp slipped from her mouth at the next flash, and Claude used the remote on his key ring to get one of the huge doors open before they arrived. Delia skittered to a halt as soon as her feet touched concrete, chest heaving.

She'd been in there a few times before, insisting that she didn't need to wait on the porch for Claude to roll up in one of his many, many cars just so he could open the door all suave and smooth for her. The warehouse mirrored the guest apartments—long, grey, rectangular— though instead of bland suites it was two long rows of vehicles of every shape and size. The far wall was covered in tools and spare tires and whatever else the Grimm mechanics needed to keep the cars in prime condition.

"What the hell is this storm?" Delia asked, wringing out her hair as she peered around Claude. Rain pounded the metallic roof above, each drop a booming echo. When her gaze shifted to the vamp before her, she expected him to turn and snag the light switch nearby. Instead, he tossed his jacket aside and ran a hand through his hair, his expression a little too serious for her liking. Delia crossed her arms as a chill started to creep across her skin. "Everything okay?"

When he finally looked at her, those bright blue eyes actually made her draw in a sharp breath. It was like seeing them for the first time again—like turning around and finding them watching her behind a ridiculous mask. Magnetic. Entrancing. Lusty. She knew now why they had so much power over her, but knowing didn't change anything.

"Claude…"

He descended upon her with all the ferocity of a starved man, grasping her arm as his lips hungrily found hers. She stumbled back, but he followed, snaking an arm around her waist to keep her from falling. Electricity buzzed through her, as if the bolts of light lurching across the tumultuous sky had hit home. The raindrops on the rooftop fell like thunder, louder and more present now as she succumbed—happily so. Her hands ran up his chest as their lips parted against one another, her eyes fluttering closed as a welcome familiarity sunk in. A needed familiarity. A wanted one.

She didn't care that she was drenched, soaked to the bone. The cold barely touched her—Claude's warmth kept it at bay. She wanted more. More of him. His hands on her skin, clothes gone and storm forgotten. So Delia let herself fall. She let herself give in with no thought of the consequences, no thought of the future. Embracing the here and now was so *difficult*, but Claude made it feel easy, made it feel right.

Her fingers threaded through his thick wet hair, tugging at it as he walked her backward. Suddenly her feet were off the ground, and Claude's hands gripped the backs of her thighs as he lifted and set her on the hood of a nearby car.

She took a much-needed gasp of air, their lips breaking apart but only *just*, as Claude dragged her to the edge and wrapped her legs around his body. Hot breath mingled between them, Delia's hands sliding up to cup his face. The look shared between them was like wildfire—so wrathful, so destructive, not even the relentless rain outside could stop it. When their eyes met, hers heavy-lidded and his flecked with need, she murmured his name like a prayer.

He swallowed what little sounds she made, their lips parted in a kiss of desperation. Claude drank her in like a parched man would drink at the watery paradise of a desert oasis. Heat flared between her thighs as their bodies pressed together, fitting perfectly; it was impossible not to feel him stiffen against her.

It would have been so simple from here. His hands would wander to her jeans and pop the button open, pull down the zipper. She could picture him cupping her, stroking her beneath the fabric, enticing her, reminding her of what they'd had for one night. Delia would stretch her legs out, beg him to undress her. Her fingers would fumble as they went for his track pants, for the ties hidden in the waistline, for the elastic band of his boxers. It would be hard and fast, the way he'd fuck her, right there on the hood of the car as thunder rumbled deafeningly overhead. She'd cling to him with all she had, arms around his neck, head thrown back in bliss, until he pushed her over the edge and she cried his name in sweet release, not caring who might hear her...

Her needy daydreams came to a hasty end when Claude's mouth dragged over the two marks he'd left on her neck. Her skin was already a prickly mess, his tongue and teeth getting a rise out of her as he worked his way along her jaw, then down to her neck as she fisted a hand in his hair. But the moment his lips brushed the marks, it was like someone had seared her with a cattle prod. Delia's eyes shot open, the fog of lust clearing in an instant, and pushed frantically at his chest.

"I'm sorry, I'm sorry," Claude whispered, bringing his mouth back to hers.

Their kiss was over before it started, Delia ducking her chin down and taking a few calming breaths. With his forehead resting against hers, she realized fear had made her react as she did—and she wasn't sure how she felt about that.

Sighing gently, Claude brushed her damp hair back and cradled her head in his hands. She let him because it felt good, calming, her eyes drifting closed as she took a moment to collect herself.

"I won't do it again," he told her, the seductive purr replaced with something else, his voice straddling the precipice of strain and comfort. She couldn't blame him, given the hardness that still pressed against her thigh.

"I don't know why I..." Delia let out a shaky breath. "It was like you shocked me."

Claude kissed her cheek, lingering for a long moment as warmth bloomed across her skin, before pulling back and meeting her eye. "I should have realized it would affect you. Sincerely, Delia, I do apologize. It shouldn't... I shouldn't have done it in the first place."

She nodded, swallowing hard as she brought her hands to his chest and pressed her palms to him, then watched as he ducked down and kissed her fingertips. When he straightened again, some of the desire had started to fade, replaced with what Delia interpreted as concern.

"It won't happen again," he told her with a nod to her neck. "Not unless you ask me."

Unable to stop herself, Delia let out a hollow laugh, which he mirrored with a somewhat forced smile.

"Let's..." She shifted closer to him when she started to

shiver. The cold and the damp had finally won, regardless of the warm vampire between her thighs. "Let's forget about it for now." Her hands fell to his waist, gripping his shirt. "Maybe you could just drive me home?"

After another brief closed-lip kiss, Claude's arms wrapped securely around her to ward off the cold, he offered to let her change into something dry before they left.

"You could even sleep here if you wanted," he insisted as she eased off the car's hood. "I'd be happy to drop you off wherever you need to patrol."

"I feel like that maybe sends the wrong message," she said with a smirk. Her jeans had hiked up and were downright impossible to fix with how wet they were, but her sex tingled with want as she tried.

"What? Don't most hunters bring their vampire boyfriend out on patrol?" He scrunched up his shirt to twist out some of the excess water. "I think you should all have a vampire partner. It would probably make things much smoother."

This time her laugh was more genuine. "Yeah, I'll float that at the next meeting. See how popular it makes me."

"It's worth a shot, given your current popularity ranking."

"Hey!"

He dodged her hand when she took a good-natured swipe at him, then caught it and laced his fingers around hers. Delia followed behind him with heavy feet, dragging her motions out until he darted back to kiss her again and promise he was only teasing.

"I know," she assured him as they made their way to his soccer mom van. "Just like I'm about to tease *you* for the vehicle you're about to put me in. Brace yourself."

"I can take whatever you throw at me, huntress," he said once he had the door open for her. "I'm more than prepared for everything you've got in your arsenal."

Delia swallowed thickly and forced a smile, then

clambered in and tried to keep the worrisome thoughts at bay.

All the while trying to figure out the best way to sit without leaving a huge wet butt-print on the seat.

*   *   *

"Are we still on for tomorrow?" Claude asked as Delia settled back in her seat, trying to catch her breath from their most recent kiss in front of her building. This one had been the hardest to break, hot and heavy and beyond intoxicating—she would feel Claude on her lips well into her patrol the following morning.

"Yeah," she said brightly, picking at her hair in an effort to revive it from its current flat, scraggly mess. "Why wouldn't we be?"

Tomorrow was a League-assigned date. There was no backing out of that one—not that she'd want to or anything.

"Sure you're not sick of me yet?"

She matched his grin with an impish one of her own. "I'm on the verge, Claude Grimm. Don't give me the final push."

"No, we can't have that, can we?" he mused, leaning across the space between their seats to kiss her again. Delia shifted to make the angles better, but at the last moment spotted something that made her pause. Someone, more like. Her usual grey-haired tail from the League had just settled on the bench across from her apartment, his umbrella on his lap. He certainly didn't look like he'd been caught in the storm, which had of course stopped the moment Delia and Claude started driving.

"What is it?" Claude asked. She looked back to him and shook her head, but her smile must not have been convincing. Moments later he was looking out the window for himself.

"It's nothing—"

"That man follows us on our dates," Claude remarked, voice tinged with anger. When he faced her, she noticed the way his jaw clenched briefly before he spoke again. "I've seen him on numerous occasions. Is he bothering you?"

Delia shook her head. "It's fine."

"No, it isn't." Scowling, Claude went for his door, but stopped when she placed a hand on his arm. He exhaled deeply, the window catching his irritated reflection perfectly. "Delia, let me speak to him—"

"No," she said forcefully, "don't. It's League business. He shouldn't be here, but I can handle him."

It took some more convincing, more than she'd expected, but she eventually managed to soothe his temper with one last kiss.

"I'll call you tomorrow," she insisted once she was out of the car. The temperature had plummeted since the storm, and she entertained the idea of climbing back in and blasting the heat. But on top of getting a half-decent sleep, Delia had another issue to deal with—because *she* hadn't noticed the grey-haired watcher following them on their dates before, and it made her insides squirmy.

Claude lingered at the curb, minivan humming, and took one last look between her and the elderly man on the bench, a man Delia suspected wasn't a hunter at all. Probably an informant—rats tended to actually reach old age, recent murders aside. Forcing another bright smile, Delia waved Claude off and watched until he was beyond the nearest intersection.

Drawing a deep breath, Delia jogged across the street. The rainy hike had already ruined her runners, her socks thoroughly soaked, but she still winced when one foot landed in a puddle at the curb. Cursing softly, she shook it off before stalking up to her shadow, eyes narrowed.

"What are you doing here?"

"I could ask the same question of him," the man said, his voice crackly and gruff. "Date's tomorrow, not today.

You aren't scheduled today."

"I got my days mixed up," Delia said flippantly. "I didn't realize until after we met up."

"Made the same mistake on Sunday and Monday, did you?" He gave a throaty laugh and stood, and Delia hoped he wouldn't see the pink in her cheeks. "Or Wednesday last week? Or Tuesday and Friday the week before? Lots of mistakes you're making lately. Got some sort of calendar dyslexia?"

She pressed her lips together tightly, refusing to respond. The man's eyes swept over her, his skin crinkled around the edges, and he shook his head.

"Well, at least you've had a bit of fun, eh?" Popping open his umbrella, he raised it over his head as a light misting started to coat the city. Delia blinked the rainwater out of her eyes.

"What's that supposed to mean?" she asked, but he was already gone, sauntering off into the stream of people around them. She could have chased him down, but Delia just stood there, gawking until his umbrella disappeared around the corner of the building at the intersection.

Arms wrapped around herself, she dashed back to her building, weaving around cars stopped at the light while her teeth chattered. Once she was inside, chills continued to plague her—and Delia knew, as she peeled off her drenched clothes and hopped in the shower, that the cold outside air wasn't completely to blame.

CHAPTER 14: EXPECTATIONS UNMET

"Did Grimm do something to you, you know, *psychologically*, or are you actually this stupid?" Wentworth practically simmered with rage as he stared Delia down from behind his desk. For once, it was just him and her in the room. No Kain. No other members of the High Council with their midnight-black robes and sullen faces. Just good ol' Don Wentworth in horrific khaki from head to toe, and Delia wishing she were anywhere but here.

After she had fixed herself up from her hike in the rain last night, Delia found an email from the League waiting in her inbox—but it didn't contain the specifics of her next date. Instead she found a formal request from the office of the High Council; Delia was expected to report in after her patrol the following morning.

Funny how only a few lines of text can strike so much fear into a person. The order read quite succinctly, mechanical even, and was not the first Delia had received in her hunter career. She knew right then and there that she was going to be disciplined.

Her nerves had made sleep infrequent and breakfast impossible, so she went on patrol with two cups of coffee and a handful of oatmeal–chocolate chip cookies coursing through her system. It was no surprise that she'd felt like absolute shit by the time she arrived in the reception area outside Wentworth's office, but that was nothing compared to the way she felt now: hungover but without the night of fun drinking beforehand.

If only she could stop her hands from shaking. Even with them clasped together, Wentworth could probably see it.

She drew in a shallow breath as his eyes burned holes right through her. "Sir—"

"No," he barked, a hand raised to silence her. "No, you listen for a moment. What did you think this special assignment actually entailed?"

Delia swallowed hard. Even though he paused, it was a rhetorical question. If she spoke now, he'd chew her out even harder.

"In no way, shape, or form was this assignment *permission* for you to actually *date* Claude Grimm!" He slammed his hand down on the table, making his mason jar of pens rattle. "I was willing to let the terribly crafted reports slide. I hoped that you would grow into the role. I wanted to give you a *chance,* after all these years, to prove that your continued employment hasn't been a mistake, that you were more than just a grunt. But time and time again, you prove me wrong."

Sure, the reports weren't her best work. Hell, they weren't even real reports, just a mishmash of archive intel and whatever was on Delia's TV docket for the day. She planned to take whatever verbal lashing she got for the quality of her reports without a word because, well, she knew she'd fluffed every last one of them, preferring to shirk her shady assignment and just enjoy her date with Claude instead.

But the notion that she had proved him wrong time and time again, that she made him look like some fool for believing in her, felt far-fetched. Anger pooled in her gut. Delia hadn't proved him wrong—Delia hadn't been given any *chances* to prove him wrong. She did her boring work as instructed. There were a few hiccups along the way, but every hunter had more than a few notes on their personnel file. She wasn't the League's worst employee—not by a long shot—and she was sick of being made to feel that way by a handful of men.

Her arms crossed over her chest at the thought, and she started taking deep, even breaths in and out of her nostrils.

"This was supposed to be easy, Miss Roberts," Wentworth remarked, scowling. "It was clear that Claude Grimm had an interest in you. There was a relationship established without our knowledge, the kind of relationship *highly* frowned upon. Those disgusting bite marks on your neck are more than reasonable grounds for termination and then some." She stiffened at the thought. "Yet I saw a use for you. Claude Grimm and his people have been the most isolated clan in Harriswood for decades. No informants have ever successfully penetrated it. This was the perfect opportunity for us, yet you squandered it for what? A handsome face?"

She kept her silence as he stared at her, his brow raised.

"So that's why I have to ask if he's done something, because I was under the impression you were lazy, not stupid."

This time the pause dragged on a little too long, like he was waiting for her to defend herself. And for once, she did.

"With all due respect, sir," Delia said, voice wavering with frustration this time, not fear, "I'm neither."

Lazy hunters didn't have hours of archive reading time behind them. Lazy hunters didn't research hand-to-hand combat in their free time, or seek out an unlikely mentor to train them. Delia might be lazy in a lot of ways, but when it came to the League, she liked to think Claude was right: she'd just become apathetic over the years, passive to her experience when her efforts never panned out.

"Really?" Wentworth leaned forward, hands clasped on his desk as he eyed her. "I've yet to see you do anything to prove otherwise. Did you think you were clever, scheduling all those extra dates in secret? You reported nothing on them—"

"It would be weird for two people starting a relationship not to see each other whenever they wanted to," she argued, face blanching when she realized she had cut him off, "sir."

"Weird?" he said, as though the word personally offended him. "What's *weird*, Miss Roberts, is that you invited Claude Grimm out on several unsanctioned visits."

"Kain said it isn't out of the ordinary to have a vampire contact—"

"For hunters like Kain, yes, it isn't." Wentworth sniffed and shook his head. "Hunters like Kain have more experience with how this world works. Hunters like *you* do not play willy-nilly with clan leaders because there's a *spark*."

"There isn't—"

"I've seen the pictures, Miss Roberts." His voice cracked like a whip, and Delia pressed her lips together, cowed.

Wentworth stood, his chair scraping the floor, fingertips resting on the edge of his desk. "Consider your special assignment terminated and yourself suspended. Your breach in conduct, along with your poor work, cannot go unpunished."

"Sir, I—"

"You will not see or speak to Claude Grimm until the High Council has decided what we are going to do with you." He looked her over from top to bottom, then back up again. "Until we have determined your worth."

Her tongue felt too big for her mouth. No matter how hard she swallowed, everything was dry and scratchy.

"Yes, sir," Delia managed, her voice barely above a controlled whisper as a storm of sudden *feeling*, a hurricane of anger and fear and desperation, tore through her.

"It will be in your best interest to follow directions," Wentworth remarked. "All of your upcoming patrols will be covered. Consider yourself on thin ice until we have completed our review."

"What will happen if I'm...asked to leave?" When she'd considered that possibility on the night of the masquerade, Delia had dry-heaved into a bag, tears streaming down her cheeks and her whole world spinning. Today, somehow, the thought only sent a rush of prickling anxiety through her. The thought of forcefully keeping herself away from Claude, on the other hand...

Maybe that was a sign.

"That will be determined when the time comes," Wentworth said with a soft *tsk*. "Know that your whole history will be evaluated. Given your lack of clearance, you can breathe easy that I see no reason to have you *permanently* silenced."

Her lips trembled as the thought sunk in, but she was determined to at least look in the general direction of his face. "Thank you, sir."

"Hardly worth a thanks, Miss Roberts," he said curtly. "We're done here."

Knowing there was nothing she could say to persuade him otherwise, Delia dipped her head and turned. As she was about to reach the door, Wentworth sighed heavily.

"A disappointment," he said when she glanced back, "that you couldn't even do *this* effectively."

Shoulders slumped, Delia muttered an apology before slipping out the door.

*   *   *

"Come on..." Delia groaned and tapped the Refresh Page button. The internet was absolutely killing her—today, the day she just wanted to get lost in a twenty-episode binge of a space opera TV classic. A favourite from her teen years, it had been ages since she watched it. Today felt like a good day to try.

As the page slowly reloaded, her phone vibrated on the other side of the bed. Delia glanced toward it, then brought her attention back to the screen. Still loading. Another round of vibrations. Huffing, she rolled over and grabbed the black rectangle, meaning to turn it to silent. She paused, however, at the sight of a missed call from Claude, followed by a text message asking if everything was okay. There was one from Kain too. *Obviously* Wentworth had filled his protégé in on the verbal beating he'd given her early that morning.

Of all the people in her life at the moment, Claude was the only one Delia actually wanted to talk to. But she couldn't tell him why she'd been disciplined without admitting that the League had ordered her to spy on him. If she could help it, Delia planned to keep that little tidbit to herself until the dust had settled. The trust they'd cultivated over the last month and a half would be shattered in an instant if she told him. He wouldn't care that Delia bullshitted her reports, or that she stopped slipping the High Council's questions in after the second date, or that she considered her biweekly outings with him as real dates and not assignments. It wouldn't matter. All that would matter would be her deceit. His anger would be perfectly justified.

She'd made a mistake, in her love life and along her career path, and now it was coming back to bite her. Things were falling apart, and Delia had no one to blame but herself. She had agreed to lie to Claude, all the while developing a frustratingly fierce attachment to him. Sure, the High Council had used her situation for the League's gain, but she had let them.

Yes, she'd been in a precarious situation when Kain tattled on her. If she'd refused the High Council's assignment, what would have happened? Would they have sent her away, called her a traitor—or worse? There was no telling, but the fear of all those things had pushed her into accepting the card she was dealt. Maybe if Delia had been braver then, things would be different now.

But things weren't different. She couldn't change the

past. Delia just had to sort out her future, and when she realized that, she grabbed an unopened tub of cookie dough ice cream and barricaded herself in her room, hoping that TV would distract her.

As usual, instead of finding a logical, mature solution, she opted for petty distraction.

Her phone buzzed again as the show started to load.

The electronic characters you've texted seem troubled.

She bit her lip, eyes fixed on Claude's name and profile picture at the top of the text conversation screen. It was unfair to him, this whole thing. But so was radio silence. Drawing in a deep breath, she sat up cross-legged and fired off a quick message to let him know she was fine, but couldn't make it tonight for their date.

Do you want to talk? was his response.

She ran a hand through her hair and wrote, *No. Not now, anyway.*

Once she hit send, a heavy knot settled in the pit of her stomach. Delia typed out *I'm sorry*, but then deleted it and put her phone on silent. Maybe it was better this way. Until she got her life in order, a break from the man who consumed her and the job that used her might be necessary to get some perspective.

Miserable, Delia flopped back on her bed and pressed play. For a second, even though it looked like the stupid thing had loaded, the sound started but the video didn't.

"Come *on*, seriously?" She groaned, unwelcome tears resurfacing. "Come *on*, you piece of *shit…*"

When her next few attempts to get things going failed, Delia slammed the laptop shut and pushed it down her bed. It stopped just at the edge, half an inch from toppling over, and she took what she hoped were calming breaths to ward off the impending bout of tears.

She was so sick of crying—yet, after each storm passed, Delia was a tiny bit better.

CHAPTER 15: SAFE CHOICE IS AN OXYMORON

"Welcome to Safe Choice Grocers. Would you like a coupon booklet?"

Delia contemplated blitzing by the teenager stationed by the entrance as the doors whooshed shut behind her, then thought better of it. Although the work *she* used to do was boring, this was worse—no point in treating the poor girl like she didn't exist.

"Thanks," Delia muttered, taking the thin booklet from her.

"That'll be five dollars."

They stared at one another, both equally expressionless, and Delia slowly handed the coupon book back. The teen took it, then faced the newest arrival with the same mechanical speech.

"Welcome to Safe Choice Grocers. Would you like a coupon booklet?"

"No," the man muttered sharply in passing. Raindrops rolled down his wide-brimmed hat and coat. Delia looked through the Plexiglas doors, marred with fingerprints at roughly kid height, and frowned. Perfect. Exactly what she wanted—to carry her groceries home in the rain.

Sighing, she grabbed a basket from the pile nearby and headed in.

Three gruelling days had passed since Wentworth ripped her a new one in his office, and so far, silence from the High Council. Delia couldn't decide whether that was a good thing or not, but tonight was the first time she'd ventured outside her apartment since it all happened.

Earlier that day she had finally confided in Devin over the phone, needing to talk to *someone* or she'd blow a gasket. Claude was the one she actually wanted to talk to, but seeing as he hadn't replied since her rebuff via text a few days before, Delia thought it best to exclude him. Although just the sound of his voice would lift the funk following her around, it would also complicate everything.

Devin had been supportive after the initial shock of her story wore off, and not once did he sound judgey about the fact that she'd accidentally let a vampire bite her.

"Why didn't you come to me, D?" he'd asked when they met up at one of their usual twenty-four–hour diners, face riddled with concern. "I could have helped you. I don't know how, but you shouldn't have had to deal with this alone."

While Delia hadn't wanted to tell him, the bite incident was integral to the overall story—it was why Kain's betrayal stung as much as it did, and it was why the High Council had leverage to use her. Everything Delia hadn't known about the League, all its secrets about Claudia and day-walking vampires, was news to Devin too. His response to Claudia being fake had certainly been more humorous than hers.

"I fucking *knew* it," he'd all but shouted, banging his hand on the table and making the waitress side-eye him. "I *knew* that bitch wasn't real. That's some bullshit, man."

Somehow, him being just as in the dark as she'd been made Delia feel a bit better.

"Wait for the axe to fall, D," Devin had told her when they'd moved onto her suspension. "Wentworth already told you it won't be a death sentence. You'll survive, one way or another."

It wasn't exactly what she wanted to hear, but Delia rationalized it was probably what she needed.

Devin had no thoughts on her romantic problems, but

only because Delia hadn't shared them beyond the fact that a prominent vamp had bitten her months ago and she was now forced to spy on him. She knew that no matter how awful she felt, her situation with Claude should be worked out by the two of them, not an outsider. Besides, even if Devin hadn't been judgemental over the bite, she knew his prejudices wouldn't let him accept the idea that she'd actually *fallen* for a vamp.

That was just too much to ask of him.

While she hadn't wanted to leave the house that night, the lack of food in her fridge and pantry forced her hand. Dressed in an old hooded high school sweatshirt, black wool tights, knee-high brown boots and a thin army-green jacket, she'd braved the chilly temperatures and trekked down to the grocery store three blocks over to stock up on supplies. Her heart wanted chips and ice cream, but her body demanded at least one vegetable—*any* vegetable. All the contemplative moping lately had made her feel like sludge.

Given the hour, gauging how busy the grocery store would be was a crapshoot. Sometimes she'd wander in before closing and the place would be swamped. Other times, nothing. Tonight fell closer to the latter, though Delia counted maybe one person or couple in each aisle she passed. It wasn't the largest grocery in Harriswood, but given its location downtown at the base of a residential apartment complex, it was a palace.

After tossing a few pre-mixed bags of salad in her basket, Delia grabbed a pack of frozen chicken thighs, then made a beeline for the comfort food aisle. Chips. Chocolate. Salted caramel chews. It would be a miracle if she hadn't packed on a few—or ten—pounds between the last time Wentworth saw her and the next. Come to think of it, her waistband *was* a little tight.

Just what she needed. Weight gain on top of the downward spiral of her professional life, followed shortly by her romantic one. No word from Claude for more than a day spelled trouble, but as she squared her shoulders and pushed on, Delia forcefully reminded herself that she had brought on any tension between them all by herself. Claude was the innocent victim in all this.

The thought only worsened her mood, and she resisted the urge to pull her hood up and skulk around the discount candy section.

She paused, however, at the row of name-brand popcorn boxes. The last time she'd had it was when Claude came over for a movie date—horror movie marathon, lots of zombies and found footage films and snuggles on her couch. A soft smile touched her lips as she lifted her hand, but Delia paused before she grabbed a box. She'd been so nervous about showing Claude her teeny one-bedroom apartment that she'd detail-cleaned the place from top to bottom for the first time in months. It had practically glistened when he arrived.

Yet Claude barely noticed. He'd been so interested in her that she was sure if she asked today, he wouldn't even remember the colour of her couch. True to his nature, Claude hadn't for one second focused on the little things—the pointless things. Just like he never pointed out when her windswept hair looked a wreck or her t-shirt had a stubborn food stain. He struck her as a big picture thinker, letting the little things slide. She needed a man like that in her life.

Her arm fell to her side, her smile fading as she stared at the popcorn label. Delia needed a man like Claude, but here she was, pushing him away. And for what? For a job that had steadily crushed her spirit over the years?

Shoving her mounting quarter-life crisis to the back of her mind, Delia left the popcorn behind, on a sudden quest for juice cartons to replenish her stock. In the next aisle over she spied a mom with her two kids, one dozing in the shopping cart's baby seat, the other pulling boxes of pancake mix off the shelf.

"Kyle, stop," the woman said as Delia passed. The little

boy grinned toothily at her, which Delia returned halfheartedly, before knocking four boxes off the shelf in one fell swoop. Delia looked away as his mother snapped his name again and crouched down to tidy the mess.

As she rounded the end of the aisle, pausing at the display of discounted cereal, someone at the front of the store screamed. Delia's gaze shot up, a shockwave passing through her. Another scream, followed by the sound of glass shattering. Moments later, all hell had broken loose—and, amidst the chaos, not all the voices were fearful cries. No, there were bellows and barked orders too, deep and gruff. As Delia dropped her basket and peered around the shelving units, she saw people running, men in black leather jackets hot on their heels. She pulled back when one started down the aisle she had just been in, heading straight for the mom and her two kids.

The music cut out. Glass shattered somewhere again, and the sound of blunt tools hitting shelves and cold storage units alike sent her scurrying in the opposite direction. It quickly became clear that there was a robbery in progress, and as Delia shot to the fruits and veggies department at the far end of the store and crouched down behind a tower of stacked watermelons, she suspected the ones committing the crime were rounding up shoppers.

With trembling hands, she unzipped her purse to grab her phone.

Only to find it missing.

She'd left it at home.

Delia knew precisely where it was, too. Sitting on the armrest of her couch, plugged in and charging at the outlet. Her wallet was also missing, most likely in her other purse. She'd grabbed this one because the other's strap was starting to fray. All she had was her newly acquired stake—an item she made sure never to bring on dates with Claude—and   her   keys.

"*Fuck*," she hissed.

"Get on the ground!" a man bellowed nearby. It wasn't

214

directed at Delia as far as she could tell, so she hung low and crept along beneath the produce bins, using the brim laden with produce to hide as best she could. The fresh food section was closest to the main doors. If she could slip out while they were distracted with other shoppers, she could find help.

That plan went out the window pretty fast. Two men, thickset and square-jawed, stood guard by the door. One rooted through his duffle bag, then straightened with a can of spray paint in hand. Delia watched, biting down on her cheek, as he shook it, then started drawing something on the doors. They must have disabled them somehow—the doors were automatic, set to open once someone stepped on the sensor beneath the carpet in front of them.

Okay, new plan. There was always another exit. Turning, Delia shuffled toward the back of the store again, recalling a door marked for employees only and another with hanging plastic flaps covering the entrance to the in-store bakery. There had to be an exit somewhere.

She didn't make it far enough to investigate either. With the employees-only door in sight, she was forced out of hiding when heavy footfalls thundered toward her. She tried to skirt around to the other side of the display bins, but was cornered in front of the cucumber, celery, and lettuce display lining the wall.

"Get up," the hulking man ordered. Delia turned to flee, but a viselike grip clamped down around her arm and hauled her to her feet. She noted the crowbar he carried on her way up, and sucked in a breath when she came face-to-face, not with a man, but a vamp. Her heart hammered harder and faster than it should. Delia hadn't expected to run into one here, his face so dreadfully pale and his eyes bloodshot.

"Let go," she grunted, using that moment to cop a feel of his wrist. Ice cold. Frigid like death. She pressed her lips together firmly, the reality of the situation hitting hard. *Definitely* a vampire.

He shook her off, then dragged her toward the aisles again. By the looks of it, another vamp stood waiting there, a third in the baking supplies aisle he thrust her down. Meanwhile, a herd of frightened shoppers clustered together, Delia shoved into the middle of them. The mom she'd passed before stood in the middle crying, clutching the smaller of her two children to her chest. The other, Kyle the mess-maker, was nowhere to be seen. Most of the people, humans judging by their complexions, appeared roughed up in one way or another. Some cradled their hands; others sucked at swollen and busted lips. One shopper had what she guessed to be a broken nose, another a steadily darkening eye. The mom's purse and jacket were gone and her shirt appeared ripped. Meanwhile, the child in her arms had red cheeks and watery eyes, but the pacifier between his lips seemed to be keeping him quiet—for now.

One of the vamps pushed through the crowd while the other two remained at the rear, barking for everyone to move forward. They were rounding everyone up. Corralling them all into one place. Delia squared her shoulders and took a few deep breaths to focus herself. It was time to start looking at this situation from a hunter's perspective. It wasn't enough to cower with the others and hope the police arrived soon.

She'd faced and killed vamps in the past. Not many, but her stake *had* seen a bit of action during her five-year career. Generally, though, she seldom found herself in a situation where she needed to kill anyone. Arrest. Detain. Sanction. Record. Those were the duties of a mid-level hunter. But now wasn't the time for any of that. The brutes had already hurt people. She couldn't let it escalate. She wouldn't. Nobody was going to die on her watch.

Delia had knowledge of the enemy, an advantage the shoppers around her lacked. She had a stake in her purse and Claude's training at the back of her mind. If the High Council was going to kick her out tomorrow, she might as well go down swinging.

And if she died in the process, maybe in the afterlife, if there even was one, Delia could feel like she had done her duty. She had saved the lives of the innocent—the real reason she'd taken up the hunter life in the first place. Now, staring down three enemies armed with spiked clubs and crowbars, a cluster of terrified people between them, Delia wasn't so sure she had it in her.

Well. No time like the present to find out.

Discretely slipping her hand into her purse, she pushed the little button at the end of the metallic stake to elongate it, then cleared her throat as it clicked into place. The captive group was almost at the end of the aisle—the vamps must have wanted to hold hostages at the front of store. Or maybe they planned to casually devour them near the discount nacho chip stand by the cash registers.

Head down, Delia made her way to the front of the group as inconspicuously as she could, using the sniffling, crying, panicky humans as her cover. When she had the vamp in front of her, she took a deep breath and lunged. Seconds later, her newly sharpened stake buried deep into his back, right down to the hilt.

Right into the heart.

She had missed when she'd made a snap decision to try and stake Claude on the night of masquerade, but Delia had learned since then. A woman behind her shrieked as the vamp crumpled, his skin already starting to lose what little colour it had. Delia went down with him, hand wrapped around the stake so tightly that his weight dragged her to the floor.

"Hunter!" he cried, the word gargled as a dark reddish-brown blood seeped out his mouth and onto the linoleum.

She looked back to the stunned group behind her. "Run!"

With some effort, she yanked the stake out, stumbling back and into the shelves. Her heart pounded hard—quick and sharp, rattling against her ribcage. She'd expected the other two vamps to be on her in a second, but her show of courage must have roused the troops. As most of the human hostages scattered, four human men had charged the other two vamps. The attack was useless—they were woefully unprepared for the strength and ferocity of their vampire foes—but it gave Delia a few precious seconds to compose herself.

She snatched a container of frosting off the shelf beside her and hurled it at the nearest vamp scuffling with two rather large men in bloodied suits. Her aim had improved since working with Claude, if only thanks to the fact that he thought her hand-eye coordination was something in desperate need of improvement. The hit knocked the vamp off his game, giving the two men a chance to drag him to the ground, and Delia fired off two more frosting cans before turning and scaling the shelves behind her.

It wasn't right to leave a handful of humans to fight *two* vamps, but Delia wasn't going to be much help. She'd been lucky to catch the first vamp off-guard. Staking the others would be more difficult now that they knew they had a hunter in their midst.

With all the grace she could muster, she clambered up the shelves, knocking products off as she went; a bag of flour tumbled down and exploded as it hit the floor below. Delia hopped down to the other side, crossed the aisle in two steps, and climbed up the next shelf. And then the next. She went until she was at least three aisles away from the staked vamp, then did a quick sweep of the store before climbing down again.

If she had counted correctly, there were two vamps at the front, two left in the baking aisle, and one prowling around the frozen food aisle. Five vamps. One Delia.

Fuck.

It wasn't until she wormed her way in behind a row of paper towels, pushing and wriggling onto the shelf so that she was well hidden, that she even acknowledged what terrible odds she was up against.

But if she could take down one or two more, maybe it would give the other shoppers a chance to find an exit. She hoped for their sake they had found suitable hiding places around the store instead of running blindly toward the vamps spray-painting the doors.

It was a miracle the metal shelf was holding her. Larger than the usual foodstuffs shelf, it was meant for towering packages of paper towels and toilet paper—and now a vampire hunter who needed to catch her breath and calm her mind. During training, Claude had said he could see her thinking, like her eyes were windows to the gears in her brain turning away. And they were always on overdrive, apparently. Socializing had always come naturally to Delia. Working through a spur-of-the-moment League scenario? Her brain bounced all over the place until she sat down and forced it to focus on one thing at a time. But she was getting better, utilizing Claude's calming techniques to collect her thoughts.

Eyes closed, Delia concentrated on her breathing. Any vamp walking down the aisle would hear her in a second if she didn't. Slow and even. She took all the time she needed, listening to the sounds of subdued humans around the store. After a while, it all went quiet, but so too did her breath.

With that under control, she rotated her body—*very* slowly—so that she was on her belly, then inched along the dark shelf, thin metal shelving above and below, careful not to knock into any of the stacked items shielding her from onlookers. She crawled along, worming her way across the cool metal, mind relatively clear save for the task at hand, until she made it to the end of the aisle. From there, she listened again. Vamps were shouting to one another, demanding they find the hunter, that there wasn't supposed to *be* a hunter, that one of them hadn't signed up for this.

Whatever. Neither had she.

Rolling her eyes, Delia eased the package of paper

towels in front of her aside, then paused and listened again. Nothing. No footsteps along the aisle. No heavy breathing around the corner. She was as shocked as anyone that her hiding place had actually *worked*, but she knew she couldn't hide forever. They'd tear the store apart to find her.

Jaw clenched, she eased off the shelf and dropped into a crouched position. More waiting. More listening. When it sounded like the coast was clear, she peered around the end of the aisle, scanning the yogurt, egg, and dairy coolers along half the back wall of the store. The other side was for the bakery and deli—stocked full of knives and other sharp things to arm herself with.

Without a vamp in sight, Delia crept around and stood, pausing at the endcap full of discount bottled vinegar. Probably not a bad idea to make it a slippery path behind her, as long as she didn't forget the floor was greased. Stake tucked under her arm, she grabbed a bottle and popped it open, spilling the clear liquid across the floor as she took a few steps back.

"Hello, hunter."

She looked up in a panic. Some ten feet away was a vamp she hadn't seen before, maybe the one who'd been loitering by the milk earlier. They stared at one another for a tense moment, then Delia fled as he lunged for her.

Seconds later she heard a hard body hit the ground like a ton of bricks, and she looked back to find her little trick had worked. The idiot had slipped on the puddle of vinegar.

Seizing the opportunity to stake a vamp when he was down, Delia surged forward, slipping a little herself when her boots hit the wetness, and splashed the remaining vinegar in the bottle across his face. Then she dropped on top of him and wedged the stake into his chest just as he swung his crowbar at her. The steel missed her face by a breath.

She didn't get a chance to see blood weep from his

nostrils and mouth. Mere seconds later, a hand dug into her hair and yanked her off the body, dragging her back across the vinegar. Delia's feet flailed out, managing to catch the hooked end of the fallen vamp's crowbar and pull it with her. Her scalp burned at the manhandling—and her stake sat squarely in the other vamp's chest.

Thick fingers slipped under her chin and wrenched her head back hard, and as Delia gawked up at a vamp, she saw the flash of pointed teeth. Pulling the crowbar toward her with her foot, she grabbed it and swung back blindly, hoping to hit him right behind the knees. Delia heard a grunt on impact, and she hit again and again, her scalp on fire as the vamp's grip tightened. His knees finally buckled after repeated blows with the crowbar, and Delia stabbed the end of it back and up into him as he toppled down onto her. It didn't pierce through to the other side like her stake would, but it gave her a few seconds to scramble away, bloody crowbar in hand. She swung it again when he dove after her, a crowbar-width chest wound oozing blood, and after a brief scuffle, Delia somehow managed to flip him on his back.

Use your opponents' strength against them. Claude had told her that. She vaguely remembered League trainers mentioning opponents' weight, but Claude had explained it in a way that she understood. She actually retained what he told her—probably because he wasn't a patronizing ass when he taught.

Delia managed to get a few good hits to her opponent's face with the crowbar. When his arms fell to the floor and his jaw went slack, she crawled off and stood, leaning on the crowbar for support as she surveyed the situation. This…could have been worse. The vamp wasn't dead like his friend, but he was out cold for now.

Fuck the weapons in the bakery and deli. Dealing with these two alone had exhausted her, and Delia switched gears to finding an escape route. The Employees Only door was nearby, but when she turned, she saw that she was being watched. Two little eyes had seen the whole thing, the whites wide like saucers. Delia wiped under her nose as something dribbled out. Blood. There were probably more injuries that her adrenaline kept her from feeling.

She brought her finger to her lips, nodding at the little boy—Kyle. His mom was probably distraught with him missing, but the kid had had the sense to hide under the bakery display case. Small enough for a little person to fit—probably not a place the vamps would look right away.

He just stared, traumatized, and Delia vowed to grab him on the way out. Crowbar in hand, she jogged across to the Employees Only door.

Which was locked.

With a punch-in passcode required.

"Damn it," she muttered, jiggling the handle a few times. Was there anyone inside hiding? Were they just going to let everyone face the music out here? No sense in knocking. Every vamp would hear—

Suddenly, Kyle was screaming. It wasn't one of those screams you hear kids make in movies, either. It was a high-pitched, shrill, piercing scream that only got higher and shriller as it went on—a scream of pure terror. Delia whirled around and spied the vamp she'd thought she left unconscious crawling toward the kid. His face was a bloodied, mangled mess thanks to her crowbar. Not that it mattered—vamp healing abilities were unrivaled.

She rushed forward and grabbed Kyle by his jacket's hood, dragging him across the floor so that he was behind her, not caring if she hurt him along the way. The vamp rose on shaky legs, glowering at her as she held the crowbar between them.

"It's not a stake, but you better believe I will make do," she warned. For once, her voice stayed even when she wanted it to, though her arm trembled under the weight of her weapon. Kyle clung to her leg, both arms wrapped tight, and she wanted to shake him off.

The vamp inched forward, and just as her adrenaline spiked, glass shattered at the front of the store as if the dusty windows by the line of registers had been blown out all at once. Several people screamed. Sirens wailed outside, flashing red and blue lights washing across the store. Delia kept her gaze on the vamp in front of her, smirking. The cavalry had arrived. Even if they were only human cops, at least they had weapons and numbers.

The vamp looked between her and the front of the store, then shook his head and raised his hands. "Fuck it. I'm out."

Seconds later he leapt over the deli counter like the hounds of hell were on his tail. Delia stood there, her arm shaking, until she heard the sound of gunfire. Then she tossed the crowbar aside and threw herself over Kyle. He sobbed beneath her, clutching at her jacket as Delia forced herself to take even breaths.

When the shooting stopped, she stood and kept a hand on Kyle's head, surveying her surroundings again. Only when she heard the radio chatter of police walkie-talkies and heavy booted feet entering the store did she hoist the boy onto her hip and make her way to the front. An officer raised his gun at her when she rounded the corner, making Kyle emit another high-pitched shriek right next to her ear. Delia winced and lifted him off as his mother came running over and the officer slowly lowered his firearm.

"I'm with the League," she told him. The uniformed man considered her with a quick up and down sweep of his gaze, then went back to the other shoppers. Kyle's mother, meanwhile, practically ripped the boy away from Delia, not saying anything as she blitzed back over to the elderly woman holding her other kid. Delia watched her go with a frown.

She was too tired to care that the woman hadn't thanked her for keeping her bratty kid safe. In fact, as she took in the scene before her, exhaustion, fear, panic—they all hit her in waves. The adrenaline was slowly fading, leaving her drained and shaken, her head a little woozy. All around her, familiar sights drifted in and out of focus. Faces. Food bins. Cash registers and their little conveyor belts.

Then, slowly, her knees gave way. Down she sunk, settling on the ground. It didn't matter that it was dirty, soiled by wet feet and wheels; Delia stunk of vinegar and blood—that was infinitely worse than whatever might be on the floor.

Paramedics arrived shortly after the police stormed the grocery. Half the uniforms had gone off in pursuit of the fleeing vamps while the medical personnel checked on each former hostage, treating their minor injuries before ushering them out. One headed for Delia, calling out to her as he approached, but he was directed away by a police officer. Apparently being in the League meant she didn't require medical care. Blinking heavy eyes, Delia slowly lowered her head between her knees.

Her fellow shoppers would leave with cuts and bruises, battered noses and split lips, but it was the emotional trauma that would sit with them, probably for years to come. In a way, she almost envied them. At least they could just accept the horror they felt—Delia knew she'd need to swallow it, forget it, and move on. She shouldn't feel this way. Fighting vamps was her job.

For now, anyway. There was no telling her fate beyond tonight.

"Did you say you were with the League?"

A tired voice posed the question some time later, as the clamor of sirens and crying people lessened. Delia lifted her head sluggishly, her neck stiff and tight, and offered a weary nod to the officer crouched in front of her.

"You okay?" he asked. Another nod. "You look a little, uh…"

"I'm fine," she said, voice thick. "Really."

"Good." He stood and stepped out of her line of sight. Delia's eyes followed him, fixed on the way he stuck his thumbs through his belt loops. "Care to tell me what they put on the doors?"

She frowned, confused, then looked to the front doors. Someone had closed them after directing the other shoppers out. Green spray paint marred the Plexiglas, hiding the usual fingerprint smears and splotches of bird shit she'd seen on the way in. Her eyes narrowed, studying the design, then slowly widened in recognition.

"It's…" She swallowed hard and pushed to her feet, wanting to be absolutely sure before she told him anything. The officer offered his arm when she wavered, but she politely declined.

It couldn't be.

Nobody would be that bold.

Or that stupid.

Delia licked her lips as the officer stared, his impatience palpable. "It's the Donovan clan emblem."

He too fell quiet for a long moment, both of them staring at the design. It was a crude rendition, sure, but it was unmistakable. Even with some of the paint dribbling, Delia could make out the tree, the stars around its full branches, and the serpent at its base.

"Christ," the officer muttered. Delia nodded. Christ indeed.

Were the attackers Irish? Did they have an accent like their clan leader? Her head lowered as she frowned, trying to recall the voices she'd heard. No accents that she could remember, but her brain was probably already distorting the incident. Plus, not every member of the clan had the accent. As she recalled, Bella Donovan, daughter of clan leader Shane Donovan and a notorious troublemaker, a vamp whose iron grip had lingered on Delia's wrist for weeks after the masquerade, sounded local.

"This is bad." The officer glanced at her, then pulled out a small pocket notepad and a pen. "Give me your

LIZ MELDON

information. I'll need to report all this to the higher-ups. I'm sure they will want to discuss the situation with the Council."

She hesitated, then took the pen and pad at his insistent look and scribbled her name and hunter ID number. Once she handed it back, the officer hurried toward a small cluster of policemen, barking at them to get all the security footage and bring in the CSI guys.

Delia wrapped her arms around herself and fended off the urge to faint.

CHAPTER 16: WEARING MY BIG GIRL PANTS

"And while I believe it is a poor decision," Wentworth said as Delia stood across from him in her usual spot, her insides knotted and her palms sweaty, "it is the decision nonetheless. If it were up to me, you would be packing your bags right now, Miss Roberts."

The eyes of every man in the room—all the High Council members and Kain—fixed on her for a long moment, until she realized she was supposed to say something. Clearing her throat, which was painfully dry, she nodded and managed a "Yes, sir."

"Your little stunt at the grocery store was…" Wentworth leaned back in his chair, fingers steepling. "It was noble, but foolish. I cannot be sure why the Donovan agents fled when the police arrived, but I can only assume that had the boys in blue showed up a few minutes later, you would have been dead and I could have been spared this conversation."

Not exactly the glowing praise Delia had always hoped she'd get from the High Council after pulling off a near-impossible task against a handful of vamp enemies. She bit the insides of her cheeks to keep from arguing that despite her few slip-ups, she'd held her own that night.

When she'd arrived home the night of the Donovan assault on Safe Choice Grocers, there was a message in her inbox from the League. Stay put. No contact with anyone. If she must leave the house, do so under a guise to distort

227

her features. Delia couldn't imagine why that was necessary until she logged on to her social media the following morning. Somehow footage of the attack had been leaked. Internet commentators far and wide criticized her fight stance, the way she climbed the shelves—everything.

Once she realized what she had done, Delia had melted into a puddle of nerves. After all, she and the Donovan henchmen, together, had potentially spilled the secrets of their world into the general public. No one on the news had cried vampire yet, but the online conspiracy theorists who analyzed every second of footage were certainly howling it.

Delia had had no idea where she was headed at that point, but she'd had a sinking feeling that simple banishment might be off the table.

So, she'd come to the High Council that afternoon fearing the worst. Instead, Wentworth had reinstated her *and* given her a promotion. Apparently powers higher in the League hierarchy than the High Council thought it would be reckless to get rid of her. Should they need a public liaison to help manage a crisis if the internet conspiracy theorists caught traction, a situation already being handled by various inter-organization PR teams, they had a somewhat familiar face to put in front of the cameras.

Delia took the news with an uneasy smile.

"Kain will bring you up to speed on your new assignment," Wentworth told her with a dismissive wave toward the Irishman, who sat on the edge of the same couch he always did, a heavy look on his face. "This is your chance, Miss Roberts. Either you shine on the task force, or a Donovan vamp will take care of you at the compound."

Delia drew in a deep breath and tried not to scowl at how carelessly they threw around her demise. The look on Wentworth's face told her she was unsuccessful.

"You will also cease all contact with Claude Grimm from this day forward," he told her. "We cannot have him tipping off Shane Donovan about the impending attack."

Delia's gaze drifted just above Wentworth's head as she nodded. "Understood, but—"

"But what, Miss Roberts?"

Claude had tried to reach her relentlessly since the footage of the attack went live, but Delia hadn't been in the right frame of mind to talk to *anyone* over the last two days. His calls and texts, therefore, went unanswered.

"He's been trying to reach me," she admitted after some hesitation. "I can't keep blowing him off."

"You can and you will."

"If I may, Wentworth," George Heston interjected, placing a hand on Wentworth's shoulder before hastily retracting it. "I hate to agree with Miss Roberts, but I do. Claude Grimm is quite intelligent for a vampire." Anger surged through her at his words, like he thought Claude was some kind of animal. "One who has always maintained a steady truce with the League. Should we take away his favourite toy, I don't want to imagine the tantrum he might throw."

Delia bristled at the sentiment, but if it meant getting what she wanted, she could stay silent. Lips pursed, Wentworth's stare seemed to pass right through her, his eyes distant and unfocused. After what felt like an eternity had passed, he placed his hands on his desk and sighed.

"I can see the validity there," he admitted, though it sounded like it pained him to do so. "Claude Grimm has been the most compliant clan leader in the history of Harriswood." His gaze darted to Delia, then narrowed. "Should you see him, do it under the pretense of ending things. Tell him work has gotten too busy, that you don't care for him, that you're frightened he'll bite you again. Whatever it takes to lose him. We cannot have anyone spoil this operation for us."

Delia nodded mutely. When she had received her

promotion only minutes earlier, Delia had become privy to the fact that the League, paired with the Warwick clan and the Harriswood PD, was going to attempt a raid on the Donovan estate. All Donovan clansmen were to be arrested for questioning. Any aggressors were to be killed on sight. The grocery store stunt had pushed the League too far, and it had been unanimously agreed during another all-night meeting that the Donovan clan needed to be subdued—perhaps permanently.

Several squads of hunters, roughly half of those employed locally, were selected to work on the assault. Delia was now one of them, assigned to Kain's alpha squadron. Whoever was higher than Wentworth had seen the Safe Choice footage and deemed her worthy, apparently.

"You are dismissed, Miss Roberts," Wentworth said, hissing her name in a way that made her skin crawl. "You will receive a message shortly about your training schedule."

The raid was to take place in early December, almost two weeks away, and she was sure there was a boatload of information she needed to learn.

"Thank you, sir." She dipped her head down slightly before heading for the door. Behind her, Kain's footfalls followed, but stopped when Wentworth told him to stay. She glanced back and found Kain's expression unreadable, then left without another word.

Out in the hallway, Delia moved listlessly toward the elevators. She should have been thrilled, elated— overjoyed. Not only had she skirted a severe reprimand for risking their secret world—even if she did it to save lives—but she'd been promoted to a position that she had wanted for years. She'd be suited up and given weapons, not dressed down and armed with a smile. She'd be on par with hunters like Kain and his boys. Apparently Devin and Ali had also been assigned to the raid, albeit on different squads. For once, she wasn't left in the dust.

So why wasn't she more excited? Why did it feel like a bus had parked on her chest and refused to budge?

She swallowed hard and veered away from the elevators, heading for the bathroom instead. No cameras in the bathroom—at least not overlooking the stalls. Once she barricaded herself inside one, she pulled out her phone with shaky hands and fired a quick text to Claude, immediately breaking the rules she'd agreed to only a few minutes prior.

Hi. Wanted to write and say that I'm fine, but I can't talk. I think we should take a break for a little while. It isn't something you did. It's all me, I promise. And not in the it's not you, it's me kind of way. It's actually me. She hesitated, thumbs hovering over her screen, before replacing *break* with *breather*—it sounded less permanent, less serious—before finishing up with: *I'm so sorry.*

With the message sent, Delia exhaled deeply and leaned back against the stall door, knocking her head against it a few times before closing her eyes. She wanted to talk to him. Desperately. He was the *only* person she wanted to talk to about any of this.

But she knew she had to take a chance on the League this time, when she finally had what she'd been chasing for years. This could propel her up through the ranks and garner the respect she'd always wanted. She'd have the ability to save more lives on higher profile cases. Delia might even be able to make a *difference.*

Deep down, however, Delia just wanted to dial Claude's number and tell him all about it—about the attack at the grocery that had left her battered and bruised and shaken, about how she felt unsafe in her apartment, about the way shadows made her twitchy and the High Council discussed her like she was a thing, that they'd been using her to monitor him. All of it. She needed to unload it all on someone who she knew could take it and give it back frankly without pulling her apart.

Not wanting to bawl in the bathroom again, Delia left

the stall. She washed her hands only because one of the HR girls was there reapplying her lipstick, then left, dragging all the bus in tow and hoping that once the anxiety that had ballooned since the Safe Choice attack lessened, she would finally feel the way she wanted.

Once she'd calmed down, she might finally be excited about her new prospects, and the feelings she had about her brief romantic dalliance with Claude Grimm would be dwarfed by her new career mobility.

Right?

*　　*　　*

But the excitement never kicked in. Not during weapons training, not during field drills, and not when she met her tactical team. It wasn't that Delia was completely unhappy. It was a whole new world getting treated like an equal by hunters who generally didn't give her the time of day—Devin and Ali felt the same way. Low- to middle-ranked hunters were suddenly rubbing elbows with the big dogs. All they did for the last week was train, day in and day out. The social interaction totally boosted her mood, and not once had the High Council called her in for any special assignments. She was just one of the crew now—finally on a team that mattered.

But Delia wasn't ecstatic. She didn't wake up each morning with a spring in her step and a Cheshire grin on her face. The work was tiring. The training was difficult. Claude's lessons were probably the only reason she could keep up in terms of hand-to-hand combat. For once, her shooting skills were decent in comparison with some of the other hunters—a feat she probably owed to Claude as well. For once, she wasn't at the bottom of the barrel. For once, Delia stood by awkwardly as a superior chewed somebody *else* out in front of everyone, stomach knotted because she knew precisely how low that person would feel when it was over. But even that, even the not-being-singled-out thing didn't do it for her.

If the excitement hadn't kicked in during training, it certainly wasn't going to happen tonight. Whoever had decided that a camping trip to the frigid Harriswood hillside was a good bonding experience for the Donovan Task Force hunters ought to be shot.

"Did you bring anything for the bonfire?"

Delia glanced toward the mouth of her tent and spied Devin crouched down outside, his hulking frame filling up most of the opening. She'd been layering up for the cold night ahead, adding an extra sweater and two pairs of socks for good measure. Ali hadn't left her tent since they arrived, cuddled up next to her portable heater texting Steve with zero intention of joining in on the drunken festivities—and no amount of coaxing from Delia and Devin had made her budge. Kain and his boys were drunk within ten minutes of set-up. Devin had brought all the ingredients for s'mores, while Delia had loaded up two reusable grocery bags with chips.

They'd already bonded, the lot of them. Every day she'd seen the same faces for hours of drills and training, yet when the High Council instructed them to have a formalized group bonding session the weekend before the big raid, some idiot proposed a camping trip.

Delia would have been happy with a bar night, but apparently all suggestions paled next to a dozen tents, frigid late-November temperatures, and ten layers of clothes.

As she stumbled out of her hastily purchased one-man tent, the nippy air making her throat burn, she couldn't help but wonder if Kain and his boys had had it right from the beginning. She wouldn't be this cold if she had half a bottle of vodka circulating her system. She made her way over to the roaring bonfire, the flames about as tall as Devin, and found a seat on a log. Devin sidled in beside her, and the pair distributed some of their provisions to the hunters around them. Delia lost her salt and vinegar chips in a heartbeat, so she settled on hoarding the sour cream and onion all to herself.

Ali eventually joined them, pouting at the cold, with a six-pack of local ale and a cheesecake. Food was devoured. Drinks were had. Laughter encircled the group of hunters around the bonfire, smiles coming easily and jokes flowing freely. It might have been colder than sin, but everyone seemed to be having a good time.

Delia tried to. There she was, surrounded by people she'd finally clicked with. Good food in her lap. A half-finished bottle of beer by her foot. Body relatively warm under all the layers. No one talked about the mission. No one brought up the Donovan threat or clan politics. For today and tomorrow, they were all just people—not hunters, not scouts, not team leaders. Regular men and women. Coworkers enjoying a little time together.

Yet Delia wanted the company of one person above all else, and being in this part of the woods was a constant reminder that his home wasn't actually all that far away.

She and Claude hadn't spoken since she'd sent him the we-need-a-break text two weeks prior—and the silence was killing her. Every day she had something she wanted to share with him but couldn't. Delia wanted to be good. She wanted to focus on being the best hunter she could be with the legitimate opportunity provided for her, yet that proved increasingly difficult when the vampire she was crazy about was on her mind anytime she had a second to breathe.

Delia missed Claude, and for the first time, she wasn't afraid to admit it to herself. She missed the smell of his cologne and the crinkle around his eyes when he laughed. She missed his lighthearted jokes. She missed his hand on her lower back, both steering her and letting her lead the way. She missed those bright blues and the feel of his lips.

Most of all, Delia missed the way he made her feel. Claude made her feel worthy in a way no one else could. He made her feel wanted. He made her feel like she mattered, even if she felt a like screw-up half of the time.

And she kicked herself that she hadn't given as much back to him as he had given to her. It wasn't fair. It wasn't right, the way she handled things. Claude deserved more than that, even if it meant he broke things off completely.

She still wasn't sure when she wanted to tell him that she'd been tasked to spy on him, but that was a decision for another day. Tonight, surrounded by hunters with good food and great beer, Delia realized that this wasn't where she wanted to be. It was the place she'd always imagined when she pictured her future at the League, but now that she was here, this place didn't feel like home.

Claude felt like home.

The thought struck her so forcefully that she dropped her fork onto her lap, cheesecake crust crumbling across her pants.

"You okay?" Devin asked over the ruckus. Across the flames, Kain and his boys were singing, their arms stretched across each other's shoulders as they rocked from side to side—a sight Delia wished she would film. But she wouldn't. Not now.

"Yeah," she said as she stood and dusted herself off. She stepped over the log and placed a hand on Devin's muscular shoulder, ducking down to speak in his ear. "I have to go do something."

His face twisted with mock disgust. "D, if you need to go dig a hole behind the trees, I really don't need to know about it."

"No, I…" She chuckled, a flutter of nerves washing over her. Good nerves. The kind that meant she was actually doing something right for once. "I need to go take care of something. Don't worry about me. I'll call if I run into trouble."

"What do you…?" He swiveled back on the log as she left him. A few steps away, Delia pointed to the unopened chip bag she'd left.

"You can have that."

With a smile, she set off into the trees, jogging until she reached the road without feeling even slightly winded. From there, it was like following the old path home.

She swallowed hard as she looked up and down the road to ensure she wasn't being followed, that there was no one trailing behind to stop her. Nothing in either direction.

Teeth chattering, Delia hesitated at the hidden driveway to Claude's manor. But the rustle of the leafless trees and the unflinching moonlight cutting through the thick grey clouds gave her courage, and she pushed onward.

It was time to stop hiding. It was time to be an actual adult and own up to her mistakes.

And it was time to kiss Claude again, even if only for a moment.

CHAPTER 17: FINALLY

"Wait here." The bleach blond vamp gave Delia a once-over, hauntingly dark eyes running up and down her body at his leisure. If she'd been wearing something remotely attractive the stare might have felt sexual. As it were, she had on two pairs of pants, four shirts, and three layers of socks under her cold-weather gear. When he was through, the vamp headed for the door and added, "Try to resist the urge to touch anything."

"Sure thing."

She watched him close the door, and only when she was alone did she exhale the tension that had hitched a ride from the road to Claude's front door. There, an unfamiliar vamp had greeted her instead of Claude. It had been odd at first to explain why she was there and who she wanted to see, but once she was in, Delia wondered why she'd expected the Harriswood vampire king to answer his own front door, especially in the middle of the night.

The vamp with a heavy accent, perhaps German, took her to Claude's study without much interrogation; apparently he recognized her name.

Claude's study was a whole new experience for her, but it wasn't unlike any study she had been in before. Like many powerful men, Claude had a grand mahogany desk, the woodwork and carvings so intricate—a naval scene with roaring waves and fluttering sails aplenty—that it was quite breathtaking. Two huge windows overlooked the forested area outside, framed with blackout curtains, and a fireplace nestled into the stone wall near the desk, small flames crackling in the hearth. Bookshelves filled with tomes. A thick carpet situated between two leather armchairs. His desk was *much* more cluttered than she'd expected, with stacks of papers and file folders and opened notebooks scattered across it. The latest Apple desktop sat at the corner, and while Delia wanted to turn the screen for a better look, she did what she'd been told and kept her hands to herself.

While the walk there had been cold, the wind biting and bitter, Claude's study was pleasantly toasty, made warmer by all her layers and the small fire. The longer she stood there, the more her body heated. In less than a minute, a thin sheen of sweat had broken out across her forehead. Delia wiped at it with her sleeve, but just as she was about to remove a layer, the door opened behind her.

There stood Claude, dressed casually in a pair of dark jeans and a black knit sweater. Delia's gaze swept over him appreciatively, though it stopped when it caught the scowl on his face. Clearing her throat, she clasped her hands together and tried not to fidget too much—an impossible task with the way he looked at her.

"Hi," she offered as the silence dragged on. Her voice seemed to rouse him, because moments later he shut the door and crossed the room to stand by his desk, arms folded and scowl fixed. Her eyes followed him as he went, pausing at the windows: it had started to snow. Fat flakes whizzed by the window, caught on the wind.

Delia swallowed hard as she tore herself away from the view and faced Claude.

"What are you doing here?" he asked. While his voice wasn't hostile, it certainly wasn't friendly. If anything, it was neutral, distant, and it made Delia's stomach turn.

She lifted her chin a little, determined not to falter. "I came to see you."

"Why?"

"Because I miss you." She didn't have to think about

her answer, not for a second. Still, she waited with bated breath for his reaction. Claude's gaze shifted to the window, and he too seemed taken with the first snowfall of the year. His distraction was temporary, and soon he moved to the fireplace and crouched beside it. Delia watched as he added a few thick pieces of wood from the bin to his right. There he stayed, sparks crackling and jumping as the fire took to the new wood.

"Did you walk here?" he asked, eyes still fixed to the flames.

She nodded. "We're having this...hunter camping retreat thing not far from here. I came from that."

"Ah, yes, the one illegally hosted on Grimm property," he mused, adopting a hardness that didn't sit well with her. She noted the flicker of his jaw as it clenched and unclenched. "Strange that you would be pitching tents in November."

"It wasn't my idea," she insisted, dropping her hands to her sides and rubbing her sweaty palms on her pants. Good grief was it ever hot in here. The logical thing would have been to take off her jacket, but Delia thought it might distract from the conversation. "Someone suggested it and everyone jumped at the idea. We usually just get drunk together at a bar. Now they're all getting drunk in the snow."

Delia paused, worried she was rambling. It was then that she caught a fleeting smile on Claude's lips, one of those little grins that starts suddenly and disappears just as fast. And then the dreadful silence returned, marred only by the spitting fire and the howling wind outside.

"Look," she said as she took a few steps toward him, "I'm sorry I've been...gone lately, I—"

"Delia, let me stop you there."

He raised his hands as if warming them by the fire, then stood and faced her. With her voice caught in her throat, all she could do was nod.

"I want to be perfectly frank with you so we'll have no

misunderstandings going forward," Claude said. Much to her surprise, *his* voice seemed to catch too. "I'm not interested in being jerked around. I have no desire for a hot and cold relationship." Delia's cheeks flamed when their eyes met. "Perhaps it doesn't seem like it because I'm usually free whenever you want to see me, but I have a life of my own too. I would very much like for you to be a part of it, but only if you're an active participant. If not, if you'd prefer to jump in and out whenever it suits you, I think it's best we sever...*this*."

The idea of ending things had never felt so real before. While Wentworth had instructed her to permanently break the ties between her and Claude, she hadn't seriously considered doing it. But from the expression on his face, Claude had. The noticeable bob of his throat was a mild comfort, as was the way his eyes averted hers and fixed to a place over her shoulder.

"I am happy to be a friend to you in time," he told her softly, "but I can't..." Drawing in a deep breath and letting it out, he shifted his gaze back to her face. "I think I've earned more than this, or, at the very least, some sort of explanation for why you decided to cease all contact with me."

She bit her lower lip, holding back what she had to say until he raised an eyebrow at her. Delia sighed. "I can't tell you that yet."

Theoretically she could. If she did, she'd be following Wentworth's directions precisely: end things. But she wouldn't do that. Delia didn't want an ending—she wanted a fresh beginning.

"I saw the footage of you on the news," he remarked after a slight pause. "How are you doing after all that?"

"I was a bit shaken up when it happened." She shrugged away memories of her scalp injuries, of the nightmares that had plagued her in the nights after. "But I'm fine now, I guess."

Outside, the storm pummelled the windows, quickly

ramping up, and Delia couldn't help but think back to the other hunters. Had they retreated into their tents, into their cars? Or did they plan to ride it out in true drunken hunter stubbornness?

She banished the thought with a few hard blinks, eyes to the floor. The other hunters shouldn't even be crossing her mind. There were more important things to focus on.

"So tell me then," Claude said, his tone forcing her to look up. "Right here, right now… What is it, exactly, that you want?"

Him. She wanted him.

Wordlessly, she closed the distance between them in a few strides, placed her hands on his chest, and kissed him. He was a little stiff at first, his arms rigid by his sides and his mouth only *just* responding to hers. But as Delia tightened her grip on his sweater and pulled her body closer, so many layers of clothing between her and what she wanted, Claude's hands rose to gently cradle her face. This kiss reminded her of the last they had shared the night of the masquerade: sweet, gentle, cautious. Her eyes fluttered closed as she leaned into him, the warmth of his touch flooding through her body—bringing it to a boiling point.

"You're so hot," He pulled away and pressed the back of his hand to her forehead. "Are you ill?"

"No." Delia laughed, flushed and smiling. "No, just really hot… I'm wearing a lot of clothing."

"Might I ask why?"

"Did you forget some idiot suggested we go camping this weekend?" She stepped back and unzipped her jacket, shrugging it off so that it landed on the floor behind her. Next came the shirts beneath, one at a time, until she was down to her bra as Claude watched, the familiar notes of desire starting to trickle across his features.

Delia swallowed hard as her hands fell to her pants, but she continued on, stripping away all those layers, right down to her underwear and a single pair of socks. Free from all that fabric, her body felt like it could expand, finally taking up the space it needed without restriction.

Dropping her arms to her sides, she raised her chin to meet Claude's eye, almost naked. Hot. A little sweaty. Flushed. Desire pooling between her thighs.

"I want you, Claude Grimm," she told him softly. "It's taken me a little while to get my priorities in order. I think... I think I've been chasing the wrong thing for a long time."

You. I should have been chasing you. She almost got it out, but Claude swallowed the words as he took her with a kiss that was anything but gentle. His hands pinned her arms to her side, fingertips leaving a smattering of bruises over her flesh as he ravished her mouth, months of pent-up need flooding between them.

With an unseen grin, Delia slipped her leg around his under the pretense of hooking it around his hips, but instead used the distraction to knock his foot out from under him, throwing her full weight on top of him. Claude went down with a grunt, landing on his back while she giggled.

"I think I've taught you a little too well," he managed as she crawled up his body and straddled his hips. Her heat pressed against his hardening length, and without thinking, Delia bucked against him. Pleasure tingled up and out from her core, a shiver running through her body as goosebumps scattered across her skin.

They came together like they'd done this a hundred times before, Claude rising up and Delia easing down, lips meeting in the middle. Even if he was beneath her, sprawled out on the floor, Claude set the pace, taking charge quickly and assertively in a way that only made her panties dampen more. Her hands cupped his face, thumbs brushing over the slight stubble across his cheeks as they rocked back and forth together, clothes only getting in the way of what they both wanted.

While Claude possessed her mouth like it belonged to

him, his hands roamed her body tentatively. For a time they lingered on the small of her back, but eventually one quested upward and the other went down, smoothing over the generous curve of her backside. Delia moaned when he gave it a squeeze. His approval rumbled deep in his chest as his other hand grasped the base of her neck, working its way under her mass of brown waves.

Delia pulled back with a gasp when he spanked her. Not hard, but sound enough to earn him a look.

"I couldn't help myself," he murmured with a devilish grin, rocking his hips. A fresh jolt of pleasure shot through her as his cock, hard and straining against his trousers, rubbed against her swollen bud. Delia responded by threading her fingers through his hair and tugging. He licked from the dip in her neck to the tip of her chin with a hushed growl. The look shared between them rivaled the storm raging outside, all blustery winds and pelting hail. It hammered the windows now, the once-fluffy flakes turned hard and dangerous.

In one swift move, Claude rolled them both onto their sides, then used his arm to push upright. With Delia wrapped around his neck, arms and legs clinging to him like she feared she'd lose him, the vampire king strolled over to his cluttered desk, kissing her lazily, and set her on the edge. Her fingertips slipped beneath the hem of his sweater as he settled between her thighs, and she yanked the garment up and over his head. It found a home on the floor with her things, followed shortly by her bra—Claude all but ripped it off.

Miraculously, it was still intact when he tossed it aside, but before Delia could chide him—didn't he know how stupidly expensive bras were these days?—he dropped his head to her breast and took her hard nipple in his mouth. A slight brush of teeth made her whole body clench, and she let loose a breathless moan as he suckled her skin, his hand dipping between her thighs to rub her.

It didn't take much for Delia to dissolve into a

LIZ MELDON

trembling, whimpering, panting mess, her muscles tightening ever so slowly as Claude worked her into a frenzy. He hadn't even slipped his fingers into her—all he needed was to stroke her aching nub over her panties and she was gone, pleasure pulsing through her. His mouth roamed her skin with wild abandon, brushing over her collarbone and kissing up the nape of her neck, nibbling at her earlobe before dropping back to toy with a nipple. She'd forgotten how good he was at ruthlessly tormenting her. No wonder she'd fallen for him all those months ago, even with his terrible choice in masks.

"*Oh...*" Her eyes clenched shut. So close. So deliciously close. "Claude... I..."

His lips claimed hers roughly, smothering her whimpers and cries as he finally pushed the damp fabric aside and thrust two fingers into her slick, wet sex. It was almost too much when he curved them inside her to rub her inner wall, finding the sweet spot that sent her spiraling. At first she tried to pull away, to squirm out of reach, as she climbed ever higher toward a climax, too overwhelmed with the sensations to stay still, but Claude held her in place, his pace steady and constant.

Her head tipped back when she came, giving a soft cry as the levies broke and pleasure flooded her system. She shuddered, her skin kissed with a pleasant chill, as Claude pulled his fingers gently from her, slowly, milking every last bit of ecstasy from her before he was through. Blinking the hazy post-orgasm fog away, she noticed he'd gone for the zipper of his pants. Yes. *Yes.* Just what she wanted.

Claude had a knack for making her insatiable.

Her hands soon joined his in an effort to remove his pants, followed quickly by his form-flattering black briefs. His cock fell toward her like a lead weight, heavy and hard and desperate for her attention—it would be rude not to oblige. As much as she wanted it pushing into her, filling her, claiming her, Delia took the time to stroke him. Much to her delight, Claude's eyes seemed to flutter as she dragged her hands up and down, smearing the wetness at his tip down to the base.

"I guess I didn't need to make you wear a condom last time," she muttered, then laughed at his grunt of a response. As far as she was aware, there were no diseases transferable between vamps and humans beyond the main one, nor had there been any record of a vamp impregnating a human, or vice versa.

"No," he agreed as she continued to stroke him, giving extra attention to the smooth, rounded head of his cock. "I suppose not."

"But you did anyway."

"That I did."

"To humor me."

"Of course."

"Because you always humor me," she noted. Even outside of the bedroom, Claude was fairly pliant to most of her requests. The edges of his mouth quirked upward as he gave a handsome smile.

"Probably because I rarely find your desires unreasonable," he told her, the lust noticeable in his voice—it had all but melted into a seductive growl by now.

"Good," she whispered, throwing an arm around his neck and dragging him down for a kiss. Their lips parted as he drew Delia's hips to the edge of the desk so that she was forced to wrap her legs around him—or lose her balance and topple over. But her lack of balance in that moment didn't matter, not when he eased into her, slowly filling her until their hips touched. Delia wasn't the only one to moan this time, with Claude burying his face in her neck, the sound muffled.

He stayed still as she adjusted to him, shifting her legs to a more comfortable position and encircling her arms around his neck to keep herself up. One of his hands pressed to her lower back to help.

"I've missed you," he rumbled in her ear, and she

hugged him tighter. As the slight edge of pain faded, replaced swiftly by a renewed lust, Delia rolled her hips as best she could to encourage him to move. She needed it, the movement, the force of his body against hers, the glorious sting mingled with pleasure as he took her.

"Claude…" She breathed his name like he was her personal deity, a hand clutching at his thick black hair. "Please…"

"Are you sure this is what you want?" he asked, fingertips digging into her thighs. She groaned and tried to move again, earning a sharp exhale from him.

"Yes, fuck me already," she begged as she pulled at his hair. Claude straightened and withdrew his hand from her back, taking with it most of the support that kept her from falling back on his messy desk. Cheeks flushed and breath uneven, Delia looked up at him with a slight frown. "Do you mean…?"

"Yes."

He meant overall. Was *he* what she wanted. Was she sure.

Again, she didn't have to think about it. Claude was the only part of her life that made sense. Her latest League accomplishment confused her and her social life was hit-and-miss outside of work. But staring up at Claude… Things just fell into place.

"Yes," she whispered, nodding. "I'm sure."

"As long as you're…" He closed his eyes and seemed to be gritting his teeth when she clenched around his cock as hard as she could. "Damn it, Delia."

"Fuck me," she breathed, lowering herself toward the desk. "Please, Claude, please…"

In one swift motion he removed the clutter beneath her, papers and notebooks and pens scattering to the floor behind his desk, and as soon as her back touched the cool wood, Claude finally followed through. He took her hard and fast at first, drawing breathy gasps and heady cries from her, any and all words totally incoherent. As she felt the pleasurable tightening of her muscles again, he slowed to a more excruciating pace, each thrust hitting right where she needed, his hips working her inside and out.

"Faster," she whimpered, already close again. Claude seemed happy to comply, trailing his lips down her neck with groan. This time, his teeth brushed her marks. Delia couldn't help it—she panicked. *"Don't—"*

"Hush, love," he murmured, carrying on downward with gentle, soothing pecks to her flushed skin, so sensitive to the touch that each whispered kiss was torture. "I won't. Not unless you ask me. I promise."

She nodded and let her head fall back against the desk, eyes closed as she tried to banish the fear, hands gripping his muscular shoulders. Before long she was crying his name again, her whole body quivering as he continued to fuck her like he wanted to possess her. He didn't need to try that hard. Claude Grimm already possessed her, mind, body, and soul—and she let him willingly.

Her second climax was short and sweet compared to the first, and by the time she recovered, Claude was thrusting hard and fast again, until he stopped with one final groan, eyes clenched shut as he spilled himself into her.

He fell forward, his warmth radiating between their bodies, hands resting atop the desk on either side of her head. When their eyes met, his smile matched hers in a heartbeat, and rather than let him go, Delia tightened her legs around him and pulled his head down to hers. Even if fucking on a desk made her hips and back and shoulders ache, she'd put up with it, all of it, just to kiss him again.

And again, and again, and again.

CHAPTER 18: THE TALK

Delia awoke to a pleasant soreness between her thighs and a slight chill across her skin. She sighed heavily and buried her face between two pillows—two pillows that smelled like Claude. Smiling, she breathed him in for a few moments, slowly bringing herself out of sleep rather than jolting upright. That morning she knew precisely where she was—it was exactly where she wanted to be.

Eventually she pushed herself into a seated position, rubbing any lingering sleep out of her eyes. The king-sized bed was empty, but she'd almost expected that when she fell asleep beside Claude in the wee hours of the morning, exhausted. She'd never had a sex marathon before, but a few hours of on and off fucking had to qualify. No wonder she was sore. Delia grinned at the memory.

She was still naked. After Claude slipped away, she must have kicked his duvet covers down; the thick material pooled at her feet, leaving her exposed.

While his bed was enormous, Claude's modest bedroom wasn't much bigger than hers, despite his home being ten times the size of her apartment and then some. Beyond the king-sized bed sat a closet with no doors, in which he hung his suits. A waist-high wooden dresser housed the rest of his clothes, though the laundry hamper beside it had a pile of dirties poking out the top. Slate tile covered the floor and there was a large, thick black carpet—upon which he'd taken her on all fours—by Claude's side of the bed. Two sets of wall-mounted shelves sat on either side of the huge bay window, upon which were framed pictures and a few stacked books.

Not exactly the bedroom of a king, but then again, Delia had nothing to compare it to. Crawling to the end of the bed, she leaned over to dig her phone out of her purse. A few missed calls from Ali greeted her, followed by a text that told her most of the hunters had left the campground once the storm picked up. If Delia needed to be picked up from anywhere, Devin offered to swing by. Delia rolled onto her back to reply, thumbs flying across the touchscreen as she told Ali not to worry but thanks for the offer anyway, then tacked on an invite to lunch tomorrow if she was free.

As she drifted to the ensuite bathroom to freshen up, Delia noted that there wasn't an ounce of trepidation in her that morning. Sure, she was a little nervous to find her tent and belongings scattered amongst the trees when she went back for them, but that was pint-sized compared to the usual dose of uneasiness she woke up with each morning. All things considered, she should have been lying in Claude's bed, covers pulled up to her neck, ruminating about what they'd done and how they'd complicated things and that she was making a huge mistake...

But Delia didn't feel the need to do any of that. Falling asleep beside him and waking up in his bed felt right. No relationship was perfect, and there would be a lot to work out, but this was the start of something good—she knew it.

A niggling thought at the back of her mind whispered that the High Council could punish her severely for disobeying a direct order, but that was only if they found out. Wandering back to bed, Delia wondered if she could have both in her life: Claude and the League. Claude made her happy. The League gave her purpose. Was it possible to live with one without sacrificing the other? Did she even *want* the other anymore now that she'd finally let her heart take the lead?

Moments later, the bedroom door creaked open.

"Well aren't you the sweetest vampire king ever," she teased as Claude made his way in, fully dressed and carrying what looked like breakfast.

"And aren't you the most naked hunter my bedroom has ever seen," he said with a chuckle, clambering onto the foot of the bed as Delia tugged the blankets over her. "Now, now, don't cover up on my account."

"In case you haven't noticed, it's freezing in here." She accepted the carry-out drink tray, a piping hot cup of coffee with her name scribbled hastily on the side looking better than ever.

"The snow stayed," Claude remarked. He kicked off his shoes before climbing back to settle against the massive engraved wood headboard. "About an inch, I think."

She scooted beside him, placing her breakfast on the bedside table so she could arrange a pillow to lean on. "Great."

The thought of storming the Donovan estate in a week's time with snow on the ground made her cringe. Delia was already worried she'd trip over her own feet— she didn't need snow and ice to help her out.

"I figured you'd be hungry," he said when she dug into the takeout bag, "and I couldn't recall what bagel you liked, so I got a few. Each has a different cream cheese."

She hummed, pleased, as she leaned over and kissed his cheek. "You're my favourite."

"And you, my dear, have very pungent morning breath."

Hand over her mouth, Delia laughed and pulled back, then grabbed her coffee and took a tentative swig. It burned the whole way down her throat and needed a serious helping of milk and sugar, but she figured coffee breath was infinitely better than morning breath.

"Thank you for breakfast," she said as she dug out one of her bagels, legs stretched out, the takeaway bag on her lap.

"Some of my clansmen forget that their human counterparts need to eat when they stay the night," he told her while she chowed down on what seemed like an everything bagel with chive-flavoured cream cheese. "I vowed not to make the same mistake. I don't think I'd hear the end of it if you had to trudge down to the dining hall by the guest suites."

Delia shook her head, smiling. "No, you wouldn't."

They sat together for some time in an easy silence, both enjoying their breakfast. Delia hadn't noticed until she started on her second bagel—a pumpernickel bread with spinach and artichoke cream cheese—that Claude was nursing a white Styrofoam coffee cup of his own, but his lid had traces of red on the rim instead of brown. She watched him take a sip, then returned to her bagel, yanking off a good-sized piece and shoving it in her mouth.

When they were together, Delia usually forgot Claude was a vampire, never mind the *king* of all the Harriswood vamps. Warm to the touch, he acted as her own personal furnace in bed last night. He could walk around during the day, seeming alert at all hours while Delia juggled a wonky hunter schedule. He made it easy to forget she'd been told vamps were the enemy, that they were to be monitored closely, that the fragile truce between the various Leagues and vamp clans could shatter at any moment.

That vamps were only out for one thing with humans—blood.

The Grimm clan had disproven that, with the sizeable human population living on their property to be nearer to friends and sweethearts alike. Maybe it was just League dogma. Maybe it was necessary jargon to prepare hunters to stake a vamp, who, despite their disease, looked very similar to humans.

"Delia?"

She jumped, Claude's voice sounding louder than it probably was while she was deep in thought. "Hmm?"

"Do you want to talk about last night?"

Her gut response was no, *no* she wasn't interested in having a mature conversation about what all the sex meant. But she was trying to make positive changes. Talking about things with Claude had to be on the list if she wanted to see any improvements.

So, she crumpled the empty bagel wrapper and stuck it in the takeout bag, then grabbed her coffee. "Sure."

"I believe I made my position on things fairly clear," Claude said as she took a sip. Letting it sit had brought the drink down to the perfect temperature, but it still needed some tempering. Black coffee wasn't her thing.

"I think you did," she remarked. He wanted her in his life, but only if she didn't pull a disappearing act. Totally fair. Delia slurped another mouthful of coffee. "But you have to consider that I want to give the League one last chance."

His eyebrows raised slightly, a mere flicker to show his surprise. "Do you? Even with all the…grievances?"

"I think so." Delia pressed her lips together briefly, suddenly less confident than she had been a second ago. "I mean, I hope so. Maybe. I've been assigned to a new case. Kind of another promotion, but better."

"Congratulations." He meant well, but the dry quality to his voice was hard to ignore.

She shifted onto her side to face him, coffee nestled between both hands. "I'm not as excited about it as I thought I'd be. I mean, it's great. In theory, this is what I've always wanted."

"But?"

"But I don't feel how I thought I would," Delia admitted with a sigh. She fiddled with the coffee cup lid, picking at it until the plastic cracked. "I still want to give it my all. At least if I really try at it and don't like it, I won't have regrets later. If I don't enjoy this, I think I'll know the League isn't for me, but I should give it a chance before I start hunting for a new career."

And turn her whole life upside down. But if she had

Claude by her side, the exploration seemed a little less scary.

"I suppose that's a reasonable way to approach it," he said slowly, tipping his head back to rest against the headboard.

"I'd like to think so," she said. "I know it complicates things for us and dating. The High Council already knows we had a relationship and have asked me to end it." Her cheeks flushed when their eyes met, a certain other League assignment at the tip of her tongue. But she knew now wasn't the time to tell him. One day, of course. She owed him that much and more. "They told me dating you was a conflict of interest."

He made a noise that was a cross between a scoff and a growl. "Hardly. It only is if we let it be. I have no interest in League business... You know that."

"I know." They'd talked about it at such length already that the topic felt tiresome. "But I don't think I can publicly defy them by dating you around town. They let it slip, but I don't know if they always will." When Claude rolled his eyes, she added, "And I don't want to, I don't know, wake up in the middle of nowhere one day, vultures circling, because I broke the rules."

His gaze hardened. "I would never allow that to happen."

"Still though," she pressed. "I definitely want to be with you and... I *maybe* want to keep my job. I know it's a lot to ask, but if we can find a way to make it work, I want to try. It might only be for a little while longer anyway."

Claude proved to be a good sounding board for her concerns. They sat together for an hour or so, half of which Delia spent venting her frustrations with herself for not being over the moon about the promotion, to which Claude responded that it was perfectly normal. Expectations are made and not met all the time—that's life. The rest of the conversation centered on how they would move forward together, keeping in mind that she still wanted to see if she could ever enjoy her job again.

As Delia lay against Claude's chest, her head tucked under his chin while her finger traced random shapes along his arm, they decided they would keep their relationship as secretive as possible for the time being, at least until she decided if she'd stay on as a hunter. All date activities would be held on his property or outside of Harriswood to lessen the risk of being caught.

"It will be complicated," Claude murmured.

Delia shook her head and tried to sit up, but he kept her against him. "No, but—"

"All relationships are complicated," he continued, his voice a soothing rumble deep within his chest. She snuggled closer, enjoying the faint vibration. "Ours is, historically, one that begs for complication. A vampire and a hunter. We should be enemies on principle."

The thought made her quiet, a heavy lump settling in her throat, until Claude chuckled and pressed his lips to her forehead.

"Luckily I am one of the more progressive clan leaders," he offered, smirking.

Delia agreed with a kiss, a lingering one that made the hairs on her arms stand and the heat between her thighs grow. It probably didn't help that she was still naked, wrapped in his arms, his hands wandering everywhere and anywhere.

"I think it will involve a lot of work to make this successful," he stated, as if the thought had just occurred to him. It wasn't something Delia wanted to agree with— no one wanted to face an uphill battle, especially when it involved a person they cared about.

"But," she said in a small voice, "I think it will be worth it."

His arms tightened around her in response, which made her smile. Something that made her feel this good had to be worth it. Work never made her feel the way Claude did. Junk food was a comfort, TV binges a distraction, bar nights a giant black hole. But what she had right now felt tangible—more real than any of it.

Sometime later, as she hovered between falling asleep and feeling Claude up, Delia wriggled out of his arms and sat upright, brushing her hair back over her shoulders. Claude's bright blues wandered her figure appreciatively.

"Do you mind if I take a shower?" She nodded toward the ensuite. "I should probably go get my tent and stuff if the storm didn't carry it away."

"Of course," Claude said. He reached out and cupped her breast, then pinched her nipple lightly before she swatted him away. "I can drive you out there and bring you home… Or call for a car?"

"Car will probably be better," she told him as she crawled across the bed away from him, purposefully on all fours as the blankets fell from her body. "Less noticeable, especially if the other hunters are still there. I'm sure a few would actually know your face."

"Glad I've made an impression," he muttered somewhat distractedly.

Delia grinned as she clambered off the bed. Hands on her hips, she rounded on the spot and pointed an accusatory finger at the vampire king. "And don't you dare think of sneaking into the shower with me." She bit her cheeks to keep from smiling as Claude eased forward and made his way to the edge of the bed, eyes fixed on her, looking more predator than man. "I have a reputation to consider, sir."

Nose in the air, Delia tiptoed toward the bathroom— only to squeal and make a mad dash for the shower at the sound of Claude racing after her.

CHAPTER 19: IT'S GOING DOWN IN DONOVAN TOWN

"It's a guy, right?"

Delia looked up quickly from her phone. "What?"

Beside her, Devin leaned against the light blue locker with a smirk, arms crossed. "The person you're texting," he said, nodding down to the phone.

Delia hastily pressed the lock button and shoved the phone in her backpack, then slammed the locker shut harder than she meant to. And here she thought she'd been subtle with all her Claude-texting. Apparently not. Pre–Donovan raid nerves were getting the better of her. Devin's expression morphed into full-blown smugness, his smile infectious.

"It's nothing," she muttered as she drew her hair into a low pony, then stuffed the tail down the back of her shirt. The last thing she needed was some vamp getting a hold of her hair again.

"Is he cute?"

The way she blushed was answer enough. "Yeah. He's cute."

She and Claude had been texting back and forth all night. While she should have been sleeping, her ticket to the dream train must have been invalid, because it never came. Now it was a sunny Saturday morning, cool and crisp in the early days of December, and Delia probably had about four hours of mediocre sleep to keep her going. She couldn't help it. She'd been assigned to Team Alpha with Kain for the Donovan estate raid that day. Expectations were high, just like her blood pressure, and she'd been fidgety since about 4 AM.

A part of her wished she could actually talk to Claude about what she was doing today. Still, her loyalty on the issue belonged begrudgingly to the League, so she'd kept her mouth shut beyond telling him it was a huge project with dozens of the best hunters working it. He pointed out that *she* was one of those hunters, and Delia resisted the urge to tell him she was only there because she'd been a hit on the local news.

His confidence in her, though somewhat misplaced, was appreciated.

"Don't forget to suit up," Devin told her, handing her a tin of black paint to decorate her face with.

"What should I do?"

"Zebra stripes, all the way. Forehead to chin."

"I'm one hundred percent going to sweat that off," Delia said with a nervous laugh as they made their way to the bathroom area of the unisex locker room, Devin hovering nearby as she used a mirror over the sink to apply her war paint. Lacking creativity, she added two stripes to each cheek, then handed him back his tin. Her hand trembled when it brushed against his, but he had the decency not to comment on it—probably because he was a little jittery too.

Dressed in breathable cotton t-shirts and cargo pants, the two left the changing room together, accompanied by a few other hunters. Rendezvous was scheduled for 9 AM. Each team, Alpha to Omega, would leave HQ by eleven with the aim of reaching the Donovan estate by noon—when the sun was at its highest.

"I really can't stand that these fuckers are coming with us," Devin muttered as they navigated HQ's underground hallways. Delia glanced around him at the cluster of Warwick vamps, all outfitted in sleek black gear, not an ounce of skin showing beyond their faces. One of them blew her a kiss when he caught her looking. Delia kept going, too hopped up on pre-mission adrenaline for a bit of verbal sparring.

"Well, it's not like they'll be in the same van," she noted. As they drew nearer to the meeting hall, a giant space roughly the size of an airplane hangar with a ramp leading up to Harriswood Library's rear parking lot, the sound of dozens of voices assaulted her ears. All Delia's senses had been heightened from the second she jumped out of bed hours earlier.

"They might as well be," Devin said with an irritable sigh.

Delia shot him a quick look. "We all voted on this. Try not to pick a fight with them."

"No promises."

Not like he'd have the opportunity to do so. While Johnathon Warwick was sun-resistant, as were his turned children, the rest of his clan would burn severely the second they stepped foot outside. Sun-proof transport had been arranged to take them to the underground tunnels leading off the Donovan property, the blueprints of which were supplied by Johnathon Warwick himself. They were to stop any of the Donovan clansmen who thought of hightailing it out of there as soon as the coalition arrived. For once, Delia didn't mind the extra vamp muscle, though she would have preferred the muscle be Grimm rather than Warwick.

When they reached the hangar, the hunters in front of them split off, each going to meet up with their respective teams. The Omega crew was stationed by the doorway, their table set up with all the items they'd need for clean-up duty once the task was done. Ali's face lit up when she spotted them, her thin blonde locks swept up in a tight ponytail like Delia's. She waved as she continued to pack her gear bag, a gesture both Devin and Delia returned.

"Well…" Delia inhaled deeply, filling her lungs, then blew it all out. "See you on the other side."

"Take care of yourself, D," Devin said. They'd need to go in opposite directions to meet up with their teams. Team Alpha was closest to the transport vans and had the largest table to hold their various weapons—Alphas were responsible for bringing in the immediate Donovan family, whom they'd been assured were all on location by scouts. Team Charlie, Devin's crew a few tables over, were to extract all the Donovan humans and dispense with whatever security they might meet along the way.

Delia's gaze swept over her friend briefly. He was exactly the kind of man she'd want coming to her rescue if she were vamp property.

"Hey," she said as he started to turn away. As a few hunters watched, men mostly, she pulled Devin into a quick hug, standing on her tiptoes to wrap her arms around his muscular neck. Even with the jeers from onlookers, Devin hugged her too, his grip cracking her back.

"Sorry." He gave her a lopsided grin when they pulled apart, and Delia brushed the apology off. It felt good, the cracking. "You come out of that house, Miss Roberts. Y'hear me?"

"Done." They did a quick fist bump. "Take care of the people inside."

"Of course."

With one last smile, they went their separate ways. When Delia looked back to him, he was being greeted by his crew. It was all smiles on Team Charlie.

Team Alpha had a decidedly frostier reception for Delia. Kain was the only one who even glanced up as she approached. The others went on loading their guns, polishing their stakes, and checking their scopes in silence. She placed her fingertips on the edge of the weapon-laden table, looking around with an uneasy smile, one that weakened when no one greeted her besides Kain.

"Tense around here," she said as she sidled up to him and nudged his arm. He might not have been her favourite person lately, but he was the only one she could word-vomit her nerves on without getting glared at. "How're you doing? You ready for this?"

The Kain who stared at her wasn't the Kain she knew. No, this Kain was all business, his brow furrowed and his lips set in a tight frown. She swallowed hard and crossed her arms, suddenly aware of just how poorly she fit in with her team. All the crews taking part in the assault had trained together. Sure, each team had had separate meetings to prep for the day of, but for the last few weeks, Delia had been working with everyone. That had been fun. This was uncomfortable.

"Are *you* ready for this?" he asked, his tone lacking her playfulness. Delia initially assumed it was a rhetorical question, but hastily nodded when it seemed like he was waiting for a response.

"Yeah, I'm good. Nervous, but good."

"Well, get your jacket and gear," he told her, returning his attention to the crossbow in his hands. "And stick close to me."

Struggling to keep a snippy comment to herself, Delia went for her jacket, which was the only one left hanging: bulletproof with added protection around the wrists and neck. It zipped all the way up to her chin and her helmet would cover the rest. She'd been training with it over the last few days to adjust to its weight, but it still made her shoulders sag when she put it on.

While the rest of her team had a whole slew of weapons assigned to them, Delia only had one outside the usual. Finding her name card on the table, she inspected her handgun—lightweight and responsive—and loaded it with ammunition, leaving the safety on for now. The bullets were armor-piercing silver with a wood core, perfect for immobilizing a vamp until the hunter could finish the job. A part of her hoped she wouldn't need to use it, but the Donovans didn't strike her as a family who would come quietly.

She stuffed additional ammunition bundles into the various pockets of her cargo pants, and then added the five stakes she'd been assigned to their holsters around her waist and calves. When she caught the eye of the hunter next to her, Gregory, she offered a small smile, but all he did was stare at her blankly before going back to his gear.

Awesome.

She rolled her eyes and finished suiting up, then returned to Kain's side at the other end of the table. They stood together in silence, Kain with his arms crossed as he surveyed the hangar while Delia sat on the edge of the table and picked at a stubborn hangnail, wishing her stomach would settle already.

At ten thirty on the dot, a siren went off to settle the hunters. Standing by the transport vehicles with a megaphone, Wentworth, flanked by the High Council, looked as grim as the Alpha team. The sight of the five men in their traditional midnight-black robes made Delia's insides twist again. Meanwhile, Johnathon Warwick, gaunt as ever, stood on Wentworth's right and looked positively giddy.

"Okay, listen up, folks." Wentworth's voice boomed throughout the hangar. Delia winced at the short-lived, high-pitched whine of the megaphone. The older man smacked the device a few times before speaking again, this time without the feedback. "Busy day ahead of us. Team leaders, brief your squad, then check in with me before loading up. It's time to remind the Donovan clan that Harriswood isn't their personal playground. Today, we make our city safe again."

Cheesy as it was, Delia joined in on the clapping and cheering—she couldn't help herself.

*　　*　　*

"I know that face…" Bella Donovan snapped at Delia like a rabid dog, the ice-blonde vamp's teeth a mere three inches from her face as two hunters held her back. They'd managed to capture the vamp in her bedroom, an enormous room overlooking the estate's well-maintained courtyard. Clothes were scattered across the floor and hanging from bedposts, while necklaces and shoes decorated various door handles. It was the bedroom of a spoiled, and perhaps much-loved, heiress.

Bella Donovan, eldest daughter of Shane Donovan, was set to inherit the clan should anything happen to her father. Her picture, along with those of her two sisters who were close in age and appearance, hung in the staff room at League HQ with a warning for new hunters not to approach. Delia had had the misfortune of falling into her clutches briefly at the masquerade ball this past spring—and apparently her face, even beneath a lacy mask, still stuck in the vamp's memory bank.

She swallowed hard but stood still, determined not to flinch as the vamp struggled to get at her. Delia had faith that the two hunters holding Bella, who looked very much a predator with her ruby-red lips peeled back in a snarl, would keep the vamp from ripping Delia's throat out.

Claude's bite marks prickled beneath the fabric of her dense protective gear, but Delia resisted the urge to scratch at them.

With some effort, the hunters holding the wild vamp cuffed her and hauled her out of the room—but only after Kain threatened to put a bullet in her skull to make things easier. Bella scowled as they dragged her out, lips pursed in a childish pout while her eyes blazed with hate.

Team Alpha had already captured her sisters, Gwendolyn and Kerrie, though Bella proved to be the toughest to physically restrain. She would join her sun-resistant siblings, all turned by their father's bite like the Warwick kids, in the transport truck waiting in the front yard. Team Bravo stood at the bottom of the stairwell that led up to her tower, waiting for the Alphas to hand her off so they could secure her.

Delia did a quick sweep of the room. It shouldn't surprise her that Bella Donovan had a whole tower to herself, with a bedroom at the peak of the spire and several floors of parlors and TV rooms and bars below.

The Donovan estate could engulf the Grimm manor if it wanted. While Delia had seen pictures and blueprints of the place before the raid, they were nothing compared to the real thing. *This* was a palace. Situated at the top of a hill beyond the lake at the farthest reaches of Harriswood's city limits, surrounded by high stone walls and orchards, it was an impressive piece of architecture. Unfortunately, there wasn't much time to appreciate its gothic beauty. As soon as the transport vans had pulled up, it was *all teams go*. Wentworth had given the raiding squads two hours to complete the assignment—Kain insisted they could do it in half that time.

Teams Alpha and Bravo had headed for the rooms allotted to Shane Donovan's immediate family—their job was to acquire, capture, and restrain Shane and his girls, then bring them in for questioning. Team Charlie had gone for the humans. All the other teams were responsible for bringing in the lesser clansmen and subduing daytime security, while the Warwick vamps caught and killed anyone trying to escape through the underground tunnels.

It had been airtight and thus far executed perfectly.

Delia barely had time to think, much less feel the nerves that had made it difficult to sleep last night. She knew her role—shoot a non-fatal shot should the immediate family try to resist—and she was determined to follow through. So far, Team Alpha was a well-oiled machine of awesome.

"No word that Shane's been spotted in the tunnels," Kain remarked when the two hunters moving Bella returned. The others were searching the bedroom, Delia included. "There's a chance he's gone into his panic room, but if the codes Warwick's guys gave us are viable, that won't be a problem."

How did one woman have so many dresses? Delia's eyes wandered over the sea of flowy gowns, a rainbow of pastels and glittery fabric—and stopping suddenly when a few of the tulle extravaganzas moved.

Delia brought her gun up and took a step back. "Guys…"

The room fell silent, save for the loading and cocking and lifting of weaponry. Swallowing hard, Delia eased forward, adrenaline blurring out the obnoxious DANGER sign in her mind's eye, and slowly pushed a few of the gowns to one side.

"No!" It wasn't the cry of another Bella Donovan lookalike. No, it was the shriek of a girl—a little girl with blonde ringlets and fiercely blue eyes that made Delia immediately think of Claude. Thick milky tears rolled down her cheeks, round with lingering baby fat, smooth and white.

It was clear the second the sunlight hit her from the nearby windows that she was a Donovan offspring—all of Shane's were, like Claude, immune to the sunlight. But that didn't stop her from shrieking in terror.

"When the hell did he have another kid?" Gregory shouted over the noise.

"Get her," Kain ordered, and it took Delia a second to realize he was talking to her. Holstering her weapon, she moved inward to pick the girl up, but she scampered away in her little Care Bear pajamas, wailing.

"Shoot it and shut it up!"

But she couldn't. The hunter in her knew the little girl could actually be older than Delia—the vampirism disease slowed aging to a crawl, giving the illusion of immortality. Looking at her, however, Delia saw a blubbering five-year-old in cartoon pajamas. She couldn't *shoot* her.

"Come here," Delia said softly, arms outstretched. "It's okay. Nobody's going to hurt you."

"Stop it!" And just like that, the little girl was on her feet and racing for the door. She almost made it—until

Kain netted her. He'd been bragging about the newly issued net gun for most of their training—and seemed to get a sick thrill out of using the crossbow lookalike. Its shot emitted an obscene *crack* that made Delia's ears ring.

Capture didn't quiet the young vamp down, however. The crisscross of silver burned her face, legs, and arms, leaving bright red lacerations across skin that tried to heal on its own, only to be marred again as the girl struggled. And did she ever scream. As a pair of hunters closed in on her, she let out a high-pitched screech that reminded Delia of the one little Kyle had given at the grocery store when a bloody-faced vamp crawled toward him. Pure fear.

And Delia just stood there, watching as two grown men hoisted the silver net up with a squirming vamp child inside, numb. She turned away when the girl started calling for her mother between agonized screams, ones that echoed throughout the tower as she was hauled out of sight.

"Maybe Bella's kid?" one of the other hunters suggested. Delia, arms limp at her side, could feel him staring. "Why did you let her go? This is why women shouldn't be hunters. You get one crying kid and they go all maternal and shit—"

"Shut up, Travis," Kain growled.

Travis complied with a heavy sigh, then ducked down to look under the bed, presumably for more hidden children. Delia, meanwhile, pulled out her gun and examined it, her adrenaline fading, leaving her with an unsettling nothingness. When Kain said her name, she looked to him, but already knew what he was going to say well before he said it.

"Seriously Dels, what the actual fuck?" He shook his head when she opened and closed her mouth wordlessly. "You know how much flack I've taken for defending you to these guys, and then you go and do that?"

"Kain, I'm sorry, but she's a kid—"

"She isn't a kid though," he snapped as he buckled his

net gun to his hip and lifted his helmet's visor. Delia did the same, both their eyes narrowed when they met. "It was a vamp who could have probably put you through a window given the chance. She's a kid... Are you serious?"

"Kain—"

"But I guess I shouldn't have expected you to notice the difference anymore, between human and vamp, right?"

Travis glanced up slowly from his spot on the floor at the foot of the bed, then hastily went back to pushing through bedazzled boxes when both Delia and Kain fixed him with a glare.

"I'm sorry, what's that supposed to mean?" she demanded. The numbness had passed, leaving a simmering anger in its place, one that worsened when Kain scoffed.

"You know what it means." He rolled his eyes. "Look, we'll talk about it later."

"Probably with the High Council, right?" Delia gave a few hollow chuckles. "I mean, you broadcast my every move to them, so I guess that's where I'm headed."

"Any one of these guys could report you for what you did—"

"I made a mistake," she fired back, cheeks red. She'd fucked up and she knew it. No sense in denying it now, not with so many witnesses. "But I'm on Team Alpha *with* you, so why don't you treat me like I belong here?"

"Because you don't," Travis said, voice muffled from under the bed. Footsteps thundered up the stairwell at the return of the other hunters.

"You're here," Kain said slowly, as if trying to keep his voice even, "so I can make sure you don't die. I'm a team leader *and* a babysitter, and all because you staked a few vamps and got on the news. You're here because you've been given special treatment over hunters who have actually worked hard for years to move up the ranks."

Delia's jaw dropped before she could stop it. Only then did Kain's tone soften. Behind him, the other two hunters strolled in, not realizing what they were walking into. "Just keep your head down, Dels, and don't get in the way."

The silence was overwhelming. Delia's hands shook as she watched Kain lower his visor and instruct the others to do one final sweep of the room, walk-in closets included, before they moved on.

"Sorry to be such a burden," Delia managed, tucking her gun away.

"Room's clear," Travis muttered as the trio of non-bickering hunters headed for the door. "Can we press pause on this therapy session already? We've still got Shane Donovan to capture, or did you forget that?"

"I'm good to go," Delia said gruffly, pushing through and heading for the stairs. Halfway down, the quietest hunter of Team Alpha, Francis, met her eye fleetingly before moving in front of her to lead the group to Shane's purported panic room in the basement cellar.

Delia followed, red-faced and humiliated, and told herself not to break down until she was alone. Because this mission wasn't about her, even if had taken a brief detour in her direction. Because this mission was more important than her and her failings. And because she was determined to show that she could pull her weight, even if that meant staying out of the way until it was over.

CHAPTER 20: BOYS 2.0

"Congrats to you, Team Alpha," Arthur boomed as soon as Delia stepped into his accounting domain. Her cheeks flushed when a pair of hunters glanced at her on their way to the door, but once they were gone, there was no one left to judge her—or Arthur for his enthusiasm. The League accountant actually stood and gave a teeny bow as she approached, his grin stretching ear to ear.

It felt incredibly unnecessary, given her meager contribution to Team Alpha on the Donovan raid yesterday morning, but Delia let him have his moment. Anyone else who came by to collect their pay probably hadn't given him the time of day so far.

"You have to tell me all about it," he insisted as she leaned against the counter, arms crossed with a painfully fake smile on her lips. Arthur, ever her cheerleader.

"It was…" She let out a sigh and shrugged, watching as he counted her pay, this time in hundreds instead of twenties. When he looked up expectantly, Delia gave him the story she'd been telling all day. "Yeah, it was awesome. Everything I could have hoped for and more."

"I told you things were going to start looking up," he said brightly as he pressed the wad of bills into the money counter and pushed the count button. In seconds, twenty hundred-dollar bills whizzed through and into the tray at the bottom—the most money she'd ever seen at one time. Her bank account practically salivated at the thought of the deposit.

Delia nodded when Arthur beamed up at her, his wispy hair askew over his forehead, the usual pit stains glaringly apparent on his salmon-pink button-up tee. "Yup, you predicted it."

"Well, go on then," Arthur prompted. It seemed like he was holding her money hostage until he got the story he wanted. "Tell me everything."

"Right, uh…" Delia wished she could be more enthusiastic about it. "All the snow and ice melted by the time we arrived, so I didn't fall flat on my face the second I hopped out of the transport."

"Always a plus."

"Seriously."

Delia did her best to share all the highlights: she wove a story about capturing the notorious Donovan patriarch and his gaggle of bloodthirsty daughters, spicing up the details as best she could to satisfy Arthur's ceaseless curiosity. He was like a proud mom after their kindergartener went through their pointless graduation ceremony.

In actuality, the day had been a huge letdown after Kain gave her the talking-to in Bella's bedroom. Delia had done what she could to support the team, pointing her weapon at Shane Donovan and making her most intimidating glare while the others did all the work. It probably would have gone down the same whether she was there or not. The hunters assigned to the raid knew what they had been doing. They were a hardcore unit, moving as one in the face of the enemy. Delia had just been along for the ride.

The entire clan had been taken in, the coalition between the local police, the League, and the Warwick clan proving to be a successful one. There'd been two police casualties, one for the League, and none for the vamps in the tunnels. They'd finished the job in an hour and ten minutes, irking team leaders but impressing the High Council. Delia suspected the clan had been so easy to take in because they were attacked when the sun was at its highest—and they had actually been surprised. Had the Donovans been ready for an assault, perhaps the day would have had more serious hiccups. Instead, capturing a bunch of unprepared, sleeping vamps was hailed a brilliant success.

Scary Donovan clan was off the streets.

Police officers and League hunters had proved they had control of their city.

Warwick vamps had solidified a strong truce with local hunters.

And Delia had fallen asleep in the locker room. After returning from the raid, she'd showered and then fallen asleep and woken up much later on a bench between the rows of lockers, still miffed about the role she'd played. Too tired to walk home, she'd stayed in for-rent HQ dorms, eaten alone in the cafeteria—minus the occasional pat on the back from younger, clueless hunters—then had gone to collect her pay shortly after Arthur started his shift. By then, she was ready to go home and call Claude about her decision.

It was time to officially re-evaluate her position at the League. Not contemplate it. Not hem and haw and dance around it. Maybe this, maybe that. No. The revelations made during the raid had clarified things for good.

She'd already missed her shot to do better. No one who mattered could see beyond her shortcomings—and that wasn't an environment she wanted to be in for much longer. Maybe she would ask for a transfer, or try her hand at a different department. Maybe she'd quit, though where was she supposed to go from there? It wasn't like she could take a corporate gig with *vampire hunter* on her résumé. If someone outside of her world asked her what she'd been doing between the retail nightmares of her teens and the last five years, what was there to say?

What did she even *want* to do outside of vampire hunting?

Delia still wasn't sure the exact path to trod, but this one wasn't making her happy like it used to. Even if it gave her a unique purpose in the world, was that enough of a reason to sacrifice her mental and physical health?

Did it make her a quitter to walk away?

Delia hadn't decided yet. All she knew was that she was more than a little sick of being put down for trying—and tired of feeling guilty if she didn't.

"I can't believe you looked the Donovan daughters in the face," Arthur said with an overly dramatic shiver. "Those pictures of them in the break room give me the willies."

Delia laughed. "You mean you actually use the break room? Don't they have you chained to this desk from the time you start to the time your shift is over?"

"Sometimes I wiggle loose," he told her, finally sliding over the white envelope. She hastily stuffed it in her purse—it was more money than she was comfortable carrying in public. Still, with her winter coat hanging over her arm and yesterday's outfit clinging to her body, she needed to get some cold, fresh air soon. HQ was starting to feel claustrophobic.

"So, you going to that big party thing at the end of the week?" Arthur asked as she started to slip her coat on.

Delia frowned, tugging her hair out from under the cuff. "The what?"

"Party," he repeated somewhat unsurely with a nod toward his computer. "They sent an email about it this morning."

"Haven't checked mine yet."

"It's to celebrate the raid, I guess," he told her, cheeks going a faint shade of pink. The colour spread brightly to the tips of his ears when she grinned. "Everyone's invited, hunters *and* support staff. Seems like…kind of a staff party."

"Oh. Right." It would have excited her a few months ago, but now the thought of coming back to live it up with her coworkers… It made her feel nothing. Delia could see Arthur, Ali, and Devin, plus any casual acquaintances, outside of work if she left. Still, the hopeful look on Arthur's face broke through the nothingness. She was probably one of the few people he'd ask about going; Delia suddenly had the strange urge not to disappoint him. "Sure. Sounds fun. It'll be nice not to have to cab home if I get too drunk."

"Yeah, okay, great," he said, his voice catching. She grinned again as he cleared his throat. "Should be a good time."

"Definitely." The more the idea ruminated around in her head, however, the more she suspected she'd probably bail—but she'd tell Arthur first, of course. Delia just needed the space to get some perspective on things, and drunken partying with the few people who made her work-life enjoyable wasn't the best way to go about it.

As a new group of hunters arrived, Delia said her farewells and headed for the door, bypassing the ones who congratulated her on the mission with nothing more than a friendly smile. A stabbing sort of headache was starting to develop behind her eyes—the sooner she got out of HQ, the better.

Unfortunately, her departure would be delayed by at least a few minutes. With a hand pressed to her forehead, eyes clenched closed, Delia accidentally hit the wrong floor button, and rather than going up, the elevator shot down to a level she'd never visited—holding cells. Even if she and a team of other hunters brought in a vamp for questioning, Delia was never the one to do it.

Huffing irritably, she punched at the correct button as the doors started to open—and petrified screaming blasted into the elevator the second they were an inch apart, growing louder as they opened completely. Delia's hand hovered over the *close door* button. They were the same screams from her nightmares.

Bella's daughter—the little girl they'd found in the

Donovan heiress's room. Her wails for her mother had haunted Delia's dreams from the second she slipped into them until the moment she bolted upright that morning, sweaty, panting, and exhausted.

She should have pushed the button and left it at that. Instead, Delia slipped between the doors as they started to close. Seconds later the rotating gears signaled the elevator's ascent, leaving her alone in an empty hallway. The light flickered overhead, casting shadows over the barren walls and the linoleum tiles. The décor was on par with Arthur's floor—nothing—but the screaming gave it an extra touch of depressing.

But then again, Arthur would probably scream all day too if he could.

Sweeping her hair behind her ear, catching a whiff of the HQ-provided lavender shampoo she'd used in the process, Delia ventured forward. No cameras in this hall, nor the next, when she rounded the corner and faced a long, dimly lit corridor with a row of wide metallic doors on each side. It was like being in a funhouse where the mirrors gave the illusion that a hallway went on forever—only this one actually did.

And standing in front of one of the doors was the last person she had any interest in seeing, let alone speaking to.

Kain's head snapped in her direction as soon as she stepped around the corner, and his hands dropped slowly to his side from their clasped position behind his back. His stern glare shifted to something more recognizable, and they stood there, staring at one another, as the screaming carried on. Finally, Delia gathered her nerve and pressed onward, but Kain met her before she reached the door. The shrieking stopped briefly when they met, only to resume when Delia glanced toward the spot he'd been guarding.

"What are you doing here, Dels?" he asked, sounding more tired than anything. If she wasn't mistaken, he too was wearing the outfit he'd worn to the raid—only, unlike her, he didn't look as though he'd had the luxury of a shower or much sleep.

"Hit the wrong button on the elevator," she said distantly, her brow creasing into a frown. "What's... Who's screaming?"

"Who d'you think?"

She met his stare evenly, in no mood for another patronizing lecture. "It was a rhetorical question."

"Go home," he muttered after rubbing at his eyes and sighing. "Get some sleep."

What appeared to be crusted blood under his short fingernails held her attention.

"Why are you here?" she asked.

"Guarding the door," Kain remarked, then grinned, "and telling nosy fuckers to go home and sleep while they can." She didn't return the smile, and within seconds his own faded. "Dels, look... I'm sorry for what I said yesterday in front of the boys. It was uncalled-for."

She pressed her lips together tightly before muttering, "Was it?"

"Yes."

"Or was it something you've wanted to say for a while now?"

"It's not..." He looked away, agitated. "Look, we get on, you and I. I care about you, but my personal and professional feelings are separate, and worlds apart, if I'm being honest. I was the team leader, but I said what I thought I needed to say without thinking. I'm sorry if it hurt your feelings."

Her grip on her purse strap tightened. "Okay."

Behind Kain, the screams were at a zenith, sounding more and more like words now. *No. Stop. Please stop.* It all sounded like the pleas of a single person, a woman—a Donovan daughter, probably. Her eyes drifted to the door again, wondering if she'd hear the cries in her dreams tonight too. They were nothing like the sniveling of a homeless dirtbag vamp she and a few other hunters had bagged somewhere downtown and were bringing in for questioning. These cries were those of real pain—real fear.

And they affected her more than they should.

Shaking her head, Delia hurried for the elevators. Kain's footsteps didn't follow.

"Where are you going?" he called when she was nearly at the end of the hall, elevators around the corner.

"Home," she said without looking back. "To sleep. Like you told me to."

He cursed softly, the word floating down the hall in a ghostly echo, but when Delia spared him a quick glance, she found herself looking at his back, his hands shoved into his pockets. She stood there, unsure, before carrying on and jabbing at the elevator button.

Her retreat from League headquarters through the library was a blur, one that her phone's shrill bleating snapped her out of once she was on the stairs—the stairs where the Donovans had strung up the rats only a few months earlier. Flustered, a flushed Delia dug through her purse, struggling briefly before finding her phone at the bottom of all the junk she carted around in that particular bag.

Claude. The mere sight of his name brought a relief she'd never thought possible.

"Hey," she said, lower lip wobbling, the tears evident in her voice. "How's it—"

"Delia," Claude said curtly, "were you part of the assault on the Donovan estate? Was that the big assignment you told me about?"

She wiped under her nose and headed for one of the pillars on the library front steps. It took her a few long seconds to process what he'd said, the odd feeling of worlds colliding knocking the wind out of her.

"Sorry, what?" was the best she could do.

"The Donovan takedown," he repeated. Something was wrong. This wasn't the tone of the Claude she knew— this was the frustrated Claude of whom she'd only caught glimpses. "Were you a part of that?"

"I…" A chilly blast of air wormed under her jacket, and she held the phone to her ear with her shoulder as she zipped it up. "Yeah, they put me on it. I didn't know until recently it was because I'd made the news and some higher-ups thought it'd be good to include me—"

"Do you have any idea what you've all done?" He exhaled noisily in tandem with the sound of a car door slamming shut.

"What are you talking about?"

"Delia, are you at the League now?"

"Just leaving—"

"Under no circumstances should you interact with any vampire your High Council has seen fit to work with. Do you understand?"

"What? No, Claude…" She hurried down the steps and merged into the usual mid-morning downtown foot traffic. "Where are you? I'm coming to your place—"

"Don't," he told her. "I won't be there. Go home. Wait for me to call you."

"Claude—"

"Please tell me you weren't a part of this. That you didn't know."

Delia stopped amidst the sea of pedestrians, the headache that had started in the accounting wing threatening to explode into a full-blown migraine. "What are you *talking* about? We apprehended a clan who was butchering people, vamps *and* humans, in case you've forgotten."

He was quiet for so long that she thought he'd hung up on her. After checking, she said his name once more, her cheeks wind-kissed.

"Go home, Delia," he said, softer this time. "Don't let anyone in until you hear from me."

"But—"

"Even if you think you know them," Claude added sharply. "Lock the doors and keep your phone on you. Do you understand?"

"Can you just tell me what the fuck is happening right now? Claude, you—"

"Please trust me," he urged. "Can you do that?"

"I trust you to tell me what the hell this phone call is about the next time you call," she said tightly as she started walking again, this time in the direction of her apartment. She moved with purpose, easily gliding around the slower walkers in front of her. "But I'll do it. Just don't keep me in the dark."

A hypocritical request, she realized.

"I'll do my best," Claude told her. "Now hurry home and lock the door."

And with that, the line went dead.

*   *   *

The ringing in his ears continued long after the wailing stopped. Kain stood there, like he'd been told, because he was a good soldier. He followed orders. He looked to his superiors for guidance. Hunting was the only thing in his life he hadn't shot straight to hell. It was his mission, his purpose.

The fact that he felt like complete shit right now was probably because he hadn't slept in twenty-plus hours— not because he'd listened to the torture of a vamp who reminded him of his little sister.

They'd been switching them out all day and all night, the Donovan family. First Shane, then Bella, then the next in line. Kain watched each one go in. He listened to their defiance—and then he tuned out their screams. There was no delighting in torture. There was only the celebration of a victory when all was said and done. This was a victory, just not the kind the other hunters thought. Only a few knew what the decimation of the Donovan clan meant for the big picture. And Kain was one of them.

Kain would survive this.

Because he knew how to obey. How to fight. How to be an asset, a weapon.

He wasn't sure how long he'd been standing there. His phone had died a few hours ago. Delia had been the only one down to this level since the interrogation had started. He had no point of reference. But still Kain stood there, hands clasped behind his back, staring straight ahead, and waited for it to be over.

And it was. In a hail of gunfire and screams, it was finally over.

He stepped aside when the door behind him unbolted. Out came the High Council, Don Wentworth at the helm with Johnathon Warwick at his side. Viscous brown blood-splatter painted their faces, their hands, and the stakes gripped within them.

"Now, do be so kind as to show my son and daughter the armory again before they leave," Warwick insisted, patting Wentworth's cheek with a barbed smile. Kain's insides turned at the sight, but he kept his features expressionless. "I'd do it myself, but I'm afraid I have a monarchy to dismantle, a king to crush, all that."

"Of course," Wentworth replied with a slight nod. "Be in touch when you're through."

There was a flash of something across Warwick's face—annoyance, maybe. But it was gone before Kain could get a better look, replaced once more by the vamp's shark-like smile.

"Talk soon, Donny boy," the vamp mused. His bloodshot eyes swept up and down the cluster of High Council members, as if appraising livestock, then darted briefly to Kain. That unnerving smile grew for a moment before he stalked down the hall, footsteps echoing in his wake.

"Tidy the chamber," Wentworth ordered Kain with a nod toward the room. "Burn the remains."

The reply was automatic by now. It had been for years. "Yes, sir."

Stepping into the interrogation room, Kain was hit with the rank scent of death. Six bloody bodies lay against the wall, brownish blood smeared behind them where they'd been shot. It reminded him of the photos he'd seen of the old Russian monarchy—Tsar Nicholas Romanov and his family. Gunned down. Brutalized. What the hell had Shane Donovan done to Johnathon Warwick to warrant such a merciless death? Kain didn't need to know. All he needed to know was that it was time to clean up the mess.

After moving the brutalized bodies into a single pile, he hurried out of the room. Through the empty corridor he went, off to find the necessary supplies to sweep the murder of a clan leader and his family under the rug.

At least these ones would be burned *after* they'd been staked; Kain couldn't say the same for the rest of the vamps in the clan. Good thing the incinerator was soundproof. There were more than a few hunters who wouldn't be able to stomach the screams.

Those were the ones who wouldn't make it to Christmas.

And he wouldn't mourn for them—he couldn't. This was natural selection at its finest.

*   *   *

The last time Claude Grimm had been forced to deal with a crisis as king of the Harriswood vampire clans was… Well, in the near three hundred years he'd been living in the area, never. He had heard the stories from other kings around the country: clans squabbling, rogue vampires swooping in to usurp the monarch, discovery by the general populace that real vampires were in their midst.

Harriswood had had a brief brush with the latter, but the human political and law enforcement beast had a brilliant PR team to keep the story from sticking. They spun it and spun it and spun it until the Safe Choice grocery incident was no more than a common robbery, and his darling Delia a woman with an unquenchable thirst to survive a bad situation.

In his opinion, he'd had a pretty easy go of things as elected ruler. For the most part, the other clans had listened to the edicts he set. Rules were generally followed—it was the best he could hope for, given the brutal nature of his subjects. Hunter leagues were created to maintain order amongst unruly American vampires, so detached from the old European ways that they required a *little* extra monitoring to keep the peace.

Unfortunately, the fact that he hadn't ever needed to assert his authority may have been the cause of all this. He had too much faith in the clan leaders. He had always preferred a hands-off approach, hoping that these vampires, all well into their first or second century of existence, could handle disputes like adults.

Apparently he was mistaken. Apparently he had a band of unruly children in his kingdom instead.

"*Are you sure you don't want me to come in with you?*" Elov posed the question in Swiss German to keep their hired driver from understanding. They'd traveled from the estate to Jimmie's Place in relative silence, nothing but the unobtrusive classical music tinkling from the radio to break the tension. Claude's gaze shifted from the back of the driver's seat to Elov, his closest confidant and oldest friend; Claude had turned the man himself centuries ago, sharing with him his ability to walk in the daylight. Where would he be now without him? Bookkeeper, spy, clan liaison, historian—Elov wore many hats, almost as many as Claude.

"*It will set a better precedent if I go alone,*" Claude remarked, falling back to his mother-tongue with ease. "*Show them that I don't need the numbers to put them in their place.*"

Them. Claude suspected it was only one clansman who needed to be put in his place.

Funny. After all this time, he'd always thought Shane Donovan would give him the biggest headache. The

Irishman had been a pesky thorn in his side for years. As the head of the largest regional clan, his people were all over the place. His daughters made headlines for all the wrong reasons. He was purposefully disrespectful whenever he and Claude were in the same room together. If anyone was going to drag Claude out of the easy comfort of his day-to-day living, he'd always expected it to be a Donovan.

Instead, he had been summoned by Johnathon Warwick—of all people—for a meeting with the clan leaders. Johnathon Warwick, leader of the smallest Harriswood clan. Johnathon Warwick, who raced greyhounds and invited Claude to high tea at least once a month and showed his prized tulips at flower shows every spring. Johnathon *fucking* Warwick.

The vampire had sent an envoy to Claude's door yesterday, hours after word reached him that the League had arrested the entirety of the Donovan clan—an absurd and most certainly *illegal* act—with the message that the king's presence was required at a meeting with all the local clan leaders the following afternoon at their usual place. The way the message had been worded left Claude thinking that somehow there would be severe consequences should he not heed the summons.

The fact that the clan leaders had the sheer *gall* to threaten their *king*…

Something was wrong. Something had felt wrong for a few months now, but he had hoped the others could work it out amongst themselves without needing a king's intervention.

Clearly he had miscalculated.

"*I can be there in an instant,*" Elov reminded him as the driver pulled into the back lot of the bar.

"*I'm not worried,*" Claude said, though the look his old friend gave him suggested Elov was harder to fool than the rest of the Grimm clan's advisors. He cleared his throat. "*For my physical safety, anyway.*"

"No, that's something for me to worry about, highness."

"Keep the car running," Claude said to the driver in English, placing a gentle hand on the human's shoulder. "This won't take long."

Their eyes met briefly in the mirror, Claude's bright blues holding the muddled hazel gaze. "Yes sir."

"Good." He climbed out of the town car's backseat with ease, smoothing a hand down the front of his pressed jacket. He'd opted for red, a visual reminder for the vampires in attendance of the title he bore, paired smartly with a crisp white dress shirt and a pair of grey slacks. The sun glinted off his shoes—all he needed was his crown. It hadn't seen the outside of its carrying case since the night it was given to him, but perhaps it could have served a purpose now.

"Let me at least sweep the area before you go in," Elov requested from the other side of the car. His door slammed shut in tandem with Claude's, mouth fixing into a thin, exasperated line when the king waved him off.

"Stay," Claude ordered, tapping the car's roof before heading for the bar's back door, thick chunks of de-icing salt crunching underfoot. Elov did as he was told— undoubtedly with much tooth-gnashing and knuckle-cracking. He shot the blond vampire a grin before yanking the door open and slipping inside.

Jimmie's Place, known in certain circles as the it-place to drink for vampire hunters—and the local clan leaders had chosen it for team huddles long ago for that very reason. Who would think to check upstairs while having a pint? Still, Claude would have preferred something a little better maintained. As soon as he stepped inside, the scent of cheap draft beer pummeled him even harder than ever, and the floors looked noticeably sticky. Old photographs lined the walls, years of dead hunters immortalized.

With a quick glance down the back hall, past the bathroom doors and the dusty ATM, Claude fixed his jacket and hair once more before grasping the railing and

282

jogging up the familiar rickety wooden staircase. Second floor, private lounge room—third door on the right. It was unnervingly silent as he approached, overhead lights twitching in and out of brightness. His title gave him a reason to be confident, but he wasn't naïve. Should he need to pull someone's head from their shoulders to make a point, Claude would do it.

It seemed he was the last to arrive. Once inside, he found himself faced with a sea of clan leaders, all of them seated on one side of the usual long wooden table. Half-full glasses of blood sat before them, and their whispered conversations died as soon as he shut the door, though the air was thick with words unsaid. Claude's jaw clenched as he surveyed the scene before him, each and every alarm bell going off in his head. There was only a single chair on his side of the table. Not his usual one at the head. Just one in the middle, directly across from Johnathon Warwick. The rest were stacked in the corners.

Franklin Belmont sat on Warwick's right. Alaric Hewitt on his left. Enrique Reyes stood behind the chair at Belmont's side. And then there was an unfamiliar face. Not totally foreign to him; it was Mercy Sorrows, sole female head of a very small clan allied with the Warwicks—if one could consider six members a clan. Well, five now: the vampire who'd been found beheaded and staked downtown this last summer, Donovan markings on his body, had belonged to the Sorrows clan.

"All hail the king," Warwick crooned. Five glasses were raised, but no one drank to his honor. Claude would have preferred to stand, but when Warwick gestured to the lone chair across from him, he obliged.

He could humor this game for now.

No one spoke for a long moment, the others swirling their glasses and fiddling with their nails. Only Warwick looked him in the eye.

"What have you done to Shane Donovan?" Claude asked, his tone conversational but his gaze hard—and his question met with silence. He folded his hands together and set them on the tabletop, head cocked to the side as he waited. Children. He was dealing with children.

"Shouldn't you be asking the *League* what they've done with him?" Mercy Sorrows piped up finally. Claude's pinned her with a look that made her lower lip quiver. The brunette sat up tall, her plum-purple mouth parting slightly as she drew a breath. "They're the ones who have him in custody, as far as I'm aware."

She was a skinny thing, her collarbones prominent and her cheekbones high. This was the longest conversation they'd ever had, and Claude hadn't yet said two words to her.

"Do not make me ask again," he said coolly, shifting his attention back to Warwick. If there was a mastermind in the room, Johnathon Warwick held the title; that much was clear by the way he held himself, effortlessly relaxed while the other clan leaders squirmed in the presence of their king. Warwick and Sorrows looked like they could be siblings, both angular and slim—easily snapped with enough pressure.

"We dealt with our opposition," Warwick announced finally.

Claude watched the other leaders break out into knowing smiles. He let out a long sigh. The game had become tiresome.

"Opposition to what?" he asked.

"Why, to the future," was the response he didn't want to hear. He pressed his palms flat to the table to keep them from curling into fists.

"Listen to me quite clearly." Claude leaned forward, his voice low. Kings who shouted were kings no one took seriously. "I have given you all an incredibly long leash over the years, but I will not stand for this—"

"You see, no one *cares* what you will or won't stand for," Warwick interjected, sounding bored. He shrugged when Claude's eyes narrowed, then took a quick sip of his drink. "We outnumber you. With the Donovan clan subdued, we, a unified whole, are the largest clan in the region, and we're going to move forward whether you agree or not."

"I am your *king*," Claude hissed, each word tight, simmering with barely restrained anger. "I am—"

"So behind on the times, I'm afraid." Warwick exchanged a look with Reyes, both of them smirking. "The Americans had the right idea… Shirk the English king, create a place to call home. Their rules. Their laws. With no one using them for their own purposes. That is the future we foresee, and in it, we are all equals."

Claude's eyes darted from face to face incredulously. There were many hidden truths between him and his subjects, that much was obvious, but Warwick's professed equality was a lie that the others seemed to have swallowed.

"There's going to be a new world order in the coming days," Warwick remarked, his eyes glinting with a kind of malice Claude was unaccustomed to associating with him. "It's very simple. Those who aren't with us are against us. It's been a long time coming with vampire colonies across this nation. You'll find that clans like Donovan's are in the minority."

"I don't believe you."

"Believe what you like," Warwick said, purposefully omitting Claude's title. They had always addressed him as *highness*, even in informal settings. "I don't really care, honestly, nor do my companions. All that matters is where you plan to place your loyalty in our new world."

Claude leaned back in his chair, disgusted. "What new world?"

"Isn't it obvious?" Reyes asked, all whispery hisses and cruel undertones. "A world where we must no longer hide ourselves. A world where we, vampire, the genetically superior species, can finally claim what is owed to us."

Claude's stomach roiled. Vampires seldom felt sickness,

yet its presence was always extra potent when it reared its ugly head. Claude swallowed hard and said the only thing he could think of in the face of such recklessness.

"This is insanity."

What a fool he had been. Shane Donovan had tried to warn him—months ago, in fact. Something was afoot in their city, but neither could put their finger on it. Claude's distrust in the vampire ran deep, hardened by years of misconduct and disrespect. He'd almost been pleased to see such a mighty leader fall on hard times, hoping it would teach him humility, and that it would curb Claude's suspicions that a Donovan-born vampire was always out to take his crown, one way or another.

When Shane had come to him, no more than a month after the masquerade and the body of the first dead vampire was found, Claude had insisted he handle the mounting problems surrounding his family name by himself. After all, at the time it had seemed strictly a clan issue. Punish the misbehaving Donovan vampires and be done with it—because if Claude had to step in and quiet the law-breakers, the Donovan clan would be getting a new name and a new leader.

Claude should have believed in him. He should have lent his support, done a little digging on the issue, rather than letting his personal prejudices guide him. Besides, what had he been doing in the meantime that had kept him so busy? Going to business lunches? Meeting with entrepreneurs hoping he'd invest in one thing or another? Blood bank negotiations? Pursuing Delia?

Meanwhile, all around him, deceit had eroded his once peaceful city. And he'd let it happen, too blinded by his distrust in Donovan and too distracted with his love life to notice.

He should have done his duty. Claude should have been a king.

His hands finally curled to fists, nails biting into his palms. When he caught the flash of Warwick's smile,

Claude eased out a strained breath and forced his hands to relax.

"I have heard this story a thousand times over," he mused, lifting his gaze to meet the treacherous vampire across from him. "Revolutionaries plan to burn the whole world and then rule its ashes. It will never work. The world's too big, Johnathon."

A faint ripple of alarm passed through the line of clan leaders, starting at one end and working its way to the other. Claude hoped the message might have sunk, but there was Johnathon Warwick leering at him like a man who had already won the war.

"It is unfortunate you are of that opinion, Claude," the bony vampire said with a heavy sigh, as if it truly, *truly* bothered him. "I'd hoped your little hunter pet might have perished by Donovan hand when I assigned her to the raid. Had it been so, I'd like to believe your loyalty to the cause would have been absolute."

"Strange." Claude rolled his shoulders back as he observed the vampire. "Have I done something to make you think that I would be so short-sighted?"

He'd wanted to see Claude prickle at the mention of Delia—at the thought of her being used to sway him. While it certainly made the ache in his gut worse, his expression remained unchanged. Love was a weakness Claude had willingly adopted once he decided to pursue her. Lesser men would think the best way to hurt him was to hurt her. It was only natural.

And now that he knew who the real enemy was, he knew how to protect her. The League was compromised—that much was clear.

"Well, you seem to lack your usual judgement and reasoning when it comes to a Miss Delia Roberts," Warwick countered, his smile grown sickening. "After all, I've had the League High Council use her to spy on you for *months*..."

Claude withheld what was bound to be a humorless

laugh. Delia was many things in his eyes, some deliciously wonderful and others an acquired taste, but a master of espionage she was not. It had been quite apparent from their first date that someone had been feeding her questions to ask him. Thankfully those had popped up less and less as time passed, disappearing altogether at one point, allowing them to grow more comfortable with one another without her job interfering.

Claude didn't hold it against her. He had known what he was in for when he chose to pursue a huntress. Still, he wondered when exactly she planned to share with him what he already knew.

"Fight by our side," Warwick continued as he reached forward across the table, a hand outstretched. A mockery of an olive branch. His lip twitched. If Claude had had a knife, he'd stab it right through Warwick's palm. "Join us. Become a master of the new world—"

"This new world will bring about the annihilation of our kind," Claude said tersely. "Humans still outnumber us. Why do you think the ancient houses keep to themselves? They know the cost of exposure. Vampire is a term still feared in popular culture—"

"The *ancient houses* in Europe are fossils," Warwick spat, retracting his hand. "They are no longer models of existence for a modern-day vampire to follow. Stop living in the past, Claude."

"The human population will not stand to become cattle, or whatever you envision them in this *new world*—"

"Many humans have embraced our model," Warwick said, sneering. "Senators, governors, police commissioners, High Councils… They bring their sheep into the fold at our command. We offer wealth and influence to mankind as well. We have *use* for them."

"This is madness."

"This is the *future*." Warwick brought his hand down on the table solidly, making Mercy Sorrows jump. He then pointed an accusatory finger at Claude, who briefly entertained the idea of snapping it in half. "We give you a choice, then. Bring the Grimm clan in line, or we wipe it out." Claude's jaw clenched. "Look to the smoke rising from the Harriswood Library chimneys and know that as we speak, the Donovan clan is being erased from the history books. Make no mistake, the Grimm clan is not a house of warriors. You're intellectuals. Modern-day men and women who simply *exist*. We wouldn't need an elaborate scheme to trick the hunters into sanctioning you. We will just show up in the middle of the day and set your home aflame."

Claude stood, chair legs scraping across the floor. "I will not stand for this, Warwick."

"Haven't you been listening?" The vampire rose slowly, fingertips resting on the table's edge. "It doesn't *matter* what you will stand for. It's over. Your kingship is done. We free ourselves from the grip of a monarchy—"

"For an oppressive oligarchy, I can only assume."

"—and we give you a choice. Bring your clan into this fight, or face the consequences of your refusal."

The silence was suffocating. Claude would never join such a foolhardy errand, but he refused to put his clan at risk. These were his people, some born again from his bite, others flocking to him for security. They had given him centuries of ceaseless loyalty and support, companionship and love.

"Shane Donovan shared your same objections when he and I spoke at the masque ball," Warwick remarked casually. "Now he and his children are dead."

"I will need time to discuss this with my advisors." Not a single one would go for this vampires-rule-the-world scheme, but he could use their guidance to navigate the thin ice before him at any rate. "Give me a week to respond." His eyes met Warwick's unflinchingly. "I believe I am owed that much."

A week left him no time to call in favours from his allies overseas, nor would he be able to bring in enough continental muscle if other American kings were onboard with the scheme. Still, he had to explore all his options—and get as many of his people to safety as possible.

"One week, Grimm," Warwick agreed, flashing a hint of fang as he did. A clear sign of aggression. Claude's lips twitched again, wanting to return the gesture. "We'll be waiting... and watching."

He didn't need to hear anything else. Claude left the room without another word.

There were so many who relied on him for protection. He needed to get them out of Harriswood—yesterday. Delia too. A world where vamps ran rampant wasn't a safe one for a hunter, even if she had grown lukewarm to the profession. Their previous phone call must have left her wanting to know the truth, but he would need to keep her in the dark for now, for her own safety.

While he'd kept his cool when Warwick threatened her life, Claude wasn't sure what he would do if something actually happened to her.

But he knew it would be foolish.

Claude thundered down the wood stairwell and headed for the bar's back door. In its window, he caught the reflection of his red jacket, meant to mirror the velvety red cape of kings in an era gone by. The colour looked cheap on him. And why shouldn't it? Claude Grimm was a kingly fraud.

His people were owed more than a fraud. As he pushed through and headed for the awaiting car, which Elov leaned against with a smoke in hand, Claude vowed to do what was best for the people he loved most in this world, a certain huntress among them.

Even if it meant he had to run.

CHAPTER 21: YULETIDE LETDOWN

"This is the best champagne I've *ever* had..." Delia swirled the sparkling liquid around in a slim flute, the motion taking her back to the masquerade, then downed it in a single gulp. Claude's deep chuckle reverberated along her skin, his lips pressed to the crux of her neck and shoulder. Warmth coursed across her body as the alcohol trickled through her, cool in its descent down her throat yet bringing out a heat deeper within. It was especially potent where Claude touched her, mouth to her bare skin and hand spread wide and flat over the boning of the black, corseted back of her strapless dress.

Stupidly expensive, the dress fit like a glove around her waist, pushing and lifting her chest to support cleavage she seldom had. The lower half ballooned out, yet the front stopped at her knees while the back trailed down past her feet—like a mullet, Delia had offhandedly remarked when the shop assistant first showed it to her. It was the last garment she tried, pushing it aside in favor of the others. But this was the one. Like the vampire king touching her, caressing her, kissing her neck, the dress had waited patiently on the sidelines until she was ready to be claimed. Paired with comfortable red heels and ruby red lips, plus some thigh-high sheer black stockings, the whole get-up made her feel like a million bucks.

"Would you like another one?" Claude's words were like a purr, seductive and soft, uttered in her ear as if to share a filthy secret. Delia crumpled against him with a giggle, bringing her hand up to cup his face, cheeks stained in a permanent blush from both the king and the champagne.

"No," she murmured as she tipped her head back across his shoulder, neck on display in a room of vamps. "You... I'd like *you*."

He hissed against her skin. "Intoxicated minx."

She wasn't—not really. At least, not from her several glasses of bubbly. No, Delia was drunk on him, on the night, on the atmosphere of the most elegant, elaborate party she'd ever been to. After hearing only sporadically from Claude for a few days, she had arrived at the Grimm Winter Gala a bundle of nerves—and went straight for the alcohol to soothe away the jitters.

An unnecessary tactic, she had soon realized, when Claude swept her up in his arms and kissed her in front of his entire clan, vamps and their human companions alike.

"We'll talk later," he'd rumbled in her ear when she started her line of questioning—what was up with that phone call, why hadn't he been as reachable as usual, why throw a lavish party and *insist* she attend? It took place the same night as the hunter shindig at HQ, which Delia had no plans of attending anyway. Arthur had seemed mildly disappointed, but insisted there was a Star Wars marathon he could watch on TV instead. He'd brightened considerably when she asked him out for dinner the following night to make up for her bailing on the hunter party.

Because, in her week away from League duties, her work schedule empty, Delia had decided what she was going to do with her life.

Well, she had a vague idea of what she was going to do with the next six months of it, anyway.

She was done with the League—or, at least, *this* League. Her resignation letter sat on her laptop, drafted ten times over the course of the week, and she'd been using the resources at HQ to read up on other Leagues around the country. She considered transferring—locations and departments—but first things first: Delia knew she needed a break from work to really clear her head. She'd done what the High Council had asked of her, for the most part, and she needed time to reassess her life goals. Her drive to climb the hunter ranks wasn't as strong as it once was, and she had Claude to thank for that. He'd shown her that life wasn't a straight line, but rather twists and turns and loops—and that was okay.

It was time to breathe again, to find herself. And she couldn't do that while working for the Harriswood League. Too many bad memories. Too many uncomfortable feelings. So, first thing Monday, she planned to print her resignation letter and hand it in to HR.

But she needed the weekend to find her courage.

And she needed Claude to help her manage the potential fallout.

The party helped her forget. Claude's hands on her body, roving and touching and grasping, *definitely* helped her forget. Tomorrow would be a time to talk, for her to press him about his reaction to the Donovan capture, to explain her career decisions, and to ask for support in the days to come—if he wanted to give it.

For now, Delia planned to enjoy the way she looked in her dress, with her hair a shiny brown sea of controlled waves and her eyeshadow perfectly natural to offset such a bright lip. She would bask in the ambiance of a true yule gala, with its decorated dining hall, velvety red and green and gold as far as the eye could see; with its floor-to-ceiling Christmas tree, decked to the nines and glittering with lights; and its exuberant guests, vamp faces alight with mirth, human cheeks pink with intoxication.

And most importantly of all, Delia planned to lose herself in Claude, in the man she'd denied herself for too long already.

"Come on." Delia wrapped both hands around his

wrist and tugged him toward the huge door at the far side of the hall, weaving around clusters of partygoers. The most elaborate garland she had ever seen outlined the arched doorway, with red baubles and gold tinsel and velvety purple ribbons threaded throughout. She'd admired it when she first arrived, escorted into the hall by the same tall blond vamp who'd walked her up to Claude's study the night of the hunter camping trip. Elov, apparently Claude's right-hand guy, had been much friendlier this time around.

As she pulled the vampire king through the corridors, her champagne-addled brain having only a vague idea where she was headed, her heart thrummed rapidly against her ribcage and her smile made her cheeks ache. This was where she wanted to be. Only Claude coaxed out this side of her—this willfully happy side, untouched by sarcasm and snark.

After teetering up a set of narrow stairs, they found themselves in a dark and empty hallway, still close enough to the gala that the muffled music and chatter made the walls hum. Delia turned on her unsteady heels and dragged him into a kiss.

Dragged—the word implied she had to encourage him to touch her. Rather, Claude all but pounced, his fingers threading through her bouncy brown waves as his other arm yanked her close.

"Do we have a time limit here?" Delia asked with a giggle as soon as Claude's lips left hers and pressed heatedly down her throat. "Are you, I dunno, *expected* to make an appearance or anything?"

"My absence will be noted," was his muffled reply, and she let her head fall back with a breathy moan when he nipped at the shell of her ear. Suddenly her back was against the wall, his hands and mouth everywhere, her stance widening instinctively so he could nestle between her thighs.

Even though she was eager to show off how

phenomenal her thigh-high stockings made her legs look, especially paired with the heels, Delia had something else in mind. As much as it pained her to even *think* about wriggling loose from Claude's skilled hands, she did so with surprising finesse. Grinning, Delia gripped the front of his black dinner jacket, then pulled and pushed and positioned them so that they were reversed—he against the wall and she bearing down upon him. Surprise flashed across his vibrant blues, but it was hastily replaced by dark desire.

"Well, if you need to get back to your people," she whispered, fingers dropping to his belt, "I'll be sure to be quick."

His lips shifted into a sinfully handsome smirk. "Delia, what…?"

She answered his unsaid query by dropping to her knees and making quick work of his pants, not once stumbling over the buckle or getting caught up with the button or the zipper. Considering the glasses of champagne circulating her system, it was a noteworthy accomplishment.

Delia found him almost ready for her as she pushed the cumbersome fabric down, letting it all rest on his muscular thighs—which quivered at her tentative touch. The slightest twitch of his skin, wonderfully warm and scattered with dark hair, sent a throb of need straight to her core.

When his fingers curved beneath her chin, their slight pressure encouraging her to look up, Delia obliged with a mere flick of her eyes, her mascara-laden lashes poking the skin beneath her eyebrows. Claude inhaled sharply, his jawline seeming tight. The control she had, the power she exercised over him even from her knees, was thrilling. Her lips parted as she drew in shallow breaths, her gaze returning to his steadily hardening cock, her chin jutted outward as if she was still watching him.

Grasping him at the base of his shaft, Delia trailed her

tongue along the heated skin, then wrapped her lips around the head. His hushed cry when she took him as deep as she could, lips meeting her hand, was an incoherent mix of her name and some other affection that sent another jolt of arousal through her—the moan she gave in response made him grip her hair a little *too* tightly. It was hard not to feel proud at that; she wanted him to know she could give too, that their intimacy wasn't all about her.

And that thought alone encouraged her to set an even, steady pace, her head bobbing up and down in tandem with her hand. He seemed to especially like the way her tongue swirled around the sensitive, engorged skin at the head of his cock—and Delia especially liked the way his breath quickened and his groans grew hoarser.

"Wait," he murmured, stilling her with a slight tug of her hair just as her jaw started to ache. She glanced up with an arched brow, unable to keep the coy grin off her face. This was the most undone she'd ever seen him—and it was surprisingly attractive.

"Are you sure you want me to stop?" She pumped her hand back and forth for added effect, blooming inside at the way his eyes threatened to drift shut. Her mouth was almost back on him when he pulled her away again, gently this time.

"That mouth of yours is going to end things before I have a chance to return the favor," he argued, though he didn't sound quite as convincing as she assumed he wanted to. His hand left her hair to curve around her chin again, thumb brushing her lower lip. "I think you deserve a little—"

A shrill giggle cut him off, and Delia looked sharply toward the stairwell they'd stumbled out of earlier. Apparently they weren't the only ones in search of a little privacy. Drunken laughter echoed up toward them, and the second Delia was off her knees, Claude dragged her down the hall and pushed her into a dark room. As she scrambled for footing, Claude closed the door quietly behind them at the sound of giggling voices, both male and female, tumbling into the hall.

Moments later he switched on a light, bringing to life a forgotten room, all its furniture covered in white sheets. She took in the room quickly as Claude locked the door, her hands on her hips. Tables, dining chairs, couches—all covered. Black shutters on the other side of the room looked locked and coated in a layer of brownish dust, though the sound of the gala below had grown infinitely louder here. One could probably pull the shutters back to admire the festivities in the party hall.

When she heard Claude exhale deeply, Delia turned on the spot, cheeks flushed and mouth set in a thin line. He ran a hand through his hair, looking like a little boy who'd only *just* escaped punishment. When their eyes met, his smile went unreturned.

"Not that I didn't want to be caught with you," he told her, as if reading her mind. "So stop that frown before it starts. I don't want *any* member of my clan to see…quite so much of me."

Her smile was slow to form—if only to make him squirm a little. "Huh. A bashful king…"

He held out his arms and rotated in a quick circle. "Here I am."

When he faced her again, they fell silent, studying one another across the distance. The smiles disappeared, replaced with something dark and tinged with want. Outside, the muffled groans reminded her that they had unfinished business to attend to—that neither were satisfied with such an abrupt departure.

Claude's eyes wandered her figure, leisurely, taking his time, drinking her in. He then nodded to her knees. "You've ruined your stockings."

"What?" Apparently the stone floor had worn a hole in each knee, tearing them like they were dollar-store finds, not boutique treasures. She looked down at them briefly, then gripped the front of her dress, slowly dragging the fabric up, inch by agonizing inch, until cool air brushed the skin exposed at the top of those thigh-highs. "Shame. I was so excited to wear them for you."

He was on her before she had a chance to look up, lips crushing hers with bruising force, pinning her to what felt like the back of a couch. His mouth was like a punishment, a delicious penance that Delia happily paid. Not long after, he bent her over the draped couch, and they both clumsily hiked up her dress, shoving all that billowy fabric aside.

She'd never been taken like that before—hard and fast, with little foreplay or pretense. She'd also never climaxed that fast either, wrapped in Claude's arms, helplessly trapped between his hard body and an antique piece of furniture. When he came, groaning into her hair, a hand cupping her breast hard enough to hurt, Delia half-turned and claimed his lips, fingers threaded through his hair. He sagged against her somewhat, one arm propping him up on the back of the couch, the other secured snugly around her corseted waist.

In the hall, the drunken giggling had been replaced with loud, long moans. Delia clapped a hand over her mouth to keep from laughing, but she couldn't help herself. Easing out of her, Claude grinned too, and as they sorted themselves out as best they could, the sex serenade outside reached its crescendo.

"We weren't that loud, were we?" she asked. Claude rolled his eyes.

"I should hope not."

With her dress in order, she tried to help him with his tie—which Claude immediately redid; Delia's tie-knotting skills were beyond subpar.

"Hey," she whispered, clutching his tie and tugging. "You wanna scare the absolute shit out of one of your clansmen?"

She wiggled her eyebrows when Claude grinned slowly, then took his hand and let him lead her to the door.

*   *   *

"Why did you go after me at the masquerade?"

She heard the rush of water from the sink, the old pipes in Claude's bedroom walls creaking and groaning with the effort. Moments later, he poked his head around the bathroom's doorway, brow furrowed.

"What was that?"

"At the masquerade ball," Delia repeated, legs dangling over the edge of the bed. She tilted her head to the side, sitting back on her elbows. "I wanted to know why you went after me. I mean, you said then it was because of my back in the dress…" Her cheeks prickled unnecessarily as he grinned and ducked back into the bathroom. "But I'm pretty sure that was just a line."

"It was," Claude agreed as he breezed into the bedroom. They'd popped into his room after surprising the two noisy canoodlers, vamp and human, who'd thought they were alone in the empty hallway. Claude had insisted he show his face a little more at the gala before they headed to bed for good, but only after they washed the sex out of their appearances, even if only a little.

"It was a bit of a corny line," Delia said, stopping his advance on her by sticking her leg out, pointed toes poking his thigh. "But I guess I bought it at the time."

"That you did."

He looked to the door briefly, as if to encourage her to go. Her shoes were set neatly beside her, ripped stockings hanging over a chair by the window. She'd see if they were salvageable in the morning. Ali probably had a bunch of torn-stocking fixes up her sleeves, given her obsession with DIY projects for the wedding.

"Delia, we should—"

"Not until I get a straight answer," she said as she sat up, hands settling on her lap. They'd barely ever discussed the night they met, besides remarks made in passing by

Claude, ones that always set her off—and not in his favor. His large hands fell to his hips, then slipped into his pocket as he gave a shrug.

"I'd seen you before," Claude admitted after a long pause, his eyes wandering along her bare leg. A prickle of apprehension skittered across her skin at the confession, and Delia dropped her foot to the floor.

"You did?"

"I'd seen you working," he told her softly. "Only a handful of times. I'd gone along with my men to check up on League activity, you know, make sure no one was doing anything illegal on either side. I mostly saw you driving a car or sitting somewhere I assumed you thought no one could see you. I thought you were beautiful."

The apprehension slid away. "Oh."

"Beautiful and bored, I suppose," Claude added with a chuckle, reaching out and pinching her chin. She tugged her head away, unable to fend off the small smile creeping across her features. His hand hovered there between them, until it returned to his pocket and he sighed. "I too was bored. It's been so quiet for so long, you see. The same thing, day after day. The same tasks, year after year. I've been king of the region for almost three centuries. I think I became too lax with the clans. I'd become absent."

Delia fidgeted with the voluminous black fabric gathered around her waist, sensing that his story had very little to do with her. This was a side unseen by her, a Claude who came across as a man touched by self-doubt, by regret. For a moment it read plainly across his face, but it vanished as she stood, replaced by a more recognizably affectionate expression as she touched her palm to his cheek.

"So you went after me because you were bored?" she asked, trying to keep her tone light.

"I thought we had that in common," he offered, his hand blanketing hers as he pressed a kiss to her wrist. He lingered there, his eyes closed, before threading his fingers around hers. Their clasped hands hung between them, and as Claude moved in, their bodies finding one another in a perfect fit, he pressed her arm behind her back, nudging her hips closer to his.

"I'd watched you for some time that night once I realized who you were." His whispered words smoothed over her skin, willing her eyes to close. "It started as curiosity, then interest. I couldn't help myself. But know that I had every intention of dancing with you, showing you my room, and keeping you for myself until morning."

A welcome shiver traveled down her back, beneath the tight lacings of her corseted top and straight to the tips of her toes. Suddenly the rest of the world ceased to matter. She didn't care about the gala or the face Claude had to put on for his people. She only wanted him—again and again, until exhaustion forced her to stop. Delia stood on her toes, trying to capture his mouth with hers, but he evaded her with ease. Even as their bodies touched, he still felt so far away.

"I ruined it for myself by tasting you," he murmured, twisting and turning so that it seemed as though he was going to kiss her, lips so close that hers buzzed in response, but Claude stopped just shy of touching her. "I thought I'd ruined everything. But you surprised me. Ensnared me."

"Staked you," she whispered back.

Claude smirked, his free hand reaching up to stroke her cheek while hers hung at her side. He nodded slightly, eyes alight with want once more. "Yes, you showed me you could be brave, even in a desperate moment. Fierce and beautiful, that's what you were from then on. No longer bored. And neither was I."

Her grip tightened around his hand. "So you chased me to stop being bored?"

"No," he said, his voice a hushed dream, hypnotic and comforting, delicious and desirable. "I pursued you because I thought we had something. I wasn't lying about that. There was a spark. A moment. I couldn't be sure, but it seemed worth the effort." He kissed her then, sweet and soft, and retreated when she tried to take more. "You are worth the chase."

"Am I?" His words touched on a niggling little fear at the back of her mind, one that had started to fester ever since they'd made their relationship more official: that she was too much work for him. "It's been kind of a bumpy ride so far. Your patience seems infinite."

"I can assure you it isn't," Claude remarked gently, then brushed her hair back, tucking it behind her ear, "but no great love story can grow in lifeless, *boring* soil."

It was as their lips found one another again that the floor rumbled. Vibrations tickled her legs, hummed beneath the soles of her feet. Delia pulled away with a frown, eyes to the ground.

"What the hell was—" She cried out when another set of tremors rocked the manor, the windows rattling this time. Claude held her tight until they stopped less than a minute later, and Delia wriggled out of his embrace and went for the windows. Smoke rose over the trees, far in the distance. Thick grey smoke, stark against the otherwise clear night sky.

It was spiraling up from Harriswood.

"Wh-what…" Delia pointed to the glass pane, then looked at Claude, her mouth hanging open. "What's happening?"

"Let's go back to the party. I'm sure it's nothing to—"

"Something's happening," she pressed. "Something…isn't right."

He crossed the room to the window and peered out, squinting, hands falling to her hips. "Probably a fire, judging by the smoke."

"Fires don't feel like an earthquake," she shot back shakily. Then she went for her purse, which she'd left on Claude's bed when she arrived—no point in carrying it around all night when her hands had more interesting things to touch. Phone in hand, she sat on the edge of the bed again, finding about a dozen missed calls from Kain and a few texts from Devin. She swiped her hair back as she scanned the messages. Devin was at the League party and wanted to know where she was. Hadn't she said she was coming? Did she want him to save her some *oysters*— yeah, the League went all out on the food, and she was missing it.

Delia swallowed hard. Kain left no messages, voice or otherwise.

The smoke seemed to be spiraling on the side of town that housed the library and government buildings. And which local organization of the whole lot was bound to have the powerful enemies?

"Delia, I really should get back and make an appearance. We've been gone a little too long."

She held up a finger to silence him as she tapped Devin's number and pressed call. Straight to voicemail. Shaking her head, Delia tried again—three times more. Then she tried Ali's number. Then Kain's. Arthur's rang but eventually went to voicemail too. Frustrated, she called every hunter number she had stored in her contacts list, not caring if they'd even spoken in the last year. Nothing. Nothing from anyone.

Delia went back to the start, calling everyone again. Nobody's phone rang besides Arthur's. Her breath came in short, panicked gasps. "Claude, I don't—"

Suddenly he was crouched in front of her, gathering her hands in his and holding her gaze. "Relax. You've had a bit to drink, and this has understandably startled you. I'm sure everything's fine. Let's go back to the party."

Her brow creased as she stared into those beautiful blue eyes, eyes she had come to trust implicitly, and then slowly freed her hands from his. A sick feeling had taken root in her gut and was working its way up her throat, leaving a scorched trail behind.

"Why don't you care about this?" she asked, the gears

slowly turning as she worked through the sudden turn of events. "Why are you…?"

"Delia, please, now isn't—"

She stood abruptly and stepped around him, heart pounding. "I want to know what happened. I… I should go back to town, or something. Devin isn't answering his phone. Ali isn't either and that thing is glued to her hand. I should check on things."

"Why? Is it really so crucial at this moment in time?"

He'd snapped at her. Claude Grimm had never snapped at her. Frown deepening, Delia went for her shoes, jamming them onto her slightly swollen, sore feet. When she tried to open the door, Claude closed it before she got very far, his hand lingering on the dark wood, gaze cast down. "Delia…"

Her grip tightened on the doorknob. "Why don't you want me to go?"

"Why don't I want you to rush blindly toward a natural disaster?" His eyebrows shot up when their eyes met. "Is that a serious question?"

"Stop it." She tried to open the door again, but he continued to hold it shut. "Stop. Whatever *this* is that's happening right now, stop it."

She glared up at him, not entirely sure how to navigate the choppy seas of *this* Claude, but she wanted to check on her friends. They all lived with their phones. Some even took them in the shower. Reception could be hit or miss at HQ, but it wasn't *that* bad. Someone should have answered.

Over his shoulder, the smoke had started to spread across the cityscape. There was quite a stretch of land between Harriswood and the Grimm estate, but she'd always been able to see the tops of the tallest skyscrapers over the trees outside his bedroom. Now it was just smoke. Smoke, and if she looked hard, the flicker of fire.

"No one is answering their phones," Delia snapped. "And now something's happening downtown where all my friends live and work. I want to—"

A third quake cut her off, less powerful than the second but stronger than the first, and Claude steadied her when she wobbled in her heels. She clutched at him until the vibrations stopped, until the windows ceased their rattling and the books stopped inching toward the edge of their shelves.

"Delia," Claude said, taking her head in his hands firmly, "it is not a good idea to go back to town tonight. It's safer here."

Carefully, she peeled his hands from her face and held them by her sides, struggling to draw even breaths. "Do you... Do you know what happened?"

"I didn't know this was the way. I..." Claude gave a slight shake of his head. "But I know now. At least, I can guess what's happened."

"Is it about the clans? The Donovans?" She let go of his hands when he nodded. Her voice caught in her throat as she asked, "Does that smoke have something to do with the League?"

The answer was obvious from the look on his face. There it was again. The regret. The self-doubt. It practically doused him, clear as anything, and Delia stepped away with a shaky gasp, tears stinging her eyes.

"Oh my *god.*"

"Delia, I'm so sorry. I didn't know this was to be the outcome of all—"

But she was gone before she could hear the rest of his apology, blitzing out the door and down the hall. The burning feeling had made it to her mouth now, tasting like sickness, like death. She was halfway down an unfamiliar corridor when she realized her feet had been moving, but not in the right direction. Her fingertips ghosted over the wall as she stopped, and when she turned around, trying to get her bearings and find the front door, she spotted Claude jogging toward her.

With her coat and purse in hand, his dinner jacket back

on those beautifully broad shoulders.

"Come on then," he said, feeding her arms through her jacket's sleeves. "You're in no mood to wait for a cab, nor would I ever let you drive anywhere tonight."

"You don't have to—"

"No, I want to see it for myself," he insisted gruffly as he guided her down the hall. "I want to see the carnage with my own eyes…"

*   *   *

Because he wanted the images to haunt him. Johnathon Warwick owed him three more days to respond to his offer. Tonight was supposed to be one last hurrah for the Grimm clan. Tomorrow he'd tell Delia. The following day the manor would be abandoned, all his nearest and dearest safely aboard private planes destined for Switzerland. He had friends there. Friends who would keep him safe.

He hadn't known something would happen tonight— not for certain, anyway. Elov had heard whispers that the new order of vampire clan leaders intended to slot the League into their plans for the future—Claude thought it best Delia was with *him* when that happened. But after what sounded like a bombing, he could only guess that Johnathon hadn't offered the hunters the same chance to join him as he'd given Claude.

So he'd go into town with her and keep her safe, leaving the warm glow of his decorated home behind. Because Claude wanted to know, wanted to see and remember forever, the flames of hellfire he had fanned with his inaction.

With his… *boredom.*

CHAPTER 22: BRB EMOTIONALLY SHATTERED

Red and blue lights washed over the crowd at the police barricade like waves lapping at the surf. Officials had closed off the street, blocking pedestrians from the usual path Delia took to get to League HQ from her apartment. Flames engulfed the historic building. The old town library, a Harriswood monument—victim of some sort of terrorist attack. That's what the news would say, anyway. They'd find human culprits and plaster their faces across television screens and online news articles.

But Delia knew they weren't human and they weren't targeting the library—not really. The curt whoop-whoop of an incoming ambulance forced her and other onlookers to shift aside, the boxy vehicle easing headed for the wounded. The crowd was pushed back to the end of the street, a good hundred feet from the wreck, but the heat was palpable. Sometimes her breath caught in her throat and she'd cough out the smoky air with a wince.

Firefighters were doing their best to contain the blaze, battling it back so it wouldn't spread to other nearby historical buildings and apartment complexes. Scores of people had been evacuated, many waiting in their slippers and winter jackets, demanding to know what had happened. On the other side of Claude, an elderly man held a fluffy Persian cat to his chest, paunchy cheeks slack and jaw hanging open.

Hands shaking, Delia watched the flames as she tried to

reach the people who'd been partying beneath the building. No response.

Devin. Ali. Arthur. Kain. All the HQ staffers, from the hunters to the human resource folks, had been invited to celebrate the Donovan capture. There were at least a dozen emails in her inbox encouraging her to attend, to bring a bottle of wine, to dress festively—the High Council was planning to merge it with their annual Christmas Party, so prepare for karaoke and eggnog.

Claude hadn't said a word since they arrived on the scene. He'd been unusually silent on the drive into town too, not a word said about Delia flipping through local radio channels frantically. Silent and stoic, he'd nudged people aside to help her get to the front of the steadily growing crowd.

And now he just watched. She cast her watery gaze toward him. A tight fist gripped her chest, crushing her. It was no longer her racing heart she felt, but the high-pitched whine in her ears, accompanied by some invisible fluff that muffled the chaos unfurling around her.

"What is this?" She sounded like she had something in her throat. Claude continued to stare ahead, watching. Not even the soft hand she placed on his arm roused him. "Why did this happen?"

"There has been a coup," her vampire king remarked stiffly, eyes sweeping across the paramedics wheeling a gurney toward the scene. "A rising up against the established order."

Teeth starting to chatter, Delia slipped her hand into her coat pocket, only then noticing how the cold affected her. Her bare legs had gone numb—but so had the rest of her, physically and emotionally. Before she could say anything, Claude wrapped his thick jacket over her shoulders. Her body wanted to sag under its weight.

"Are *you* the established order?" she asked thickly.

In the distance, firefighters shouted at one another, the blaze stronger than ever. A little closer, uniformed officers barked at the encroaching crowd to get back, to go home, to get out of the way. Beside her, Claude merely nodded, his jaw noticeably clenched.

Delia hesitated, unsure if she wanted an answer, then cleared her throat. "Is this why you insisted I come to the gala at your place? Did you know this was going to happen?"

Her stomach did a few somersaults in the silence that followed. She shouldn't have asked. Sometimes not knowing was better. But he had been so adamant on her being there tonight...

"I'd heard whispers that the new powers that be had plans for tonight," Claude told her at long last, each word sounding forced, pained even. "I didn't know what, so I wanted to keep my clan close. Keep them out of the blast radius... metaphorically speaking, of course. I'd no idea they were going to do *this*." Delia looked away when he glanced down at her, tears clinging to her lashes. In her peripherals, she saw him shake his head, his huff of air fogging in front of him. "It was my understanding that they were *using* the League for their own purposes, not that they were going to destroy it."

"And butcher all the people inside it." Her voice sounded far away, even to her own ears, and she tried not to blink, tried not to let the tears fall. "There was a huge party in there tonight. Was supposed to go well into the morning. Devin said in a text they went all out... Oysters, champagne probably." Her face screwed suddenly as the true gravity of the situation hit her—like running face-first into a brick wall. This time she let the fat wet streaks roll down her cheeks and drip onto Claude's coat. "You couldn't have given me a heads up?"

"Telling you something before I knew the whole story would have been like throwing you into the fire." Claude touched her shoulder, but she shrugged his hand away, arms folded beneath his huge jacket. He sighed. "I was trying to keep you from getting burned."

Life hadn't prepared her for this. As she stood there, openly weeping, Delia wasn't sure how she was supposed to feel. Sad? Angry? Horrified? All of the above? Hunters liked to tell themselves, and anyone who would listen, that this life was a gruelling one: that at one point or another, all your friends would die before their time. That was the nature of the business. Fighting vamps. Protecting the free human world. It was supposed to be this very rock and roll, live-hard-die-young lifestyle. Delia had told herself time and time again that this job came with hardships, that the possibility of no tomorrow was a very real one for her and anyone she cared about.

But, in a single night, they had all been snuffed out.

Just because she wanted to quit or apply for a desk job didn't mean she wanted to see it all go up in flames. She'd never hear Devin call her D again. There'd be no early morning pancakes at the diner watching the sunrise together. In that moment, she'd kill to hear Ali talk about wedding plans—Delia would happily look at every fucking inspiration board on the woman's phone. You never know when it will be the last time you hug someone, smile at them, tell them you'll see them tomorrow...

When she brought her hand up to muffle her sobs, Claude pulled her to him, and this time she let him. Tears mixed with eyeliner and mascara peppered the front of his white shirt, but he let her cry, a hand rubbing up and down her back while the other cradled her head.

For a time, the rest of the world faded away save the pounding in her head and the sounds of her smothered sobs. When the tears finally dried up, she wiped at her cheeks, eyes swollen and nostrils red from the cold and the misery.

"We should go," Claude murmured, brushing her hair back before steering her away from the wreckage. "You'll catch your death out here."

The cold. The smoke. The possible lurking vamps. Delia would catch her death from a few different sources if she stayed for long, but her feet were heavy as she shuffled along, toes cramped and aching in her heels, her thoughts everywhere and nowhere. The people around her, faces illuminated by streetlights and distant flames, looked understandably distraught. Many had their phones out, filming the breakdown of a public treasure to post it online later—maybe hoping the news would buy the footage.

Her stare moved from face to face, seeing but not registering, until finally it stopped on a face she knew better than the rest.

"Arthur?"

He looked toward her, his expression mirroring hers— lost, confused, broken. It took a moment, but before Delia threw her arms around his neck, she caught a flash of recognition across his features.

"I-I didn't go to the party," he croaked in her ear, and she nodded, pulling him to her tightly. "You said y-you weren't going, so I did the m-marathon…"

She pulled back and sniffled. Blood oozed out of slits on his face, and he twitched back when Delia reached out for them. "What happened to you?"

"I live in the blast radius," he told her. She noticed the way he glanced warily at Claude hovering behind her. "My windows shattered when it…."

"Oh my god." It was like something in her brain clicked back into place—like seeing Arthur all scratched up, shredded but familiar, snapped her into reacting. "Okay. We need to get you to a paramedic. We should flag one down and—"

"No." He pulled her arm down when she tried to catch the attention of a nearby officer. "No, Delia, we can't."

"But—"

"I'm a League employee," he argued. A shivering, twitchy, teeth-chattering employee. She shrugged off Claude's coat and threw it around him.

"*I'm* a League employee," she said, noting that Claude's

jacket swallowed Arthur just as it did her. "We can't—"

"League employees don't seem to be the most popular kids on the block tonight," Arthur pressed, lowering his voice and leaning in. "Obviously we're being *targeted.*"

"He's right," Claude said, easing an arm around Delia's waist. "It isn't safe for you here should anyone recognize you."

She frowned. "But—"

"You can both stay with me," he continued, "but we should leave now."

"And who are you?" Arthur's studied Claude's face with a frown, as if trying to place him. The vampire king—if he could even be called that anymore—dipped his head with a little half-smile.

"Claude Grimm," he said, and Delia grabbed Arthur's hand when he blanched. "Head of the Grimm clan. Former regional king, and in a few days… Wanted traitor to the new regime."

His words hit her hard, willing her knees to buckle again. Arthur looked between them as he half-heartedly tried to tug his hand from her grip, but moments later he was trudging alongside them. Before long, Claude was marching sandwiched between Delia and Arthur, holding them both up as they pushed through the crowd.

With the car in sight and Arthur babbling about the heat, about the hunters turned to ash, Delia stole one last look over her shoulder. It was meant for her to take a mental picture so that later, when she was more together, more functional, she would remember what had happened—and it would fuel her personal fire.

Instead of looking at the crowd, at the roaring flames and the billowing black smoke, she saw a vaguely familiar vamp grinning at her from the edge of the crowd. William Warwick, thin and gaunt and vile like his father.

As Claude ushered Arthur into the backseat of his car, that vile Warwick son offered her a sneer of a smile and a wave, then drifted back into the sea of gathering humans.

And Delia suddenly knew that when she thought back to this moment, all she would remember was that smile. Not the carnage, not the fire, not the mixed storm of emotion raging within her—but that awful, awful smile.

*   *   *

"So the Warwick clan was just using us to get at the Donovans?" Delia slumped in one of Claude's bedroom armchairs by the huge windows overlooking the forest. A few candles burned low on the windowsills, and the lamps on either side of the bed provided a soft, calming yellow light, but otherwise the rest of the room was dark. Claude stood before her, his hands clasped behind his back, his expression harder and graver than she had ever seen before.

"So it would appear. My best guess is that Johnathon Warwick needed the League manpower and resources, and to get that, he needed a just cause to unite all the hunters, to make you all agree to ally with his clan." His gaze lifted to the windows behind her. "It has taken me a few days to connect all the pieces and ensure this isn't some elaborate hoax to oust me. But it seems clans have banded together nationwide for this foolishness. The Donovans were the most powerful clan in the region, given their size and flagrant disregard for our rules. I have only been able to control Shane Donovan over the years because of my title *and* the backing of the other clans. If he disapproved of something going on behind my back, he could have crushed any of the smaller clans on their own in a second."

She blinked slowly, tiredly, her body yearning to crawl into Claude's huge bed and sleep away her sorrows. But while physically she was on the decline, mentally she was as alert as one could be in a situation like this. Once they'd returned from Harriswood, Claude pulled Elov from the gala to tend to Arthur's injuries. While her friend hadn't looked thrilled to be carted off by a vamp, both she and

Claude had assured him of his safety. From there, Claude led her up to his room, closed the door, and sat her down in one of the hard-backed armchairs. He'd taken off her shoes, gently, careful of her aches and pains, before telling her everything.

Everything he had kept from her. The clan betrayals. The move for mass human subjugation—coupled with human alliances. The partnership between Warwick, the lesser clans, and the League.

It was a lot to take in. Delia was sure she'd need a few days to wrap her head around it. Even if she wasn't a key player at the League, she'd always thought she had some idea of how things worked in Harriswood—she thought she knew what purpose her organization served, if anything. Now, she wasn't so sure.

Not once did it occur to her to be upset with him for keeping secrets. Delia had kept a number of things from him since they started seeing each other, if only to spare his feelings. It was quite clear to her rational mind, which was getting ganged up on by wild fantasies and wayward schemes, that Claude had withheld the truth to keep her safe. Not for one second did she believe he had anything but her best interest at heart. He was a vampire king, a man responsible for the lives of everyone in his clan and all those opposed to this new vampire-run order. Delia didn't blame him for his absence. He had a crisis to manage.

But she was pleased that he'd told her everything now. Not because the knowledge set her mind at ease, but because there was a simple comfort in being on the same page as one's partner. It would have been kind to return the favor, but her little reports for the High Council seemed silly now—inconsequential. All those reports, digital and not, were burning in the basement of the Harriswood Library, never to be seen again.

Like Devin and Ali and Kain and…

Everyone.

Like everyone.

"I made sure to get my clan to safety," he told her, starting to pace. He'd rolled his sleeves up to his elbows, jacket cast aside, his hair mussed from the winter wind. "Tonight was a farewell party. I am sorry that you came here under false pretenses, but I *did* plan to tell you everything tomorrow."

"I get it," she said quietly, her hands in her lap. "You don't have to apologize."

"You say that, yet I feel profoundly responsible for everything here."

Suddenly, Claude knocked a row of books off a nearby shelf. They fell noisily to the ground, spines bent and pages folded. "I *am* responsible for everything that has happened. It was my responsibility to control these leaders, and I've failed."

Delia watched him, wishing she could pull him into her arms and stroke his head. To her, Claude Grimm was the perfect man, but it would do no good to voice her opinion. Her knowledge of inter-clan relationships was spotty and based on League intel. Hell, up until this year, she, like most, had been under the illusion that a murderous vampire named Claudia ran the show. What could she possibly say about any of this that would make him feel better?

"Shortly I'll be moving the entirety of my clan back to Switzerland. Warwick gave me a week to decide my allegiance, and our disappearance will be my answer. Now that he's dispensed with the League, I have no doubt he will come for the Grimm clan next." His words made her straighten in her seat, her brow furrowing. "As far as I know, this *virus* has only infected North American clans. My people will be safe in Europe."

"W-what?" His words hit her like sludge, like feet sinking into thick mud. Delia raised her gaze to him, hating that it took her so long to process this. "You're leaving?"

Claude exhaled softly, then knelt before her and

gathered her hands in his. "After I'd told you everything tomorrow, I planned to ask you to come with me. You should, Delia. It's my understanding that clans across the nation have united in this foolhardy endeavor. It's dangerous to stay behind. Dangerous to be a hunter, even if you have grown cold to the profession."

"But…" What about Harriswood? What about the people in it? Was he just going to leave all of them in the hands of the other clans?

"Delia, come with me." He stroked his thumbs over her skin, his touch warm and soothing. "I'm sure this will pass. All foolish revolutions do. Until it does, I can keep you safe with me. Bring your accountant friend if you wish. I've made arrangements with an old companion for temporary sanctuary. It's open to you as well."

"So you want me to…pack a bag and go?" It'd be so easy. Take an extended vacation while her home, her country, fell in and out of vamp rule—while thousands might die. Claude drew a breath, his expression full of hope, but she shook her head. "I know about vamps. How can I leave all these innocent people to die when I can *do* something about it?"

"Delia, this isn't a war for you to fight alone."

"I'll find others. You could help me to—"

"I have an entire clan depending on me," he reasoned, his tone gentle and calm and so damn comforting. "There are military forces that I have no doubt will combat this plague. Johnathon Warwick thinks his reach is farther than it is. Come with me. Ride it out elsewhere."

"It'd be wrong," Delia said, ignoring the way her heart screamed for her to stop, to give in and go with him. "I can help people here. There are no…" She closed her eyes, momentarily overwhelmed. Claude caught the tear that fell when she opened them again, his hopeful expression quashed. "The hunters were eliminated in a single night. There's me… Maybe there are more of our outpost agents, but we need to do something. I can't run away."

"Delia—"

"I know I'm not the best hunter out there," she continued forcefully, sniffling, "but I have *some* knowledge. I have stakes I can give. I know what the hell is actually happening thanks to you. I… I have to try to help. It w-wouldn't be right to just let people die."

"They're going to die anyway." She tried to pull her hands from his, but Claude held tight, seeking out her eyes. "Please. I can't stand the thought of you staying behind. This country will fall to darkness for a time. I know it. They are so *determined* to see their vision come to fruition."

This time he let her hands go when she pulled back, but they stayed on her lap, limp, her fingers close enough to his to feel the heat of his skin.

Of course she wanted to go with him. Delia wasn't one to play the hero. If anything, she was the one to freeze and let someone better swoop in to save the day. Beyond her vamp-killing spree at the grocery store, which she chalked up to a combination of surprise and luck, she had limited credentials to back up such a stupid mission.

But that didn't matter. People didn't deserve to die because she was scared. She had a responsibility to get the word out. She had a brief stint of news fame with the grocery mishap—maybe she could use that to her advantage.

She had to try.

"I don't blame you for going," she whispered, then pressed her lips together when they quivered. A steady hand reached out for Claude, cupping his cheek lightly. "You have a lot of people to take care of. You should do that."

He kissed her palm, the words that followed murmured against it, so soft that she had to strain to hear. "This is my fault. I owe it to my clan to protect them from the mess I've created."

Unable to find the words again, Delia gently coaxed him forward until his head settled on her lap. Finally, she was able to stroke him like she'd wanted, but it brought neither any comfort. Instead, beneath the weight of his head on her thighs, Delia felt her heart breaking.

This wasn't how the night was supposed to go. She'd bought sexy stockings to show off for him. Delia had planned to pick his brain about her career, but only after they'd had their fun together.

Why couldn't that have happened instead?

When she was on the brink of tears again, Claude sat up and pulled her to him, lips claiming hers before she could protest. They stayed like that for some time, Claude on his knees and Delia at the edge of the chair, holding one another, kissing one another, wishing that things were different for the other. When they broke apart, they lingered, foreheads pressed together. Her gaze raked across his face as she tried to commit every feature to memory, from the blueness of his eyes to the square line of his jaw to the rise of his cheekbones.

"Come with me," he whispered. "Please, Delia."

"I want to," she told him, her voice breaking. "Honestly, there's nothing I want more right now, but..."

But she couldn't. She had to stay and fight. Years ago, she'd entered this secret world because she wanted to keep people safe. Even if this League hadn't worked out for her, Delia still felt in her heart that that was her purpose in life. To help people. To protect them. Somehow. Even if she could keep one family from feeling the overwhelming loss that she felt tonight, she would have done her duty.

If only letting him go was easier.

"I can ask those staying behind to watch out for you—"

"If they're staying behind, they aren't exactly on my side," she said with a slight shake of her head. "Don't. Get your people out of here. I-I'll need to find *my* people, whatever's left of them, and see what we're going to do."

See what they *could* do. There was no telling how many clans were involved in this mess. How many vamps were likeminded in their thinking that humans ought to be relegated to second-class citizens?

"When things are settled on my end," Claude said fiercely, cradling her face in his hands, "I will come back for you. I will find you and I will do what I can to protect you."

She blinked slowly, the closing of her eyes forcing her tears out, and offered the best smile she could manage. "Thank you."

But Delia had no expectations that he'd return. If things were about to get sucked into a churning black hole of awful, she couldn't put that kind of demand on him. Claude needed to stay safe too. Warwick and the others had already proven what their manipulations could do to those who stood against them, powerful vampire or not.

"It pains me to say," Claude muttered tersely, "but you should leave tonight. There's no telling who saw us downtown, and if you wait and leave when I take the others, you may become a target."

Numbly, she nodded. This was happening. It was *actually* happening. As she drew a breath to tell him that his affection these last few months meant more to her than he'd ever know, the bedroom door opened slowly, and Arthur tentatively poked his head in, face covered in bandages.

"Come in," Claude said wearily, gesturing for her friend to enter. As he did, Delia stood and smoothed her hands down her dress, then pressed a hand to Claude's shoulder and squeezed. When he looked up, she tried and failed to smile.

"Are all those people downstairs...vampires?" Arthur asked as she moved toward him, grabbing her heels on the way.

"Most," she told him. "Don't worry. We won't be here long."

His thick eyebrows creased. "What? Shouldn't we stay the night?"

"Anyone could have identified us," Delia said, her throat tight as she brushed her hands under her eyes. "One of the Warwick boys waved at me as we were going." Behind her, she heard Claude exhale noisily. A quick glance back was all she needed to read his fury. "We need to leave tonight. Now, I guess. See who is alive, if anyone else didn't go to HQ tonight."

It didn't take much to convince Arthur. Somehow it seemed he'd rather be out there in the world than in a house full of vamps—but Delia knew that the reality of the situation, once she shared it, would change his mind.

"Take one of my cars," Claude insisted as they headed for the door, once again her feet slow and heavy, laden with unseen mountains of lead. She shook her head.

"I couldn't—"

"*Delia*," he said sharply, causing even Arthur to flinch. Claude paused and drew in a breath. "Take one of the cars. It's the least I can give you."

Another numb nod. What else was there to say? She and Arthur had no transportation otherwise and the thought of braving winter's biting edge on foot made her want to lay face-first on the floor and not ever get up.

As the trio moved through the Grimm manor, with its boughs of holly hanging in doorways and strings of garland hugging the bannisters, Delia felt like she was in a dream. Maybe if she pinched herself hard enough, she'd come jolting back to life in her bedroom, coated in sweat and her chest heaving.

But the here and now was all too real.

Claude stopped them by the front door, telling them he'd be a moment to get the keys. As Delia watched him go, wondering what it would feel like in a few minutes when he *actually* walked away from her, the sounds of the gala crept down from the great hall—the music, the laughter. There were so many people in there. So many people who now depended on Claude to spirit them away from this mess.

Would the humans go with their vamps? Were they invited into Claude's Swiss sanctuary too? Swallowing hard, Delia faced the front door with her arms crossed, the tight pinch of her pleather jacket bothering her more than it should. Out of the corner of her eye, Arthur seemed in a world of his own too. She reached for his arm with a sigh, gripping when he jumped at the contact.

"How are you feeling?" she asked.

He blinked at her slowly, then looked down. "Everything hurts."

"Yeah…" Delia retracted her hand. "Same."

She wasn't sure how long Claude was gone for, but minutes felt like hours as they waited for him. When he eventually returned to her side, he stuffed a car key with a fat grey remote dangling off the little metal ring into her hand, then handed what looked like a pile of coats to Arthur.

"Take this too," he insisted as her hand closed around the key tightly. It took her a few seconds to realize what he was handing her—a black credit card. Delia frowned, but took it with shaky fingers. "Buy what you need. I don't care what it costs you. Do it fast, before things…disintegrate."

"Okay."

Before she knew it, they were all moving out the front door and onto the porch, with Claude telling Arthur where they could find the minivan.

"It's inconspicuous," he insisted, his hand on Delia's lower back, "and it gets surprisingly good gas mileage. Good for holding supplies or passengers."

"Thank you," Arthur said, stumbling a little as he stepped off the porch. "Really. This is good of you."

"I'd do more if you would both…" Claude trailed off with a sigh. Delia couldn't hear him ask her to come with him again. She just couldn't. Her mind had been made up since she saw the burning library, but that didn't mean her resolve was strong. It was weak, frankly. Ready to snap at any moment.

So Delia eased away from him because she had to. Gravel crunched under her heels as she marched off the porch, crossing toward the garage with Arthur by her side.

God, she was so weak.

Delia made it halfway across the driveway before she turned and awkwardly jogged back to Claude, the little bits of rock catching her heels with every step. Claude met her in the middle, sweeping her into his arms. She buried her face against him and breathed him in one last time. This patient, wonderful, loving man. This vampire who had proved her stereotypes wrong, who showed her there was a different world simmering below the League's polished surface level. This lover who had taught her to fight, to believe that she was capable and strong.

How was she supposed to do this without him?

"I'm so sorry," he murmured in her ear, and Delia hugged him tighter.

"It isn't your fault." Even if he felt like it was, Delia couldn't—wouldn't—blame him for what happened to her friends tonight, nor would she for whatever the future held.

"I will come back for you," Claude whispered. "I promise."

She closed her eyes. "I know. I'll be here."

"You'd better be, huntress."

They held one another in an embrace neither seemed inclined to break. But eventually she did, as the cold seeped into her marrow and the feeling started to fade in her fingertips. Clasping Claude's face, Delia kissed him, just a quick peck, and then another, and another, and another, until she had to push herself off his chest to get away.

"I know you can survive this," Claude told her as they stood a few feet apart, her fingers itching to thread around his. In turn, he reached out for her, but then quickly dropped his arm to his side. This was it. The end of things.

Delia tried to swallow the painful lump in her throat with no success.

"Look after your people," she said, rubbing her arms to conserve heat, "and then get your ass back here."

The corners of his mouth twitched. "You have my word."

Drawing in a deep breath, the cold air cutting through her lungs and burning her throat, Delia nodded and forced herself to join Arthur across the circular gravel driveway. But when she was beside him again, her legs threatened to give out entirely, and her friend had to hold her up with an arm around her shoulders.

After locating the minivan inside the garage, she handed the keys over to Arthur, in no state to drive anything. He made a face but said nothing as he headed for the driver's side, Delia for the passenger's. She cranked the heat once he got the engine going, and they drove out of the huge hangar with a bit of jostling over the uneven ground.

Claude stood on the porch as they passed, hands in his pockets. There was no dramatic wave this time, none of the playful farewells of the past. Instead, Delia watched him in the rearview mirror, her gaze becoming steadily blurrier. Before long, the forest swallowed them—and Claude was gone. Leafless trees filled the mirror, and Delia doubled over, crying softly into her hands.

When the van came to an abrupt stop, she sat up, eyes wide and searching, and found them loitering at the edge of the Grimm estate, the road a few feet ahead. Overhead, a full moon shone through the branches.

"Delia, I don't know how to do this," Arthur said. He was white-knuckling the steering wheel so tight that even the slightest shift of his fingers made noise. "I'm not a hunter. I'm a desk guy. I don't know what to do... I don't know what I'm doing."

"You think I do?" She gave a hollow laugh when he looked at her. "Arthur, I do patrols. I sit in cars, on rooftops, and film vamps. Sometimes I get to bring in low-level criminals with a *team*, and they usually made me drive." Another laugh, this time sounding a little more high-strung. "I was on Team Alpha on the raid because someone above the High Council *ordered* them to put me there, not because I was good enough, and the grocery store thing was a huge stroke of luck. I have no idea what the fuck I'm doing on a good day, and this… *This* is not a good day."

His hands fell from the steering wheel to his lap. "Oh."

"I don't know what I'm doing, but I know we need to make sure a group of insane vamps don't start the apocalypse," she told him, her head back against the headrest. He cleared his throat, face screwed with confusion when she glanced at him. "I know we need to find other hunters who *are* good at this kind of stuff. I know we can't stay by ourselves. And I know we need to keep people safe."

In her peripherals, she saw him nod slowly. "Okay."

"And I'm going to keep you safe," Delia said. "And before long, you'll be just as good as me with a stake."

"Something we don't have."

"Something we will get tomorrow when the sun's out," she told him, and then drew a deep breath. "One problem at a time."

How did she turn into the rational one here? Couldn't he see that she was a huge mess?

"D'you promise?" he asked, and when she looked to him with a slight frown, he cleared his throat again. "To look after me."

"Yes." Delia reached across and touched his arm, giving it a squeeze when she felt him trembling. "Arthur… I'm going to make sure no one hurts you."

It took some gentle persuading to get him going again, and as soon as they crossed off the Grimm property, Delia officially felt her heart break in two. But she swallowed her cries, shoved her hands against her eyes to hold back the tears, and focused on her breathing.

She needed to keep a semi-level head here. Once they were somewhere safe and secure, she could let it all out. Now wasn't the time.

Because when she sat up, Delia noticed behind them, in the rearview mirror, a set of headlights steadily growing larger. Delia's brow crinkled, taking a few seconds too long to understand what she saw, then turned in her seat to confirm it. It was rare to see another car at any point driving on these backcountry roads.

"Arthur," she said, forcing her words out calmly, evenly, as she faced backward, "you need to drive faster."

"Hmm?"

Suddenly the vehicle, some huge four-by-four, was about a car's length behind them, and Delia grabbed Arthur's shoulder hard at the thunderous revving of an engine.

"Go!"

THE QUEEN

It's the end of the world as Delia Roberts knows it,
and she is absolutely positively not fine.

Enjoy an unedited snippet of the prologue of the second
book in the Games We Play duology, then snag it next
year.

THE QUEEN: PROLOGUE

"Claude?"

Harriswood's former vampire king lifted his gaze from the wall-mounted television. At the sight of Elov loitering in the doorway of his study, he sat up, the stiff leather couch creaking beneath him, and muted the news. Every day he watched the morning and evening cycles. Still no word on America—nothing new, anyway. There'd been nothing since the entire country went dark, cut off from the rest of the world in every sense of the word.

"Yes?" Claude stretched an arm out across the back of the couch as his right-hand man hurried in, noting the stack of file-folders in hand. He barely noticed that Elov hadn't used his formal title—because in Switzerland he wasn't a king. Hell, in America he wasn't a king either. The two vampires were equal, yet Elov's loyalty had never once waivered. He continued to work for Claude, tirelessly and ceaselessly, from the day they loaded the clan onto Gregor's private jets to this very moment.

He wasn't sure what he had done in a past life to warrant such unwavering loyalty. Some days—most days—he felt as though he didn't deserve it.

"Xavier and his human—"

"Tracy," Claude said absently, an image of her neon coordinated outfits flashing across his mind. Elov faltered, looking up from the folders in his hand, and nodded.

"Yes, Tracy." He cleared his throat as Claude's gaze wandered back to the TV screen. Nothing of interest this morning. Not even a whisper of America's situation. "They've been accepted into the Bucharest clan. All their paperwork just cleared. Anton's man called to let me know they can move into the manor this weekend."

Claude's head bobbed up and down on its own accord, the screen shifting in and out of focus as he stared. "Good."

While he might not have sounded enthusiastic, each time a member of his clan was accepted into one of the old European vampire families, it was like one more weight could finally lift. He had fought for their placements from the moment he arrived in Gregor's lavish Swiss palace. After all, there were nearly a hundred members in the Grimm clan—plus the humans who fled Warwick's "new America" alongside them. Gregor's palace quadrupled the size of his old home, but Claude couldn't ask him to host so many extra mouths for long.

His old friend had welcomed them with open arms. At nearly nine centuries old, Gregor Leutzinger had been the one to turn Claude all those years ago. Struck with a fated illness—cancer, as he now realized—and on death's door, Claude had been saved by the vampire, a family friend and the only legitimate cure possible at the time. Since then, he'd felt indebted to the man, yet to Gregor, Claude was like a son. He'd opened his home to the Grimm clan without question when they'd fled Johnathon Warwick's wrath.

But Gregor's generosity didn't extend to every Grimm-aligned vampire. From Christmas a year and a half ago to now, Claude had been petitioning various European vampire clans relentlessly. He'd traveled across the continent to speak on behalf of the vampire or two he wished to integrate into the clan. American clans were quite fluid, all things considered. European lines dated back to the ancients. They were very particular about who joined their elite houses. Those who were fortunate enough would live in comfort and safety, physically and financially, for the rest of their days. Clanless European vampires had to fend for themselves—hence the

European Leagues.

While Leagues in America persecuted his kind, the Europeans worked alongside government agencies to hide vampires without hunting them. Jobs were secured. Housing was devised. Blood was procured. For vampires welcomed into the hundreds of old established clans, there were officials within the clan to do all that for them. In Europe, vampires did not exist to the general public. Everyone, from the highest member of a clan to the lowliest office worker in a League, shared that singular vision for the protection of the species. Rogue vampires were a threat to all and were treated as such by human and sane vampire alike.

Claude refused to let a single one of his people become a clanless drifter, relying on government assistance to exist. He fought hard for their placements, putting his reputation, his money, and his name on the line in order to see their futures secured.

And how could he not? He was the reason they'd been run out of their homes in the first place.

"Xavier was the last." Claude looked to him sharply, Elov's words creeping through the dense fog his exhausted mind had been in for the last few months. His friend nodded, the edges of his mouth twitching up. "Well, besides myself, but I—"

"You will always have a home here," Claude insisted. If his heart could pound with excitement, now would have been the moment he'd feel it hammering against his chest. "Xavier is the last… Do you mean…?"

"They've all been placed," Elov told him, hugging the files to his chest. "Every last member of the Grimm clan has a new family. You've done your duty."

It hit him harder than he thought it would. All this time, all these many months, he'd been fighting so hard for his people; the guilt drove him to it, naturally. But there was another guilt gnawing at him, one that he felt in his bones, in his very soul.

Delia was still in America—a nation under vampire rule, or so the rumors went. A nation with no media, no international transit. Like Russia behind the Iron Curtain, no one knew what went on within its borders.

And she was there, his little huntress. He'd left her behind to save his people, as much as it killed him. Claude had admired her drive to stay and help, foolish as it might have been, but the moment his plane left American soil he'd known he should have just thrown her over his shoulder and dragged her kicking and screaming from the conflict. She'd had no idea what she was up against, what sort of collective entity had formed with rebellious clans across the country. There wasn't a less safe nation in the world to be a vampire hunter—and Claude had just left her there.

Why? Because she'd sounded reasonable that night? Because he'd thought her desire to avenge her fallen comrades seemed noble, like it was the right thing to do? He'd been a fool, blinded by a desire to make things right, to give her *something* to cling to that awful night—hope, passion, *anything*. He'd handed her a credit card and some coats and his minivan and just sent her off into the night. He'd left her to the wolves.

And now he had to find her.

ABOUT LIZ

Liz Meldon is a Canadian author who grew up in the Middle East. She has a degree in Bioarchaeology from Western University, and when she isn't writing about her own snarky characters, she is ghostwriting romance novellas, working on her fanfiction, loitering on social media, or taking care of her many animals.

As a freelance ghostwriter, she has written dozens of romance pieces, some of which have been published and are doing well. She loves writing realistic characters in fantastical settings.

More from Liz Meldon:

Lovers and Liars – a Paranormal Romance Serial
Manhattan (2014) – Book #1
Vancouver (2015) – Book #2
Westwick College (2016) – Book #3
Tuskin Island (2017) – Book #4

Lovers and Liars: Immortal Wars Series – a fantasy and paranormal romance series based in the Lovers and Liars Universe
Court of the Phantom Queen (2017) – Book #1
Apollo's Priestess (2018) – Book #2

It Begins Here: An Anthology (2015)
Til Death (Lovers and Liars Prequels, #1)

It Ends Here: An Anthology (2016)
Do Us Part (Lovers and Liars Prequels, #2)

Games We Play – a Paranormal Romance Duology
The Fool (2015) – Prologue
The King (2016) – Book #1
The Queen (2017) – Book #2

Erotic Short Shorts – an Erotic Short Story Series, free to newsletter subscribers
Happy Hour (2016)
Bliss (2017)
Captive (2017)

Connect with Liz online:
Website: www.lizmeldonwrites.com
Twitter: @lizmeldon2
Facebook: facebook.com/authorlizmeldon
Instagram: @authorlizmeldon
Pinterest: pinterest.com/lizmeldon

Subscribe to Liz Meldon's monthly newsletter on her website for pub updates, freebie coupon codes, and exclusive access to ARCs and paperback giveaways.

www.ingramcontent.com/pod-product-compliance
Lightning Source LLC
Chambersburg PA
CBHW020228180626
46810CB00006B/2083